GOLD
DIGGERS

SANJENA SATHIAN

**SIMON &
SCHUSTER**

London · New York · Sydney · Toronto · New Delhi

First published in the United States by Penguin Press,
an imprint of Penguin Random House LLC, 2021
First published in Great Britain by Simon & Schuster UK Ltd, 2021
This paperback edition published 2022

3 5 7 9 10 8 6 4 2

Simon & Schuster UK Ltd
1st Floor
222 Gray's Inn Road
London WC1X 8HB

Simon & Schuster Australia, Sydney
Simon & Schuster India, New Delhi

www.simonandschuster.co.uk
www.simonandschuster.com.au
www.simonandschuster.co.in

A CIP catalogue record for this book
is available from the British Library

Paperback ISBN: 978-1-3985-0905-4
eBook ISBN: 978-1-3985-0903-0
Audio ISBN: 978-1-3985-0904-7

Designed by Meighan Cavanaugh

Printed and bound in Great Britain by CPI Group (UK) Ltd, Croydon, CR0 4YY

For Usha, Krish, and Tejas Sathian

PROLOGUE

In the middle of Bombay there was, for many years, a certain squat building that served as a beacon for the city's ambitious. It was smog-licked and wedged between a halal butcher and a chai shop, with a sign that flickered neon blue: THE GOSWAMI CLASSES. Underneath, in faded lettering streaked with bird droppings: PHYSICS STUDIES CHEMISTRY STUDIES MATHS STUDIES | BEST CHOICE FOR SCHOLARS. A practiced eye could spot the sign from the Dadar flyover, or from the pedestrian bridge above the train station.

One evening in 1984, thirteen-year-old Anjali Joshi pressed herself against the balcony of her family's fifth-floor flat and examined the neon from her elevated angle, fiddling with her two long plaits and smoothing her plaid school uniform. Anjali hoped to glimpse her older brother Vivek exiting the school after his extracurricular tuitions, his figure knocking shoulders with the clever neighbor boy, Parag. All the strivers shaded blue.

Vivek had lately stopped paying her much mind, and the world had become suddenly lonely. Once, her brother and his friends in the housing society had played cricket with her behind the building, bowling the ball with noodly and forgiving arms. But now,

Vivek's afternoons were reserved for studying, often with the wolf-ish, swarthy Parag, who was overgrown for his age, with a habit of grinding his teeth as he did problem sets, as though chomping hungrily on tough meat.

Anjali did not see Vivek, so she returned to her own chemistry papers—ordinary papers, unblessed by the legendary Ratan Goswami, who handpicked his students, anointing those who would matriculate at the Indian Institutes of Technology and later make their way to the highest echelons of the nation's industry—or to America. Anjali's parents had not entered her into such a pool. She was a daughter. It had never occurred to the Joshis that Anjali might want for herself what they wanted for Vivek. It had never occurred to Anjali to want very much at all.

On this particular day, she chewed on an eraser, lying on her stomach on the dusty floor and wishing for some relief from the heat. Even the drench of the monsoon would be preferable to the dryness of April in Dadar, where you could forget that Bombay bordered the sea, that a few miles away the air might salt your skin and you might see something like a beyond.

Anjali's eyes drooping, she righted herself so she could see the highest curves of the letters in the cram school sign. Inside, the bulky figure of Ratan Goswami would be rat-a-tatting his chalk on the board as he drilled students. *Young's modulus is? Atmospheric pressure is? External torque is?* At this hour, Vivek would be scribbling his last lines on graph paper before trudging home to inhale a small molehill of rice, then plunging back into his bedroom for more swotting. His body was growing slender, like a mongoose's, the longer he studied.

Anjali lifted her head at the click of a key in the lock. Her mother glanced at her daughter only briefly, then made for the kitchen. In the afternoons, while Vivek was under Ratan Goswami's supervision, Lakshmi Joshi mingled with the other ladies in the housing society, bragging about her two sons—Dhruv, who was in America, and Vivek, who would soon be abroad, too. Anjali heard her mother coming and going, the boys' names always on her tongue, her own name never uttered.

In the kitchen, Anjali's mother reached into her sari blouse and deposited something on the Cuddapah stone counter. As Lakshmi squatted to fidget with the rusty petroleum gas cylinder, Anjali padded closer to see the glint of the furtive object: a small, plain gold coin, the sort a family member might give a young boy for good luck.

"Ithna nigh, out of the kitchen while I'm doing this," Lakshmi snapped.

Anjali obeyed, retreating with her chemistry papers to the dining table, but stealing glances. Her mother boiled water in a saucepan, reached for the masala dabba, shook some soil-brown powders into the hot liquid, and began to sing something like a prayer, passing through each phrase as though passing the beads of a mala from finger to finger. At one point, Lakshmi left the kitchen and stepped into the alcove in the hallway, where the family kept their altar—pink and blue gods and haldi and kumkum and bells on a bronze plate. She returned to the kitchen pressing two figurines against her breasts and set them on the shelf above the stove. The sandalwood eyes of the goddesses of prosperity and education surveyed the proceedings.

Lakshmi tilted the pot, just enough that Anjali could see the coin slip from her fingers and splash on the surface. Anjali stood on her tiptoes in time to see the liquid in the pot react—a little yellow whirlpool formed and swallowed the gold, as though the brew had been awaiting this addition.

"Aiyee," she ventured. "What is it?"

"This has nothing to do with you," Lakshmi said. "This is for Vivek."

With practiced ease, her mother lifted the pot with tongs and held it high above a steel tumbler, like a street tea seller. Liquid ribboned out between the two vessels: a perplexing, deep-yellow flicker. It caught the muted evening sunlight streaming through the flat.

The door opened, and there came the sounds of scuffling in the hallway, Vivek and Parag, briefly unburdened of their studies. Anjali heard them making plans for a round of cricket, then lowering their voices before a burst of conspiratorial laughter. There would be no cricket; she knew Vivek would fall asleep over his coursework before there was time for games.

"Aiyee!" Vivek called, kicking off his street-dirt-streaked chappals. Lakshmi swiveled, hand still inches from the fire, and her flinty gaze fell on Vivek. He straightened, and Anjali swore he shuddered as he saw what swished in the tumbler. He glanced back over his shoulder, as though hoping Parag might call him away. But Parag had gone. The open door swung on its hinges. At the drift of outside air, the gas stove shuddered. Its flame hued the same witchy blue as the Goswami sign. Lakshmi switched it off.

MANY YEARS LATER, Anjali stood in her own kitchen in Hammond Creek, Georgia. Her daughter slept upstairs. Her husband was miles away. In the suburban somnolence, the only noise was of a long metal spoon clinking against a glass pitcher as she stirred. She brought just the edge of the spoon to her mouth. A small pink tongue darted out to taste the thing that still seemed forbidden. Was it tangier? Too sour? She had tried her mother's drink only once, briefly, surreptitiously. But she suspected her iteration was not yet right. That seemed to happen in migration. The old recipes were never quite the same on this side of the world.

PART ONE

GOLDEN CHILDREN

May this gold which brings long life and splendor and increase of wealth, and which gets through all adversities, enter upon me for the sake of long life, of splendor, and of victory.

—FROM THE *Grihya-Sutra of Hiranyakesin*, VEDIC TEXT

As in metal, so in the body.

—*Rasarnava*, HINDU TREATISE ON ALCHEMY

1.

When I was younger, I consisted of little but my parents' ambitions for who I was to become. But by the end of ninth grade, all I wanted for myself was a date to the Spring Fling dance. A hot one. The dream was granted, by chance. Finding myself unaccompanied in the final days before the event, I begged my neighbor and childhood best friend, Anita Dayal, to take pity on me. Fine; I could be her "escort," she allowed, putting the word in air quotes as we readied for that rather fateful night.

Before the dance, I was set to meet Anita and our crowd at the mall. We'd take photos outside the TCBY, all trussed up in our Macy's finery. My mother deposited me on a median in the middle of the parking lot, early, then sped off to my older sister's picture party. Prachi had been nominated for Spring Fling court and was living a more documentable high school life. Prachi, the Narayan child who managed to be attractive *and* intelligent *and* deferential to our cultural traditions to boot, was headed to Duke, we were all sure. Earlier that day, cheeks blooming with pride, my mother had fastened a favorite, slim gold chain of her own, gifted by our ajji, around Prachi's neck. My sister kissed my mother's cheek like an old, elegant woman and thanked her, while I waited to be dropped into my own small life, in an ill-fitting suit.

I waited on the median, growing anxious. There was no sign of Anita. I paced and fidgeted, watching the others pin corsages and boutonnieres, and readied myself, after fifteen minutes, then twenty, to give up and trek down one of those horrible sidewalk-less stretches of great Georgia boulevard back home to Hammond Creek. I was already turning away from the fuss, attempting to loosen my father's congealed-blood-colored tie, when Anita and her mother screeched up in their little brown Toyota. I knocked my knee against the concrete dolphin-adorned fountain and shouted, "Shit!"

A wall of mostly Indian and Asian parents regarded me with a collective glare. Yes, I consisted largely of my parents' ambitions, but some part of me was also made of the ogling, boggling eyeballs of the rest of our community.

And another part—a significant part—was Anita, who was now stepping out of the double-parked car, smiling blithely. Anita had bright eyes: muddy brown, lively, roving, liable to flick over you quickly, as though there was something else more interesting or urgent in your vicinity. It made you want to stand squarely in her line of vision to ask for her full attention; when you got it, it felt like the warming of the late-morning summer sun.

"Neil, I *told* her we were late, but stubborn girl wouldn't listen!" Anita's mother, Anjali Auntie, said. She was dressed like she planned to attend the dance herself, in a bright green sheath framing her breasts, a dress that reminded me she was unlike other mothers.

"I got invited to Melanie's picture party first," Anita said. "I IM'd you!"

A betrayal: cherry-cheeked and universally admired Melanie

Cho had laughed off my invitation to the dance weeks before, leaving me itchy with self-loathing. Anita's grin—the grin of the newly anointed popular—matched the crystal studding along her bright blue bodice.

Anjali Auntie positioned us shoulder-to-shoulder. Anita linked her arm through mine so the insides of our elbows kissed. This was how we'd been posed in Diwali photos as kids, when our families got together and Prachi dressed Anita up as Sita and assembled a paper crown for me, her spouse, Lord Rama. The posture suddenly seemed foreign.

There was no time to be angry. I smiled. In the photos, I am washed out. She, in electric blue and crystal, beams, her eyes settled somewhere just above the camera lens.

The dance: People were learning to inch closer to each other, and some girls didn't mind the short guys' heads bobbing below theirs, and some guys didn't mind the girls with braces. The teachers on chaperone duty patrolled the bathrooms, where kids who were not my crowd might engage in "nonsense," as my mother put it, *nonsense* that was inaccessible to me at the time.

As with any other event at Okefenokee High School, the room was semi-segregated. A handful of white kids mosh-pitted in the middle of the party; others made their way to those nonsense-filled bathrooms or the parking lot. The good-looking Indian and Asian girls hung by the long banquet table. The debate, math Olympiad, robotics, etc., Indians and Asians were the likeliest ones to be bopping around, because though none of us could really move, the dancing offered a prescribed activity for the evening, a script. I depended on scripts in those days, before anyone asked me to invent my own life.

I followed Anita onto the floor, expecting to join the circle dancing around Hari Chopra, who was attempting to prove his B-boy abilities to the Kanye song that was ubiquitous that year, flicking a finger across an imaginary flat-brimmed hat in the warm-up. But Anita veered toward a cluster of girls that included my sister and Melanie. I stopped at the edge of the squeaky gym floor in my dress shoes, which were vast, boatlike, slippery, and made me sweat.

"Anita," I whispered frantically, but she mouthed, *Just a second*, and darted into the girl cluster—as though she was crossing the finish line in a race I hadn't known she was running. She'd grown spritely and uncatchable lately, always squinting at a secretly looming horizon line.

I didn't see my date again until the end of the evening, let alone dance with her. The ghost of her touch on me—the inside of her elbow against the inside of mine—lingered on my skin. I felt insubstantial.

I spent the party with Kartik Jain and Manu Padmanaban and Aleem Khan and Jack Kim and Abel Mengesha (who was Ethiopian but clocked most of his time with the Asians), avoiding Shruti Patel, with whom Manu had agreed to come, and whose electrified bristly hair and eager gopher teeth discomfited us. Jack was counting the girls he'd made out with at computer camp the year before, in an effort to overcome the fact that he was here tonight alone. I had been at that camp and knew the single kiss he'd received was dumb luck, the result of a double dog dare.

I was supposed to return home with Anita and her mother at ten—their house sat catty-corner from ours in the Hammond Creek cul-de-sac. Ten; I only had to last till ten. I watched the egg-shaped clock on the wall above the banquet table tick. I drank the sugary punch; it stained my tongue Coke-can red.

Just before nine thirty, people began to gather for the announcement of Spring Fling royalty. At the swell of a tantalizingly sex-infused slow song—*Crash into me, and I come into you*—I went looking for Anita. I wound through the gym, all elbows and too-long hair that curtained the top of my vision. No Anita. No Prachi. I sidestepped out of the gym and down the hallway carpeted in green and gray—the swampy colors of Okefenokee High School. It occurred to me that I might find the girls in the parking lot. The parking lot, full of *nonsense*.

I pushed open the first door I encountered, missing, in my annoyance, the sign that read EMERGENCY EXIT. The alarm wailed. People's hands flew to their ears, and heads turned toward me. A white guy gripped a handle of some clear verboten substance. Someone cursed. Someone shrieked. Someone laughed. I stood mute as they scattered. When Coach Jameson came striding outside to bust up the party, he noted my presence, held up a large, meaty finger, and said, "Wait there." I froze, darkened by the shadows behind the gym.

Girls were crying. Not Anita, I don't think. It took a lot to make her cry. From somewhere came my sister's voice, in the buttery lilt that never failed her: "Coach, I just came out here to find my necklace, it fell off, it's my grandmother's, you know I don't drink—"

"I'll ask, missy," he said. "What were you doing to cause you to, ahem, lose a necklace?"

I shuddered and didn't catch Prachi's reply because Anita stood behind me, propping open the door whose alarm had at last been killed.

"Neil, get inside, you'll get in trouble," she whispered. Her glossed lips quivered and for a moment I was suffused with a premonition that something phantom wished to be spoken aloud but that no one—not me, not the people around me—could find the language. Anita clamped her mouth shut and blinked very fast, as though beating back that ghost, and there we remained, still rooted to our finite asphalt selves.

I said Prachi was out there and it didn't sound good. "The coach already saw me," I added. "I'm not supposed to move."

"Are you *kidding me*, Neil?" Anita was framed in the doorway as the hallway light streamed out around her. "My mom's waiting, like, right now."

"I wasn't drinking."

"I *know* you weren't drinking," she said. No, more like—"I know *you* weren't drinking." I wondered how she had come by all her new wisdom, how she had grown so fast, so far ahead of me. "Did *you* set off the alarm?"

I nodded miserably.

"Dude," Anita said. "People go out the food delivery door." She pointed. She spoke rapidly, percussively, with a bravado that might have masked her nerves at being so near *trouble*.

"C'mon, kid." Coach Jameson led his small troupe of prisoners inside, beckoning me with that meaty finger, holding the alcohol pinched in his other hand like a used rag. The captured students followed, heads bowed—two white guys I didn't know, Katie Zhang, Mark Ha, Prachi. My sister mouthed, *What?* at me while Coach Jameson looked Anita up and down and added, "And you, rubbernecker."

"I just got here, Coach," Anita said. Her voice caught in her throat before she switched to a clipped tone like the sort my mother used on work calls. I could feel her straining to be someone with whom she had not yet become fully acquainted. "Actually, we were trying to leave. My mom's outside, you can ask her—"

"Y'all well know not to be in the parking lot."

"I just got worried, see," she tried again, in a slightly sharper pitch. "Because—"

"What's your name?"

"Anita Dayal."

"And yours?"

"Neil Narayan."

He repeated. "Anita Dial. Neil Nay-rannan. Y'all're freshmen?"

"Yes, sir," Anita said.

"Stay away from this crowd," Coach Jameson said grandly. "Getcherselves home."

He escorted his captured cool kids past us. The scent of our innocence—or mine, anyway—was strong enough to overpower everything else.

Some kids my age drank alcohol, but I was afraid to, not because of the things the health class teacher cautioned would happen to your body and brain but because of my mother's warnings that engaging in *nonsense* could abort all you were supposed to become, could in fact abort the very American dream we were duty-bound to live out. Take the case of Ravi Reddy, whose parents had shipped him to Hyderabad to finish high school upon smelling beer on his breath. No one had heard from Ravi since, but my mother had hinted that she and my father were not above taking a leaf out of the Reddys' book.

I would not have wished such a fate on anyone, let alone my sister, so I said to Anita, "Can you get your mom to wait two minutes? My sister lost our grandmother's gold necklace, and she'll be even more screwed."

Anita bit her lip. Something shifted in her posture, brought her into a new alertness, like when she was asked a question to which she knew the answer in algebra.

"Oh." She retrieved her pink flip phone from her fake-pearl-encrusted purse. "Mama. Coming. But Prachi lost this gold necklace, and Neil—" A pause. She hung up. "My mom says be quick."

"My sister doesn't drink." I held up a flashlight that connected to my Swiss Army knife and house keys. Nothing showed itself on the asphalt, just the black Georgia ground beneath the black Georgia sky. Puddles of yellow lamppost light revealed the riddled texture of the parking lot. There were no secrets here; in this stupid place, what you saw was what you got.

"All of them drink," Anita said, peeling away. "You can't run in that crowd and not drink." Did *Anita* drink? A pang in my chest— for wasn't she now in *that crowd*? "She ditched with Hudson Long because she knew she was going to lose Spring Fling Princess."

"She lost?" I sighed. Even if Prachi escaped Coach Jameson, she'd be smarting from defeat. I didn't fancy enduring one of her performances of grief, wherein she refused to make eye contact with us for days, or ensured I overheard her vomiting in the bathroom. "See anything?"

"Nah," Anita called, a little nasally.

I cast my light beneath the dumpster, knelt and got a smashing stench of cafeteria chili and old bananas and a number of other smells both animal and human. I covered my nose, stood, ran the beam in a long line like a searchlight hunting a fugitive in desolate farmland, sweep, one, sweep, two, but nothing on the asphalt glinted like gold. "Nothing?" I called.

"Nothing." Anita was kneeling by the wretched emergency exit door and reaching for something on the ground.

"Is that it?" I half jogged over.

"Nope," she said. "It's not here."

I was right next to her now. "You didn't find it?"

"I just said I didn't. My mom's gonna be mad; we have to go."

"Your mom's never mad." I waved my hand dismissively. Anjali Auntie was *different*—a given—and Anita could not believably invoke her as a threat. "What's in your hand, Anita?"

For her fist was clenched, her knuckles bloodless. She looked ready to slug me.

Her jaw tightened. Then she growled through her teeth, as though she'd been trying to tell me something and I'd been too dense to hear it. "Neil, you are such a *freak*! Prachi lost her necklace because she's *drunk* and making out with Hudson Long, and I've got enough to worry about without helping you fix *her* shit."

She opened the door and stomped over the green-and-gray carpeting. I followed. I couldn't do anything but slide into the back of the Toyota. Anita and her mother sat in wooden silence up front. Anjali Auntie's eyes landed searchingly on mine in the rearview mirror a few times before settling sidelong on her daughter's taut expression. Her own face remained impassive; I could not tell if she was surprised at the coldness between Anita and me.

Back home, in my room, I wrenched myself free from my father's tie and tried to fall asleep as the landline rang and heels sounded below me—Prachi coming home, Prachi in trouble, my parents' voices rising. ("Who were you with?" "Open your mouth, show your breath!" "Where's Ajji's—?" "Ayyayyo!" "You'll jolly well tell us—!") Prachi, the golden child, fallen from grace, some essential blessing lifted from her.

I dreamt in shards, and I encountered Anita in my sleep—an Anita who had Melanie Cho's red lips and was wearing a bright green dress like her mother's, an Anita who removed said dress to display the body of one of the porn stars I had become familiar with, which meant a white body, ivory skin, and dime-sized, pert nipples. I woke up and found that my boxers were wet. In the bathroom, I tried to scrub away all that had happened that night.

I SAT AT THE DINNER TABLE one evening the following week, poking my bisibelebath around with my fork, listening as Prachi stood in the kitchen and called our grandmother to issue a formal apology with regard to the necklace. ("Ajji!" Prachi overarticulated, glancing pleadingly at our mother, who had mandated the call. She wound her fingers through the cream-colored curlicue phone cord. "Ajji, it's Prachi! Can you put your hearing aid in?") I looked up to see my father poking his food around, just like I was. My mother furiously scrubbed the white Formica countertop, which was irrevocably stained with splatters of hot oil and masalas, and glowered at Prachi.

In our house, it took only one gesture in the direction of India to compound an already grave situation. The accusation was that Prachi had flouted her responsibility as a daughter, a sister, a former Spring Fling princess, and yes, a *granddaughter*, too. She had imperiled the very nature of the sacrifice of crossing oceans. My parents relished that phrase, "crossing oceans," as though they had arrived in steerage class aboard a steamship instead of by 747, carrying two massive black suitcases with pink ribbons tied around the handles and the surname NARAYAN written in blocky letters on masking tape along the side.

My father, miffed, gestured at the two empty plates on my mother's Walmart imitation-Indian paisley-print place mats. The bisibelebath and reheated aloo sabzi were all growing cold. I reached for some potato, but my father shook his head, and I got the sense that poking food around was the way we were going to ride this out, so back I went to that.

As Prachi continued her breathless apology, I looked out the breakfast room window, toward the Dayals'. Anita might step outside at any minute.

"It just got lost at a dance, Ajji," Prachi was saying. "It was a very bad mistake, and I'm really sorry about it." I could picture widowed Ajji on the other end of the line in Mysore, her long graying hair pinned against the nape of her neck, puzzled, perhaps unable even to remember what had been lost—she was forgetful these days—or if she did remember, thinking: Why are you calling me about a lost *necklace* when bigger things were lost in the move to America? Prachi signed off. "Love you, Ajji, see you soon. No, I *don't* know when, but soon, right."

We could now start dinner, which had gone completely cold.

Heroically, Prachi began to talk about the summer's pageant as she heated everyone's plates. My sister planned to be Miss Teen India Georgia and then Miss Teen India Southeastern Region, and then Miss Teen India USA. The prior November, she had placed second in the region, narrowly missing out on a spot at nationals, and was a favorite going forward. Prachi truly believed she was on her way to solving the riddle at the heart of the MTI: *What does it mean to be both Indian and, like, American?* One more shot at the tiara and she'd have the answer at last. She would communicate all this, and what it signified thematically and emotionally, on the Duke application she was to spend the summer filling out.

"Who's Miss Teen India-*India*?" I inquired.

She glared. "The point is to empower Indian girls in *America*. Incidentally, your girlfriend's going in for it, too."

My parents' eyebrows furrowed. They could not comprehend the utter impossibility of Prachi's accusation that I, at five feet five, as brown, as *me*, could have a girlfriend.

"Who?" I said. My fist tightened around my fork.

"Anita Dayal." Prachi sniffed. "She's trying for MTI, too. Not that she's ever been interested in exploring Indian American identity be*fore*."

"She's not my girlfriend," I said, feeling a revolting feminine blush beneath my skin. "We're barely friends anymore."

"What happened?" This was my mother, surveying Prachi and me.

I twitched, looking not at my family but at what I thought was a figure stealing up the driveway of the Dayal house. I blinked; she, or it, was gone, or had never been.

"She's a little climber," Prachi said, accounting for my silence.

And my mother said, forgetting her anger for a moment, "Just like her mother."

My father remained stoic the rest of the meal, but my mother thawed; that banter reunited the Narayan women. Gossip is to my mother what South Indian classical music is to my father—the virtuosic amalgamation of years of a community's becoming. For as long as I can remember she has been a connoisseur of gossip, of the sounds it makes, the musicality, the overall gestalt, which is one that causes her to use the pronouns *us* and *them*, and the phrases *these people* and *our people* and *such people*, with confidence. One might call her ears—which are extremely large and loose lobed, with openings to the ear canal the size of a thumbnail—the place where the Indian immigrant public sphere gathers. In between wax and bristly dark hairs, the diaspora unscatters and lodges itself in my mother's oversize hearing organs.

When I was younger, Anita and Anjali Dayal were held in per-fectly fine favor at my house. Our two families mingled pleasantly; as a latchkey kid whose mother was less prolific in the kitchen than Anita's, I often let myself into the Dayals' house to rummage around in the fridge. The key beneath the watering can behind the azalea bush was mine to use. Our parents—the four brown adults in a largely white subdivision—collaborated to create a simulacrum of India in a reliably red Georgia county.

But over the past few years, Anita's father, Pranesh Uncle, had grown conspicuously absent, discomfiting the other desi mothers. No one pronounced words like *separation*; it was stated only that Anita's father was working in California, where he had founded a company with his classmates from the prestigious Indian Institutes of Technology. The official reason for Anita's father living across the country while her mother remained in Hammond Creek was the daughter, and a desire not to interrupt her schooling. Which is why my mother was overtaken by a frisson of judgment when I came home at the end of May, weeks after Spring Fling, with the news that Anita would be leaving Okefenokee and, in fact, inter-rupting her schooling.

"California?" my mother said.

I could almost see the RE/MAX realty signs in her eyes as she dreamt of an open house, overdone chewy sugar cookies and fruit punch and information on the neighborhood's property values. My mother adored open houses, their mild festivity, the red bal-loons, the way the houses were held in presentational limbo—vacuumed carpets and potpourri in the powder rooms—until the owners' current unsatisfactory life had been traded out for a bet-ter one.

"To Buckhead," I said.

Anita had been accepted to a posh private school in Buckhead, one of the neighborhoods inside the perimeter. The perimeter, referring to Interstate 285, which neatly locked the suburbs away from Atlanta proper, was one of those things to which my mother sometimes mystically referred while in that open house headspace—a state of mind that I swear caused her very large ears to droop and soften, implying that she was listening to something otherworldly, something more splendid than terrestrial gossip. Someday, we might live *inside the perimeter*, she suggested. My father scoffed; in Hammond Creek we were close to my parents' jobs, good public schools, and other immigrants. Inside the perimeter, he grumbled, were crumbling houses that white people would spend a million bucks on because they seemed Margaret Mitchellian.

Anita's destination was a school I'd faced at debate tournaments a few times. They never failed to intimidate, showing up with four coaches from the best college teams huddled around them. They strutted about in blazers and ties and pearls and heels, while we mopped our sweat with our swamp-green Okefenokee High School T-shirts. Her school sat near the long low lawns of country clubs and the governor's mansion. Its female students would be debutantes, and its alumni seemed—from my position outside its brick-winged gates, anyway—to waltz into Harvard and Princeton and Vanderbilt and Georgetown.

It made sense. Anita's only plan in life, as long as I had known her, was to attend Harvard. What followed Harvard was a vaguely crimson-tinged blankness; Harvard was sufficient, would propel her into some life thereafter. The first step in achieving that life seemed to be leaving Hammond Creek, Okefenokee High School, and me.

Anita and I had been avoiding each other since Spring Fling.

She now traipsed around the hallways ensconced in Melanie Cho's pack, making it impossible for me to catch her eye. But I had not forgotten the dance. I wondered if by ditching me—or by stealing a queen bee's coveted piece of jewelry?—she had completed some hazing ritual. I sought signs of change in her. Did her hair shine more than it used to? Had she grown lankier? I looked for her on AOL Instant Messenger, one of our regular sites of communication. She logged on only once. I began to type: *wtf where u been?* Then I deleted it, trying the softer, *r u mad @ me?* I cleared that out, too: *sup*, I wrote. Then came the heartrending sound of a door slamming. She'd signed off. Her avatar never reappeared. I guessed she'd blocked me.

So I did not learn the news about the school from her, but from Shruti Patel. Shruti was in all the gifted classes, and already taking Advanced Placement Physics as a freshman. She told me during Honors American History, the only class where she did not regard me as a flailing moron. (I liked English and history and scraped by in most other subjects.)

"How do *you* know?" I whispered as Mr. Finkler handed back the previous week's tests.

"Ninety-four, good job," Shruti said. Mr. Finkler had written the number in red and circled it twice on my blue book. She waved hers.

"Ninety-eight," I conceded.

"*Her* mother told *my* mother at Kroger," Shruti said. "I didn't even know she was *applying* to private schools."

I shrugged.

"You didn't know either?" Shruti pressed. "Aren't you two, like . . ." And she pulled an appalling face, aping something she had seen on television, a knowing-teenage-gossip face.

Desperate to put a stop to the way she was pouting her lips and

raising her eyebrows, I said, "No, *definitely* not," and it was true—
we weren't, like, anything. Not anymore.

ANJALI DAYAL DID NOT WORK in the way my parents worked.
My mother was a financial analyst. My father spent eight hours a
day on his feet, in a white coat behind the counter of a Publix
pharmacy. He had suffered years of study for that job, in India and
in America, but in my eyes as a kid, I had a father who "worked at
the grocery store." When I said that once in front of my mother, I
was swatted on the butt and duly corrected. My father was a *pharmacist*. The word clunked in my mouth—but never again would I
say he worked at the grocery store.

Anita's mother, on the other hand, would tell you she ran a "catering business." She filled in for working Indian mothers who
wanted to serve their families proper home-cooked fare but who
lacked either the time or the skill in the kitchen to do so. Occasionally she would do a graduation or birthday party, but for the
most part, Anjali Auntie answered calls placed in response to flyers she hung up at the temple and in Little India strip malls—
those two-story off-the-highway structures housing Kumon math
tutoring centers and restaurants called Haveli or Bombay Palace
or Taste of India and threading salons where women pruned themselves of excess ethnic hair. She drove all over the suburbs and did
much of her cooking in other people's homes, as though the women
hiring her wished to think of her the way they thought of *the help*
back in India. To admit that the prettier, younger mother was the
"proprietor of a small business" would have been strange and modern and white.

Surely Anjali Auntie did not need this job—based on everything my mother said about Pranesh Uncle, money was flowing from the West Coast. But she did it nonetheless, perhaps because she was afraid, herself, of being left to do godknowswhat.

It was this job that threw me into close contact with the Dayal women for the first time in a month. At the end of May, my whole family donned our Indian clothes and headed to a big party celebrating the Bhatt twins' graduation. I scratched at the blue kurta my mother had made me wear. Talk on the way there focused on the honorees: Jay was Ivy League–bound in the fall, while Meena would attend a state school, and not one of the "better" ones, in my parents' eyes. Meena's fate offended my mother.

"She fooled around all high school, didn't she?" my mother said to Prachi. This was the latest tactic in the wake of Prachi's Spring Fling moral miscarriage. My mother would ask her to recite the fates of those who "fooled around"—which might, in her view, include anything from neglecting to take AP Biology to shooting up hard drugs. She educated us about the wider world by assembling a kind of shoe-box diorama of other people's lives—a cardboard drama. She arranged the characters, moved them about, and showed you how they were doing it wrong, turning the diorama into the set of a morality play.

Upon arriving at the Bhatts', I prepared to abscond to the basement. Basements were the safest places to survive an Indian party in the suburbs. In a basement, the itchy clothes could be loosened, the girls' dupattas dropped on the floor and trampled upon, the guys' kurtas removed to reveal that all along someone had been smart enough to wear a T-shirt beneath the fabric, and jeans rather than churidars below. In basements you never encountered garish images of multiarmed gods, or family portraits shot in the mall photography studio—sisters draped in lehengas and brothers' hair stiff with gel. In basements you found foosball and Ping-Pong tables, big-screen televisions, and, depending on the benevolence of the parents, video game consoles. In basements, I learned the secrets of sex, according to information curated from older brothers who were certainly still virgins. In basements, a semblance of our due—American teenagedom.

The Narayan family basement was, by the way, unfinished.

"Lavish-shmavish," my mother whispered as I made for the underground. This was her general opinion on the Bhatts, and on any carpeting or televisions below the earth.

New graduates kicked back in oversize leather recliners. Meena Bhatt sat on the lap of George Warner-Wilson, who had spent high school as one of the only white people among Asians. He was going to Georgia Tech in the fall, where he might continue dwelling at this demographic crossroads.

"Neilo, Neilium, Neilius," he said through his sinuses, saluting me. I waved. "Your crew's in the exercise room." He pointed.

As I opened the door, I heard Meena sigh, with a voice less damned (per my mother's diorama) than insouciant: "Can someone bring me something that's not frickin' Indian food?"

The gym looked unused. Half the walls were mirrors. Folded up against an un-mirrored wall was a treadmill draped in plastic. Mounted in one corner, a television, and beneath it, a video game console. A report of gunfire went off on-screen.

"Fuck you, Osama, this is America!" yelled Kartik Jain, as Aleem Khan's avatar, a square-jawed white soldier, expired.

Anita sat cross-legged on the floor, examining a glossy magazine. She hovered a pencil above the pages, marking off answers in some quiz.

"Oh, good, Neil! Everyone was wondering where you were,"

she said in that brisk voice of hers. Her eyes alighted on me for only an instant. Anita was a bit like a windup toy, capable of spinning fast for a period—laughing easily, tending to social niceties—only to run out later, in private. When it was just the two of us, she'd always been slower, laxer.

Amnesia, I thought viciously. Ignoring me all spring, and now here she was, bending over the magazine so that I spied the top of her newly grown chest.

Now Anita was turning to Aleem, saying, "You got 'mostly B's,' so your future wife is Lauren Bennett . . ." (giggles from Manu at the improbability). "But really, don't take it too seriously—these are designed for girls."

Anita loved these games and quizzes—anything that offered a prognostication, anything to help her better articulate her future, no matter how trite. I understood why. A positive result—you'd marry Melanie Cho!—could turn you briefly dreamy with a picture of a life to come. The worst result you could land in one of these divinations? Shruti Patel.

"Who'd you get, Anita?" I asked.

"Jake Gyllenhaal." She smirked.

"Doesn't count."

"That's what I said," Isha Arora put in. "No celebrities."

"What*ever*," Anita said. "It's not like we know the people we're going to marry *now*. Like, what about the whole rest of life? I could meet Jake Gyllenhaal sometime. Or whoever."

"My parents met when they were sixteen," Juhi said.

"Yeah, and got an arranged marriage." Anita gave a little shiver of revulsion, one I'd seen before when she spoke about the parents of Hammond Creek, whose lives she roundly disdained. "Anyway. It's not like I'm going to marry an Indian guy."

Everything hung dead in the air for a moment, and then Juhi and Isha started to guffaw, looking around at me and Manu and Kartik and Aleem. The video game was forgotten; a soldier spun on-screen, displaying his machine gun impotently.

"I mean, no offense," Anita said to the air.

"Yeah, well, it's not like I'm going to marry—" Manu was saying, when in came Shruti Patel. The room stiffened at the sight of her, standing there in her wiry, frizzy manner. Her presence fractured a party. You were too aware of the sounds of her mouth-breathing, the way her face contorted when she tried to participate. It required emotional labor to include her, and it was simpler to dispense with all the kindergarten rules of engagement and ignore her. That day, Shruti seemed to know more than ever these facts about herself. Those bushy eyebrows, which so often met in the middle of her forehead as she considered a problem in class, raised almost to her hairline and then flattened. She wanted us to believe she had never given us any thought at all, though behind her Mrs. Bhatt was saying, "See, Shruti, I told you all your classmates were hiding out down here."

Which was when Isha, eyes on Anita, said, "Guess who *you're* going to marry, Shroots?" She and Juhi snickered. Manu's eyes met mine as we both considered intervening. But you had to save your ammo for yourself; the derision could land on you anytime, and even among friends, it had the effect of total destruction. It took so much to gather yourself up into some semblance of a person every morning. A rash of mocking could undo all that in an instant. I sat with my back against the wall and laughed as quietly as possible.

Shruti, always quick in her own defense, quick enough that you could believe she didn't mind the banter, retorted, "I'm not planning on *getting* married, Isha. I happened to punch the last guy who asked me, you know." And if we hadn't all heard the strain in her rebuttal, seen the whitening of her lips, it might have been funny.

Anita stood, and though she had frequently used Shruti as a punch line, this time she spared a withering glance for Juhi and Isha. She could afford to, from her new position above the rest of us. "Come get some food with me, Shroots," she said.

I remembered the day Shruti arrived in seventh grade, fresh off the boat. Anita made me cross the cafeteria to sit down with the new girl, who rolled her *r*'s too hard. The three of us ate our white-bread sandwiches. Kraft singles in mine, peanut butter and banana in Anita's. Red and green chutney with potatoes in Shruti's, emitting a distinct spicy smell. "It's easy to make this yourself," Anita advised Shruti, opening her triangles to reveal the smush of browning fruit and crunchy Skippy. "But I like mine," Shruti had said.

We had since distanced ourselves from her. But you could never properly avoid, shun, renounce, extract, or untangle yourself from any other desi in Hammond Creek. You were all a part of the same mass. Some days you trampled on one another. Other days, you hid in the same basement, seeking shelter from the same parental storms.

"Yeah," Isha called as Anita and Shruti made their egress. "Anita, enjoy the food—I mean, you must be so at home, eating this stuff."

Aleem turned to me. "You hear my middle sister didn't get into any schools?"

"*None?*" Manu gasped.

"What's she going to do?" I had a vision of Shaira packing up the Khans' station wagon and zooming west, a female Muslim Sal Paradise (I'd recently read—and treasured—*On the Road*). What if she just went . . . anywhere? Sought out *the mad people*? "She could do anything."

"She's applying again. More safety schools. This time she's writing her essay on 9/11."

"Why are you all so gay for college?" Kartik fiddled with the video game controller. School didn't come easily to him. So, soon enough, we let him redirect the conversation to one of those teenage-boy brain trusts: "You know the secret to getting any in high school?"

We asked him to enlighten us.

"Avoid the Indian girls."

"Why?" Manu said.

"They're afraid of dicks. Every one of them. That's what my brother says."

"What the hell does that mean?" I said.

"Three reasons to not fuck with Indian girls," Kartik continued. "One: they're afraid of dicks. Two: they're hairy, like, gorilla hairy. Three: they bleed a lot."

"What do you mean *bleed* a lot?" I said.

"I mean it's a biological fact that they have the thickest—what's it called—the thing that breaks when chicks get reamed for the first time."

"The hymen," Manu said professorially.

"Right, they've got the thickest in the world, so blood everywhere." He emitted an explosive, diarrheic noise, making fireworks with his hands, puffing cheeks out, spewing air.

"Who's that girl you debate with?" Aleem asked me. "Wendi Zhao? *She's* kind of hot."

Kartik leaned against the mirror. "Wendi Plow," he said. Then he added, in case we didn't get it: "I'd plow Wendi Zhao, all I'm saying."

"Dude," Manu said, turning to me, and I cringed, because he was about to do that thing—the male version of that thing Shruti did—where he deepened his voice and tried to access the patois of our generation. "Dude, I bet Anita totally likes you, though."

"What did I *just say?*" Kartik moaned.

EVENTUALLY I GOT HUNGRY and excused myself. I passed, on the way out of the basement, the sixty-inch television, on which home videos of Meena and Jay streamed. Currently, a little Jay was holding up a piece of construction paper to the camera. It featured a stick figure standing atop a mountain of green rectangles—dollar bills. Below, written in red marker, with a few letters facing adorably in the wrong direction: WHEN I GROW UP, I WANT TO BE . . . RICH!

I reached the buffet table in the Bhatts' emptied three-car garage. Anita's mother was there, reaching one of her slender arms up to a wire shelf to grab something. I ached to be tall enough that I could reach a shelf she could not. On the table were chaat fixings and mango lassi in a sweaty glass jug and yellow fluffy dhokla and a pile of mini cheese pizzas, in concession to the littler kids' whitewashed diets.

"Neil!" she said. "Ani's just gone home. She wasn't feeling well."

"Gone home with who?" You couldn't walk back to our neighborhood from this side of Hammond Creek; you could hardly walk anywhere in Hammond Creek.

"Shruti's parents decided to leave, so they took her."

"She gets tired," I said, thinking of that windup key in Anita's back slowing, threatening the vigor of her public persona. These days I couldn't imagine who she was in private, what she dreamt of or loved.

"You haven't been coming by," Anjali Auntie said airily. "Are you sick of my food?"

"It's been busy."

She raised her eyebrows. "Anita might like some company soon. She's been busy, too. Here, you want to come help? I lost my best set of extra hands."

I joined her behind the buffet table and began piling up napkins from the package she had pulled from the shelf. People had mostly come through for their first round of food already, so though the dishes were hot and everything was still laid out, our corner of the party was quiet. From inside, high-pitched Hindi music sounded, and I knew some auntie would try to get everyone to dance and some uncle would give a speech about Meena's and Jay's futures and then the party would end and we, the non-Meenas and non-Jays, would go home to begin our summers of striving to become Jays and not Meenas. I would be spending my break up to my ears in debate research and, at my father's behest, suffering through supplemental Kumon math courses. Thinking about this made me want to linger in the garage, to postpone the coming months.

"Have some dhokla," Anita's mother said, placing one on a Styrofoam plate. She drizzled it with tamarind and coriander chutneys. It melted into my gums.

"It's good," I said.

"I offered to make ice cream, but they said no. I should have said *kulfi*. Should have said, 'I'll make some saffron or pista kulfi,' and then the Bhatts would have said oh yes oh yes please." She said that last bit in a put-on accent. Anita's mother did not speak like the fobbier parents; her vowels were wide and practiced, and she did not strike her consonants too hard. Her voice was all mongrel, almost English on some words (you *knooow*, she'd say in a pinched pitch) and mimicked American drawl and zing on others (you *guuyz*). My parents referred to this accent as "pseud." They had kept their *r*'s and *v*'s and *w*'s just the way they had been when they crossed the ocean.

"Can you start boxing up leftovers? I have to get the cake from their basement and bring it upstairs for after their toasts. Know what? They made me put those kids' *faces* on it." She rolled her eyes. "These *people*."

Someone with more sense of society than I possessed at the time might have called her bitter. But to me, Anjali Dayal was a minor thrill. She laughed at those who most annoyed me—the ones who so scorned her—and in that way, she debilitated them a little.

When the party wound down and the twins' face-cake had been consumed—I got the corner of Meena's kajal-lined eye—my family found me in the garage, still putting away accoutrements. Anita's mother was carrying containers into the house so the Bhatts could freeze leftovers. My mother waved hello.

"Congratulations," she said, a bit icily. "You and Pranesh must be very happy."

Anjali Auntie blinked. "Pranesh?"

"About Anita's new school."

"Oh, yes," Anita's mother said, her voice suddenly at a steeper pitch. "Yes, I—we're very excited—you know Pranesh, always so focused on her academics, good IIT man."

"How nice that Anita has his brains," my mother said. "We

haven't seen him in quite a while, isn't it? Tell him Raghu and I say hello." Before Anjali Auntie could reply, my mother turned to me. "Neil, come. We have to go to the Nagarajans'."

"You're kidding me," I said. "*Another* party?"

Prachi gave me a look as if to say, *I've already tried.* But I had something in me at that moment, something copped from the careless way in which Meena Bhatt had been draped over George Warner-Wilson, some absorbed averageness.

"No," I said. "I don't want to go to another party. No one will miss me. I'm not going."

My parents were, for a moment, rendered immobile; we rarely bristled against them. They must have felt dread, sensing the emergence of adolescent rebellion, must have feared it, in the wake of Prachi's Spring Fling missteps. But I was thinking about the constrictions of the rest of the summer, of all I was supposed to achieve or become in the next three months, and I felt choked, and I reacted. I threw a finger in Anita's mother's direction. "Auntie can take me."

"Neeraj," my mother hissed, using my damned real name. "Anjali Auntie might have things to do. Come."

"Auntie," I said, turning to face Anita's mother, who was feigning deafness. She glanced back, her arms piled high with paper plates. "Would you mind bringing me home? I can help unload the car and stuff, since Anita's not feeling good."

She seemed to want to resist intervening, but I mouthed *please*, as though I was talking to one of my own friends, and she sighed.

"I can do it, Ramya," she said. "It's okay."

My parents appeared torn, afraid to display disharmony, and Prachi glared, seeming to feel she couldn't tag along since it had been *my* brilliant escape plan. And so they left. I packed up Anita's mother's Toyota with her, and answered her questions about debate, back in a Neil-and-adult script that excised me from the situation and concerned itself only with the exoskeleton of a human, teenage boy. When that had run out, silence filled the car and I watched the suburbs flail by—in the distance, the flank of I-285, that perimeter, and somewhere beyond, a city. From here, all I could discern were the churn of asphalt and concrete, a single white cross piercing the sky, and the flash of a few green highway signs.

At the Dayals', I hauled in the leftovers the Bhatts had told Anita's mother to take back for herself. The house was silent. "Anita sleeping?" I asked, and her mother said she must be. I went back to the car to grab the last bags, a couple of grainy cloth totes in the front passenger's seat. Anjali Auntie arrived before me, brushing past so quickly I startled.

"I've got those. Thanks, Neil," she said brusquely, reaching out to hoist them onto her shoulder. She stood in her driveway, watching me expectantly, framed by their house—mustard yellow with a red roof, comical in our neighborhood of brown bricks and gray stucco.

I'd made it home when I realized I didn't have my Swiss Army knife on me. I'd taken it out while loading the trays into the Dayals' refrigerator, because the Saran-wrapped dish of dhokla needed separating into two containers. I'd slashed the plastic open and put the knife—and the key chain it was attached to—on the counter. I had been distracted, wondering if Anita could hear me in her kitchen.

I crossed the cul-de-sac again and knocked. The red door was framed by a few petal-shaped pieces of glass, as though the door were the pistil and the rest of the house the flower's bloom. I didn't see any light filtering through. But they couldn't have departed so quickly. I knocked again, louder; no answer. I padded behind the out-of-bloom azalea bush, lifted the red watering can, and retrieved the spare key. In the foyer, I didn't remove my shoes, only kicked any spare summer dust from their soles against the doorframe.

"Just gonna get my knife," I said to no one. Anita's house opened wide in either direction: to the left, her mother's room, and a living room filled with formal stuffed chairs. To the right, a dining room with a long wooden table and a mahogany cabinet stocking china. Farther along, the lived-in parts of the place: the kitchen, a den with a plaid sofa and an unobtrusive television.

I made for the kitchen. But as I passed that china cabinet, I noticed an open door to my left, in the middle of the hallway—the door to the basement, which I knew to be unfinished, like mine, just cement floors and boxes and storage. Through the open door, light—the only light I could see anywhere in the house—was flowing.

I took one step toward the door, edged it further open with my toe, and listened for voices. All that came was a peculiar whirring and glugging. Something like a drill seemed to be buzzing, and I heard it the way you hear a dentist's tools in your mouth: in your temples, in the space below your eyes. The sound lifted. Footsteps were coming up the stairs. I hurried to the kitchen and located, on the countertop, in the darkness, my knife.

The lights flipped on. Behind me were Anita and her mother. The door to the basement was flung open behind them. Anita looked perfectly vital, completely well. From Anjali Auntie's arm dangled one of those totes that she had kept me from grabbing. In

Anita's hand was a glass that at first I thought was empty. But I looked again and saw that the bottom of it was filled with a kind of sunlight-yellow sediment. Some bubbles popped in a column. Anita quickly drained the sediment. That otherworldly yellow was gone through her lips in a moment.

"You look healthy," I said. I held up my Swiss Army knife. "I left this."

Anita was very still. Her breath seemed to be coming intentionally, as her chest rose and fell slowly.

The open basement door swung in my peripheral vision. Anjali Auntie took a step back and kicked it shut with her toe. She and Anita glanced at each other for the briefest moment. They really were starting to look alike. Anita was becoming a new creature and her mother had never looked much like a mother, anyway—no wrinkles, no crow's feet, not a sprinkling of silver or gray in her hair. As Anita grew taller, grew breasts, it was as though they were not getting old and older but moving toward a prearranged meeting point in the middle.

"I was just making Ani some of the stuff my mother used to make me when I was sick," Anjali Auntie said. I looked again at the glass. "You know turmeric milk, right, Neil?" she said.

I knew it: a horrible dark yellow thing my mother brewed whenever someone came down with a cold or cough or stomach bug. I knew turmeric milk, and I knew it had never and would never look like what had been in Anita's glass just then.

"Sure," I said. "Guess it perked you right up."

I lifted my knife in the air again to remind them I had gotten what I came for, and walked to the door without saying anything else. I spent the rest of that night home, alone, attempting to wend my way through the gilded sentences of *The Great Gatsby*—my summer reading book—but instead staring out my bedroom window at Anita's front lawn, where there was no seductively blinking green light like Daisy Buchanan's, only a mustard yellow house with all its lights on, as though its denizens were having a party for just the two of them.

2.

In summers past, I'd traipse down to the neighborhood swimming pool with Prachi and Anita and Kartik and Manu, toting sunscreen that someone's mother had prescribed, which we would all ignore, opting to become the color and texture of bottom-of-the-bag raisins. There had been a few day camps—one where I went trout fishing with a pink-skinned park ranger, to my Brahmin mother's chagrin. In those summers, my dreams followed me into my waking hours, their logic lingering, turning the humid days magical, overlaying the season like a very thin net.

But this summer was cold with reality. I'd been grounded, due to my public display of impertinence in telling my parents I preferred not to attend the Nagarajans' party. I was banned from Kartik's, the only place I could play video games, and allowed to go only to the Kumon math center and to the library—the latter when accompanied by my debate partner, the acidic Wendi Zhao, who oversaw my work and berated me for my mediocrity. In the evenings, I was to sit in my room, doing my reading and math. If I wanted proof that summer had descended on Georgia, I had only to open my window. The insects were out, katydids and cicadas and flashing lightning bugs, little green constellations.

"Don't you have assigned reading?" my mother said when I complained.

"The thing is, *The Great Gatsby* is a really short book," I pointed out.

My father shouted from the bathroom, over a trumpeting fart: "In our schools, you never got hundred percent in anything!" He flushed. In the kitchen, hands washed, he continued: "Sixty percent was considered very good! You should jolly well never be done!"

I suspected that I had become a casualty of Prachi's Spring Fling misbehavior. But my sister, the perpetrator herself, was allowed to roam free due to her pageant activities. It seemed immensely un-fair. Perhaps my parents feared my descent into averageness more than they feared Prachi's tumbles into vice. They trusted Prachi. My sister telegraphed her ambitions in the Duke poster on her wall and the Duke T-shirt she tugged on whenever she had a test, for good luck. She had a dream to lose. Me? I had no college poster, no talisman.

On the first evening of my imprisonment, I grabbed the up-stairs cordless in hopes of calling Kartik to arrange a covert video game rendezvous. But my mother was already on the phone.

I heard Mrs. Bhatt's voice on the other end of the line saying, "And that Anjali Dayal!"

"*How* would she go do something like that?"

"*Why*, mujhe toh pata nahi, but Ramya, I *saw* her going into my bedroom during Manav's toast, and I waited, soch rahi hoon ki, maybe she just needs to use the bathroom—"

"She should have been using the powder room! Who enters the master bathroom like that—"

"But just wait, I sent Meena in, usko maine bola, 'Meena, go see if Anjali Auntie needs something, or if she's looking for me,' so Meena went into my bedroom."

"And?"

"Toh, that woman is just *standing* in my closet!"

"That's what Meena said?"

"Yaaah, yah! Not only that, looking at all my clothes, my jewelry!"

"She *opened* your jewelry cabinet?"

"I had left it open, I remembered later, because I kept trying to choose, which earrings—"

"Itnaa nice-nice earrings."

"And also I kept trying to get Jay to wear the gold *Om* his daadi gave him, but these boys won't wear necklaces, saying 'Mummy, I look like a girl,' and then people started ringing the doorbell and I never shut it all up . . . anyway, *strange* behavior—"

My mother tutted. "She's *jealous*, Beena. She goes to all these parties-schmarties as *catering*, no husband in sight, and you're always wearing those niiice saris and stoles and—"

"Skinny-mini gold digger shouldn't need my saris."

"Gold digger? Kya matlab?"

"*Ram*ya—you know. All these kids listening to that song these days, you must keep up with them or you will lose them. *Get down, girl*, it goes, some such thing. Anyway, my cousin Rakesh was Pranesh Dayal's senior at IIT Bombay. He only told me. She went round with all the boys. Then chose Pranesh because people said *he's* the class topper, going to make lots of money, going to America and whatnot."

"Hanh—" my mother paused. "Thought I heard something on the line." (I muted the phone.) "Lekin, back there marriage *can* be a little *transactional*, na? *Gold digger*, bahut American way to think about it, Beena."

I heard footsteps coming up the stairs; my mother liked to pace around the house, complementing gossip with exercise, so I returned the cordless to its cradle and rushed back to my bedroom to stare out at the Dayals', beginning a pattern that would define the summer. I ran through hypotheses as time rolled by, as I squinted through the heat and fireflies and the low glimmering of the suburban streetlights. Did the Dayal women need money— money to be garnered from Prachi's necklace, or something in Mrs. Bhatt's closet? Was a divorce pending? Was Pranesh Uncle not funding the fancy-schmancy school? Or was something else altogether setting in?

I watched that Crayola yellow house that night and all summer, not knowing entirely what I was looking for, but aware that it deserved my attention.

My vigils over the Dayals' were interrupted by library trips, where I was stuck researching the upcoming debate topic. A bunch of high schoolers would spend the year discussing the fossil fuel crisis, something that felt distant, even invented, from my perspective amid Atlanta's gas-guzzler-crammed highways, where all seemed quiet, the apocalypse staved off in the comfort of concrete suburban stasis.

My parents had feared debate at first, because of the tournaments that took students out of town on weekends. Surely my mother imagined *nonsense* playing out beneath the noses of the chaperones in Howard Johnson hotels. But they relented when talk at Indian parties centered on the clarity of purpose that debate offered—you have one job, and it is not to tell the truth about the fossil fuel crisis. It is simply to win. Debate gave children ambition, the Indian parties concluded. Ambition: the substance to settle the nerves of immigrant parents. Ambition: the point of that summer, for me, was to acquire some.

I'd set up in a light-filled corner of the Hammond Creek Public Library in the mornings, at a table with a view of a slippery pine-needled slope leading to a ravine. There I took direction from Wendi Zhao. She was rumored to be among Harvard's top choices for debate recruits the next year and did not need a partner so much as a "tool" (as the debate kids said)—someone to do as she demanded amid the high heat of a tournament's elimination rounds. She had reduced female teammates to tears too many times, so the coaches decided she'd pair best with a guy.

I was uninterested in the policy papers Wendi forced me to read. Stuff about planning for a distant future. Solar wind capture. Hydrogen fuel. I found myself wandering the library, seeking higher-order material, in hopes of becoming the kind of competitor who opted for a philosophical approach over a wonky one. We called the former kritik debaters, or K-debaters, and their ranks were populated by enviably nonchalant potheads from alternative private schools, some of whom would grow into Harvard humanities professors. I spent my days aspirationally tunneling into the work of Slavoj Žižek and Giorgio Agamben and Martin Heidegger, sneaking these texts under the table until one day when Wendi approached silently—she had assassin's footsteps—and caught me.

"What's that got to do with alternative energy?"

I jumped as she slammed her palm down on *Being and Time*. "I was reading online," I stuttered. "I—I was reading about how sometimes policy making is the wrong thing to do because we have to, like, address the philosophy? Erm, ontology. Ontology. Behind the policy?"

She scowled. "I don't trust the abstract. Read this shit on carbon taxes."

It was during those library days that I encountered the imported grandfather. He was a huge guy, perhaps six feet, over two hundred pounds. He hulked in the corner over his books, reading with uncanny stillness, twitching only to turn a page, taking no notes. Sometimes he'd lean toward a closed hardback and press an elephant-flappy ear to the cover as though the pages had some secret to whisper. He was always there before I arrived around ten, remaining in his reading posture when I departed at one or two.

The day after Wendi pried *Being and Time* from my hands, the man whispered, with a shimmer in his eye, "I rather think she likes you."

"Weird way of showing it." I drummed my fingers on my laptop.

It began, then—the Neil-and-adult script. I told him, somewhat monosyllabically, about the debate team, Okefenokee, math classes, my sister.

"This debate business," he said after I had explained the basics, "it's fun for you? You enjoy the rush of testing ideas?"

I frowned. "I guess?"

"I have put words in your mouth. What is it you like about it?"

I sighed. I was thinking about my father's face when he picked me up from the novice state tournament, how his expression had been vacant when he pulled up to the curb but then suddenly animated at the sight of my trophy—a gold-colored figure opining atop a wooden block, one hand lifted, unspooling some brilliant oration. "That is *yours*?" he'd said, and the whole way home, our normal car silence had been somehow warmer than usual, like the feeling of pressing fresh-from-the-dryer laundry against your skin.

"Winning," I said. "That part is nice."

He pointed at the book that I'd tugged back down from the shelf after Wendi confiscated it, and spoke in an accent more British than Indian. "I have always wanted to visit Mr. Heidegger's home in the Black Forest. It would certainly be something."

Then he turned back to the American Revolution and I blinked vaguely, wondering how this peculiar old man knew all about Heidegger.

I found out over the next few weeks that Ramesh Uncle, a retired professor, had been imported unceremoniously from his prior life in West Bengal to suburban America. "Calcutta is a place alive with the past," he said one morning when we bumped into each other at the water fountain, near the children's section—away from Wendi's probing gaze. "You cannot walk outside without running into ghosts." He could not live in Hammond Creek, in America, without knowing its history, so he was absorbing American history like a second language.

"So, were you a history professor?" I asked, taking my sip of water and brushing my lips on my sweatshirt sleeve.

"In a way." He grinned. "I am a physicist. Which makes me a philosopher of time."

Wendi, on the other side of the library, would have had little tolerance for this exchange. I pressed on the water fountain a few times to watch it spurt. "What's that mean?"

"There is a little philosophy that was once considered heretical," he said, folding his arms and leaning against the corkboard that advertised, in primary colors, toddlers' story time each afternoon at four. "It is, however, the sort of thing a Calcuttan knows to be true." He paused, as though to gauge whether or not I was following. I nodded. "Eternalism," he pronounced. "The idea, see, is that the past and present and future are all equally real. Perhaps even coexisting."

"How *old* are you?" I suddenly asked, then flushed. There was something mesmerizing about the way Ramesh Uncle spoke of history, as though he'd witnessed it firsthand.

"I am one of those trees with so many age rings round its middle that you cannot really tell anymore. Come," he said. "We must both get back to our books, mustn't we?"

Each morning, I'd wait for Wendi to retreat into her work, and then I'd turn to Ramesh Uncle to be briefed on his day's pursuits. He wound through a self-made syllabus on America—on where we'd been, and where we seemed to be going. W. E. B. DuBois and Walt Whitman and the Wobblies; Thoreau and Twain and Tippecanoe.

"Are you writing something?" I asked after a while, as I'd been wondering what reading a bunch of books about America would add up to.

"Why should I write something? There are so many good books already to read."

"So, what do you, you know, want to do with . . ."

"The books?"

"Yeah."

"I would say I would like to read them, and then think about them, and maybe come back and read them again some more, later. Would that be an acceptable plan?" A smile was always inching across his face when he said stuff like that, as though he was inviting a challenge.

Soon, Ramesh Uncle began to take on more specialized pursuits. One afternoon, as I helped him carry a few fat volumes from the nonfiction section to his desk, he told me he was now looking into the early histories of Indians in America.

"Uncle," I whispered, depositing the books with a clunk, "I think you're supposed to say Native Americans."

"No, no, Indians like *us*."

"How much history could there be?" I said. I'd thought we were new here—hence all the unsettledness, all the angst, all the striving.

We sat down in our glass-window corner. Nearby, Wendi Zhao worked in a study carrel, surely blasting G-Unit in her noise-canceling headphones.

Ramesh Uncle smoothed his short-sleeved collared shirt as though he had been awaiting this question a long time. "*Very* much," he said. "You just see."

June rolled on. I hated math, I saw few friends, Wendi whacked me upside the head. And Ramesh Uncle ordered books from afar. The Hammond Creek library plugged into the college and university loan systems, making that little stretch of table where we sat gorgeously expansive, containing much more than our cramped lives. While other kids were splashing in the pool, shooting hoops, making out, I was listening to this old man tell stories in throaty whispers of Swami Vivekananda, showing up in Chicago to lecture Americans on Hinduism at the World's Fair, and of Bhagat Singh Thind, who went to the Supreme Court in 1923 to sue for the right to be considered "white." I learned, too, that Indians weren't allowed to enter the United States for decades. He even showed me, once, a 1912 clipping from an Atlanta newspaper. It mentioned *the Hindoos* who had come to town, peddling exotic fabrics, trinkets, and jewels—*dark as the Negroes, yet somehow different in complexion and mannerisms.*

I'd never had an urge to muse on my *roots* in the way Prachi and the girls in the Miss Teen India pageant liked to obsess over their *heritage*, like, *What does it* mean *to be both Indian* and *American?* That kind of thing seemed simpering, and I suppose if I were to ruminate honestly on it years later, such questions only magnified certain inconvenient truths: that despite our bubble of brownness in Hammond Creek, we were, in fact, the minority. That the white kids were still, on average, considered more attractive, more popular. More essentially at home in themselves. That sometimes America baffled us teenagers as much as it did our parents. That every emphasis on achieving a certain future came from the anxiety of simply *not knowing*, none of us *knowing*, what life here could be. There was no room to imagine multiple sorts of futures. We'd put all our brainpower toward conjuring up a single one: Harvard.

But. If I had roots in American soil, if we had not all so recently *crossed oceans*, if our collective past was more textured than I'd been led to believe, then, well, maybe there were other ways of being brown on offer.

Of all these historical yarns, I most remember the one about the Bombayan gold digger.

It was the middle of the afternoon in late June, and I was growing drowsy. A Jenga tower of books was piled on the old man's table that day, and he rapped the top of it as though to announce something. The tower collapsed, sending books skittering.

"Neil," he whispered, unfazed by the thudding of books landing on his table. I yanked my headphones out. "I have found something incredible. Would you like to hear it?"

I said I very much wanted to hear. He shuffled through the

fallen books to find the original, but then swatted the air, giving up. He leaned back in his wooden chair, stretching his legs in front of him. Through the window, the bloom of brown and green, hickory and pines, darkened. A midday Georgia storm began. As Ramesh Uncle talked, the thunder rolled on.

The Tale of the Bombayan Gold Digger

The man in question goes unnamed, known only as the Bombayan or, otherwise, the Hindu. The Bombayan has been in California for some-odd amount of time in the summer of 1850 and has picked his way to the goldfields, where he, along with Americans, Australians, Chileans, and Chinese, has been trying his hand at panning. This Hindu may be one of the only—if not *the* only—men of his race in the region. Solo, he must survive by wits and ambition.

Having had some luck in the goldfields, the Bombayan has on his person about nineteen hundred dollars' worth of gold in the form of dust and nuggets. One night, he makes camp beneath an oak tree in the valley of Douglas Flat, a region where more fantastic tales of riches mount every day, where ravenous men come seeking that sight—the yellow-gold flash in the shallow pan as the silt falls away. Come one early, blue-black morning, he awakens in his canvas tent after a night of raucousness to find that his gold has gone missing. Frantic, he uses his limited English to flag down a passing caravan of whites, some of whom claim connection to local government, though "government" of any kind in 1850s California is scarce. It's an unformed place, Calaveras County, full of unformed men.

"I have lost everything! Everything!" he weeps to the whites, who at first wonder at his origins—his skin is nearly as dark as the Natives', but his dress is thoroughly European. Establishing that he hails from the port city of Bombay, that jewel of the British Empire, they at first pity him—"So far from home . . ."

But then discussion commences. The whites form a briefly united nationhood: Germans, French, Scottish, Irish. Between them they purport to comprehend the colonized world. On horseback, gazing down at this peculiar Hindu, they review what they know—the Indians burn their widows over there, don't they? And is there not some decree prohibiting Asiatics from touching gold at all? Was there not a scuffle in the Deer Creek mines of late, against those impudent Chinese? They must not be fleeced by such a wretch, who himself may have gotten this gold by unsavory means. They decide to distrust the foreigner. But they do not tell the Bombayan this. They invite him to come along while they attempt to find the thief who stole his gold. They will collect the goods themselves and deliver the Hindu to justice for violating this ban: no brown or yellow fingers to touch sunny gold.

He traipses alongside the party as they ride, but then, suddenly, something gives him a fright. Perhaps he looks at them and suddenly, blisteringly, grasps their suspicion and disdain. Perhaps he possesses some last stores of gold on his person and fears these strangers might take it from him. Perhaps he is just made existentially aware of his aloneness in this land—a Hindu: not a white, not a Negro, not of the Natives or of China, but a man out of place and out of time. A man who becomes incomprehensible to history because he is an aberration.

He begins to run for his life. This sprint the whites take as proof of guilt—"He was trying to trick us! It is he who's stolen gold."

They catch him. A trial follows, and people arrive to testify against the Hindu. He'd been seen drinking brandy, growing rowdy, in someone's tent the other day; count him a black rogue, to be sure. In the end, the judge decides to spare the man his life but to have him whipped and banished. "How's a person supposed to get back to Bombay from here?" the whites wonder. But that isn't their concern. They beat him efficiently and search him for gold. As he is hunched over on the earth, his face and gestures obscured from view by splatters of blood and kicked-up dust, he begins to wail something in a horrid foreign tongue. Having found no metal on him, they decide they will let him loose and warn him with a few shots in the direction of his uncomprehending rump.

They untie him from the pole where he has been kept for the duration of the trial. He flees into the wilderness, and they shoot after him, one, two, three. He disappears into the woods. He should get himself home as soon as possible, the whites agree to one another. Otherwise, he'll earn himself a bullet or a noose, soon enough.

"Found that one in a German travelogue . . . but I can't for the life of me remember which . . . it was *green*, I think," Ramesh Uncle said, scratching his head, watching the mess of books with bemusement. "But. It sticks with you. I had thought the first Indians showed up much later—but think: the gold rush! Such an American phenomenon and one of our own kind running about in the middle of it. Makes you a bit proud, doesn't it?"

I saw him, the Bombayan, a small-built man, sinewy from years of labor, snapping his suspenders against his billowy once-white shirt, pushing open two big clanging saloon doors. Something primal that I never knew was in me suddenly came alive. Recognition, is that what it was? Kinship? I had never much cared about *ancestry* the way my parents spoke of it when we went back to India. There, ancestry meant unpronounceable names and impenetrable orthodoxies. But this gold digger felt viscerally like my forebear. What if *this* was my land, after all?

"I wonder if he survived."

Ramesh Uncle shrugged. "I shall to try to find out. Sometimes it takes luck and magic to track down someone history has ignored or gotten wrong. This German fellow didn't know a lick about the poor man. We would never call him a Bombay*an*, for instance. To us, he'd be a Bombay*kar*." Ramesh Uncle tapped one knobby forefinger on his right eyebrow. Then he turned to the window. "Do you know? There was a gold rush here in Georgia before California."

I remembered a class field trip to the Dahlonega gold mines in middle school. It was one of those strange Southern vacation towns that insisted on peacocking its heritage at you. Kitsch and crowds and turkey legs and gold (chocolate) bars, the past shrugged on as costume—not what Ramesh Uncle meant when he said *eternalism*, not the real resurrection of history, but the echo of it. I recalled getting in trouble for pocketing a glittery fool's gold rock that the tour guide passed around; the memory of my childhood gullibility and greed still stung.

"They ran out, out here," he continued. "Then they heard about more in the West, and off they went. Kicked out all the Indians— the other type—along the way. Same old arrogance, no matter where you look in history." I had the distinct impression that he was, in fact, looking in, or at, history, as he peered out into the pines and the sunny ravine. Like the past was within sight for him.

By the Fourth of July, Wendi separated us. She said, "Sir, I need Neil here to do his work, and you're distracting him," and set me up on my own. Ramesh Uncle winked on his way to and from the bathroom, but Wendi stood and coughed if he lingered too long.

Then, in mid-July, he vanished. I did wonder where he had gone. The truth is, though, that I was young, and preoccupied with myself. I began to google pictures of Jessica Biel and Lucy Liu in the study carrels, both of whom served as a fine replacement for history at the time.

AT NIGHT, I continued to keep an eye on the Dayal house. Anita and Anjali Auntie frequently got home late, often clutching things as they debarked, perhaps leftovers from catering events. I kept watching, unsure of what I might see, but hoping for an explanation to account for Anita's metamorphosis.

Anita's world had changed before. Pranesh Uncle had started "traveling for work" to California when we were in fifth or sixth grade. A few years after that, he founded a company out there, and was gone more often. Anita and Anjali Auntie spent most of the summer before ninth grade in the Bay Area. When Anita got home, we met up at the pool. Everything about her was different. She kept her arms folded awkwardly around her stomach, like she was trying to hold her intestines in. The gesture emphasized her new breasts. I would have gladly observed them all afternoon if Anita hadn't also been teary-eyed and tenuous the whole day, finally admitting as we lay on our towels during an adult swim that she might have to move. "I don't *like* him," she'd said fiercely.

"Your dad?" I was bewildered. "Can you *say* that?" It was the wrong response. But how could I have known that Anita had never seen, up close, two adults making a happy life? That her ignorance of the domestic stability I took for granted in my own home was a blank spot in her otherwise assured worldview?

Anyway, that was all I grasped about change: that it occurred above me, around me; that by the time I noticed it, it was too late; that I would always be catching up to it.

Case in point: after more than a month of being grounded, I remained unsure why my parents had reacted so restrictively to the insolence I'd displayed at the Bhatts'. I got my answer when an invitation arrived for Shruti Patel's birthday pool party at the YMCA. She was turning fifteen, and her parents had called around inviting everyone on her behalf. A sad existence, having grown-ups handle your social calendar. But I'd been isolated for weeks and I thought I'd go.

My mother shook her head. "I don't trust what goes on at these parties."

"At *Shruti Patel's* birthday?" I contorted my features into a Shruti-esque expression to remind my mother who we were talking about here. I pulled my hair up and out from both temples and bared my teeth like a gopher.

"Anyone can get into all kinds of nonsense these days."

My mother wanted Prachi and me to endure apart from the corrupting influences of American society—drinking, drugs. And dating: "Americans learn how to break up with each other very easily, all of them with endless baggage, exes upon exes. . . ." I first received the dating diatribe on the eve of Gabby Kaufman's bat mitzvah in seventh grade. "Mrs. Kaufman, I have called her on the phone," my mother had said, wagging a finger. "There will be no close-close dancing." I spent that night being taught how to grind by Gabby's spunky cousin from New Jersey, who informed me that she had kissed two Indian boys already and liked the chocolate look of us. In order to keep in contact with the thrilling Jersey Kaufman, I created an ill-fated screen name that followed me into high school: neil_is_indian. It would be years before another girl displayed interest *because* of my race, rather than *despite* it.

Some of these topics came up with my father one afternoon that summer, after he had finished pushing the lawn mower across our front yard. He surveyed his work with a sense of defeat. The grass looked like his back, little tussocks of fur sprouting here and there, unevenly.

"Mom's being insane," I complained, standing barefoot in the driveway, feeling the heat scald my foot soles. "She's, like, pre-grounding me for stuff I haven't even done yet."

He lifted his Braves baseball cap, one of those articles of clothing that my immigrant parents had amassed unthinkingly through the years, part of the assimilationist wardrobe; my father could not have recited any of the players' batting averages, or performed the fans' highly questionable "tomahawk chop." The southern sun knocked against his bald spot, reflecting merrily. He wiped the ring of his sparse hair with a hankie, deliberately, then shook the cloth out in front of him, as though looking for a premonitory guiding pattern in the sweat.

"You know what they say on the trains in India when it gets very crowded?"

I sighed to make clear my disinterest in whatever parable that was to follow. "What?"

"*Ad*-just." He pronounced each syllable separately. "Ad-just. No matter how many people are there, someone wants to sit; they'll say, 'Ad-just, sir, please ad-just.'"

"Uh, okay?"

"We are all still ad-justing to this place, see?"

"*I'm* not. *I'm* American."

"Your mother—she's protective."

"I don't get into trouble, though."

"What do you mean, *trouble*?" my father said.

"You know. Drinking, whatever."

He inhabited a grave silence for a moment. Then he said, "That is hardly the only kind of trouble."

That was a loquacious exchange between my father and me.

NOTHING WOULD EXCUSE ME from attending the Miss Teen India pageant in July, which was held in the convention room of a Ramada Inn in Duluth. I'd not been forced into a kurta this time, but I shriveled inside to think of stepping into a lobby full of white people as a member of the Indian pageant caravan. It turned out the hotel was owned by desis, and the only non-Indian in sight was the paunch-bellied Black security guard who kept asking, "Are y'all having some kind of *festival* or, like, *traditional* thing here?"

The ways in which the pageant was traditional were more American than Indian. The owner of the MTI Georgia was a Gujarati businessman with beady, roving, salacious eyes, proprietor of a chain of liquor stores across Alpharetta and Gwinnett, who introduced the twenty-some pageant competitors as they filed from the crimson-carpeted hallway into the yellow-wallpapered room: "Give it up for our contestants, beautiful inside and out, isn't it," he said, his vowels those mutt noises, folding in on themselves in an effort to keep the speaker from rolling the ensuing *r*'s or clacking the *t*'s too hard.

There were perhaps fifty chairs laid out for the audience, surrounding a long judges' table. About half were filled. A toddler in a gold-and-maroon lehenga waddled laps around the seats. Some auntie leaned over me, her sequined dupatta falling on my face, to say hello to my father. My mother stood in the hallway with the other mothers, armed with bobby pins and safety pins and concealer. I hadn't spotted Anita or Anjali Auntie when we came in.

The pageant opened with a column of brown girls balancing on spiky heels as they runway-walked a makeshift stage about two feet off the floor. Last in line: Anita, wearing a lemon-lime, yellow-and-green number splattered with mirrors and tie-dye. Her whole belly was visible—it was a little soft, like an inviting pillow. I caught her eye for an instant and noted nerves there, in the wideness of her gaze, the way all her concentration seemed to be devoted to stilling her facial muscles. I mouthed *hi*, and then regretted it.

Applause sounded and the contestants retreated. The MTI owner was muttering to someone next to him, but the mic had not been removed from his lapel, so we all heard him hissing, *Tell that very fat one to cover up little more.* It echoed, and a shushing auntie came to unclip him while we awaited the next episode.

A scrawny man manifested beside my father and pressed a pile of glossy magazines into his hand. My father, ignoring, passed them to me. They were those diaspora rags, the kind piled up in the front of Indian restaurants and salons, which stay afloat through advertisements that purvey immigrant necessities and nostalgia: an article featuring a profile on the Scripps National Spelling Bee champion (CAN YOU SPELL JUGGERNAUT? INDIAN AMERICANS DOMINATE BEE!) running next to an advertisement for KAJOL BEST LADIES' FINERIES and MEGA DESI WEDDING EXPO, ALL SHAADI NEEDS: ORLANDO, DALLAS, SAN JOSE.

I flipped through and saw one of Anita's mother's catering ads—ANJALI DAYAL: ALL TYPES DESI KHANA! and a black-and-white picture of her that stretched her out dishonestly, making her look pleasantly plump, turning her into another safe auntie. An insert labeled ACE COLLEGE APPLICATION SEASON fell out, featuring an interview with the Chinese mother who had authored the bestseller *Harvard Girl.* In the back, a column ran from a "Hindu activist" under the headline WE MUST BE MORE LIKE THE JEWS.

My father prodded the college insert. "Keep that aside." I did. Later I would find it contained a workbook to help you build your college essay "Mad Libs–style." *My name is . . . My dream is . . . When not studying I . . . My most important experience between ages 10 and 18 was . . .*

There were the question-and-answer sessions, during which the ladies skirmished to offer the inanest possible response to that platitudinous question and its many manifestations: *What does it mean to be both Indian and American?* To wit: *How should this generation ad-just to the New Country?* Prachi faltered trying to explain why we didn't speak an Indian language at our house; we had Kannada and Tamil and Malayalee roots, and a mother who'd grown up among Hindi speakers, so settling on any regional identity had never been an option—"My mother, see? Speaks about six languages? And my father two? But when they moved here, they wanted us to only learn English?"

Better was Uma Parthasarthy's response to a question posed by judge Manisha Fruitwalla: "Miss Uma, which place would you most like to visit, and why?"

"Um, for me, to Tirupati, because God has, um, been very calling on me, recently . . ."

There were the talents: too often Bollywood-infused hip-hop or Kathak-infused tap. Prerna Mallick, fifteen, of Clay County was the highlight of that year's program, as she twirled a folded umbrella about like a cane to some old filmy monsoon song, which subsided into "Singin' in the Rain." As the English interrupted the Hindi, Prerna snapped open the umbrella to face us: Ah! The instrument! It was patterned in the colors of the Indian flag. She rotated it in front of her, legs lifting into many chubby Rockette kicks. Then she began to do Kathak chakkars, twirling and twirling to a beat not audible within "Singin' in the Rain." Finally, Prerna set down her umbrella, stumbled, covered her mouth, and ran out of the room, having dizzied herself into nausea.

A few people followed her anxiously into the hallway. The judges went on making notes. The audience kept elbowing each other, eyeing the glossies, undertaking college-application Mad Libs. And my father began to emit deep, ursine snores.

The most important part of the pageant, apart from the (known but unstated) primary point of judgment, the quality of its contestants' features and curves, was the Charity Presentation. That was where Prachi lost. Her charity project for the past six months: a clothing drive that gathered discarded T-shirts and sent them to villagers in Karnataka. But the room shifted when Anita took the mic, her Sprite-can-colored outfit jangling with mirror work, and began to talk about her fund for battered South Asian women in Queens.

I don't think I'd ever heard the phrase *South Asian* before. I definitely hadn't heard of *battered women*, nor did I know of *Queens*. I had the sense Anita was not relying on her own knowledge of the world. How could she have suddenly come into such an adult, global perspective?

"I had this desire," she said, "to do something here, in America, because people have this idea that when you get to America everything is all of a sudden okay."

She launched into a barrage of statistics, speaking in a practiced staccato reminiscent of Wendi Zhao's debate voice. I craned my neck to see where she was looking. In the very back of the room stood Anjali Auntie, wearing a tatty gray T-shirt that read IIT BOMBAY. Her hair was pulled into a messy ponytail. All of her attention seemed to have gone into Anita's looks rather than her own that day. Her hands were pressed over her heart in a gesture that might have looked loving if not for the furrowed brow, the clenched jaw, the neck tendons bulging. I suddenly felt *bad* for Anita. The intensity of Anjali Auntie's focus on her daughter just then seemed obliterating, like a too-bright spotlight. Anjali Auntie's lips trembled as though she was reciting some enchantment to cast victory over her daughter.

It worked—something worked. Anita sounded unlike the other competitors. No one else had arranged a charity in the US. It was all *send this or that to the third world.* It was as though Anita had suddenly convinced the judges that there was such a place as Indian *America*, that she'd drawn up its borders and rerouted the foreign aid to the new domestic front; they had no choice but to honor her patriotism.

When the businessman placed the dinky crown on Anita's head and informed her that she'd be going to the regional pageant that November in Charlotte, she lifted her hands in a namaskar and said thank you to the community and to her mother, who helped her see all the ways in which the Indian immigrant experience is complicated.

As she gave her valedictory, people were dispersing, mothers bitterly helping daughters from the stage, daughters pulling off heels and looking relieved to be barefoot. A photographer knelt, snapping shots from a lewd angle. A hotel employee stood in the doorway, eyeing her watch. But Anita was untroubled by her lack of audience. She turned, her bargain-basement tiara winking, and looked at Prachi, who had begun to unpin her dupatta.

"Thank you also," she said, "to the fellow contestants, who have been such an inspiration, and whose best qualities I will try to incorporate into myself."

On the ride home, my mother went in on Anjali Auntie's activities backstage. The moms had been in close quarters all afternoon, pinning and making up, and now my mother reported that Anjali Dayal had been "behaving like one *cow*, only."

Prachi sat glumly, her made-up face pressed against the station wagon window. She drew back. Whatever cakey stuff she was wearing left behind a ghostly print. Through Prachi's window I made out a looming church sign—STOP, DROP, & ROLL DOES NOT WORK IN HELL—and past it, silhouettes of two buildings on the meager Atlanta skyline. But they were smeared by that makeup stain, so I felt I was seeing the city as through a shaken snow globe.

"Not only that," my mother was saying. "When Prerna Mallick got sick, no one could find water for her, na? Someone's asking those hotel employees, water please, water, and no one's coming, and poor Prerna Mallick's mother is asking Anjali, 'Can you just give her some of your daughter's water?' and she reaches for this bottle, and Anjali grabs it and says, 'Germs, she did just get sick,' and everyone back there, we're all thinking, 'Just let her pour it in her mouth, no lips-touching, like a proper Indian.' Shameless woman."

The car went quiet. I was developing a migraine, and leaned forward, pressing my forehead into the back of the driver's seat.

"What is it, Neil?" my father inquired, feeling me headbutting him. "Why so sullen?"

"I'm so tired," I croaked. "I'm just *so* tired."

My mother whipped her head around. I feared a shouting match would begin, that she might demand to know what right I had to be tired, that she would recite all she and my father had been doing when they were my age. Instead she reached her hand back and cupped my kneecap, and then did the same to Prachi. "You are both working very hard," she said.

She switched on the CD player. A bhajan filled the car, "Raghupati Raghava Raja Ram." My parents hummed along to the prayer song, both off-key. Where it all went, what gods might have been listening in that land of church signboards, I couldn't have said.

Next to me, Prachi stared out the window toward the Spaghetti Junction, where the veins of Atlanta converged into a Gordian knot of concrete and cars. The shape of Prachi's forehead remained on the window, the self she had worked so hard to become left behind on the glass.

I DID NOT MAKE IT to Shruti Patel's pool party. The night of the event, as I lingered on the doorstep waiting for Kartik's mom to pick me up, my father stepped outside, waving the cordless phone, a rare fury on his face. He had just gotten off the phone with Mr. Lee, my Kumon instructor, who informed him that I'd failed to turn in any work at all for the past two weeks. What I *had* completed, Mr. Lee went on, was abysmal. I'd wasted hundreds of dollars of hard-earned immigrant income.

And so, I found myself spending my evening futzing with trigonometry at the dinner table. My father sat next to me, trying to teach me mental math tricks. I absorbed nothing. After two or more hours, I finally begged for a break. He softened.

I took a Popsicle from the freezer and tried to walk off the night as I made a loop around the cul-de-sac. I wished everyone would give up on me. Their gazes were too forceful, their hopes for me too enormous. For it felt, back in Hammond Creek, that it wasn't our job just to grow up, but to grow up in such a way that made sense of our parents' choice to leave behind all they knew, to cross the oceans. I couldn't bear to be the only one among them—Prachi, Manu, Anita—who failed to achieve anything, who ultimately became nobody at all.

I sat fiddling with the gluey part of the Popsicle stick, on the curb a few feet from the Walthams' red BUSH/CHENEY: FOUR MORE YEARS sign—which had remained staunchly on their lawn for two of the four years. Just then, Anita's mother's Toyota rose over the crest leading to our cul-de-sac. Anita stepped out of the car. She didn't see me at first; I was sitting beneath the out-of-commission lamp-post, in the dark. She wore a crimson tankini. A blue towel was slung around her hips. Her birdlike, still-childish shoulder blades pinched together as she stretched her arms wide. They looked like a hinge beneath her skin, opening something behind her sternum. In there, somewhere, was the Anita I'd grown up with.

What had we played? *House.* It wasn't, with Anita, a game of cooking or cleaning, but a game of arranging the components of a neat life. She'd grill me: *Name?* I'd pick Ben or Jake or Will. One day I said, *Neil,* and she said, *That sounds like Neeraj,* so she made me Neil. *Age?* she'd ask. *Occupation?* Having nailed down the par-ticulars, she'd then grow wistful. *Look outside,* she'd say. *Tell me what you see.* What I saw: the loops and twines of our neighbor-hood and neighborhoods like ours—trees and asphalt and medi-ans and sedans. Hot southern sky. Hot Georgia asphalt. Suburbs, endless suburbs. I'd remain frozen, afraid of making a mistake. As a child, I feared mistakes. In the face of my paralysis, Anita would lay a small hand on my shoulder and shake me. *Neil, you're sup-posed to make it up! You're supposed to* imagine*!*

Other times, she would decide we needed to be productive. Once, she had us publish and circulate a newsletter for the neigh-borhood, reporting on the Walthams' church and her father's busi-ness. When we sadly counted out the money from that endeavor—a measly few dollars—Anjali Auntie, hovering over a pot of dal on the stovetop and looking on, bemused, weighed in. "Don't kids here make *lemonade stands?*" Like she was playing, too. All three of us straining, against the heat, to figure out what American kids did. Then she boomed, her voice like a used car salesman on tele-vision: "It's a great day for a lemonade!"

That afternoon, we made lemonade. Anjali Auntie switched

between stirring the dal and helping us. Our hands were too weak to eke all the juice out of the lemons, so together we pressed each fruit against the ceramic and watched the acid consume the sugar.

All this I remembered, and mourned, at the sight of those girl shoulders. Whatever was entering Anita through that open hinge was obliterating the child I had known.

She turned, squinted, spied me.

"Oh, hi, Neil!" she called, in a voice that was, miraculously, the inheritor of the voice that had once said, *You're supposed to imagine!* All the life that had gone into imagining the landscape outside our shared *house* now went to . . . what? The Harvard pennant above her bed? "Were you waiting for *me*?"

I stood, still in the shadows, and kicked the Walthams' BUSH/ CHENEY sign behind me.

"No," I said, swallowing the lump in my throat. "I just needed some air."

"All well, Neil? They missed you at Shruti's," her mother said, hoisting a bag out of the car. I made a sort of muted noise of assent, confirming I was alive, if not well. Anjali Auntie squinted at me doubtfully.

"Ani," she said, before making for the door. "You're going to work on that dance piece tonight? Before you sleep?"

"I said I would," she said tersely. Her mother went inside, leaving me alone with Anita. "It's for regionals," she said, though I hadn't asked. "The talent part. It's stupid."

"Congrats, I guess," I said, lifting my hands over my head in the shape of a lumpy tiara.

"How's Prachi?" she said. "I really thought she did great."

I felt my voice deepening artificially as I snapped: "They're saying she was robbed."

Anita looked startled for a moment. Then she smiled. "Shruti *really* missed you today," she said. "She's just *too* excited to see you in the fall. She's getting her braces off." She smacked her lips.

"Have you ever even *been* to Queens?" I'd googled it after the pageant and learned it was in New York. "Or did you just make up all that charity stuff?"

Her face set back into the practiced public calm she'd displayed at the pageant, and it now occurred to me that perhaps her outer self had smothered her inner life. This thought frightened me only for a moment, before it morphed into envy.

"Some of us have goals. *Some* of us work hard," she said, turning away.

Anita was almost at her doorstep, in the unlit part of the driveway; the shadows consumed her, and I did not know how far away from me she'd gone, which made everything more urgent. I felt I had just moments to call out to her, to beg one final time that she bring me along wherever she was going: "Anita," I said, barely above a whisper. "Wait—please—can you talk a minute?"

I thought I made out the beginning of a reply, but it was only the croak of a cicada, and then the shudder of a firefly, and then the Dayals' front door thumped shut.

I SWEATED THROUGH a strange dream: Ramesh Uncle and I were aboard a ship making for America. I never saw my own face, or his—we were ghostly bodies with splotches of light for heads. We kept pacing the ship deck as the ocean sprayed our faces, and I kept saying, *How will we know when we get there?* and he said, *There's a big statue,* and when we berthed at the California coastline, an enormous oxidized bronze Anita loomed, one hand high in the air, holding not a torch but, instead, a very large tiara.

I woke around two. I could not imagine lying still through the night. I tiptoed downstairs and stepped outside, barefoot, making my way to the Dayals' front lawn. I stood a moment and considered the facade of that strange house, the mustard yellow and the lively red door, and I thought it was time for me to break something.

I lifted the watering can behind the azalea bush. The key was missing. So I edged around back and found, next to the cement path, a stone. I gripped it in both hands as I approached the basement, where Anita and her mother had been the night I left my knife in the kitchen. I had the sense that some boundary between my dream and my waking life had not yet fully shut.

The bottom square of glass on the basement door window shattered quickly, and I didn't think about the shards protruding when I pushed my arm through and undid the lock, making use of the digital dexterity I had been developing in hopes of one day removing a girl's bra. I dropped the rock on the earth outside. No alarm. The only sound was the house itself: the ambient noise of the air-conditioning, the hum of a refrigerator.

Last I'd been in this basement, it was unfinished, with boxes piled up by the water heater. Now, though. The first thing I thought was *mad scientist*. Three long tables, the kind Anita's mother might have used while catering, were covered with white plastic tablecloths. A mess of tools was laid out. A large stone basin. A blowtorch. Tongs. A juicer. (I thought of the buzzing I had heard the last time I was here.) A huge plastic jar of sugar. I looked down to see a trickle of blood dripping from my elbow to my wrist. I pressed my shirt to it.

I moved toward the fridge, which was also new. Sometime recently, the Dayals had added a small kitchen—a fridge, a kitchen island on wheels, a wire rack. When I opened it, still tending the wounded arm, I saw the *thing* altering Anita, like a vast shaft of light, striking her chest, growing her up.

On the top shelf were three round, yellow lemons.

On the second, several small vials of liquid, and on the lowest, a large pitcher filled with the same substance. Each vial was partially covered with a piece of masking tape, on which something had been written. The plump belly of the pitcher was also covered with tape. I made out two letters—*S.P.*—and some numbers: *81106*. I said them aloud. They were the previous day's date: August 11, 2006.

I lifted the pitcher to examine it outside the fluorescent interior. A bit of my blood streaked the handle. Through the glass, the liquid glowed yellow gold. That hue beamed through the masking tape. *S.P.*, I read again. *S.P.* I returned the pitcher to the fridge, lifted the vials. One, nearly drained, read *P.N.*, followed by more numbers—the date (because now I had in my head that these were dates), I realized, of the Spring Fling dance. I picked up a few more until I found the one I'd been expecting to see: *J.B.*, with the date of the Bhatts' graduation party.

Something taken, from each of those people—from S.P., Shruti Patel. From P.N., Prachi Narayan. From J.B., Jay Bhatt. Was *this* what had made Anita different that summer? And that gemlike glint. Prachi's necklace, on the parking lot asphalt. The jewelry cabinet, open in Mrs. Bhatt's closet.

I leaned over the pitcher, *S.P.* It smelled like—it *was*—lemonade. Fresh. Saccharine and sour at once. Not quite the same concoction we'd made all those years ago; it was now laced with something new. Something that had belonged to Shruti Patel.

I drank.

It was tangy, but sweetness followed, and followed. Bubbles were settling in my stomach. I never wanted it to end. As the liquid streamed down my throat, I felt a great sense of purpose.

And then—"Stop, stop, Neil, fucking *stop*," came a pinched, panicked voice. Whose? Which one of them? As a throbbing began behind my eyes, Anita's face materialized before me. Her hair was haloed by the eerie low basement light. A cold nausea set in, and then a fuzzing of my vision. But I was still drinking.

"Neil, you have to stop, please," I heard Anita say. Her hands closed around the pitcher; she was trying to tug it away from me, with surprising strength. "You've had too much."

3.

Anita held the pitcher above me. I heard her step away and place it on the counter. I knelt, bearing my knees to the floor, as though it alone confirmed my existence. Sharp, icy knuckles pressed against my forehead.

"Neil."

I was losing all sense of time; I could not tell if I'd been there a minute or an hour.

"Am I dying?"

"No." She waggled her fingers in front of me; her nails were painted a bright cherry red. She wore black Soffe shorts and an oversize Harvard shirt. "How many am I holding up?"

I blinked. "Ten."

"You're not dying," she said. "But the answer was four."

"Should I barf?" I folded my arms into my stomach and leaned forward. I wanted to rest my cheek on the cement—it looked so refreshing.

"It won't come out. If you don't listen, you'll feel worse." I looked up, and there was my oldest friend, speaking in a conspiratorial whisper. She waited for my eyes to settle on hers.

"How'd you know I was down here?"

"I was in the living room. Working. I don't sleep well."

"It's summer."

"My new school sent over summer homework, so I can 'catch up.' They don't think much of OHS."

I nodded, unable to respond verbally. The cement floor smelled damp; even basements sweated in the Georgia summer. I spoke to the floor: "Is this what's made you . . . so weird?"

Anita snorted, an unseemly sound she would never have made in front of someone like Melanie. She knelt. Her hand hovered above my head as though she were going to stroke my hair.

"I had too much once," she said. She didn't touch me. "I know how it feels, all acidy, your heart is racing, you'll be sick and jittery for weeks if you don't—"

"*Weeks?*"

"Get up."

Still dizzy, seeking support, I stood, stepped over the shards of broken glass by the door, and settled myself on the staircase landing. I lifted my forearm to show Anita the blood.

"That's not too deep," she said. "I'll get some Neosporin in a second. But listen to me. Just—just do what I say. Otherwise it'll be a total waste."

My head was drooping between my legs as I heaved like a spent athlete at the end of a trying sprint. Anita's hand rested on the nape of my neck. At any other point in my adolescence, that touch would have been miraculous.

"I think I can do this," she said. That furtive glance back toward the ceiling, like she was taking permission from her mother's sleeping form. "Okay. You should, um, close your eyes." I did, and watched strange neon fractals form behind my lids. "So, uh—

focus on something you want." The first thing I thought of was her hand on my neck, how it was a continuation of her hand shaking my shoulder all those weekends of our childhood: *You're supposed to make it up! You're supposed to imagine!* She amended: "Something you want to achieve."

A series of those fractals passed before me, and then something settled. I was in the car with my father, holding a golden trophy, which kept me rooted to the car seat, to the earth. My father, next to me, radiated not his usual stoicism, but rather something I can only describe as supreme understanding. I was known. The world stilled, turned briefly safe.

"You've got it," Anita said. I wondered how she knew. "Your breathing's steadier."

She was right. My pulse had slowed. But beneath my stabilized heart rate was an elevated energy that made me want to open my eyes and welcome back the world. The room came into view. Everything quivered at its edges before erupting into brighter, more saturated color.

"You're okay." Anita sounded both surprised and relieved, and then stepped onto the stairs, walking softly on the balls of her feet. "I'll get you the Neosporin and—"

"Anita!" I spoke louder than I meant to. "Tell me what I fucking drank!"

She glanced at the ceiling as toward some higher power, or maybe just toward her mother's room again, and there was distress on her face. "Technically, lemonade—but a special lemonade. Ah. Well. Gold, Neil. You drank a shit-ton of gold. Half our best stock, which is honestly pretty infuriating."

Before I could reply, Anita raised a shaky finger to her lips and hissed *shhh*. It was too late. The basement door was swinging open, and Anjali Auntie was standing in the hallway, darkened by the bright lights she'd flipped on around her. Anita stepped not up toward her mother, but down, closer to me.

"Ani? Anita Joshi Dayal, what are you doing down there?" Anjali Auntie always said Anita's name the Indian way, with a soft *t*—*Anitha*—but I heard that *th* with special resonance that night. Our parents could do this in anger, jerk us back from drawly *Anita* to terse *Anitha*, from mild *Neil* to positively spicy *Neeraj*. And Anjali Auntie reminded me of my own parents in another way just then: her voice resembled their shouts the night of the dance; running through their fury at my sister had been a vein of fear.

"If you've been meddling with my supply," she went on, "I'll—"

Anjali Auntie stepped onto the top stair and into the light, which was when she saw me. She was wearing powder blue pajama shorts patterned with dancing penguins. Her mouth was slightly agape, and her face looked puffy.

"My god, you two," she sighed. "What have you done?"

BEFORE SHE WAS ANJALI DAYAL, my neighbor, she was Anjali Joshi, just a middle-class Bombay girl.

Bombay, a city where Gujaratis and Maharashtrians and Tamilians and Parsis become Bombaykars, allegiances shifted to contemporary urban existence rather than to the regions that created them. The Joshis considered themselves modern, but in one respect they rang a bit of the bygone days: the parents—an excise tax officer and a housewife—privileged their sons' education over their daughter's.

Anjali grew up flitting about with friends in the housing society, playing with her two older brothers when they were free, reading

English novels. She did fine in school, though not spectacularly, and no one told her to put in more work. There was an understanding: her brothers were to one day become somebodies; she was to one day become married. When Anjali was in fifth standard, she watched her eldest brother, Dhruv, sweating through entrance exams, mortgaging his adolescence for a chance to study at the prestigious Indian Institutes of Technology. He made it to IIT's Delhi campus, setting the bar high for the younger brother, Vivek, who did not display the same innate brilliance or work ethic as Dhruv. As Anjali crested into her teenage years, in the mid-1980s, Dhruv was accepted to graduate school in a place called North Carolina. Vivek came under even more pressure to follow in his brother's footsteps.

The parents enrolled Vivek in the renowned Goswami Classes, the cram school meant to prepare him for the IIT exams. Dhruv had done without these courses, but Vivek needed help.

Anjali Joshi perceived something mysterious about the Goswami Classes, because they pulled Vivek toward some inexplicable newness. She used to spend hours eyeing the blue neon sign advertising the courses, waiting for Vivek to get home, hoping he might spare a few minutes to flick around the puck on a carom board.

In the height of monsoon in 1984, Dhruv came home from America for a visit, wielding gifts like arms, breaking through the barricades of the closed Indian economy. For his father, Dhruv brought a ceramic mug reading NC STATE DAD. For Vivek, a Butterfly aluminum-frame tennis racket and a Lynyrd Skynyrd tape. For his mother, melamine plates and Tupperware; she systematically emptied their steel vessels in favor of the foreign imports. For Anjali: Jolen hair-lightening cream. "For your face," Dhruv explained, pressing a pinky to his upper lip.

The women in the housing society came to ogle Dhruv. Though ungainly, he was not bad-looking, and they wanted to hear how his accent had evolved. ("You sound just like the people on the TV," said Parag.) They were ravenous for America. America: metonymy for *more*. A vast place full of all the things Dadar lacked. Nonstick cookware, Chevrolet Corvettes, Madonna, the Grateful Dead, small leather purses, Mary Kay cosmetics, Kraft cheese. And something all those trinkets added up to—*another way of being in the world.*

"A lucky girl, whoever marries him," the neighbor aunties said. But Dhruv was in no hurry to be married. He left still a bachelor.

One afternoon, before Vivek arrived home, Anjali saw her mother return from Parag's house, where the society mothers had been gathering, and set to work in the kitchen. What she saw baffled her. Had her mother *melted* gold? Boiled it? Anjali would learn the proper names for the processes later, in adulthood, reinventing some of them herself. But at the time, she gathered this much: her mother had somehow liquidated Parag's gold coin and served it to her brother. When Lakshmi lay down for her afternoon nap, young Anjali crept into Vivek's bedroom and found him there, sipping this strange drink.

Vivek, hunched over graphing paper, drawing numbers in pencil so small that he had to squint to make out his own markings. His skin blooming with dark shadows of sleeplessness. A devil's bargain, this route to America.

"Can't you tell me what it is?" she whispered, pointing at the tumbler.

Vivek folded his arms, glanced at the clock on the wall, and sighed. "I have to get back to this in three minutes," he said, his voice full of the new lonesomeness that had frosted it in recent months. But he told his sister what their mother had told *him* the first time she gave him a glass of brewed gold to drink, some weeks earlier.

"Gold," he said, "is a wise metal. It contains people's dreams and plans."

"How, bhau?"

He sighed. "Think, Anju. Think what all reasons people buy gold." She thought. At the birth of a new baby—gifts of gold. As a backup in case the cash economy failed. It appeared in poojas, at weddings. "Everybody puts many hopes and plans on gold, see?"

"Why go *drinking* it?"

"If it's brewed properly, it seems to give us . . . some sort of power."

"To do what?"

"To, na, achieve those plans."

"You're . . . stealing somebody's . . ." Anjali fumbled for the word. "Ambition?"

"Don't be dramatic. Skimming off the top, really."

Anjali stood to examine the tumbler, but she saw only the dregs of whatever her mother had been brewing earlier. She tilted it back into her mouth. It was bitter, and it stung.

"I don't like it," she said.

"Well, you don't have to take it if you don't want to go to IIT," her brother replied.

"What if I wanted to do something else?"

Vivek rubbed his eyes and looked at the clock meaningfully. "Like what?"

Anjali squatted on the ground and fiddled with her plaits. She felt very small down there, curled in that semi-fetal position. She did not know what else there was to do, or to want.

. . .

I'D BEEN LED UP TO the den and deposited on the plaid sofa while Anita ran off for Neosporin and Band-Aids.

Her mother was pacing in front of the television and bookshelves. The only sound was her occasional deep sigh.

"I'm sorry about the window," I said.

"The window," she said, disbelieving. "He's sorry about the window."

Anjali Auntie paused in front of a row of framed black-and-white photographs above the television. I'd never noticed them before. She reached out to touch one. It showed a young girl in a starched salwar kameez, with fat braids running down her torso. She was chubbier than she would be when she grew up, but the striking cheekbones and compelling eyes were recognizable through the puppy fat. She scowled at the camera. Next to her was a gangly boy in pleated shorts and a collared shirt. He grinned widely, as though to compensate for young Anjali's grouchy demeanor.

"This is a massive fucking secret, Neil," Anita said, stepping into the room, bearing a black first-aid pouch and waving the tube of Neosporin. Her mother didn't flinch at the swearing.

"What Ani means is that I would be in some trouble. If anyone were ever to find out."

Anita sat next to me and began mopping my bloody forearm with gauze. Her gestures were dispassionate, as though I were a stranger. The gel was icy on my skin.

Anjali Auntie looked again at the photo that had made her pause. It would be some years before I knew how many memories passed over Anjali Dayal that night. She seemed to resolve something in her mind. "It's all already been set in motion for you, hasn't it, Neil?"

She was correct. I already belonged, irrevocably, to this particular history.

Anjali Auntie paused and went to the kitchen for water. *Gold.* It was everywhere in our world: around my sister's neck, dripping from my mother's earlobes, adorning the statues at the temple. Even I had a few gold possessions—pendants and rings gifted by relatives, all stored safely in a box in my mother's dresser. I recalled a white babysitter who'd worked for us a few times when I was small, and how curious she'd been about parts of our lives I considered normal. She interrogated my mother: Where did she get her spices? And the steel plates with Prachi's and my names etched into them? And the gold—especially the gold—she wore every day? "You can't get good pieces like this here," my mother told Kimberly proudly. "Maybe at Jhaveri Bazaar Jewelers in Decatur. But even then, nothing like India." Gold—now it ran in my bloodstream.

"I want in," I said.

"In?" Anjali Auntie carried two glasses from the kitchen and pressed one on me. "What do you think *in* means?"

"Anita takes regular doses," I said after sipping.

Anjali Auntie turned to Anita. "You've told him all that?"

"I guessed," I said, as Anita opened her mouth in outrage.

"Oh. Well." Anjali Auntie rubbed her forehead. "Yes. I give this to Ani regularly. But this works for her because she converts the energy very quickly. She knows she *has* to."

Anita's jaw clenched. "You have to make use of this stuff," she said, then, more gently, "It's only worth it if there's something you want to *do* with it." In this response lay the thing that divided the two of us these days. Anita knew what she wanted. Every day, she worked toward it.

"What if I did something?" I said. "What if I used it?"

They were sitting on the same seat across from me, Anjali Auntie in the chair itself, Anita on the arm, posed like two actresses in an ad for a television drama. Anita's head turned slightly to the right, and her eyes met her mother's—they were united again. Neither replied. Perhaps it was just too incongruous—that Neil Narayan might want something other than a video game, or a girl, or a nap.

"Can I at least ask some questions?"

Anjali Auntie made a small hmm-ing noise.

"Have you only been stealing from Indians?"

"Who else has good gold?" she said. "White people make and buy shoddy stuff. Ten-, fourteen-karat—you're a boy, you won't understand this. But the kind your mother has, certainly the kind your grandma would wear—that's all usually twenty-two-karat. Handmade, hallmark, created with intention, beautiful filigrees, intricate designs, see, by superb artisans. Some of these aunties will even buy it on particularly auspicious days, increasing its power even more."

"So, it's good gold because of how it's made? Because of who owns it? Wears it?"

"All of that. It starts with the quality of the metal—that has to be top-notch," Anjali Auntie said. "It has to be made by the best artisans, people who have an almost sacred relationship with the gold. And then, on top of all of that, if it's owned by people who possess the kind of energy and ambition we need—"

Anita cut in. "And point is, who else is really, truly ambitious? This is immigrant shit."

I nodded, slowly, absorbing. "You get it when you go on catering jobs?"

Anjali Auntie nodded. "Mostly."

"Prachi," I said. "This is how you beat her?"

Anita's chin lifted defiantly. "It was only an assist—"

Anjali Auntie interrupted. "What Anita's saying is that all of us replenish ourselves. We *borrow*, but someone healthy and motivated keeps regenerating. Prachi, I think, was not recharging. She may have stopped wanting to win. So, Anita acquired some of her desire. But if Prachi's ambition had gone deep enough, she'd have stood a chance. See?"

I wasn't sure I did. But I went on: "And Shruti? What do you want to beat her at?"

Anita gave one of her jerky headshakes, the sort that made her resemble a malfunctioning android. "She's smart, super driven. It's not all about winning a specific competition or test. There's this larger race we're all running, you know?"

I did. "Why not hit jewelry stores?"

"That might work," Anita's mother went on, raising her voice to talk over something snarky Anita seemed on the verge of articulating. "But I'm not cut out for such a big, er, *criminal* operation. My job has made it possible for me to do these small . . . acquisitions.

"And secondly, we want something specific, yes? We don't just want generally auspicious or lucky gold, which we'd surely get from a store. We want something someone has invested with very specific ambitions. For the future. For their high-achieving children. We want something someone has *owned* already. You see?"

I felt the excess of that energy prickling along my skin again. I was trembling as I spoke. "I need something," I said. I looked at Anita. If I told her about the summer—flunking Kumon, flailing through debate research, flitting around with historical tales—she'd chastise me. "I'm afraid I'm not going to make it," I went on. "Through high school. Without some help. If you let me in, I promise, I won't waste it." My voice cracked.

"I've only been getting—making—enough for one," Anjali Auntie said, speaking low.

Anita's huge, pooling dark eyes met mine, and for a precious beat, her entire attention and understanding enveloped me.

She tore her eyes away from me. She would not look at me that way again for a very long time.

"I'll share," Anita said to her mother. "It's Neil."

She spoke so quickly I almost missed it. It took me years to understand why she said that, that night. The best explanation I've come into is that she did not want to live in this mustard yellow house with just the lemonade and her mother any longer. That she had grown lonely with the secret. That maybe she needed me next to her during the strange year that followed.

Anjali Auntie's brow furrowed. She pressed her index finger to the space where she might have placed a bindi and smoothed her skin. It was a self-soothing gesture, recalling the way my mother massaged Prachi's head with oil when my sister complained of headaches from sleeplessness. Anjali Auntie closed her eyes, and when she opened them, they looked like tree bark struck by shafts of afternoon sunlight. I realized they were shining from latent wetness.

"You remind me of him," Anjali Auntie said, looking back at the photograph that had caught her attention a few times that night—the chubby girl and the cheery boy. "My brother. I always thought so. He had those girlish, long eyelashes, just like you."

All of me clenched, as if to grasp at some invisible atmospheric manliness.

"He passed away," she added. "Very young."

Death was terribly distant to me at that point. I never imagined how, during the Lemonade Period, Vivek seemed always nearby for Anjali Auntie, sometimes laughing in the driveway so convincingly that she'd open the door to find, instead, the Waltham boys howling as they attempted wheelies on their bikes. Sometimes she saw him in the sons of the people whose houses she crept through, and sometimes she saw him peering out of my eyes. I didn't know that during this period she also often thought of Parag, the neighbor boy whose gold fueled her brother to IIT, and who grew into a middling existence as a competent but unbrilliant engineer. How the life the Joshis and Parag's family had craved for their sons never transpired, and never happened to her, either; how all those unattained lives mushroomed over the Dayals' den that night, and we were breathing them, feeding on all that had not come to pass, as we began everything all over again.

"Okay," Anita's mother said, shaking something off.

THAT NIGHT set in motion the rhythms of my sophomore fall. I woke with a headache the morning after and at breakfast admitted I did not feel well—"pounding brain," I mumbled into my Toaster Strudel—which caused my mother to suspect, yet again, that I had been drinking.

My father had his own theory: "You are socially withdrawn," he said. I blinked dimly. "*That* is one of the symptoms of marijuana usage."

Prachi was invited to give testimony on my behalf. "Mom, I don't know anyone on the *planet* who'd give Neil alcohol or drugs. You don't understand how big a dork he is."

"Chee-chee," my mother said. "I think drugs are for *dorks*."

When we crossed paths upstairs later, Prachi stopped me. Her eyes fell on my Band-Aid. "You're not a cutter or something now, are you?" she said.

I shook my head.

"Don't get all emo this year. It's only tenth grade—too early for that shit, okay?"

The *too much*–ness of that initial lemonade took days to fade—I walked around high, restless, practicing the *focus* Anita had taught me in order to channel what I'd downed. I even started going on runs.

Once school began, I was a new Neil, a Neil containing a mysterious balance of stability and energy. I found myself willing to work harder; I did not want to waste the lemonade. Math and science came more easily, and my abysmal Kumon grades were forgotten. I was buoyant in history class, and my blue books came back to me with ninety-nines, circled and underlined. Shruti's, next to me, still hung comfortably in the nineties, but often a few points lower than mine. She hid them after the first time I leaned over and said, "I win."

Anita's mother doled out new doses of lemonade every few weeks, usually on Fridays, to precede a weekend of homework or a debate tournament. We consumed Shruti's in pipette drips; a taste of her lemonade could set me up for a solid week of focused studying. Before a big math exam, Anjali Auntie gave me some from Jay Bhatt, former state math Olympiad champion. With each sip, I got better at concentrating—*You're supposed to imagine! Imagine yourself making use of all you took.*

I followed Wendi Zhao's directions flawlessly at the first tournament of the year, in Dallas, and shocked everyone by earning an individual award on top of our team semifinals finish. ("You might be more than just my tool, Neil," Wendi said begrudgingly as we helped the school chaperone unload the rental car at the airport.)

I leveraged this first success with my parents, negotiating the right to attend driver's ed before school twice a week. The teacher, Mr. Hudson, a pruny old man who had once been white but whose veins were so prominent beneath his skin that today he resembled something more like a bruise, had been at Okefenokee since "before the out-of-towners"—us. "Y'all all have this thing in your *culture*, don't you?" he'd begin, while I was trying to circle the Chick-fil-A parking lot. He would unravel a list of anthropological observations on each minority: the Indian male's plentiful chest hair and accompanying pungent scent, the composition of the Chinese stomach that allowed for consuming unlikely animals, the Koreans and the satanic rituals he believed to be secretly afoot in their churches. "There was a Nigerian kid here a long while ago," he said once, sighing. "Tall. Unforchernately, he couldn't play football for you-know-what."

I began to spend time at Anita's once or twice a week, the way I used to when I let myself in to raid the fridge. I'd finish homework and debate practice, then hitch a ride from school back to our cul-de-sac. Prachi was busy with her activities—charity clubs, the dance team, and (I had an inkling) Hudson Long. My parents worked late. So I was managing to hang around the Dayals' without accounting to anybody about my reasons for being there.

Often, I'd land at their house before Anita's carpool dropped her home. Her school was almost an hour's drive away through miserable Atlanta traffic, which meant I spent a lot of time that fall with Anjali Auntie. On the occasions Anita *was* around, she treated me like her assigned partner on a mandatory school project. The spark of connection that had seemed to revive between us on the night of my break-in had dissipated. I wondered if she regretted letting me in, or if she could sense my want, if it disgusted her.

One early fall afternoon, I was alone in the Dayal kitchen, considering the warm burst of the Japanese maple on the front lawn, when Anita's carpool arrived. She dropped her new lime green, monogrammed, L.L.Bean backpack in the foyer and looked surprised to find me at the counter, eating as usual—this time her mother's spicy phodnichi poli. Anjali Auntie was in the bedroom, taking a phone call; the door was firmly shut.

"Do you want me to go?" I leaned against the counter, about six feet from her.

"No," she said. Her eyes narrowed, perhaps out of exhaustion, but I read annoyance.

"I feel like you're mad at me. And I don't get what I did—"

"I'm fucking beat. I'm fucking hungry." It was not a reply. "Is there food?" A silly question; there was always food at the Dayals'. She edged to the fridge and pulled out a neon orange Gatorade. "I'm up every day at five," she said, addressing the vegetable crisper. "Do you know that? My mom wants me to do volunteer fundraising for Habitat for Humanity, because being a Habitat officer as a junior means you can be a Service Prefect as a senior, and *every* Service Prefect for the last five years has gone to an Ivy League or *at least* Vanderbilt, so I'm doing *that*, which means I have to be at Chick-fil-A at six thirty to help buy the chicken biscuits we sell for, like, six bucks each. *Oh,* and I've started eating meat at school, you know, because I couldn't live on their slimy white-person okra or iceberg lettuce, but even then I *can't* eat a chicken biscuit even though I'm standing over them for, like, an hour, because if one of the girls on the cross-country team sees you eating a chicken biscuit she'll give you this *look,* you know, just to make sure you know they've noticed *you* have an ass and they don't—I mean not you, I mean *I* have an ass. I have to size up on the cross-country shorts; everyone else double-rolls them. And Mary Claire Turner, the other day 'Baby Got Back' came on the radio on the bus, and she goes, 'Is this your anthem, Anita?' Oh, and on *Fridays,* I have to do the whole biscuit thing alone, because the other service kids are in Friday Morning Fellowship, praying or singing or whatever, and sometimes I think about going in there, doing the whole parade and accepting Jesus Christ because the only Asian girl they *don't* hate is the one who wears this huge cross—well, her boobs are huge, too, and anyway I think she's only half-Asian. I—I miss sleep."

It hadn't occurred to me that Anita might not be popular at her new school; I'd imagined her transitioning laterally from her position at OHS. (It also didn't seem the time to inform her that there were boobs guys and butt guys, and unfortunately she had enrolled at a boobs guys' school, but that there were plenty of butt guys out there still.) As I processed, I realized I'd waited too long, and her confession, or expulsion, hung limply in the air, unanswered.

"Uh." I glanced impotently around the kitchen before trying what Anjali Auntie did in the face of tension. "Do you want masala chai? Your mom taught me how to make it."

A small, relieved smile spread on Anita's face as she nodded. I was proud to see myself knowing her so well, giving her what she needed—the chance to release, but also to reclaim her composure.

"With ginger?" she said.

"Sure," I said. I took out the milk and Anita grabbed the spices from above the sink and began slicing the root. I set about boiling the liquid, covering it with the hairy dark leaves.

"What's new for you at school?" she asked as we watched the chai burble, as though she'd said nothing at all about her own life.

"I don't suck anymore."

"You never sucked. You're just a little lazy."

"*I* still sleep."

"You always slept." Her mouth twitched. "Too much." She reached to switch off the stove as the chai foamed over the lip of the saucepan. Her thumb brushed the hot steel and she yelped. Before my self-consciousness could kick in, I pressed my own cool hand around hers. She let it stay there.

In that instant she almost seemed to flicker back to life. For a brief flash, she was *there*, looking back at me.

Her mother's door opened. We split apart, and as the touch broke, I knew I would lose whatever had just happened in the unreal minutes before; Anita would pretend she'd admitted nothing of her life, and I would have to participate in the conspiracy to cover up her vulnerabilities. By the time Anjali Auntie came in, hanging up the cordless, we were on opposite sides of the room, strangers again.

"You made chai?" Anita's mother stood over the pot and laughed, not unkindly. "It's overdone." As she brewed a fresh pot, we got back to the activity Anjali Auntie and I had been engaged in earlier: gossip. At the Dayals', the gossip my mother so loved—who was winning what, who was engaged in *nonsense*—translated differently. When my mother gossiped, she was trying to teach herself and us something about who was living America correctly. When

Anita's mother gossiped, the question was: *Who might be worth* acquiring *a little something from?*

Anita stood with her arms folded, leaning against the dark wooden cabinets, fiddling with her ponytail. Her skin shadowed as the sun went down.

Suddenly, Anjali Auntie turned toward her daughter as if she was just noticing her. "Ani! You're filthy!" she cried. "I can smell you from here. Look at you, sitting in Mrs. Kaplan's car for an hour, stinking, and sweaty, don't fall asleep like this in my kitchen."

Anita slunk upstairs. I heard the shower running and wondered what she was thinking about as the sweat dripped away, revealing whatever was the essential *Anita* that got lost when she entered her Anita-and-adult or Anita-and-classmates script. I felt certain that no one else had ever wondered as intensely as I did about that essential Anita, that she had revealed none of it to anyone else.

PERHAPS SENSING THE generational gap between the youth of Hammond Creek and their forebears, my English teacher, Ms. Rabinowitz, an eager Bostonian transplant, decided our curriculum ought to include several short stories depicting the somber reality of the immigrant experience. Through these pieces, we learned that old people looking out windows symbolized nostalgia for their former nations. We learned that images of springtime symbolized youth, and we hypothesized that the changing of the leaves might imply a metamorphosis from Foreign to American, or perhaps from Life to Death. Having inspired us to discern the signs and signifiers that surrounded us, Ms. Rabinowitz told us to interview a family member as inspiration for our own Heritage Creative Writing Project.

Let me nod to my teacher's intentions: it was 2006, and one of my classmates bore the unfortunate name Osama Hussain. Much of what Ms. Rabinowitz did in that course seemed to be driven by an implicit desire to redeem the nomenclative tragedy. (Osama, for his part, was thriving. He'd recently talked his way out of a few class-skipping charges by claiming he was fleeing Republican bullies, when he had in fact driven off campus to buy weed from his college-aged brother.)

At any rate, I had no desire to interview my parents only to receive premasticated spiels about how much more mathematics they understood at twelve than Americans could grasp at twenty. So I brought the paper Ms. Rabinowitz had given us listing suggested questions for the Heritage Interview to the Dayals'.

"Ani?" Anjali Auntie called when I opened the door. "Oh, Neil, come, come," she said when I presented in the kitchen. "I was expecting Anita—she's late after this cross-country meet. We live so far away, poor girl." She stood behind the stove, pushing along some okra with a wooden spoon in a frying pan. "You look bothered."

"Can you help me with some homework?" I said.

"Maybe you should wait for Anita—I've never been much help to her." Then she laughed. "At least, not on the page-by-page basis."

"I have to interview someone," I said, and explained the assignment. "It's meant for family, but I don't think Ms. Rabinowitz would be mad if I asked you."

"Well. If it's for class." She glanced at the clock and sighed. "I have to make up some new lemonade. I suppose we can talk downstairs."

In the basement, the interview mingled with the action. It was late October, and I'd now witnessed the brewing of the lemonade a few times. The scene: Three plain gold bangles, laid out on the table. The stone basin. Above, weak fluorescence. The last strains of autumn afternoon light ribboning through the glass. Anita's mother shoving the sleeves of her lavender peasant top past her elbows.

I shuffled for the tape recorder Ms. Rabinowitz had sent home with each of us. "We're supposed to use these instead of note-taking so we can be *present*."

Anjali Auntie raised her eyebrows and glanced at the splay of criminal activity laid out before us as if to say, you want *this* on the record?

"I mean, I'm the only one who's going to listen to it," I hastened.

She lifted a plastic jar full of a clear liquid—flux—to remove impurities. The jar still wore its original label, SHREE BASMATI RICE. Nearby lay a few other bottles with liquids whose names I never learned; "untranslatable," Anjali Auntie always said. Everything with the feel of a moonshine job. The flux, poured over the bangles, splashing against the sides of the stone basin. The liquid taking to the gold, like watching that old mingling of sugar and lemon, the lick of liquid on solid, the solid yielding to its touch.

I turned to Ms. Rabinowitz's questions. "Would your life today surprise your ancestors in another part of the world?" I read. "If interviewee is immigrant him/herself, can ask: 'Would your life today surprise your prior self, if so, how?'"

"Hm," she said. "Well, sure, my life might surprise a younger me. I have my own business. And I have a daughter who I get along with, or who doesn't hate me, which is more than I can say for most of the other immigrant mothers around here, isn't it?"

I drummed my fingers on the table.

"Oh, Neil, I didn't mean—I'm sure Prachi doesn't hate your mother—"

"She likes them. They love her. More than me."

"They love you, too, Neil. I don't mean to belittle any disagreements you have with your parents, but let me tell you, you would know if they didn't love you. It would hurt. A lot."

I shrugged and continued. "Can you please tell me a story about something ancient from our-slash-your heritage that still has meaning to you today?"

"This is the class that's supposed to introduce you to the finer aspects of humanity?" Anjali Auntie tugged on thick industrial gloves and adjusted goggles on her head. "Tie my apron, will you?" Hands unsteady, I did as she asked, pulling the bow tight against her lower back. "Hm, ancient, huh?" she went on, now adjusting the blowtorch to initiate the smelting. "I heard something the other day. About the Saraswati River."

"Where is that?"

She shook her head. "It's a mythical river. We don't know if it was ever really real. But they say it was lined with placer gold, and whoever drank from it would become immortal."

"Who's they? Ms. Rabinowitz says we have to try to chart the way, um . . ." I double-checked her phrasing. "The way *stories get inherited*."

"Ancient history-mystery whatnot." Anjali Auntie waved her free hand impatiently.

"Did you study it or something?"

"No. No, I just have an interest." Her shoulders softened, even as she gripped the blowtorch by its neck. "I have a friend—a catering client—who studies all these things."

"Okay. Okay, so, the mythical river. Gold's supposed to make you immortal?" I glanced meaningfully at what we had laid out on the table, though kept mum for the sake of the recorder.

Anjali Auntie lowered her voice. "Not *this* type." Then she spoke in a more normal tone. "Only pure gold, they say, straight from the earth. Gold that runs in rivers and in soil, et cetera. All other gold that's been made or owned by humans"—she mimicked my glance at the table—"contains human desire or ambition. But with pure gold, well, *then* you can live forever. Oh, don't use this, Neil. I'll think of some other *ancient* story for you. Something from the *Ramayana*, maybe. Can you turn that off a moment?"

I shut off the recorder and helped lift the blowtorch. Over the low roar, she recited something foreign, hoarse, and musical: *Asya swarnasya kantihi . . .* The blue flames overtook the basin until the fire quelled. Left over: the low gleam of the smelted gold, gurgling thickly, being born. An espresso cup's worth of the stuff.

"Is that a prayer?" I asked when she was done. I'd been working up the courage to further inquire into the specifics of the ritual.

"Not to God, really," she said. "More to the balance of forces, time, the elements—we're asking for a certain power of the gold's to be surfaced. In this case, the ambition it contains."

"Can I ask something dumb?"

"Not if it's something else off that sheet of yours."

"What *is* it, really? Gold. What's the big deal about it?"

"It's old as the stars. Literally, some of it comes from neutron-star collisions."

"Really?"

"Some of it. Gold's old as you can imagine—older than your mind can comprehend. It exists deep in the planet's core, and some of it came to earth when asteroids struck. Chemically, it's unique—resistant to most acids. Stuff that would break down even silver won't harm gold. That's why it's been so valuable."

"And you can't make more of it."

"That's what they say. Too expensive." She was making her way to the fridge, where the pitcher of lemonade waited. Together, we poured the gold in. Before the lemonade, the broken-down gold smells intense and acrid, nauseating. But when that enchanted gold hits the perfect brew of lemonade, everything changes. There comes the ached-for plonk of something thick and heavy into liquid. The hiss as it diffuses into long dancing columns. The supernatural carbonation igniting the cravings. I still miss it sometimes.

In the weeks after that, Anjali Auntie regaled me with more history of the strange discipline we were practicing. Anita didn't take much interest in these tales. "Practical to a fault, that girl; doesn't think much about what goes into anything she's given," Anjali Auntie often said. I was a better audience, for I am impractical to a fault. We discussed the strange universality of gold as a cultural fixation—alchemy came to India by way of China and made it as far as Europe—and the persistent Indian obsession with it.

She loved the Western stories, too, like the one about the greedy Roman general Crassus, put to death by drinking molten gold, or the tale of King Midas; Anjali Auntie related the end of the Midas tale, which I'd never before heard. After he turned his daughter, his food, his whole life into gold, he begged for a reprieve, and it was granted. He ran to a nearby river—I pictured a necklace of blue coursing through a sun-yellowed valley of wheat—and plunged his hands into the rapids. The water lifted the curse. The river became speckled with the metal. Thereafter, people panned its waters. Like the American gold rush, I thought. Like the Bombayan.

That day, I went home, new lemonade still slicking my lips, with nothing close to what I needed for my assignment. I brought to class a Wikipedia'd summary of a section of the *Ramayana*, the part about the golden deer that tricked Sita into following Ravana to Lanka, and to her imprisonment. I claimed my aunt had told me this story over the phone as a caution against greed.

Ms. Rabinowitz looked sadly at me after I shared. "You didn't find out very much about your—aunt, was it?—on a *personal* level, did you? What does she miss about her home? What does her heritage *mean* to her today?" That assignment was the only B I earned that fall.

ON A SATURDAY EVENING in mid-November, I was in the debate trailer, highlighting files with Wendi. We were behind, because Wendi had lately been waffling between debate and community service hours, having decided she needed to augment the moral and civic aspects of her Harvard application. ("Fuck fossil fuels," she'd wailed the other day while dropping me off at home, as she dialed Jack Kim's brother. "Can I come by your church? Well, yes, I know I'm not Korean or Christian, Frank, thanks for informing me, but ask yourself, what would Jesus do? He would probably give me a recommendation about a hungry homeless person I could feed . . .") The trailer sat behind the gym and boasted one grimy window, a pizza-stained couch, and a whiteboard on which so many genitalia had been drawn and erased that there remained a perpetual shadow of dicks and balls beneath whatever text you tried to write on top. Just then it read WEAPONS OF MASS DESTRUCTION in a slanty hand over a faded green penile shaft.

We were preparing for one of the larger tournaments of the semester, coming up in Chicago. My mother was going to buy me a down jacket, which she had said might "come in handy" if I went to school in *the northeast*, which for my parents meant *the Ivy League*; my grades that semester had made them hopeful.

I was positively thrumming with a recent dose of lemonade, and therefore reading rapidly, connecting arguments, anticipating rebuttals, and feeling the surety that came with the gold. The lemonade powered me through research, yes, but more important, it provided a swagger that laced my speeches, delivered at hundreds of words per minute, and the cross-examinations, held at a slower pace, which nonetheless required as speedy a mind. Who could have imagined the power carried around in the rings and pendants of unassuming desi debaters? Who would have guessed that in such gold (even in the girls') lay what I must call an intellectual alpha masculinity? Though that strength was borrowed—and temporary— I was drinking enough such that, bit by bit, my private self was coming to resemble the person the lemonade helped me be in the aggressive theater of debate rounds.

I was spinning my pen, reading something about solar energy in Afghanistan, when my red flip phone rang. My parents had not paid for text messages on our family plan, and I didn't give the number out often. So I was surprised to see it buzzing on the table. I didn't recognize the voice on the other end at first; it was loopy and sodden.

"You're, what—? . . . Where? . . . What about your mom? . . . Jesus, Anita . . . You know I don't have my license. . . . I could ask Prachi—okay, okay, I won't . . . Where am I supposed to get a car? . . . Fine . . . Say the address again."

I put my highlighter down and looked straight at Wendi Zhao, who eyed me viciously before agreeing to drive me the forty minutes to Buckhead.

Traffic at eight on a Saturday was light. Wendi merged violently onto the highway and crossed three lanes in a frantic spurt to the HOV side. An unlikely number of tall pines lined Georgia highways, and though it was hardly nature, it still felt like air, like breath, a reminder that something beyond Hammond Creek existed.

Wendi: "This girl—do I know her?"

"She used to go to OHS," I said, and named Anita.

Wendi shook her head to say it didn't ring a bell. Then the headshaking grew vehement. "You know what I feel about this, though?" I figured she would tell me no matter what. "Like, just *wait* a couple of years to dick around. I'm going to dick around a *lot* at Harvard, trust me."

"Anita wants to go to Harvard, too," I said. That briefly silenced Wendi. We passed under green sign after green sign announcing another suburb where other Neils and Wendis were *waiting*. The interstate spat us out in Buckhead, where there were more trees— historic trees, all knotty. We turned onto a wide street where each home resembled a small plantation—enormous white houses with wraparound porches and lawns as well maintained as a golf course green.

I suddenly recalled visiting Harvard when Prachi and I were kids, on a vacation to see cousins in Boston. In the photographs, we are big squished ravioli in magenta and traffic-cone-orange coats. My father holds me up to the lucky John Harvard statue, on which, it turns out, freshman boys have an affinity for pissing. All the hope of the Asian immigrant is crammed into my father's hands as he lifts me up—though I am too old and too fat to be held—so I can scratch a little good fortune from that urine-drenched talisman.

"Wendi," I said. "What's *after* Harvard?"

"What do you mean?"

"Just that. You get there. To Harvard. What happens next?"

She looked at me like she had something sour on her tongue.

"Whatever the fuck I want."

YOU COULD ALMOST miss the entrance to Anita's school as you passed by the old-style Southern diner boasting, on a signboard, the butteriest grits in Atlanta and the sweetest tea to boot. We caught sight of the brick gates just in time. Two tennis courts loomed to our right, ringed by old magnolias. A sign in bright orange lettering congratulated the Bobcats on winning the state championship in men's and women's cross-country—Anita's team—and then cycled to add more titles collected that fall: football, robotics, quiz team, show choir . . .

"Maybe if I went to school here, I wouldn't wait to dick around, either," Wendi said bitterly as we crossed a small blue bridge running over a creek. My window was down. The water warbled. Campus was dark, but a few lights switched on automatically as we drove.

"What do you mean?" I said.

"This is practically already the Ivy League. She's got a free ticket."

I stiffened. "Turn right here, I think," I said, trying to remember the directions Anita had given me. "She said she's in the old junior high."

"She's not going to barf in my car, is she?"

"No," I said. "And she doesn't have a free ticket. She works really hard."

"Didn't say she didn't," Wendi said, and briefly that puckered face loosened. Suddenly, she slammed her horn, hard. We'd nearly hit a train of figures sprinting across the road.

"Wendi!" I said. "They have security on campus!"

"*Security?* Why are these kids drinking *here* on a Saturday, then—" but she shut up as I pulled out my phone and dialed the number Anita had called from. Three rings, four, no reply. "You got a cover story ready, superhero? I'm not taking the fall for this chick."

"You're supposed to be the fast thinker," I snapped.

I tried the number once more, and this time a guy's voice answered. It was deeper than mine, cloaked in a friendly Southern burr. "Are you Anita's brother?"

"Brother?"

"She said her brother was coming to pick her up?"

I paused. I assented.

The voice directed me where to come. "Hurry," he said.

The crowd that awaited us, in a parking lot next to a one-story brick building, was wedged against a broad tree. Two figures peeled away: a guy taller than me, and a girl leaning on him. The guy was white and had dark brown hair that fringed above his ears. He looked annoyed.

Anita grinned at me dizzily. "Neil. Happy happy to see you."

"Is she okay?" I reached out an arm so she could lean on me instead.

"She didn't drink that much," the guy said. "But I don't think she really knows how to handle it." He sounded sober. "We're all trying to get gone, though. We would have taken her home, but she wouldn't say where y'all live."

"Far," I said. "Thanks."

We found a towel in Wendi's trunk, and I sat in the backseat with a dozing Anita and laid the towel over her lap in case of emergency. We pulled out of the vast compound and Wendi lowered the windows. The air was fresh but cold and smelled like peeled potatoes.

"Can't she choke on her vomit?" I asked.

"I dunno," Wendi said. "Better that than spewing."

We were minutes from the interstate, on one of those roads with gated houses, when Anita suddenly began knocking on the door. "Pull over, pull over," I said. Wendi did, and I edged out with Anita. We knelt on the grass by a Keller Williams realty sign, and I caught her hair while she retched. Vomit splattered the sign. After expelling, she inhaled deeply. "Alcohol. It's fun, everything gets more fun."

"You're not making the greatest pitch." I pointed at the ruined open house sign. I had defended her to Wendi, and I'd meant it—she did work. But I felt betrayed. I'd thought we were both *waiting*. "Why were you guys drinking at *school*?"

"Issa cross-country thing. Haaazing." Her words ran into each other like cramped cursive handwriting.

Anita was wiping her mouth with her hand and picking at the un-vomity grass, and I got the sense from the way she was screwing up her shoulders that she was preparing to release a torrent of pent-up feelings on me the way she had in her kitchen a month ago. I wanted none of it now. I couldn't win—either she kept me at a distance, which ached, or she drew me close, which resulted in disgust that she'd shown herself to me at all, followed by an even crueler distance.

Wendi honked, unconcerned about disturbing the residents of the nouveau plantations.

"Homeward bound, Ani," I said, and she giggled. I stood. Anita grabbed my hand and hoisted herself up next to me. She linked her arm through mine and stumbled back to the car while I bore much of her weight. Every touch that might have felt sacred some other time now felt like confirmation that she took me for granted. In the backseat of Wendi's car, Anita laid her head on my lap, and I hastily shoved the towel beneath her hair to make a pillow, to separate her hot cheek from my zipper.

Wendi surveyed me in the rearview mirror knowingly, rolling her eyes, and switched on Death Cab for Cutie until we reached the Dayals'.

"It was fabulous to meet you," she said to Anita as we hopped out. "I'm *sure* I'll see you at Harvard."

Anita's eyes crossed. "You *like*-like Neil," she said. "That's why she's so mean to you."

I tugged her to her door, my face burning. As Wendi sped away, I checked over my shoulder—my house was dark. I was still, to my parents' knowledge, at debate.

"You're sure your mom's not home?" I whispered, and Anita laughed, as though the prospect was ridiculous. Inside, I put her in her bed and kept a trash can by the pillow, copying the gestures my mother adopted when someone fell sick. Anita's nightstand was piled high with school things—composition notebooks, a chemistry textbook, a Folger edition of *Macbeth*. Above all that was the Harvard shrine that had papered her walls since middle school: a crimson pennant, a BEAT YALE sign someone's cousin had donated, a page torn from a lookbook featuring a diverse array of students taking in the sun on the Yard. Anita sat up, unclasped her gold hoop earrings, and placed them atop *Macbeth* before flopping onto her stomach.

"Neil," she said, more to the pillow than to me. "He doesn't like me."

"Who?"

"The guy, the guy, Sam. Sam." She emitted a kind of horse whinny. "He likes Mary Claire Turner. Em-cee. She has *no* butt. It's flat, just *shwoop*, back there. He doesn't even *see* me, he looks *shwoop*, right through me."

"Why did you go out with those kids? Your mom would kill you if you'd gotten caught. And where *is* your mom?"

She shrugged. "I dunno." A hiccup, racking her whole frame. "She has places she goes places, I dunno, like, she'll say, 'I'm not like other moms, *I* leave you alone,' but one day I'm gonna drown in all her lemonade." A hiccup that turned into a gag.

"Do you need to puke again?"

"Never ever ever again." She shook her head violently. "I *hate* Mary Claire Turner."

"Yeah," I said.

"Say you do, too, Neil, say it."

I considered not playing along, but gave in. "I hate Mary Claire Turner, too."

"*Em-cee*," Anita said, chewing on the inside of her cheeks. I thought she was going to spit Mary Claire Turner's name right out on the carpet. "She's *spoiled*."

"*You're* acting spoiled."

"Huh?"

"No. Nothing."

"No, no, like, say what you were gonna say."

"I don't know what to say to you, Anita."

"You're *so* pissy at me."

"Yeah, a little."

"You're always *so* pissy at me."

"Not always. Just now."

Her loosened ponytail had fallen on her face. "I feel like I'm gonna explode."

I had the urge to push up her hair, clear her skin, give her room to breathe.

"You get it?" she said.

Was that all she wanted me to do, *get it*? All I could do? "I think so."

"*Sam*," she sighed. "You know, I thought sometimes, sometimes, I'm like, hey, lemme *acquire* something from Mary Claire Turner, you know." She was turning her face into her pillow, away from me. I just heard her say one thing before I left, before my hand closed around the hoops she had placed atop *Macbeth*. "But there's no point, see, because white girls, they don't even wear gold, white girls, they prefer"—hiccup—"they prefer pearls."

4.

Winter ebbed into spring, and the outside world reached my house primarily through my mother's oversize ears. At dinners, she reported on *nonsense*. Jay Bhatt's father had flown up to Ithaca to scold him when he announced he was quitting the math racket to become a film major: "Used to be sooo-so good at calculus and now failing midterms and all." ("Raghu, this yogurt isn't bad, just scrape out that greenish bit . . .") Fourteen-year-old Reema Misra: fair-skinned as a Caucasian, almond-eyed, who had, my mother said, citing no source for her omniscience, "gone round talking about all the boys she *practices kissing*—tell me," she demanded of Prachi and me, "is that how all you people are talking?" ("Coconut chutney. Ajji's recipe. Everyone eat, don't go wasting.") Aleem Khan's oldest sister, Tasneem: hospitalized for alcohol poisoning in Chapel Hill. "What shame that mother must be feeling." ("Nice mango pickle. Neeraj. Pickle, take.") Even successes got their due: "That Shruti Patel is smart, I'll give her that, but her mother won't leave me alone, asking all kinds of questions every time I see her about Prachi, what SAT studying we—she—did . . ." ("Take less rice, Prachi, who needs such a mountain?")

And then, one day: "You know what I'm hearing about Anjali Dayal?"

I stiffened. It was early March, and my pattern of attendance at the Dayals' remained roughly the same: covert visits, private, intimate, cherished.

"Ramya, don't gossip so much." My father intervening, a rarity.

"What did you hear?" I asked. I shoved my mouth full of green beans and accidentally bit on a chili. Coughing subsided, eyes watering, I waited, expectant.

"Just some very . . ." My mother eyed my father as if to decide whether or not she wanted to cross him. "*White woman* behavior."

My father was eating one bean at a time and examining the ring of flowers patterning his ceramic plate as though he had never before seen these dishes.

"Which Indian people talk divorce-this divorce-that, is all I'm saying," she muttered.

"Ashmita Pandey's aunt is divorced," Prachi said primly.

"Pah. That fellow was a wife beater, very sad." My mother waved her hand in the air. "Some such cases, yes, they happen. But not this desperate housewife wants to run off into the sunset business, that and all is very *strange*, you ask me."

"Last year Anita said they were, like, really close to moving to California."

When Prachi's eyes landed on me curiously, I felt hot.

"There's one woman at my office," my mother said, poised above the dal ladle, too enraptured in her story to interrogate me. Her mangalsutra swayed from her neck, that gold chain signifying her status as sturdily married. I thought of all that was invested in that necklace, of the artisan who had made it, shaping it to be a blessing conferred upon the wedding, and of all the signifiers of domestic security that had agglomerated upon it through my parents' long union. I imagined Anjali Auntie unclasping it and coiling it onto her tongue.

"*Katherine*," my mother continued. "American lady. Says she's a Christian-only but she's lived with three men. Meets them at bars. Can't keep one around. Then asks me so sweetly so innocently if I had one *arranged* marriage like she should feel so sad for me."

"Anita won MTI southeast," Prachi put in disconsolately. "She'll be prepping for nationals now."

My sister was eternally gloomy these days, having had her early application to Duke deferred; she'd been hanging in limbo since winter, and was terrified the definitive rejection was coming in a matter of weeks. Prachi now made a habit of tallying up other brown girls' victories in her own personal loss column: Anita had a shot at MTI nationals; Imrana Ansari, one of Prachi's frenemies from the dance team, had won a national essay-writing competition. Worst was Gita Menon, the former Scripps National Spelling Bee runner-up from Northview High School, who had gotten her Duke acceptance in December, taking the one slot Prachi was sure had been hers.

"Aloo," my father said, reaching for the mushy potatoes.

"Let Anita Dayal prance about. Nothing to be jealous. We are very proud of you," my mother said.

Preparation for the national pageant—to be held in New Jersey in April—was, as Prachi surmised, keeping Anita busy. Plus, this spring, she was playing tennis and tutoring English as a second language, while also finally turning the chicken biscuit sales into Habitat for Humanity houses. All this kept her late at school and brought her inside the perimeter on weekends.

Sometimes I held the hoops I'd taken from her nightstand in

my palm. I wondered what they—she—would taste like. If I could smelt down her powers and mysteries and take them as my own. But for now, I stowed the earrings in my wallet, behind my learner's permit, where they would remain for a long time.

STUDENTS ON THE HONORS TRACK met with the college counselor once at the start of their sophomore spring. I plodded over to Mrs. Latimer's office on the ground floor of Okefenokee High School one morning and sat in the hallway, waiting for her to finish another meeting.

I found myself staring at a bulletin board covered with photographs of OHS alumni holding up T-shirts displaying their collegiate futures: Wake Forest and Vanderbilt and UNC; sometimes Dartmouth or Caltech or Yale. The rest of the school was papered with pep rally banners and bake sale flyers; kids chewed gum and made out and bartered cigarettes and Ritalin. But here, in the *nonsense*-free honors corridors, there was a different currency. A currency that meant the unlikeliest people were rich, as I remembered when I saw who was now pushing open Mrs. Latimer's door. Shruti Patel stopped in her tracks to see me outside.

"Oh, *Neil!*" she said, in that scratchy voice. "I always forget you're an honors kid."

"What a compliment, Shroots," I said.

She plonked down next to me. "Mrs. Latimer is making some important phone calls on my behalf right now, so you're going to have to wait a little bit. There are a lot of people who might want to have me around for the summer. What are *you* doing?"

Shruti wouldn't speak to Juhi or Isha or Kartik or even Manu this way. It was me she felt comfortable poking at, and while normally I wouldn't deprive her of this rare social joy, I was irritable that day. It was the end of a lemonade cycle, and I'd been trudging through precalculus homework feeling laconic and woolly.

"A debate institute," I said evenly. "In East Lansing."

She tugged one of her springy locks of hair. Her eyes crossed as she watched it bounce.

"I wish I had a *track* like you," she said. "I have to be creative about my summers. Mrs. Latimer's calling up this *Congresswoman*—" I tried to close my eyes and ignore Shruti as she painted pictures of her possible opportunities: bustling around Washington, D.C., chasing a House member, or being flown to Hong Kong to participate in a youth entrepreneurship summit, or immersing in a program for math geniuses at Stanford, and she was pretty sure Stanford was practically on the beach, so she'd be solving integrals in the sand. "But I heard from Mia Ahmed that people have tons of fun at debate camp, too."

"Institute," I said through gritted teeth, as though that sounded better.

"Mia says there's this place in Michigan that'll deep fry a burrito, an Oreo, anything you want. And a shop for dollar pizza. *She* got drunk in East Lansing last summer. She says there are hobos you can just ask to buy you alcohol. But promise you won't, Neil, okay? Don't get drunk in East Lansing all summer, *right* when you were getting to be so smart—"

"Neil Narayan?" Mrs. Latimer, a graying woman with an air of brutal capability, stepped into the hallway. "Oh, Shruti, you're still here? I'll get back to you about Hong Kong. I couldn't reach that alum."

Mrs. Latimer spent a few minutes reviewing my file with an air of unfamiliarity. I gathered that she'd heard of Shruti before her meeting—most teachers had—but that I'd flown under her radar. Without looking up from my transcript, she suggested I begin to define myself.

"Not according to what you think a college *wants to hear*, understand," she insisted. "But according to where *you* see yourself in, say, ten years. So. Any idea? Where you see yourself?"

I said I guessed I could see myself in California. I'd been to the Bay Area once, on vacation, when we visited my uncle Gopi and aunt Sandhya in Fremont. I'd loved San Francisco—the way the gray fog met the gray water, the way the Golden Gate emerged from the sienna mountains. I saw myself roaming amid the pastel homes crowded against one another like uneven smiles, or reading in a bay window with a view of the Pacific. ("You want to live here?" my father had chuckled, noticing the pull the city exerted over me. "You better get rich. Those houses on the water, they're millions-millions.")

"California," Mrs. Latimer repeated. "Well, geography is a start. But how about your *interests*? What are you *passionate* about?"

"I'm a debater."

"That's your passion?"

Neeraj, you're supposed to imagine!

"Sure," I said.

"A debater. So, you're interested in, say, politics? Law?"

I mumbled a few more sures, and then she began sculpting the fib into a plan—I should consider doing voter registration drives, tackle a column in the school paper, found a chapter of the Young Republicans or Democrats. I should sit for the AP Government exam, though the class wasn't offered at our school—"Are you friends with Ms. Patel out there?" Mrs. Latimer asked. "She self-studied for the exam last year. Perhaps she could tutor you."

By the time the meeting ended, I'd become a committed Young Democrat, at least on paper. Though I spent my days throwing around the language of policy and politics, I practiced agility more than advocacy: in one round, I played the neoconservative defender of American imperial policy in Afghanistan; in the next, I argued for diplomacy with rogue states. Sometimes Wendi let me draw on the kritik research I'd done last summer, to argue, for instance, that capitalism was the true cause of the fossil fuel crisis. Sometimes I enjoyed how debate made my mind work. But it was the win I craved, the look of sympathy the judge gave the other team before announcing our victory. What it took to get there was not passion, but lemonade.

What I *did* love, discreetly—and what I never thought to tell Mrs. Latimer—was history. My AP European History teacher, Mr. Bakcs, was a compact, white-haired man, a former lawyer with a Tennessee drawl and a shuffle step who liked to pull me into his classroom when he spotted me in the hallways and ask for my help putting up or taking down the timeline for each unit. (I was, at last, tall enough to be of assistance to a smaller person, having hit a growth spurt over winter.) I think Mr. Bakes may have been waging a private war against Mrs. Latimer, for he never asked what my plans for the future were; instead, he batted around the past with me. He praised my essays—the one where I wrote about the scientific revolution as one of the great optimistic epochs, and the one arguing against the great man theory of history re: Napoleon. But I'd never heard of any alumnus of Hammond Creek going on to study history. Why putter around in the dead past when the future of our community required such ruthless attention?

This was why it so rankled when Shruti Patel turned around at the end of AP Euro to announce that she had been accepted to the

Hong Kong entrepreneurship boot camp and to a four-day conference for young leaders in San Diego (which really was on the beach), with scholarships for both. I could conceive of East Lansing, by contrast, only as an oversize parking garage.

I kept thinking about Prachi, pacing the kitchen all Christmas break, fuming as my mother chased her with a bowl of sesame oil, attempting to administer a calming Ayurvedic head massage. "Duke's already *got* an Atlanta suburban brown girl who wants to be a businesswoman!" Prachi howled. "They won't want me! Gita Menon! Gita fu—sorry, Amma, Gita fudging Menon!"

Shruti fudging Patel. A tiny, radical part of me had started to believe, over the course of the Lemonade Period, that one day I might be good enough to be in the kinds of rooms Anita had always planned to be in—the rooms Shruti had begun to unlock. But Shruti fudging Patel—who would want me when they had her?

"Jealous?" Shruti smirked. She did that curl-tugging thing again, and it infuriated me to see the lock bounce on her forehead. Her small marble eyes, which were too wide for her face and set too close together, bore into me shrewdly. I felt violated by the intensity of her attention.

"Not a bit," I said, but minutes later I was kicking my locker after class. Fewer heads turned than you'd expect; in the honors hallway, people were always kicking things upon the distribution of grades.

Manu passed while I was examining the metal to see if I'd made a dent. "Chemistry?"

"Shruti," I said.

"Did you apply for her summer stuff, too?" he said gloomily.

I shook my head. "I didn't know—I had no idea you could *do* stuff like Hong Kong."

"Have you talked to Mia?" Manu lowered his voice. "Be *careful* in East Lansing."

Then he sighed and went to find Kartik, whose locker was in the normie hallway, with the white kids. He'd joined the lacrosse team that spring as its water boy, and claimed he would list the sport on his college application, therefore standing apart from other Asian applicants. I wasn't seeing much of Kartik this year. The lemonade provided sharper focus, made me willing to ignore things—and people—that did not seem immediately useful. But I was afraid of wasting all this gold, spending it by kicking a locker instead of *becoming* something already.

Get it together, I thought furiously at myself. I was still failing to see my future, the way Shruti seemed so capable of doing, the way I presumed Anita must be able to, the way I knew Prachi could. How could it be that Shruti believed in her future self enough to survive the fact of her unpopularity, her date running away from her at last year's Spring Fling just as mine had, the mocking in basements, the birthday party for which her parents had to issue invitations? Was it because she trusted a future Shruti was waiting, the girl just ahead of her in a relay race, to take the baton and bolt to Hong Kong, and college, and a better life? I lacked such certainty.

"We need more of Shruti's," I told Anita and her mother. Another Friday in the kitchen, Anita fresh from tennis.

Anjali Auntie shook her head. "We've taken a lot from her already. Two—"

"Three times," Anita interrupted. I smelled the tang of her unwashed sweat.

"What's the problem? You're concerned she'll notice stuff is missing?"

"That," Anita's mother said, lowering her nose to sniff a pot of chana masala. "But also, that we don't want to overdo it. Poor girl, leave her something."

"She's got everything," I sighed.

Anjali Auntie gave me an odd look, brief, full of some knowledge she might have shared, but that I missed. "There's no shortage of others." She turned to her daughter. "Anita, why do you insist on stewing in your own stink like this? You think Neil likes to smell you?"

I blushed.

"Upstairs, shower, please. You have a lot of homework?"

"Just AP US," Anita said. "It's a joke."

"How are they filling up a school year with only American history? Neil has a millennium of Europe to study and this girl has just two hundred years of this strange country."

ANITA AND I went on in our renewed way, passing more of those afternoons, brewing the lemonade ourselves. She was letting me back in, illuminating the black space that had spooled between us. Her mother was increasingly out, inside the perimeter and around the other suburbs for what I assumed was a combination of legitimate work and *acquisitions*. On the occasions that she was home, Anita's mother was often on the phone, upstairs, padding around, speaking in an urgent voice as we made the lemonade in the basement.

Anita had once been on jobs with her mother, but now she was never brought along. And months into our routine, I was growing impatient with this division of labor. I felt like a lazy, fat lion, remaining at home while the lioness hunted. I pictured myself tearing through the Bhatts' mansion for Jay's old coins or chains. Flipping Leela Matthews's mattress upside down, seeking the lucky gold pinky ring she wore on test days. Most of all, Shruti. I pictured ripping her room apart. Absconding with all that gave her power. Those weirdly set eyes dimming. These impulses swelled in my vision, red and blinding, for minutes at a time before subsiding. Like war rage. Like bloodlust.

"How's your dad?" I asked Anita one day in the basement. I opened the fridge and pulled out the lemons.

"He's trying to get us to come to California."

"In the middle of high school?"

"He thinks the family's been split up for too long."

Anita pointed at the drawer where they kept the glassware, indicating I should pull out the pitcher. A sudden dizziness swirled behind my forehead. The thought of the Dayal women departing when they had just begun to remake my world was too much to conceive of. And the lemonade—the loss of the lemonade. It crossed my mind, not for the first time, that I should not rely on these women for my lifeblood.

"We won't go," Anita said firmly. "She wouldn't want to. My dad is not nice to her." This came more softly.

"Would they—would they get divorced?"

Anita shook her head. "Do you know any divorced Indians? *Other* than Ashmita's aunt."

She didn't wait for me to answer, just poured flux. I stepped back so she could lift the blowtorch. It was almost as big as her whole torso, but she wielded it confidently. When she recited the string of foreign phrases, I listened, more carefully than I had in the past. I tried to hear them reverberate in my mind, with enough intensity that they would etch themselves there.

"Were they a . . . ?" I groped for the phrases my mother used to categorize other people's marriages. "A love match?"

Anita laughed with a nasty maturity. "They weren't arranged," she said. "Not by their parents. But I don't think my mother ever really loved him. He doesn't even seem like he *likes* her. That sounds sad, doesn't it?"

I said I didn't know. I had never thought of my own parents as *in love* like in movies, but it didn't make me sad.

"It feels sad to me," she said. "But maybe that love stuff is just American shit."

And then *I* was sad, at Anita's cynicism. I had not realized before then that I was a romantic, but I saw how Anita seemed more engaged with a kind of crude sensate reality. She was perhaps more correct about the world. But I have, constitutionally and inevitably, always preferred the blur of mystery to the assuredness of empirical facts.

Upstairs, Anjali Auntie's footsteps came even and rhythmic. The contours of her life were inconceivable from where we stood. Love was a subtle want, to be known by more discerning minds.

I WAS NOT explicitly planning anything. No great heist in the works, no Big Idea. I was just going about my life, head down, earning A's, taking direction from Wendi Zhao. It was Shruti who presented herself to me. In the hallway, after history. She asked me, leaning with a practiced nonchalance against my slightly dented locker, blinking those marble eyes, and I said yes, and when I went home, I IM'd her—shr00tzinb00ts09—saying that on the evening of the Spring Fling dance I would like to pick her up from her house, skip all the picture parties. It was meant to sound intimate.

I ignored Prachi's raised eyebrows when I asked her to drop me off at Shruti's before heading to her own party. In the driveway of Shruti's house, Prachi said, "This is . . . nice of you."

That weekend, Anita was in coaching sessions with the pageant expert her mother had hired in advance of nationals. I'd told her nothing about Shruti or the dance. Anita seemed to have forgotten the old rhythms of Okefenokee High School.

I'd met Shruti's parents and ten-year-old sister at parties, but never been subjected to them the way I was in her living room that night. I tapped my foot and smacked my dry mouth, looking at the mantelpiece, where the Patels kept a single black-and-white image of two people in sari and kurta staring out at the camera, stiff and unsmiling.

"My parents, wedding day," her mother said, following my gaze. The sister, squeezed between the mom and dad, wore a smocked dress that made her look four years younger. Her hair was in pigtails. Her mouth hung slack as she stared at me, this weird, foreign creature, a *boy*.

"Neeraj," Mrs. Patel said. "Why this dancing needs *dates* and all?"

"It's an American thing, Auntie. It doesn't mean *dating*, dating, like . . ."

I thought I might be sick.

The father interrupted, waving his hand to dismiss his wife's questions so furiously that he nearly elbowed his small daughter in the face: "Have you taken SAT?" He pronounced the test not as *ess-ay-tee* but as the past tense of *sit*.

"Uh, not yet," I said. "I guess I'll study for it next year."

"I'm only taking it next year, too!" squeaked the girl. Her fobby accent surprised me.

"*You* are?"

The mother clarified. "There is one camp, Neeraj, see, they take only very talented students, you have to have taken SAT"—once more, *sat*—"in sixth grade only. You did not go for this?" She looked terribly concerned, if not for me then for my parents, who clearly had missed some memos on the opportunities available to aspiring geniuses. "Right now, Hema, she studying for spelling bee, you did not do that either?" Shruti's mother spoke each *s* and *sh* sibilantly, like a steaming kettle requesting attention.

Then, like some blessing from above, my "date" arrived in the living room, wearing a pink dress that made her look like a Publix bakery cupcake, tulle around the hips and frightful tissue-paper-like flower blooms on the shoulders. Her hair had been straightened. It seemed like it might have taken hours to get it as flat as it now hung, which was depressing because it looked like an ironed squirrel's tail, tamed but twitching. She had smeared something over her acne scars. Her mouth was switching rapidly between a contorted smile and an expression of terror, like one of those tragicomic dramatic masks. Her chickeny legs—long and skinny, unevenly shaved—stretched into high silver heels, on which she wobbled.

Her parents were not waiting for her with a camera, not waiting for me to put a corsage on their daughter's wrist—I had not brought one, anyway. There were no protocols for what happened when Shruti Patel was actually taken on a date. (Last year, she had met Manu at the dance.) Protocols would have made it easier—a churlish Southern father with a shotgun, threatening me. I conjured other scripts from television, from white culture, and wished to belong to any of them. Instead I stood as she took a shaky step onto the hardwood from the carpeted stairs. And I saw that in her ears were two large pearl studs. Around her neck was a silver chain with another pearl pendant. Probably not even real pearls.

She was not wearing a single piece of gold. I had miscalculated.

I said I needed to use the bathroom. Before anyone could point me to a room on the main floor, I was marching up those stairs, which smelled like cat, though there was no cat in the house. I pushed open one door and found myself in a child's room full of stuffed animals. They piled high on the bed: a twin set of bright pink teddy bears wearing bowties, a lavender elephant, a bulge-eyed green frog. I had gotten the little sister's room. I went back to the hallway and opened the other door to find a pale yellow bedroom housing shelves and shelves of porcelain dolls. The duvet looked like someone had vomited doily. There was no difference between age ten and age fifteen in this house. I was at a loss.

I heard Shruti's voice downstairs saying, "I'll tell him, Mummy," and "ouch," and "I'll take them off, hang on," and the sound of bare feet climbing the stairs, and Shruti, watching me standing at the fork of her hallway, the doors to both bedrooms wide open.

"It's okay if you don't want to go. I guess I knew . . . it wasn't fair to ask you."

"Oh, god, no," I said. "I just . . ." My hands were raised. I was still reaching for both doorknobs. "Which room's yours? Dolls or stuffed animals?"

She didn't blush. "Dolls," she said. So, my gut had been wrong. So perhaps I couldn't find my way to her jewelry box on my own.

"Show me around," I said.

"Really?"

"I want to see where the magic happens. Where you beat me at all the tests."

Giggle. "Not recently." She gulped. "I'm sorry I said I forget you're an honors kid. It wasn't true. I don't. Um. Forget."

"I'm not as stupid as I seem, Shroots."

"I never thought you were stupid," she said.

I was hot. Sweaty. I had to keep talking or I'd wuss out. "Can I see? Unless your parents have some kind of rule about me being up here."

Shruti laughed, and her ironed hair tried to join in, crinkling awkwardly but too murdered to really engage, and she said, "They wouldn't think to make rules about . . . boys." She seemed more embarrassed to pronounce the last word, to acknowledge what I was, than to find me lurking in her space.

There were many white dolls and one Native American one with a long braid and face paint, whom Shruti said she thought she best resembled, and whom she had christened Kalyani—the name she always wished she had been given.

I took each doll as she proffered them, even rocked one a bit. I stepped closer to Shruti when she opened her closet, and she shouted down to her mother, "*Coming*, Mummy," and then began to giggle.

"Wait. Can I see your jewelry?" I whispered.

"Hey, Neil," she said. "Are you, um, *gay*?" She blinked those uncannily set eyes several times, and I realized what could happen: the next time she was cornered, mocked, she could say this to everyone; you needed a way to reroute the cruelty when it descended on you.

"*Fuck* no," I said, and the panic drove me to do something else:

I put my lips on her mouth, which was slick with something sticky. I withdrew. I had done it wrong. I thought of my one prior kiss at camp last summer—it had been rough, and too wet, doglike. I had overcompensated this time, with reticence. I said, "Still think that?"

Her face grew pink. The second time, she lifted the back of her hand to her mouth, wiping away whatever lip gloss remained, and leaned into me. It was neither dry nor slobbery. If I concentrated, I could forget who she was.

She pulled back. I was supposed to say something. What had I said to the camp girl before, or after? *You're hot*, I'd muttered.

"You're smart," I said. "You're really, really smart."

The wrong choice, for now she was going in again, and then I felt her hand on my wrist, guiding me to her pink cupcake breast, and I felt it—the first breast I'd ever touched, and I was repulsed. I stopped. In her expression I saw confusion—*Is this . . . isn't this . . . what people do?* She had overestimated my experience and tried to catch up by stealing second base. Her mother's voice came again, and she shouted back, "Hang *on*, Mummy."

I moved quickly toward her closet and reached for a pink box on her shelf, next to the row of floral blouses with flappy collars. I opened it. I knew I was right this time, because the heat of the room was guiding me to the box, and when I saw the thin chain, I said, "That's gold?"

She nodded.

"Can I keep it?"

"My mom would be so mad, I lost this ring she gave me—"

I leaned in again, cutting her off—a fourth time. When I withdrew, she nodded. The wondering expression—*Is this what people do?* There was still suspicion in her face, but it was combined with stupefaction, and most of all, ignorance. I needed to bookend the scene, to make her certain that what she had just given me made sense according to the transactions of boys and girls our age, that it was some sort of love token. I went in one final time. I told myself it was good practice.

I pulled back, my tongue wet with hers—she'd gone *very* French that time. And there Shruti Patel stood in her room full of dolls, all of their bead eyes on us, all of the eyes of her childhood watching her as she took a great step toward what she thought was adulthood.

THAT I ABANDONED SHRUTI for Manu and Kartik and Aleem and Jack and Abel at the dance; that I ignored her studiously for the week thereafter; that I managed to move my assigned seat in Euro from the place by the window, next to her, to the back chalkboard, telling Mr. Bakes (not untruthfully) that I was suffering migraines and couldn't handle the light; that I ignored, too, the hoots about Spring Fling, until they subsided into a consensus that I had gone with her out of kindness . . . all this caused the incident to abate with dangerous ease.

I had thought originally that I would need to have some sort of conversation with Shruti, explaining the merits of friendship over romance at this stage in our lives, but on the first day I saw her after the dance, kneeling by her locker, her eyes narrowed to suspicious ovals, and all I could mutter was a hi. I shuffled past. She seemed unsurprised. Normal reality had subsumed her once more. She only cast a few injured looks at me across the history classroom before stubbornly turning back to her notebook. I heard her speaking to Mr. Bakes after class about some must-read books on Hong Kong. I'd become just a silly incident in her past.

Wendi Zhao commented on my glum mood over the following weeks: "Kid, don't fuck up when I need you most." She'd been wait-listed at Harvard, and the coaches had suggested that if they could tout a nationals win, she might be shifted to the "Z-list," meaning she would be offered a chance to take a gap year and enroll the following fall.

My family noticed as well. I was dull at dinners, dampening the celebratory mood—for despite all the heartache and cursing of Gita Menon over the past few months, Prachi had in the end received her glorious fat envelope in the mail. My father, never a drinker, had made a toast with his water glass several nights in a row, while my mother's eyes welled up, and I hmmed a congratulations gamely through a mouthful of saaru.

Passing my room to get to the attic after one of those toasting dinners, my father paused. "You can do what Prachi did, too," he said.

I thought I'd heard him wrong. "What?"

"We are feeling like our decision to come here makes sense, with you two doing so well."

I almost wished for him to revert to his old suspicions.

I had, if you counted it out, what I needed to not fuck up debate nationals. I took a regular dose from our competitors—Soumya Sen, and one of Anita's Bobcat classmates whose earring and anklet she had nabbed from the PE locker room, just for me. But I had come to understand that brewing the perfect lemonade was not a matter of taking luck or specific talents from another person and drinking those down. I needed whatever it was that had caused Shruti Patel to so effectively move on when I had done to her worse than what Anita had done to me the previous year. I needed her belief, her faith, and the thing that ignited both in her.

I needed something to get me through tomorrow and tomorrow, tomorrow—when I would finally, finally be able to begin the process of becoming a real person.

A FEW DAYS BEFORE she left for New Jersey, Anita's instant messenger avatar reappeared online for the first time in months. She must have unblocked me, at long last. I found the conversation in adulthood, archived in my old email. I can't remember what I felt like during or after the chat. It is like one of those artifacts of history I studied later as a graduate student—the thing the people experiencing it missed, the thing that might have changed the rest. When we handle such artifacts, we condescend about how ignorant the denizens of the past are. But we forget that the past is a blind, groping place.

> **neil_is_indian:** sup
>
> **anibun91:** guess whos gonna be in new jersey this weekend
>
> **neil_is_indian:** uh u?
>
> **anibun91:** other than me!!
>
> **neil_is_indian:** ur mom ba doom chha
>
> **anibun91:** *sigh* sam
>
> **neil_is_indian:** o shit
>
> **anibun91:** im like:OOO
>
> **anibun91:** hes visiting his cousin or something
>
> **anibun91:** who goes to rutgers
>
> **anibun 91:** n then his parents r gonna take him to see princeton lol w/e

anibun91: not that he could get into princeton (!)

neil_is_indian: thats rando

anibun91: ok ya

anibun91: but then when i mentioned the pageant he was like o maybe ill come

anibun91: (!?!!?!!?!?!?!!?!?! whaaaaat)

neil_is_indian: the brown ppl will trample him

neil_is_indian: "one of these is not like the others"

neil_is_indian: "kill outsider"

anibun91: im so embarrassed

neil_is_indian: no ur not

anibun91: what do u mean of course i am

neil_is_indian: ur gonna win its gonna be fine

neil_is_indian: & he likes u even if he is an asshole

anibun91: who says hes an asshole?

neil_is_indian: u did?

anibun91: w/e no he isnt

anibun91: but actually im like so sick of this pageant and all the fobs

anibun91: and sick of being only

anibun91: like

anibun91: pretty for a brown girl

anibun91: hey u still there

anibun91: ??

neil_is_indian: ya sorry @ debate

neil_is_indian: wendi on my ass

anibun91: oooooooooh

neil_is_indian: not like that shes anal

neil_is_indian: also not like that

anibun91: w/e u have yellow fever

neil_is_indian: ???????

anibun91: melanie, wendi, lol

neil_is_indian: theyr both twinkies and im a coconut so nothing counts

anibun91: um literally ur screen name

neil_is_indian: its IRONIC

neil_is_indian: g2g

anibun91: ok bai

neil_is_indian: good luck

neil_is_indian: this weekend

neil_is_indian: w the pageant i mean

anibun91: i might not like him

anibun91: like im not totally sure now?

neil_is_indian: sam?

anibun91: ya

neil_is_indian: who do u like then

anibun91: who says i *have* to like someone?

neil_is_indian: okok

anibun91: now i g2g

neil_is_indian: actually wait

neil_is_indian: can i talk to u about smthg

neil_is_indian: kinda important

anibun91 has signed off

THE WEEKEND Anita and her mother were in New Jersey—which was also the weekend before debate nationals—I let myself into the Dayals' house early on Saturday morning using the key beneath the watering can.

In the basement, I set about performing the routine I had been memorizing for months.

Shruti's chain piled into itself in the basin. Was this how the forty-niners felt—sweaty, exhausted, sick with themselves, having left behind all that was familiar for this gleaming element? Flux, sloshing. Goggles, the rest of the ill-lit basement obscured through the plastic.

I started to recite the string of foreign phrases—*Asya swarnasya kantihi shaktir gnyanam casmabhihi praapyataam*—but I stumbled. I started again. I watched the gold almost throbbing in the basin, like it was daring me to take it. *"Fuck,"* I muttered. Then I clamped my hands over my mouth, afraid for a moment that I'd polluted the enchantment with my cursing. I took a great heaving breath, began again, and got through it that time . . . and at last, there was the liquid, my shot of gold, the same as it had always looked at the end of this process and yet completely different—because this time it was all mine.

The lemonade: I pumped all the juice I could out of the fruit, feeling the thing release in my palm, a muscle spasming pleasurably at my touch. I picked up a string of lemon pulp with my pinky and felt its pucker on the inside of my mouth—headily, I thought,

This life contains more than I know. And at last the gold falling into the lemonade, the sigh in the pitcher, the muffled rush of the carbonation forming, the columns of bubbles like the light falling from the disco ball at the Spring Fling dance. Then I drank, calling upon the focus Anita had taught me months earlier, and I tasted Shruti Patel.

She tasted unlike the others, distinct from the baby bangles and coins and pendants and teardrop earrings and men's Om chains that I had been consuming for months.

Because she was not sweet.

Perhaps I had done something wrong with the proportions. Or perhaps—I now think—I had not successfully masked the bitterness, the murk, the complications.

Afterward, I cleaned vigorously. I poured the extra lemonade into one of the vials Anita's mother kept above the basement fridge. I put it in my backpack, wrapping it in gym socks. I went for a three-mile jog—the run had nothing to do with Shruti, who could not run a mile to save her life; that was me, converting her into all I wanted to be.

That night I watched Anita earn her crown as Miss Teen India USA, and when my parents came into the living room to see me tuned in to Zee TV, they raised their eyebrows and said, "Really, watching that?" and I said, "She's not so bad," and they sat, too, and my mother rolled her eyes when Anita launched into her charity speech—battered women, again. She had at last been to Queens; the Dayal women had stopped in at the shelter before heading to New Jersey, delivering soaps and lotions and cosmetic products. Anita told an anecdote of a Bangladeshi woman beaten by her husband, left homeless, turned to prostitution, because "we do what we must to survive, and there was nowhere for her to go, no safe place and no home for her in this foreign country."

IT WAS PRACHI WHO ANSWERED the phone Sunday night. I don't know who began the telephone tree, which aunties' voices carried the news from the Patels' house to ours. At eleven, my sister came into my room and asked me to put away the heavy Dell laptop on which I was typing frantically. I had a grand idea to premiere at nationals, a plan related to fusion energy. I was a diviner; my computer light in my dark room was the light of the gold in the rock—

Prachi, wearing Blue Devils blue, sat on my bed, took the laptop, and told me the news.

She repeated it; she did not know if I had heard. I was reduced to rabbity, muscular reactions. My cheek convulsed. I bit my lip and tasted blood, which smacks somehow of metal.

I looked out my window, past the stinking spring Bradford pear on the Walthams' lawn. Anita's house remained dark. The Dayals had not yet returned from New Jersey. Perhaps they were barreling north from Hartsfield-Jackson in their brown Toyota. For a wild moment I wished that they would crash, be plowed into by some drunk or insane Atlanta driver, so they would never know what I'd done.

At some point that night, Prachi left, and at some point that night, my parents said things, useless things. When I was finally alone, it was perhaps one in the morning, and the night outside was still, the suburbs grotesquely undisturbed. I rummaged through my bag for the remaining vial of lemonade. I removed the stopper and brought it to my nose. I tipped the rest into my mouth and gagged; I ran to the bathroom, stuck two fingers down my throat, and watched a membranous fluid splatter into the toilet bowl. Nothing sparkled, nothing bubbled, nothing betrayed a hint of magic.

I don't know what method she chose. I only know they found her on Sunday morning. She must have done it Saturday night. I have always pictured it happening in the closet, the one she opened when I asked to see her jewelry. I imagine it with rope. I see her placing her feet onto a step stool. Her brown lids closed. Watched by her many dolls' eyes, which were as alive as hers, for she had already given up, for the life had been taken from her a few hours earlier, in a basement, by a boy who believed he was shaking away pay dirt. The purple blooming around her throat, in the place where a necklace would have hung.

5.

An open house sign teetered on the Dayals' unkempt front lawn that late spring: FOR SALE, REMAX REALTY. An agent named Kent Hunt grinned out at passersby. His sticky, flat grimace faded beneath the Georgia rainstorms. Below his bald head and his blimp-shaped face ran his slogan: EVERYTHING I TOUCH TURNS TO SOLD!

I didn't know Anita and her mother were moving to California until I saw Kent Hunt being knocked about in the southern monsoon on the day I returned to Atlanta from debate nationals. I'd fumbled a crucial argument in quarterfinals, ending Wendi Zhao's high school career and ruining her last shot at Harvard. She was a mess that night, crying into her scrambled eggs at Waffle House as we ate our first proper meal all weekend, then banging on the door of my hotel room at three a.m., pushing me onto the bed, shoving her small hand down my pants to suggest I *grow up already*, only to find me limp. "You're grieving," she'd said finally, excusing herself. I smelled alcohol on her breath. "It's not your fault."

When we pulled up at my house, she gave my arm a squeeze and said it had, for the most part, been a pleasure doing business with me.

It was May now. Most flowers were dead and the knotty Atlanta trees erupted in shocks of green and the rain came down in a hot thick curtain.

"You can come visit me at UGA—before I transfer, I mean. Get a preview of college life," she said, raising her voice to be heard over the storm as I opened the car door. "Hey, your little neighbor's moving?" She pointed at the Dayals' yellow house—even its rollicking colors looked muted in today's weather.

I had to squint to make out the open house sign. Thunder rolled above. About a year ago, I was watching these storms from the glassy interior of the Hammond Creek Public Library; a year ago my world was smaller, and I'd bristled against its confinement.

"I would have known," I said. "No way."

"Life moves pretty fast, or whatever the line is. Hey. I'm sorry, again, about your friend." She screwed up her nose. "Shruti."

She zoomed her Saab up the hill, leaving me to hold that word, *friend*, like some stranger's baby I had been tasked with minding. I watched the bumper stickers advertising years of Wendi's honor roll statuses retreat out of our cul-de-sac. I stood in my driveway holding my suitcase and the quarterfinals trophy Wendi had disdained; she couldn't stand to look at anything but first place. My skin and clothes were turning soggy. I stood there until I felt like pulp.

I tugged my bag through the puddles and crossed the cul-de-sac. The Waltham children spun around beneath the family's basketball hoop, mouths open. It seemed impossible that life persisted, that people still dwelled in innocence. I blinked and tried to make my eyes resemble a man's eyes. I did not reach for the watering can behind the azalea bush. I rang the bell.

Anjali Auntie sighed to see me on her doorstep. Wordlessly, I looked at the open house sign, then back at her. She nodded slowly, and I began to cry. She pressed my forehead to her chest and her hair brushed my cheek and there she was, forgiving, as only one's own mother can. In the hours and days after Shruti's death, she had said weepy things—how it was her fault, not mine, her mistake, not mine, she was the adult, had failed me, us, failed, period.

"You'll catch cold," she said. "Come. Let me get you a towel."

"Is Anita here?" I sniffed, following her inside.

"She's here," Anjali Auntie said warily, as though to add, *That's between you two.* Because Anita had not spoken to me since the moment the Dayals arrived home from New Jersey to find me rocking madly on their doorstep, hacking and hiccupping as I tried to explain what I had done.

There had only been unanswered instant messages:

neil_is_indian: anita

neil_is_indian: if you rly didnt want to talk to me youd have blocked me

neil_is_indian: if you never wanna talk to me again

neil_is_indian: id understand

neil_is_indian: but i think u do

I lifted the trophy. The metal was cheap and covered in fingerprints. Anjali Auntie brushed it with her thumb like she was rubbing a stain from a child's face. I didn't want it in my house, couldn't bear the sudden warming of my father's expression, his monstrous validation.

She bit her lower lip. "Towel," she said again, and turned to her bedroom.

"Anjali!" It was a man's booming voice.

The Dayal house had an echoey tendency, and big sasquatchy

footsteps resounded. It had been some years since I'd seen Pranesh Uncle. To be honest, I had mostly forgotten him until he manifested in the formal living room. He was plump and entirely bald, his scalp recalling a glass egg. The skin below his eyes looked ink smudged. His lips were bloodless and chapped. He wore a baggy black T-shirt reading SF GIANTS and cargo shorts. I wondered if he had ever been handsome.

"Neeraj, you've grown," he said. "Haven't seen my wife."

"Hi, Uncle. She went to get me a towel."

"You're all wet. Been dancing in the rain like some Bollywood star, have you."

Anjali Auntie returned, handing me a huge fluffy green towel. I longed to lie on their floor and use the towel as a pillow and fall asleep, except that sleep offered no safe haven. Shruti populated my dreams. Sometimes she held my Swiss Army knife to my throat and demanded I pour out all the lemonade in the Dayals' fridge. Other times she pressed me against a wall and kissed me and I didn't resist. Still other times she sat silent, ashy, blinking; I'd wake in cold sweats and swear I saw her cross-legged at the foot of my bed, fingering the fringe of my comforter, frowning at me with that familiar chemistry class disdain—*It's really not that hard, Neil, if you'd just focus.* I'd tried to call out for Anita's help, to no avail:

neil_is_indian: i hate myself

neil_is_indian: and if u just didn't hate me

neil_is_indian: idk id be rly grateful

Anita's father looked between his wife and me and grunted. "Oh. Having a tough time, I imagine," he said. He crossed to their dining room and drummed one broad hand on the table.

"Give me your hoodie, Neil," Anjali Auntie said. I stripped it off and accepted the towel.

"Anjali. You need to—"

"In a minute, Pranesh."

She tossed the sweatshirt over her arm and disappeared into the laundry room, leaving me alone with her husband, who was blinking indifferently. There was something relieving about his gaze; it was so unlike the practiced gentleness of the teachers, the other parents, the school counselor, who had called in known "friends of Shruti" to recite the same absolutions, how we never knew what was going on in someone's mind, how sometimes there were simply forces at work beyond our control. I fled the meetings with these adults as fast as I could, trying not to look at the spot where I used to see Shruti kneeling by her locker.

Pranesh folded his arms. "This sort of thing used to happen at the IITs, you know. Some boy would come from a small town, all his parents' money spent on getting him into this school. Fellow thinks he's brilliant, then finds he's now on some altogether different Gaussian curve, and he flunks some exam and, you know." He clicked his tongue. "Calls it quits."

"Pranesh, drop it." Anjali Auntie returned to the dining room and shook her head briskly.

He waved his hand in dismissal. "They'd jump out some window or hang themselves. Nowadays it is all fashionable to blame the professors or the other students, but if you ask me—"

"*Pranesh.*"

"If you ask me," he spoke over her. "I have an unpopular opinion."

I had lost track of my limbs and my facial features. I only registered the general fact of gravity keeping me on the ground.

"Somebody wants to off themselves, they'll do it no matter what. It's a constitutional weakness."

Two sharp female voices spoke at once: "Pranesh, *stop!*" and "Papa, *stop!*"

Anita stood on the cream-colored carpeting of the front staircase. She wore faded, frayed denim shorts and a blue tank top bearing her Bobcat Cross-Country logo—a dark, slender figure running on a winding road.

Anita's father glanced between all three of us, shrugged, and walked to the kitchen. "Anjali, that idiot Hunt fellow keeps calling. For godsake call him back."

Anjali Auntie followed. I was alone in the foyer with Anita. She was glaring at the floor. *You're supposed to imagine!* How far she seemed from that little girl who'd brimmed over with myriad realities.

"So," I said. "You're leaving."

"Yes," she said, galumphing back upstairs. She was slight, but she had a soldier's marching gait. "And I'm still not interested in talking to you."

I let myself out; the rain had halted, and the sun was drying out the concrete and the asphalt. The foliage shone even brighter, glistening with raindrops; we were rich with the season, and no one seemed to know that the border between life and death had suddenly become as thin as gossamer.

I tossed the trophy in the Walthams' garbage bin on my way home.

MY PARENTS had mostly gone mute after Shruti's death, as though afraid that by comforting me they'd disturb some crucial rhythms of my newly acquired work ethic. But after debate nationals, after AP exams (which I roundly flunked—even Euro), once summer had begun, my mother turned off my alarm clock and took to waking me up by sitting on the edge of my bed and placing her hand on parts of me that must have reminded her of me as a baby—the soft skin on my neck, the cushion of my belly. "It's morning, rajah," she'd try.

"Stop doing this," I told her after a few days. "It's weird."

I didn't care that my mother's eyes filled, as though I'd pinched her hard with my fingernails, when I said that.

My father subbed in. One night he came home from work still wearing his white coat and knocked on my door. I was napping. I was almost always napping. He placed several laminated diagrams on my messy desk and indicated that I should take a seat. I obeyed and looked at the pictures. A black-and-white brain appeared in one, punctuated by brightly colored dots that marked the hippocampus, the amygdala, the cerebellum, etc. On another, a neon DNA helix and a word salad of gene names.

"I know you have not yet had your AP Biology and all," my father said, fingering the paper's laminated edge. "But just see, there are these distal factors, these family histories, these genes, all brain issues—you do not have to understand it all, Neeraj; I only want you to see how much is going on when something like this happens."

"Dad." I pushed the papers to the side, and with it, his hand. He slipped and caught himself on my chair. He placed one palm on my shoulder and I instinctively shrugged it off. "I have to pack. I'm leaving for Michigan soon." I hadn't brought down my laundry; the whole room smelled of oversprayed Old Spice and other, less pleasant odors.

"Neeraj, we are worried about you."

"I don't want to talk about it."

"These things, Neeraj, they occur sometimes, but—"

"*Dad.*" I stood so violently that he took a few steps back, tripping on the clothes strewn about. I was taller than he was now, and unaccustomed to my new size. I could see the brightness of his bald spot anew; it beamed beneath my bedroom light. His mustache quivered. He smoothed the lapels of his coat. He stood there, breathing hard, nostrils flaring, eyes narrowing. I looked on his anger as a curiosity. There was so much he didn't know—about me, about the world.

"You want me to treat you like an adult, you behave like an adult," he finally said. He looked around my bedroom. "Clean up this damned filthy place."

Guilt, grief, yes, but also the worst crash, the endless jonesing, the withdrawal that my pharmacist father never suspected as such. I shivered and sweated as my body ached for lemonade. On Kartik's advice, I approached Lowell Jenkins, who had an ADHD diagnosis, and used my leftover allowance for debate tournament meals to buy some of his Ritalin. I would find ways to acquire the stuff readily over the following years. Pharmaceutical methylphenidates could instill focus, and they kept some of the worst awareness of what had happened at bay. But they offered none of the comfort of the lemonade, none of the assuredness of identity, none of the implicit promise that tomorrow would contain in it a home.

There was no memorial service for Shruti, at least not one her classmates were invited to. But in late May, a few days after my run-in with Pranesh Uncle, Manu told me people were gathering notes to send to the Patels. "Overdue, man," he said. "I feel like shit I didn't do it sooner. Just. Exams. Killed me." He rubbed his eyes; he'd grown dark bags beneath them. It was the unlikely Mia

Ahmed, whom I'd never seen speaking to Shruti except in passing, who had trotted a big condolence card around the honors hallway during AP week, but there had been nothing more personal. We were in Kartik's basement. The other guys were playing *Grand Theft Auto*. Manu and I stood in the kitchen, drinking Pibb Xtra. I felt like I was made of bubbles and syrup and nothing else. I'd dropped several pounds in the past month, and I stood at five-ten now, a few inches taller than Manu, though haggard in the cheeks, growing irregular patches of facial hair.

"Who's *people*?" I asked.

"Juhi and Isha and all."

"Seriously?"

I'd shut down Facebook—and never came back, even in adulthood—the morning they announced Shruti's death at school. My feed was clogged with statuses from the girls who'd snickered at her, now claiming the deceased as their intimate: *Last weekend we lost a classmate and a friend*, Juhi wrote. *We will miss you and your brains and your laugh, Shruti.*

Manu's brow furrowed. He lowered his voice. "It's not their fault, and it's not yours."

"They were so mean to her," I said. All the saliva in my mouth dried out. I put the soda down and filled a glass with water. I couldn't rid myself of the bad taste. "*We—*"

"I know you feel bad, Neer. I do, too. I think about Spring Fling a lot."

I had almost forgotten that Manu had preceded me as Shruti's date. So, he had avoided her for a few hours on a dance floor. Some part of me ached to tell him he had no idea how small his unkindness had been in the scheme of things. Another part wanted him to keep self-flagellating, so everyone would share the blame.

"You didn't do much," I managed.

"That was exactly the problem, wasn't it?"

He reached into his backpack and pulled out a plastic Kroger bag full of knockoff Hallmark cards. Teddy bears and hearts and flowers. I'm sorry, in our thoughts, condolences. None of the language of the brown parents who had been squeezing out their inadequate explanations. Here was white procedure, American custom, and in it, relief.

Manu left me with a pen and a card—a mournful chocolate lab on a white backdrop beneath a cursive phrase: *sympathies*—as he went over to distribute the others. There was some groaning as he shut off the television, but it was replaced by the scratching of pens.

"Do we know how she did it?" Kartik whispered.

"K," Manu snapped. "How could that be relevant?"

"I just don't know shit about any of this," Kartik huffed. "What am I supposed to say?"

"I'm writing that they're in our prayers," Aleem said.

"Man, but you're Muslim. What if they don't want to be in your prayers?"

"I think they'll understand, dude," Abel said softly. "It all goes to the same place."

My grip on my pen faltered. I didn't want to write to the Patels; I wanted to write to Shruti. I had an urge to write backward in time, into the past, to run to OHS and shove a note in her locker, the way we used to communicate with girls in middle school—*Circle yes/no if you want to be bf/gf.* Now: *Circle yes/no if it was/wasn't my fault.* Manu was gathering the cards. He stood next to me and sealed each one in an individual envelope. I still had not written anything.

"They might not even open them, Neer," he said. "Do it so you can say you've done it."

I clicked my Uni-ball over and over. I pressed it to the paper. Manu had given me a glossy card and a too-inky pen; the words bled. *Dear Mr. and Mrs. Patel*—I didn't remember their first names to write So-and-So Auntie, Uncle. *Dear Mr. and Mrs. Patel, I am sorry for your loss. Shruti was an incredible person, smart, funny, and a really good friend. My whole family is thinking of you both and Hema. NN.*

"Write your full name," Manu said, but I was already licking the envelope.

The guys had turned *Grand Theft Auto* back on, and the roar of an animated car at 120 miles per hour filled the basement.

Abel shouted, "Fuck!" and Kartik yelled to shut up, his mom was upstairs.

Manu dug in the Kroger bag and handed me another card. "Anita was sometimes really nice to Shruti. Can you have her do one? I just have to get these to Isha's mom tomorrow."

"I haven't really talked to her," I said.

"Try."

I took it. It was one of the postcards you got for donating to the World Wildlife Fund.

"My mom said to use up these, too," he said.

On the front were a rollicking polar bear and her cub running across a slab of ice. A sheer blue cloudless sky framed them. The year of debating climate change made me think of their habitat melting away in long cold trickles.

ON MY LAST EVENING before leaving for East Lansing, I snuck over to the Dayals' when my father thought I was packing upstairs. He was semi-dozing over a textbook at the breakfast table, some continuing education. My mother and Prachi were on a Target run, buying extra-long twin sheets and a shower caddy and other dorm supplies. My mother was insisting on taking new purchases to the temple to have them blessed by a priest who specialized in educational consecrations, so they'd be out awhile.

The Dayals' lights were on, and music played inside. The door was unlocked. Milling in the foyer were people I didn't recognize, fobby-looking thirtysomething guys, white men and women, a young black couple. Pranesh Dayal was holding forth in the dining room, drinking red wine. He wore a key-lime-green summer button-down that stretched round his middle.

"Just came back to finalize all this moving business," he said to his conversation partner. "It was getting a bit much for Anjali, she settles for any old amount, can't be so generous when people are out to take you for all you're worth."

Pranesh Uncle's eyes fell on me. "Anita's in her room, Neeraj. She's sulking."

I didn't need to be asked twice. I kicked off my shoes and bolted up the front stairs. The walls were still covered in Anita's yearbook photos. The carpet looked recently vacuumed. I understood from years of tagging along with my mother to open houses that the limbo of placing a home on the market meant maintaining the illusion of life persisting within the walls.

I knocked on Anita's door. She looked unsurprised to see me.

Her eyebrows had grown bushy. The whites of her eyes were roped with red. Her thick hair was tugged into a messy ponytail. She wore smudged glasses instead of contact lenses.

"You're not at that party?"

"It's people mooning over my dad," she said. "Stupid shit."

"I'm leaving tomorrow," I said, practically bouncing on my toes, looming over her. "I'm leaving tomorrow, then you're leaving, and you can't just expect me to not say bye."

She stepped aside so I could come in. Her room was barer than it used to be. The dresser and desk remained, but the Harvard shrine had come down. She took her glasses off and tossed them on the carpet.

"Manu wanted me to have you sign a card. For the Patels."

"No," she said.

"Yeah. I figured."

She sat on her mattress, cross-legged. Her legs looked freshly shaved, inviting and buttery. There was nowhere else to sit—her desk chair was gone—so I chose the foot of her bed. My legs swung to the side, heels on the floor.

"You're not kicking me out."

She ignored that. "I took some of my dad's wine. Do you want some?"

I bit my thumbnail and nodded. She reached into her nightstand and removed a half-empty bottle, uncorked.

"You already drank all that?" I didn't want to spend another night holding her hair back.

"No, stupid. It was like this when I stole it." She took a long pull. Her whole face screwed up against the bitterness. She exhaled. "It still tastes weird to me."

I hesitated but followed suit. I was not particularly afraid of my mother's ban on *nonsense* just then. All the barricades she'd erected to keep the world out had come tumbling down a few weeks earlier. The wine stung. But I did like the warmth filling my throat and the space behind my collarbones. Anita took only a few sips.

"Are you feeling it?" I put the back of my hand on my cheek as though to test for fever.

"Just a little," she said.

"Uh, yeah. Me, too. Just a little," I lied. I inched closer. I saw myself in Anita's mirror. I was scruffy, but more substantial than I had been even months ago. I had the thought that I ought to take up more space in the world. "Why didn't you tell me you were moving?"

"Why didn't *you* tell me you were—" She stopped.

"Say it. No one will say it; just say it."

"You want me to say it was your fault."

"Yeah." The heat in my face swelled; I didn't know if it was the wine or impending tears.

"Fine, it was your fault," she said. "Do you feel better?"

I shook my head and reached for the bottle. Through the air vent: the continued buzz of the party downstairs, Beatles songs, wooden laughter. I didn't reply. Through the window by her bed, you could see the edge of my house. It was after eight and the sky was the color of dulling embers, the sunset polluted by smog.

There was a finger's worth of wine left. I chugged it. Anita shoved the empty bottle in her nightstand.

"I'll toss it later," she said, like she'd done this before. Then she stood, and I was still sitting. She stepped near me. She was tall for a girl, but I was now taller, so she had to look up.

And then I did it. I took her face in my hands, and I kissed like I knew what I was doing. Her lips were this strange combination of gentle and assured, and when tongue arrived, it was just enough. I couldn't say how long the first part went on for, but at some point, she was sitting on her bed and at some point later we were both lying down, and my hand was on her breast, then her stomach, then beneath her shirt. She made an *mmph* noise, and I didn't immediately move my hand away.

She pushed my wrist back up to her collarbone.

"Sorry," I said.

Her lips glistened and she bit the lower one and wiped her mouth with her knuckles.

"I didn't know you'd—" Her expression shaded suddenly.

And then, there, blinking at me, was not Anita at all, but Shruti, whose small eyes were considering me quizzically as I asked her if her chain was gold. I shuddered, visibly, audibly. Shruti's breath on my neck; her voice in precalc: *Neil, you can solve by substitution.*

"Neil?"

I looked up. "Oh, I mean, I haven't," I said, too late.

Anita's spaghetti strap and bra strap had slid down her right shoulder, and she tugged both back into place. I scooted a few inches away, though it required all my might. As Anita turned her head to assess me, there were Shruti's frizzy locks, catching the light.

"How many girls *have* you done stuff with?" she asked.

"Three." I closed my eyes. Shruti in my ear: *No, you're supposed to be taking the* compound *probability of two* independent events, see? "Two."

If I kept my eyes on the carpet, Shruti's voice faded. *Two possibilities, equally likely—*

"I've only kissed two guys," she said. "Never, um. Never even second base."

"Who?" I said it instinctively—I had to know . . . *Which adds up to all possible events, see.* Shruti's mouth—the smacking of her lips before the second kiss . . .

"Oren, from drama camp, remember?" I'd forgotten—a ginger, in seventh grade. "And Sam." *Say it's tails, heads, heads, tails . . .* "At this end-of-year tennis party."

"Really?" *No, what you've done here, it's very common, you're thinking about those two things as connected, but they're entirely independent events.* It was all I could do to stop Shruti from rising wholesale out of Anita. If I kept everything even—my voice, my expression—she remained on the right side of reality. Anita's eyes stayed Anita's eyes: wide, lively, their darkness illuminated by her bedroom lights. There. No Shruti. No hard, calculating pupils.

"It's only 'cause I'm leaving. He'd never date me in public. Who are *yours?*"

"You don't know them."

"I told you all mine." Anita was hugging her knees to her chest and chewing on the ends of her hair. For her, the world was easing; this terrain—our old terrain of small secrets, minor confessions—made her feel safe. "There was that girl from your computer camp. Let me guess the others." She bit her lip. She seemed to be trying to prove that she knew all material truths about me even when I had not explicitly shared them. "Wendi, right?"

"Not *that* much happened."

She laughed; she looked unthreatened, having some sense that she preceded, or superseded, all others. "And the third . . ." She tapped her chin with a finger.

I stood up. "No, it was just two," I said. *Determine the probability of this exact order, Neil.* I paced, stepping loudly to stop Shruti's high pitch from trailing me around the room.

"Don't stomp, Neil; my mom will come up." Anita giggled. Had I been sober or unhaunted I might have seen that she was happy in my company. "And, wait. You *said* three."

I was sure I heard someone—not Shruti—calling her name. "Is that your mom?"

"Who was the third, Neil? *Oh*, my god, was it Juhi? I always thought—" and then she stopped. Her fingernails dug into the bare skin around her knees. Through clenched teeth, she said, "No, you didn't. At Spring Fling."

I stared miserably at the carpet. Maybe I'd said *three* on purpose. Maybe I'd wanted her to know. Maybe I couldn't picture holding the secret alone for the rest of my life.

"So," she whispered. "All that . . . to get what you needed from her."

"I didn't mean for it to go that way—"

"Did you get what you needed from me?" she said, still in that tinny, mean voice.

"Anita, it's not the same thing, like. With you . . ."

The moment was racing past me, into terrain I had no language for, and I knew I wouldn't be able to seize the words to explain, or apologize, in time.

These are all independent events, see, so here are all the different possibilities. Shruti was done explaining. I heard the satisfying clunk of a pencil being dropped onto a desk. No, it wasn't that—someone was knocking on Anita's door, and calling for her through the wood.

"Ani, Papa wants you to say good-bye to the Shettys, please come down."

"You know *everything*," I tried again urgently. "You're the only one who can—"

"In a minute, Mama," Anita said. In her frosty gaze was a new kind of recognition. She was not seeing the boy who needed help to *imagine*, not coaxing him out of his paralysis and into the world. She was seeing the boy who was such a nothing that he had begged and stolen and finally killed in desperation to become something. For the first time, I wished she wouldn't see me at all.

The doorknob rotated. "Neil! I didn't know you were here."

Anjali Auntie was wearing a somber navy salwar kameez flecked with glitter. She looked at the rumpled sheets, and then at Anita's tank top, which was sliding off her shoulders again. Her eyes bulged.

"Uncle told me to come up," I said. "I just wanted to say bye." I gripped my belly to stop the sloshing and spoke deliberately, unable to calibrate whether she could discern my drunkenness. I glanced around the room for some sign of Shruti tugging on her curls. I felt sure I would never be able to sit in a room with Anita or Anjali Dayal without the ghost of Shruti hovering, waiting for the right moment to manifest.

"He was leaving," Anita said.

"I have to go to Michigan," I said. No one budged. "Not now. Tomorrow, I have to go to Michigan. To East Lansing. Tomorrow."

"Both of you," Anjali Auntie said tightly, "come downstairs. It's not nice that Anita's up here when we're having people over like this."

And she waited in the doorway, arms folded, as I trudged downstairs. Before I could actually say good-bye, Anita had entered her public self once more. Her voice pitched upward, and she padded over to the Shettys, saying, "Auntie, Uncle, I'm sorry I've been MIA, had some things to get done. . . ." They subsumed her, then, these aunties and uncles with their scripts: Where are you going to school in California? Will you stay in touch with all your friends? Ho, ho, it's Miss Teen India! And as I saw the last flash of her calf, I felt more alone than ever.

"Neil." Anjali Auntie glanced at her husband on the other side of the living room. He was entertaining a ring of engineers, all of whom seemed to be regarding him as the apex of something. ("This hardware versus software issue, Tarun . . .") "You'll be good. Make use of it."

I nodded, though I hardly knew what I was agreeing to. I felt nauseous, but still liked what the alcohol provided—this sense of self-obliteration, this warping.

My phone buzzed in my pocket and I took it out—my father had noticed I was missing and was frantic. I told him I was just saying good-bye to Anita. The panic in his voice quelled.

"You could have let me know," he said. "It is worrisome—to not be able to find you."

"Come, Neil," Anjali Auntie said. "I'll walk you out." She glanced back at Pranesh Uncle, who was talking over an engineer. I had the sense that just as the auntie-uncle scripts had once more subsumed Anita, many other scripts—for marriage, for a nuclear family—were waiting to reclaim Anjali Auntie as well.

As I left the Dayal house that night for the last time, shutting the door on that strange party, on that strange marriage, on that strange girl who would not speak to me again for nearly a decade, Anjali Dayal appeared diminished. She walked next to me down the driveway, barefoot, and seemed too exhausted by all that had gone wrong to radiate the kind of damning maternal energy my mother would have unleashed on any boy caught in Prachi's room.

I remembered, suddenly, her dead brother. I scanned her for signs of this early tragedy. Was some part of her always lodged in the past, in the moment when he'd been lost? Would some part of *me* always remain trapped here, in this moment, in Hammond Creek, too?

"Go home, Neil," Anjali Auntie said. She didn't sound like an angry mother—more like my sister, in the urgent tone she took when I was about to say something to get her in trouble with our parents. She glanced toward the Walthams' curb, where a tall, chestnut-haired white man was stepping out of a hatchback and considering the BUSH/CHENEY lawn sign. He'd double-parked, blocking in one of the Dayals' guests' cars. Anjali Auntie seemed to flinch at the sight of him. I assumed she needed to go negotiate for the space. "Please. Your dad must be worried."

I trudged across the cul-de-sac, looking briefly behind me. Anjali Auntie was walking toward the white man, her mouth open, her hands lifted as though starting an argument.

My father was waiting for me in the breakfast room. He watched me unlacing my shoes, trying to read me. My mother and sister didn't appear to be home yet. I made for the stairs, but he stopped me on the landing.

"You have been up to something, Neeraj," he said. I noticed again the shimmer of his bald spot, and I thought of the tender part of a baby's skull that makes it vulnerable, and had a vision of me holding my father and accidentally dropping him on the crown of his head.

He approached me. "You have been drinking alcohol, isn't it?" His nose wrinkled.

I nodded. Perhaps it was the wine or perhaps it was honest new wisdom, but I could see everything he did only as a kind of inept performance by a B-grade actor.

"Do you like looking like this? You look like a big mess. You do not look like my son."

"Yeah. I like it." I loved it, actually, when he put it like that.

A button of moonlight shone between the clouds. Through the staircase window, I could see the still-bright lights of the Dayals'. I had the mad thought that if I got up to my room, alone, before the buzz wore off, I might find Shruti waiting, prepared to talk with me.

"I wanna go to bed," I said.

"Have you been doing this regularly, Neeraj?"

My father's eyebrows, already only barely separated from each other, looked to be one long fat caterpillar.

The garage door creaked.

"Raghu!" My mother pushed the side door open. "Raghu, those Dayal guests have parked everywhere all up and down the cul-de-sac. Didn't think to invite us, did they?"

"Daddy," Prachi said. She was undoing her sandals in the doorway. "Daddy, please tell Amma I can't go to the temple every time we buy something off the college checklist, okay? Just for shower curtains, I mean—"

"Your shower will keep you clean and healthy, Prachi," my mother said. "It can stand to be blessed."

The Narayan women were padding into the kitchen, were within feet of me, would see me like this, however I appeared—sweaty, blaze-eyed, looking *not like my father's son*.

"Go up," my father whispered. "I will not tell Amma. You drink water, and you sleep."

"What's that, Raghu?" my mother called. She and Prachi were pawing through the Target bags and wondering if they'd bought too many hangers.

"Neeraj is going to bed," my father said firmly.

"Tell her," I said, and then I said it again, louder.

Prachi was hoisting the bags onto her shoulders. Her forehead was smeared with the warm sunset hues of haldi kumkum. She looked ruddy in the cheeks, terribly hale.

"Neil, what the shit is wrong with you?" Prachi said.

"Prachi!" my parents both said.

"Why talk like that?" my father said.

"Tell what?" my mother said.

The three other Narayans, the three functional Narayans, stared at me, still as wax muscum figurines. They appeared much better, more sensible, the three of them, without me. Upstairs, Shruti was waiting, pacing by my bed, ready to chide me: *A two on the chemistry exam, really, Neeraj?* I would accept all her reproofs, and then when she was preparing to depart, to slip once more into the underworld, perhaps I would ask her to take me with her. I would tell her that, as usual, she'd gotten it right, found the best answer to the complex problem we were all locked inside.

"Tell *what*?" my mother said again.

Across the way, the Dayal house had gone mostly dark but for two squares of dim light on the top floor, like the drowsy eyes of a beast preparing for sleep. And all around, that early-June Georgia night, the sultry swell of change in the air. I had been waiting to arrive somewhere for so long, and now that I was here, I wanted only to roll backward in time, to swim upstream until I sat at the font of something, to avoid ending up as this unbearable me.

"I'm fucking drunk," I said.

There were no secrets worth keeping anymore.

PART TWO

PANNING

He who steals the gold (of a Brahmana) has diseased nails.

—Manu-smriti, Hindu legal text

Had the immigrants known what a task the gold-hunting would be, their spirits might have failed.

—H. W. Brands, *The Age of Gold: The California Gold Rush and the New American Dream*

6.

Something strange was happening to my family. Of late, the Narayan definition of success had morphed. This was not to say my parents supported my professional choices—in the summer of 2016, I was piddling around as a student of history, suffering their disdain. No, rather, they had accrued additional expectations, ones I did not discover until Prachi fulfilled them.

"Shaadi-shaadi-shaadi!" my mother kept squealing—the Hindi word for *marriage*. She declaimed the triplicate in times of both exuberance and distress, in much the way my ajji used to utter the name of the Lord—*narayana narayana narayana*—in prayer.

"So long we have waited for this shaadi-shaadi-shaadi!" (when Prachi first waggled her conflict-free diamond). "This is a shaadi-shaadi-shaadi, not some country club Buckhead Betty nonsense!" (denouncing my sister's plan to wear a white lehenga rather than the traditional red-and-gold).

My mother broadcast her daughter's impending nuptials to her clients—when I was in college, she had begun a second, fated career as a Realtor. The wedding talk helped close a deal, in much the way the scent of freshly baked cookies in an on-the-market house does—the general whiff of familial completion is infectious, makes everyone hot for suburban settling.

Preparations for Prachi's shaadi-shaadi-shaadi were even impinging on my life on the West Coast. Our parents remained in Georgia, but my sister and I had each made our way to California by way of the tech bubble and academia, respectively. She lived on the third floor of a converted Victorian in San Francisco and I in a cannabis-infused walk-up in Berkeley. And on a particular foggy day in June, my roommate, Chidi, and I were running late to a party at said Victorian.

We stood by Alamo Square Park, taking in the vast bay windows of Prachi's nearly three-grand-a-month apartment, while I sucked on my vape. I discerned the shadows of her friends moving about on the other side of those cakelike window trimmings, and something about their shapes startled me. I'd told Prachi, in trying and failing to beg off that night, that I was spending my summer ensconced in my dissertation and couldn't be disturbed. In truth, I had no coherent justification for the social skittishness that had become my norm. Yes, there was the mounting pressure of graduate school, but there was also some other general allergy that erupted most acutely when I was surrounded by the hyperopic residents of my sister's version of San Francisco.

"None for me, I'd like to be *on* tonight," Chidi said, virtuously refusing a hit of my sativa-indica blend, which made me anxious that I'd already begun. "It's a useful skill to be able to walk into any room and get along with people, Neil. Especially a room with a collective net worth of"—he frowned, doing mental math—"call it tens of millions?" He rubbed his hands together gleefully, prepared, as always, to charm, persuade, finagle, and fundraise. "If you thought more creatively, you could get one of these people to endow you a chair one day, or rethink the whole *concept* of a university, really bring it into the twenty-first century. . . ."

I was already walking away.

Upstairs, inside, we found the room arranged by twos. It reminded me of the opening of those Madeline books Prachi read growing up: twelve little couples in two straight lines; in two straight lines, they talked tech shop, they ate their Brie, they swirled their wine. The betrothed, Avi Kapoor, tapped on his phone, while Prachi, next to him, picked at red grapes and chatted with one of her Duke sorority sisters. Chidi shook hands with Avi, whom he knew from incestuous, elite tech circles. I spied, with great relief, Manu Padmanaban, gripping a Blue Moon and being talked at by Prachi's friend Hae-mi. Manu had grown into himself after coming out in college. He'd briefly been Prachi's colleague at a midsize start-up, and sometimes wrangled an invite to her affairs, where he was my life jacket. He didn't see me.

"I own our tardiness," Chidi lied to the happy couple on my behalf. (I'd dozed through the afternoon following a late night out with the girl I'd been sleeping with. I remembered little of the prior evening's party, save the gas station whiff of coke and a dreadlocked white guy wearing a vial of ketamine around his neck, plucking solemnly at a sitar.) "My call with Fabian Fischer ran long," Chidi went on. "He sends his best, Avi."

Chidi had dropped out of Caltech when a billionaire awarded him a hundred thousand dollars to pursue a 3D printing venture. He'd since launched a wetware product dealing with longevity; that is, attempting to prolong the human life span to Old Testament proportions. He lived off a uniquely Californian income in the interim— exit money from the first company's sale, supplemented with Bitcoin investments. He was half-Nigerian, the product of an Oakland Hills secular Jewish mother and a transplanted Lagos doctor, and I attributed all differences between us—his proclivity for risk, his openness with his parents—to the nonimmigrant side.

Avi appeared duly impressed. "Are you guys raising? I'm surprised you're out." Then, to me: "Book going okay, Neil?"

"Dissertation. A book implies someone's going to read it. It's coming."

At that time, I was going to be an Americanist—a professional interpreter of this land and its layers. My specialty was to be late-1800s California, with a focus on the rise of immigration, the ballooning of enterprise, and the economic stratifications that buoyed the nation into the twentieth century. In other words, the aftermath of the gold rush. But these days, staring at the papers piling up on my desk, I couldn't imagine spending decades burrowing into this corner of the past. It didn't help that I stood out in this land of utopian technofuturists, committed as I was to the secular preservationist priesthood that is the history academy.

"You know," Prachi said. "We just hired an ex-academic from Berkeley for my team." She fumbled for her name, then remembered.

I knew the woman. "Oh. She's an ABD—all but dissertation," I clarified at Prachi's quizzical expression. The ABD wasn't the first to flee the academy for Big Tech's six figures and office nap pods and wouldn't be the last. The specter of dropping out—burning out—loomed over my life and the lives of many in my cohort. Few of us would land where she had. Without Berkeley, I was a Southern state school grad with two years of debate coaching on my résumé.

Prachi: "Ha! That sounds like ABCD!"

No one had applied that acronym—American-born confused desi—to me in quite some time. We'd grown out of it as we grew up; our generation had perhaps not resolved, but had at least begun to get over that Miss Teen India riddle: *What does it mean to be both Indian and American?*

Avi chortled. "Drop the C, and you're an ABD! You could follow her to the big bucks."

"I think I'll remain confused, for now."

But Avi was ignoring me to answer his phone. He worked for a Sherman Act–violating behemoth and was always nursing side startups, fielding endless calls. Chidi made for the couples playing Cards Against Humanity at the Crate and Barrel dining table, and I slipped off to greet Manu. He was a rarity in San Francisco, in that he had read a book not ghostwritten on behalf of an investor or a CEO in the past year. He quizzed me on my research and asked about my opinions on the election.

"Don't bring this up in front of Prachi," I muttered, having confessed where I'd stood in the primary. "She just calls me a sexist and a socialist."

Manu grinned. "Sorry, buddy, but I was too much of a political pragmatist to support your man. Actually"—he checked his watch—"I showed because your sister promised to introduce me to this bigwig on the *Rodham* campaign—her words, not mine—who she swore would be here. I'm *trying* to escape, I'd like to do *something* meaningful, but at the same time, I don't want to be an unpaid intern in, like, *Iowa*." He shuddered. "Imagine Grindr in Iowa."

Which was when Prachi arrived, arm in arm with one of the only unattached women in the room, who, it dawned on me then, was the reason my sister had so insisted on my attendance.

Prachi oozed hostess charm. "My brother's going to be a *professor*, as I've told you, Keya. Neil, you've heard me talk about Keya. Her new company, Dil Day, is doing super well."

"Dildo?" I coughed on my beer.

"Neil!" Prachi squealed.

Manu chuckled.

Keya, to her credit, seemed only entertained. "Dil *Day*," Keya said, giggling. "Dil, Hindi for heart?"

"I *told* you, Neil, it's the dating app Hasan and Farha met on!" Prachi cried.

"Shit," I said. "Sorry. It's for brown people?"

"It's for future-oriented South Asian professionals." Keya lowered her voice. "Believe it or not, they're—*we're*—willing to pay more in the marriage space than any other group."

"Eat the rich, right, Neil?" Manu said.

"Let's leave you two." Prachi steered him away. "Christine is coming, Manu, she *is* . . ."

I wistfully fingered my vape in my pocket. It could put me to sleep. It could eradicate me. These days I sought out things to remove me from what felt like an increasingly constricted world. There had been a few years, in college, when I'd believed in life's ever-unfolding variety. But now, as my compatriots entered the promotion and canine-adoption and splitting-the-rent and wedding seasons of their lives, reality had narrowed again, with little warning.

"I consider myself generally oriented toward the past," I said to Keya.

Keya edged to the counter to pour wine, then filled a paper plate high with cheese. "I was supposed to meet you earlier, but when you didn't show, I got drunk. Now I'm starving."

"I should say," I said, popping some cheddar in my mouth. "I'm seeing someone. Prachi didn't know."

I'd been sleeping with one Arabella Wyeth-Goldstein, of the ketamine and sitar party. I had once been her history TA. She now wrote for a leftist East Bay community paper. We'd spent three months mostly smoking weed and fucking, and we'd just reached that sharing-of-trauma phase that marks a crucial milestone in my generation's patterns of courtship. Arabella's confessions were terribly normal—concerns about the shape of her breasts, were they too eggplanty, etc. When it came my turn, I spoke of academic and familial pressures and Asian emasculation. She'd nodded as I wrapped up the perfunctory revelations and told me that she "lived entirely with people who identified as hyphenated in college" and therefore "got it."

Keya's shoulders slumped genuinely, but then she shrugged. "Same old. Don't tell your sister, but I'm on a mission. I've only slept with white men. Isn't that fucked?"

"So, I would've been an experiment."

Keya looked unabashed, which in turn made me feel unoffended. "Yeah, exactly."

"Shouldn't your app help with that?"

"Oh, I couldn't swipe on my own thing. And I can't be seen using someone else's. I am"—she sighed theatrically—"an analog spinster in the era of digital soul mates." She lifted an elbow in the direction of one smooth-skinned couple. "I've been to three bachelorettes in four months. Maya, with the huge rock? Hers was five days in Belize. I'm broke."

Before I could open my mouth to offer Keya a better definition of the word *broke*, Maya caught my eye. She was lovely, with a lithe neck and short black bob. But it wasn't her face or figure that I was looking at. It was her dangly gold earrings, which swayed like the pipes of a wind chime. I could not help it: I performed the assessment instinctively, with the intuition of an addict, though it had been nearly ten years since I'd tasted gold. But I wondered, as ever: What would those earrings yield? A tumbler of lemonade bearing . . . what? The power to found the perfect company? To pin down the perfect mate? No, remember, the lemonade delivered not just a boost for a single task, but an *energy*, a way of being that guided you toward your deserved future. The gestalt of Maya's golden earrings, of my sister's white-gold engagement ring, of the party itself: shaadi-shaadi-shaadi. Settlement. Well-adjustment.

(My father's old aphorism: *We are all still ad-justing to this place.* It had turned out to be true, clinically speaking. I'd seen a therapist just after graduating UGA, certain I suffered some cocktail of anxiety, major depression, and ADHD. I'd left with no pills, just a cruelly ironic diagnosis of something called *adjustment disorder.*)

At that instant, someone next to Maya turned. Her hair was still frizzy but had softened into gentler waves. Her skin was still acne scarred. She had smeared makeup over the crevices that used to cut so deep, darkening her. This was the clearest I'd seen Shruti Patel in some time. She was an occasional specter in my life, with a habit of appearing just when the material world felt most entrapping. She'd manifest at the periphery of my vision when I was drunk or high, or overlay herself on some brown girl. The memory of my own monstrosity? A reminder of the general futility of the games that comprised my life? Was she beckoning me to join her, wherever she had gone, looking at me through those marble eyes with that overfamiliarity I had always begrudged her, thinking, *I know you, and you belong with me*? Depending on the moment, I let her stand for all of those things, for her suicide—suicide itself— was the whirlpool swirling in my vicinity at all times, sucking into its gravity both every meaning I could toss its way and no meaning at all.

Are you making use of all you took?

Of course not.

I shook my head and Shruti slunk back into death.

The party had migrated to the kitchen. Prachi tittering with Hae-mi. Keya reaching for more Sonoma cabernet, despite swaying on her feet. Chidi all marble smile and head bobs, yammering at Maya about longevity. ("Really," he said, "people have been trying to live longer for centuries, just look at the alchemists, only they didn't have the rigorous experimental methods we do. . . .") Manu trailing everyone, attempting to bid Prachi good-bye, evidently leaving without the key Rodham contact.

"Whoops," Keya said, sloshing wine down her pale green blouse. "Shit."

"Keya came wedding shopping with me today," Prachi said too heartily, as the girlfriends swarmed with club soda. "I'd need a drink, too! I'm sure I wasn't easy to handle."

Keya did not correct my sister, only grinned amiably as Maya mopped her. Manu attempted to wave good-bye through the crooners, but Prachi seized his palm and squeezed several times as though his hand were a stress ball, keeping him from leaving.

"Did you pick something?" Hae-mi cooed.

Prachi reached for her iPhone with her free hand and began swiping to show off options, before suddenly looking up. "Neil! Oh my god. I totally forgot. Guess who we saw at that bridal shop."

"Who?" I said through another mouthful of cheese.

"I'm heading out," Manu called to Prachi, who still held his hand. "I'll email you about Christine?"

"No, *wait*, Manu, *you* won't believe this either—"

Prachi had inherited our mother's love of gossip as we grew up.

For us it was safe territory, untarnished by my views on her work in Big Tech (which I found repugnant, reminiscent of the inequality I studied) or hers on mine in academia (which she saw as a kind of performative hunger strike). Each time we saw each other, we ran through roll calls of acquaintances. So-and-so had become an angel investor, so-and-so a gastroenterologist, so-and-so a federal judiciary clerk. Many were engaged; some were spawning biracial, caramel children. This was what we had in common now, the general web that had formed us.

"Anita!" Prachi was shouting. "*Total* throwback, right?"

I swallowed my cheese too fast, began to cough, downed half a sparkling water, burped. Avi wandered into the kitchen, having finished his phone call.

"*Anita*-Anita?" I said.

"Anita Dayal?" Manu said.

"That name rings a bell," Maya said.

"This is our old neighbor," Prachi said, updating Avi. "Pranesh Dayal's kid, actually."

"Pranesh Dayal?" Chidi looked up suddenly. "That guy who sold the smart devices company last year for a fuckload?"

Avi and Chidi struck up a side conversation about Pranesh Uncle, which Keya joined. I heard her say, "Wait, do you think he's investing now?"

"Neer, you in touch with Anita at all?" Manu asked.

I shook my head. San Francisco is a small town, as is upper-middle-class Asian America. I'd been reencountering Hammond Creek transplanted into the Bay Area for years. There was Manu, and old Ravi Reddy, once expelled to Hyderabad, who'd resurfaced as a back-end engineer and was vocal about his "ethically nonmonogamous lifestyle" whenever I bumped into him. Wendi Zhao—whom I'd dated intermittently in college—headed west after graduating Harvard Law, logging time as a patent troll. I'd even swiped right on Melanie Cho on a dating app once, to no avail. Though we'd grown up in a no-place, the privilege and ambition incubated in that no-place had driven many of us to *the* place where so many with privilege and ambition flocked. But Anita, who I knew had attended Stanford and stuck around out here since, had remained steadfastly hidden, as though she did not wish to be found.

At least, not by me.

"I've seen her a few times," Manu said. "She was working at Galadriel Ventures for a couple of years, doing PR or marketing or events. I ran into her at a demo day she was organizing. She seemed, I don't know, different."

"Different how?" I asked.

"Calmer, maybe?"

Manu's mouth was still open, considering, when Hae-mi snapped her fingers and pointed at Maya. "She was a few years below us at Stanford, dated Jimmy Bansal! Ooh, I bet he helped her get that Galadriel job—"

"Didn't they break up?" Maya said doubtfully.

"Mm, yes, they totally did, at least once, but weren't they on and off?" Hae-mi said. "I remember one of the breakups because it was our commencement and she just kept calling Jimmy over and over, *freaking.* I think she dropped out after that, actually."

"*Anita* dropped out of college?" I inhaled sharply, now turning from Manu, who still hadn't answered my first question. "Like, the way start-up people drop out?"

Hae-mi looked at me pityingly. "No, not like the way *start-up people* drop out. I put her down as a case of classic duck syndrome."

"Duck what?" Prachi said.

"Duck syndrome," Maya said. "You know, someone who looks all calm and crushing it above water, but really they're paddling like crazy underneath to stay afloat?"

Prachi shrugged, as though the concept were foreign; school had come easily to her, and professional life welcomed her gracefully. If she'd suffered trauma (I still remembered the sporadic bulimia on which I'd eavesdropped through high school) she generally refused to reflect on it. I'd always thought time eventually forced even the most practical people to introspect. But my sister had cheerfully attenuated her inner life with each year.

Everyone else hmmed in recognition, though.

"You didn't talk to her at all?" I asked Prachi.

"Took me a second to place her. And I was covered in all these fabrics. Anyway, if she's wedding shopping now, she must be doing okay," she said. Which was, of course, so like my sister's particular understanding of happiness. "Don't give me that look, Neil, I just mean, that's an expensive store, so she must be doing *well* for herself."

"Or Jimmy's paying," Hae-mi said, taking her phone out. "But I definitely would have seen something on social media if Jimmy got engaged."

"Or her dad's paying," Prachi doubled back.

"Ugh," Hae-mi reported. "Jimmy's on zero apps. I can't tell."

"*Mean*while"—Maya leaned her elbows on the counter, clearly ready to be done with the talk about Jimmy Bansal's cracked-up ex—"*my* parents announced the other day that they've spent half of what I thought was my wedding fund on my sister's post-bacc. If she'd just been premed from the start—"

"I can't believe you guys are that out of touch," Manu said, edging nearer so he was only addressing me. In his gentle regard I felt recognized as the teenage boy I still was, or contained. "You two were always a unit. To me, anyway."

"She ran hot and cold on me," I said. "Did you talk? When you ran into her?"

"A little. She was pretty thoughtful, in a way people in tech aren't always. Honestly, I never found *her* very thoughtful, when we were younger. She was so into winning stuff that I couldn't have told you what she loved."

"What did you love then?" I asked, probably too sharply.

Manu blanched. "I *loved* math, Neer," he said. "I wanted to go to grad school for it. I just wasn't smart enough. I'm a very good engineer, but I'm not cut out for pure math."

"I don't think I ever knew that," I said.

"I don't think it ever came up," he said, not unkindly. "I can't remember talking about anything very real at OHS."

"But you and Anita—you talked about something real?"

"Not quite. She seemed kind of dissatisfied. Maybe I'm projecting. Galadriel's super prestigious, but they run people to the ground, and their portfolio companies start at suspect and go all the way to evil. Data theft and worse. She said she was going to quit soon, she wanted to do something *good*, only she didn't know *what*." He nodded somberly, sympathetically, for surely it was this shared sentiment that had him considering enduring Grindr in Iowa.

"Well," I said, "that's a start."

Lost on earnest Manu was my dryness.

"I've gotta bounce, Neer," he said, hugging me. "It's always great to see you. Just makes me reflect on how far we've all come, don't you think?"

I SPENT THAT SUMMER flailing through my research, in advance of the proposal defense that impended that fall—I needed an outline for the whole dissertation, plus two sample chapters, or I risked losing my funding. I'd already missed several deadlines in spring, and my exigent adviser, Irwin Wang, had let me know that I was on probation.

Each day, I grew headachy from staring at my laptop until my vision fuzzed. I was exhausted from sleeping and eating too little, subsisting on Adderall or coke, the latter of which was slowly becoming more than a party habit. My hair and limbs hung off me like peeling bark and Spanish moss. I was a ghost to myself, one of those Japanese mythic creatures—the unsatisfied self peels away from the body to haunt it.

I drove, often. My love of the road may be the most American thing about me. When I felt a crash coming on, or when I could no longer bear to be in my own brain, I'd get in my Honda, roll down the windows, and push onto the 880, winding past Oakland's warehouse edge, taking the 92 to Half Moon Bay. I'd follow the trampled grass on the bluffs above the state beach, all dotted with weathered, blister-blue clapboard houses. Untamed purple salvia sprouting up everywhere, the spring's yellow wildflowers drying out. If ever I had an open house craving to match my mother's, it was for these homes of windbeaten wood and high windows, places that seemed the right sort to hide away a writing man, shelves stocked with Great Americans, Styron and Stegner and Steinbeck. In gray-glum corners of California like this, I imagined myself not so much living—for that seemed to require a burdensome act of imagination, *living*—but persisting through the years.

Other times, I'd cross the Bay Bridge, wheezing my car up a vertiginous San Francisco hill. The sight: California splayed out around me. I'd cross the Golden Gate to the Marin Headlands, passing through the veil of fog to breathe the green-and-gold horizon line. Pockets of the Pacific bloomed out around Sausalito. The careens and curves jostled something loose in me. Every thirty minutes on one of those roads, the light and heat or chill of the air rearrange.

That June forced my head back toward the past. Perhaps the haunting began with the mention of Anita. It was aggravated by Arabella, with whom I suffered a nauseating afternoon on mushrooms one Saturday, during which a Shruti-like creature rose up from the red Mount Diablo dirt. She was inchoate yet clear, forming and re-forming into curly locks and small knowing eyes, even as I blew into the air to disperse her. I spent the trip quaking and retching and mapping my drug-induced pain onto first Shruti and then the world. (*Dear Shruti, We're all sick, riddled with holes, and you saw it first. . . .* I set down in my Moleskine, before the queasiness made writing impossible.)

Later, sober, having driven me home in brutal silence, Arabella had asked me to please, please let her in on whatever demons had manifested during the trip. I refused.

"I'm *done* trying to teach men to feel things," she huffed, her eyes trained on an addict addressing the sky by the Ashby Avenue BART station. "Just done."

"I feel things," I muttered. "More than you know."

"Well, you should probably find out how to talk about them, or no one will ever be able to *stand* being around you—you're roaming around your own head all the time, Neil, and maybe, just *maybe* what's going on in there isn't the most interesting thing on the planet." Then, accessing some reserve of cruelty I'd never before encountered in her, she added, fumbling with the key in the ignition: "I saw what's on your phone. Dil Day? That Indian marriage app? You don't take me seriously. You're waiting around for your perfect brown girl."

I'd downloaded Keya's app out of curiosity—about it, and about Keya, who'd struck me as off-kilter in a charming way. But I didn't explain.

"Yeah, well." I got out of Arabella's car and nearly plowed into the addict, who was calling passersby on Ashby to attention: *Remember!* he yelled. *If you don't, He will, if you don't, He will!* "To you, I'm just *hyphenated*, right?"

I was spending my summer attempting to explain why and how one era leads to the next, why a distant shout of gold in California draws migrants across the brutal Sierra Nevada; how gold-lust formed railroads and poisoned rivers; how the forty-niners' ache to stake their claim on the earth, to make a home in America, coalesced to change the course of the West, and the world.

My work as a student of history was the moral opposite of my work as a debater. As a debater, I'd lived in the present and made arguments about possible futures, claiming wantonly that someone's well-intentioned proposition would collapse the economy or cause nuclear war. The fact that the truth of the future never came to bear on a given round—that we were not accountable for being wrong, for defending a protracted occupation of Afghanistan, or for arguing, as I did most of sophomore year, that investing in clean coal was preferable to initiating a renewable portfolio standard—meant we were relieved of the responsibility of truth-telling at all. But when you study the past, you know how things turn out. The weight of the present demands something of you.

I was supposed to be constructing an argument about all that followed the California gold rush. But even after many hours of picking dully through papers on the abstract forces of money and power in the late nineteenth century, I found myself without interesting characters to follow through the era. And while I understood the tropes and pitfalls of narrative history, I wanted to meet someone in my research whom I could *live* with, whose voice I could hear, or perhaps had heard once before.

I had sought Ramesh Uncle's Bombayan gold digger as an undergraduate in Athens and during my first year at Berkeley. He was an obsession that seized me for a period of time, until the trail ran out and I had to give up. I'd researched foreigners in the gold rush many times, locating Australians and Chinese and Chileans, but never an Indian or a Hindu.

Finding that the genealogy of American belonging continued to exclude me, I'd taken Irwin Wang's advice to pursue economic history, a subfield in which job opportunities came slightly more easily. Now, though, with Wang accompanying his wife on her Indonesian fieldwork all summer, I found myself looking for the Bombayan once more. The hunt for him sustained me through those strange, blurred months; it tugged me back in time, or resurrected revenants, or both. For it turned out that Ramesh Uncle was right. We live alongside the past. It's our neighbor. We bump into it in the checkout line, at the Laundromat, on the street.

. . .

ONE LATE JUNE AFTERNOON, I'd returned from one of my drives and was headed to the library to investigate a file a librarian had called over from a museum in Marysville. The town, established in 1851 and a couple of hours northeast of Berkeley in Yuba County, was known as the Gateway to the Goldfields. I'd found a news clipping deep in the archives about a "Hindoo" put on "citizens' trial" for theft in a Central Valley mining camp. I wondered if he might be my Bombayan.

I wasn't paying much mind to the redwood-shaded trails north of campus as I ambled along. In fact, I almost missed her. But she collided with me, shoulder-on-shoulder. I did not at first recognize her. She now wore red cat-eye glasses, and they fell from her face. I picked them up, and choked to find myself looking at her, after so long. She was visibly older—her skin looked almost smudged, as though with inky thumbprints. Her figure was less obviously shapely beneath the loose linen flapping around her torso. Her hair grayed around the temples and in a few streaks along her forehead. She was still very striking.

"Anjali Auntie?"

We stood in the shade of those majestic redwoods, so I thought it was possible I'd gotten it wrong. A passing resemblance, another ghost; perhaps I had only drawn her up from the well of memory. But the woman blinked as she took the glasses from me, and the voice that emerged was familiar yet deeper, newly gravelly, like she was getting over a bout of bronchitis.

"My god, Neil!"

"What—ah—what are you doing here?" I asked. "Are you still in Sunnyvale?"

"Well, yes," she said. "Mostly. Yes. I'm down there. But I had an event to go to. Here." She dabbed at the corners of her eyes and I realized the slight growl in her voice was not sickness but recent tears. "A memorial, actually," she said. "I apologize, I'm a little—"

"Oh, I'm so sorry," I said, unintentionally speaking over her.

We both stood there, arms hanging like tree limbs half-severed from trunks in a storm.

"Was it—who was it?" I asked, and immediately regretted it.

Anjali Auntie seemed to consider before replying. "A friend, from Atlanta, actually."

"Who lives here now? Ah—lived here?"

"Well. He once taught at Emory, and then he shifted over to Cal. In the South Asian Studies department. Time, well." She sniffed. "So it goes."

"How's, um"—I scuffed the walk with my sneaker—"Pranesh Uncle? And, ah, Anita?"

"Oh." Anjali Auntie sighed. "I suppose it hasn't reached your mother yet? Pranesh and I are divorcing. And Anita is, well, mostly herself."

"Shit," I said. "I'm *really* sorry. . . . I'm out of the loop, I live in a bunker—I'm in the middle of my dissertation—"

"Your parents must be proud." She said it pro forma.

A few runners passed us, looking haughtily over their shoulders; we were taking up too much space on the path. We stepped aside.

"It's history," I said. "They'd be happier if it was computer science, or finance, or something more lucrative. Right now, I'm a little . . . outside their fold. Say. Anita isn't"—my voice cracked, but I barreled on—"she's not getting married, is she?"

"Not unless she's run off without telling me—wherever did you get that idea?"

It felt like a large chunk of air that had settled in my throat was dissipating. Anita Dayal was not—was *not*—getting married. A slight breeze lifted, kissing my arm hairs, and suddenly the world seemed wide and traversable, and life varied and branching, for I was *not* being left behind, for not *everyone* was folding into private couple-hood. For there was time, still, time for old figures to reemerge from the past, and to recognize you.

"Erm, Prachi is," I managed. "Getting married, I mean. And she saw Anita the other day, or, well, thought she did. At a bridal shop."

"How funny," Anjali Auntie said, though she didn't look amused.

"You remember Manu Padmanaban?" I said. "I guess he's seen Anita a few times. He said she's in venture?"

"Ah, yes." Anjali Auntie placed a finger on her forehead, smoothing her furrows, as I'd seen her do when I was younger. It used to remind me of my mother's hands on Prachi, but this time it made me think of a priest daubing kumkum in blessing. "She left that job not long ago and has picked up some *freelance*" (she pronounced the word with a grimace, as though its very sonic quality was undignified) "event-planning work while she . . . plots her next moves. Running lots of holiday parties for these big firms, but occasionally odder jobs, too. They seem to take whatever clients come their way, trying to get off the ground. Don't ask me how it'll play on a résumé, but . . ." She chewed her lip, considering her words. "Your generation, you all seem to be having these epiphanies, huh; no one thinks they should have to work the way their parents did."

I pressed: "So, Anita was in that shop . . . for work?"

"Probably. She's doing, of all things, a bridal expo right now. One of those big desi affairs." Seeing my confusion, she elaborated: "All the vendors—mehendi and caterers and tailors and photographers and everyone else you need for a wedding—come to hawk themselves. Ta*ma*sha. I'm sure Prachi will go to one. Anyway. That must've been why Ani was there."

Two more runners, coming from the other direction, swished by. Anjali Auntie teetered. She lifted one arm as though she was going to fall over, and I stretched mine out so she could catch on to me. Her hand was almost trembling. If she weren't still young, I might have called the quiver Parkinsonian. For there was something recasting her—not just grief or fading beauty. Nothing about her seemed *well*. How had time stolen up on us—on her? Did I only notice her age because it had been ten years? Or would anyone notice the spots speckling her fair skin, the gathering slackness around her elbows, the dulling of her once-bright eyes?

"I haven't talked to her," I said. "Not for a long time."

"Yes," Anjali Auntie said simply. "I know."

She was still gripping my forearm. Her shakes beat an awkward tattoo on my skin.

"What are you up to these days?" I asked.

She squinted and withdrew her hand. "I was working on a project with this friend of mine, the one who passed," she said. "Some work on old Hindu traditions."

"Like, amateur scholarship?"

"Yes, sure. But, well. I'll have to find something else to keep me occupied, won't I? Some of us give our whole lives to other people, and without them, we have to start all over."

"If you need any help, I mean, as academic writing goes . . ." I checked my watch. It was four, and the librarian I had to meet would be gone by five. "Speaking of which," I said apologetically, "I've got to get to the stacks."

"Go on," Anjali Auntie said in that still tone. "It was very nice to see you again, Neil."

I had the sense that by walking away, I'd be shutting some door that had never fully closed. I hugged her, then continued down the redwood-lined path. On my way home, I stepped off the trail at the spot where Anjali Auntie had entered, to see where she'd come from. Outside a brick Unitarian Universalist church was a sign announcing a celebration of life for Professor Lyall Pratt. The steps and the lawn were emptied of mourners. Just a single gardener remained, plucking weeds from the overgrowth beneath the dead man's name.

ANITA AND I hadn't spoken since her final night in Hammond Creek. I spent that summer in East Lansing as planned, despite the turmoil I'd caused by admitting to drinking. Quitting debate, it was judged, would sabotage my college chances, so my parents reluctantly released me into the *nonsense*-filled outside world. And how nonsensical that summer was! Wendi Zhao wrangled a job at the camp, teaching admiring ninth graders. At night, she'd creep into my dorm room bearing beer and drugs and soon dispensing with my virginity. Afterward, I'd write to Anita, woozy with weed and Wendi's smells. I'd tell her how painful the dull ache of moving from day to day was, how Shruti came to me in the darkness, how I felt tugged sometimes to follow her into the Land of the Dead, not to try to bring her back, but to live down there with her, too. Anita never replied, not even to my most dramatic declarations.

During the intervening years, I'd googled Anita here and there, usually stopping before going too deep. But that evening, after seeing Anjali Auntie, I wound my way through the tornado spiral of the internet. I clicked and scrolled. Neither Anita nor I was on social media. She was always private—having a secret at a young age perhaps does that to you. But I located a blurry image of her playing tennis on the Stanford club team, and another shot of her at a techie event next to a tall Indian guy with a sharp jawline and gelled hair; the caption identified him as Jimmy Bansal, investor at Galadriel Ventures. I wondered if Anita leaving the firm had meant leaving him. I found a site from the year prior featuring her annoyingly impressive half marathon time. I went on, as though pressing harder on the internet would puncture it, send guts oozing onto my fingertips, delivering a visceral reality of present-day Anita.

It took about twenty minutes to stumble upon a YouTube clip I'd never before seen. It was labeled "guest spkr @ 2014 miss india teen new jersy." I gathered from the text below the video that a twenty-three-year-old Anita had been invited to address the MTI finalists. Someone commented, "this video had gotten taken down few years back thank you for riposting." Someone below that replied, "she is 1 ungrateful girl."

The video, taken on a phone camera, was washed out. Behind Anita fluttered the Tricolor and Chakra next to the Stars and Stripes. The phone refocused on a Jumbotron, where Anita's face had been supersized. There, through a camera on a camera, came the simulacrum of Anita Dayal. Her features looked slathered with too much cakey makeup, and her cheeks were chubbier than they'd been in Hammond Creek. Her hair hung down to her breasts, thick and artificially curled. There were the thank-yous and the lead-ups, and then the meat of it:

"So, why did the Miss Teen India committee choose *me* as one of your speakers today?

"For one," she said, "because I won this pageant some years ago, as Miss Teen India Georgia." A whoop from the crowd, perhaps 2014's representative from the Peach State. Anita smiled wanly, waiting. She was plainly not there to cheerlead. "But I think I was invited because in the years since, I've lived up to the promise of this organization. I went to Stanford. I work in technology. Someone overly optimistic about my future once called me the next Indra Nooyi."

Her eyes darted to the wings, as though she was trying to remember her choreography. She took a few long strides. "I keep seeing how successful our community has become. Everyone wants to celebrate that. People like you all, here. And me. And your friends, and cousins, and classmates, and siblings who are getting into good schools and winning quiz team tournaments, and who go off to work at tech companies and consultancies and banks."

The camera shifted away from the Jumbotron and attempted to zoom in on Anita herself. "I remember wanting so badly to be where I stand now, when I was a teenager. I would have literally killed to be seen as successful. My mother would have killed *for* me to be seen as successful.

"I grew up in a community called Hammond Creek, outside Atlanta. It was the kind of suburb where immigrants move to give their kids a better life. It's a beautiful thing, when you think about it. These masses of Asians who all somehow collude to land up in the same place.

"Now, Hammond Creek was still majority-white. We nonwhite kids stuck together, whether we meant to or not. Sometimes you *wanted* distance, but there was just *no* escaping other desis." Titters in the audience; she was feeding the crowd a story of themselves with the appropriate amount of self-deprecation. Anita seemed to warm up at that. She began to pace more deliberately, growing lither and more leonine beneath those dramatic lights. "We sat together in the cafeteria and joined the same clubs. Our parents knew one another, and *everyone's* business. There was no room to get in trouble, because someone's auntie's cousin's sister-in-law would hear and tell your mom." More chuckles, for gossip is an easy vice to cop to.

"But sometimes that hive mind would decide that one person was . . . off. *You* weren't smart enough." She pointed an accusing finger into the crowd. "Or *you* weren't normal enough." She swiveled and did it again. "Or *you* wanted the wrong things. And that affected whether or not you were fundamentally accepted.

"For instance, what if I told you that I left Stanford for mental health reasons?"

The person holding the camera let out a little *hmm*. Nearby, people were scuffling, though not all due to Anita's confession. "When they're doing awards?" a woman in the periphery of the shot whispered.

"You might not invite me to come talk like this, for one. You'd wonder if I *belonged* in the community, let alone represented it.

"This was what it felt like growing up. Adults and kids constantly gossiping about one another, judging whether or not you were *Indian* enough, using I don't know what kind of standards. And at that point, it's worse than gossip. It's actually part of what I wrote my thesis about, at Stanford—because I went back, by the way, and graduated magna cum laude. We're talking about an organized, systematic form of social exclusion. Perpetrated by everyone in the system. Kids. Parents."

She tapped the mic clipped to her blouse. The sound rippled, as she called her listeners to more heightened attention.

"I know I'm running low on time. I wasn't supposed to talk this much. I was supposed to tell you to lean into STEM. But before I go, I want to talk about a young woman at my former high school. She was the kind of kid every immigrant parent wants to have. Such a smarty-smart girl, they'd say." (She descended into a fobby accent for that one. This time, no chuckles.) "But something happened. Something broke, or broke her. A bunch of forces we can't entirely understand converged around this young woman. I can put a name to some of them, but not all."

Only the holder of the phone camera murmured in recognition at that.

"When she took her own life, people talked. Was whatever she had *infectious*? But within weeks, people boxed it away—boxed *her* away. When she lived, all the parents held her up as the paragon. She was what the first generation wanted the second generation to be. When she died, everyone told us to treat her as an aberration. But I don't think she was an aberration. What happened to her was, as the people in my tech world say, a feature of the system. Not a bug."

Anita began to recite facts and figures, things I'd heard many times by then. That parents were going hungry to pay for kids' cram schools in Kota and Queens alike. That we, Asian Americans, dwelt in a troubling silence when it came to mental health. These stories had, through the years, filled my mother's ears: an acquaintance of an acquaintance who had, upon receiving a 1200 on his third SAT attempt, taken himself to the Edison train station, lain down on the tracks, and waited until the Northeast Corridor train rolled in from Manhattan and over him. His father was aboard, commuting home from work. A girl in my aunt Sandhya's chemistry class at Fremont High, threatened by her parents with a one-way ticket to Lucknow for screwing around with another girl—carbon monoxide in the garage. And others, and others.

"It's on us," Anita was saying, speaking with so much urgency that I wondered if someone was coming onstage to forcibly un-mic her. The person holding the phone—the person who'd decided this video ought to be "riposted"—was not steady enough to settle on Anita's face as she concluded. Perhaps if I had seen a shade of uncertainty in her expression, I would have been less furious. But her voice was so sure as she tied up the speech, as though she were wrapping up the neatest story in the world, and in doing so, gliding into the next era with no ghosts at her back. "By *it's on us*, I mean me," she said, "and I mean *you*, whether you knew her or not. *Us.* Our community, our logics, our values. *We* did that to her."

IN THE DAYS THAT FOLLOWED, I worked manically, drug-fueled, on little sleep. Chidi was still away, and the building was emptied of our frat boy neighbors. The eerie silence of a college town in the summer was mine to fill. In came my alter ego, a Neil who, with the help of an upper, was easily convinced of his own extravagant genius. My pharmacist father meandered around the back of my brain as I fiddled. Him, in that white coat, green Publix badge affixed to his chest pocket. How he had smoothed the starched lapels before leaving for work each morning. When I was young, I'd sit on the bathroom tile and watch him get ready. Years of study for that white coat. Crossing oceans for that white coat. My mother's voice in my head: Your father is a scientist, be proud. Hell, now I was my own, a homegrown expert in Little Pharma. I did the research, Asian-nerded the drugs, heeded numbers and neurotransmitters.

I wrote with the window open, listening to the creak of beech and gum trees. I poured every personal revelation I had that summer into the Bombayan, braiding my small history with his Big History. Bit by bit, I lent him my story. Imagined that he had lived some version of what we'd been through—what we *did*—during the Lemonade Period. For wasn't he also a gold thief? What would he do with his stolen goods? How could he bear them? Memories flooded me as I did tiny bumps in the middle of the day, and I channeled them into the Bombayan. I remembered Anjali Auntie telling me about the Saraswati, that holy river lined with gold, so like the rivers that ignited the California rush; I left the apartment to drive alongside those rivers, through the Central Valley, growing emotional as I imagined transposing our eastern mythologies onto the pioneering West. Could they stick?

In early July, high as the Hindenburg, having spoken to no one besides food delivery people and librarians in about a month, I opened a new page in the Marysville material and saw a dark-skinned man staring back at me from a photocopy of a university-press book. It was taken in 1868. He looked like the black-and-white photos of my nana, posed unsmilingly, almost militaristically, on his wedding day. Below his daguerreotype was a small caption. *ISAAC SNIDER*, it read. *Editor of the Marysville Gold Star, 1865–1885.* My eyes flitted between his name and his image and my breath caught. I stood up, stole into Chidi's room, pulled out his dime bags—I was running low on his party supply—and did a line.

I returned to my desk and stared down at Isaac Snider. *Snider was a Midwestern Jewish gold rush migrant and entrepreneur from St. Louis*, the page read. *Like many Jews in the California gold rush who opened stores, launched businesses, built Synagogues, and started*

*schools, he helped establish Californian society as something beyond
lean-tos and mining towns. He then became the editor of the largest
newspaper in the Central Valley region.* But I wasn't looking at his
biography. I was looking at his face. His eyebrows were thick and
unruly, and his eyelashes girlishly long. His gaze was unsettled, as
though he was sure some secret of his was about to be found out.

Snider, my ass. This dark motherfucker looked as Indian as samosas. I almost wanted to cry. I had found him—had I? Or someone like him. Someone enough like him. My gold digger—Isaac
Snider. What if he had slunk not out of view, but right into the
heart of American history? So what if he stole that gold the night
the whites nearly killed him? What if stealing was the only way for
him to make a home in this place?

July slipped by; I read as much of the *Marysville Gold Star* as possible, and slowly something invited me into the period. The paper
had printed its fair share of anti-immigrant polemics, blather I was
used to from years of studying the period. (*In the wake of the frenzy
of gold fever, is it not time for the Chinese and the Mexicans and all
other foreigners to make their polite egress, so that the new Western
states may go about settling into themselves?*) But I noticed something. Toward the end of Isaac Snider's tenure, the xenophobia
abated and was replaced by some unbylined columns denouncing
the British Raj. They were written with passion—even familiarity?
(*The brutish colonial presence recalls a period of American history
now viewed in revolutionary light . . .*)

More of those long drives down California's endless highways,
but nearly always meandering east now, through the Central Valley's flat, breadbasket landscape. Orchards bearing matchstick tree
limbs sprouted up by the highway, along with signs bearing Sikh
politicians' names—Singhs and Kaurs running for school boards.

I'd stop for fresh apricots and drive with sticky fingers through neat town squares. And Marysville itself! It persisted—a couple of square blocks, a diner, antique shops, a set of swinging doors beneath a self-consciously styled sign reading SALLY'S SALOON. Behind the saloon rose a red Chinese structure labeled the HISTORIC BOK-KAI TAOIST TEMPLE, and a sign marking the Yuba River, where it met the Feather. Pacing here gave me a sense of being close to Snider, though the *Marysville Gold Star* had long ago shuttered and there was no evidence of him—no statue, no plaque. But all I had to do was wander the little downtown, and I felt certain I was walking where he once tread.

I was in Marysville for perhaps the third or fourth time, having just digested a thickly mayonnaised sandwich at the diner, when the phone call came.

I had wandered behind the Taoist temple and up the path that led to a view of the Yuba. It was ugly: trampled sand and shit-colored rocks. Unfinished, graffiti-splattered concrete walls rose up on either side. I was standing there, looking out at the land beyond the river, the land now half-dead with drought, the land that belonged mostly to history, when my phone began to buzz. Perhaps it was my state—suspended as I was between eras and realities—that made me answer the unfamiliar South Bay number.

"Neeraj fucking Narayan," came the voice. "It's been a minute."

Below, a hunched figure emerged from a fluttering blue tarp. He began to rustle in a shopping cart stocked with miscellany—tin cans, ripped shirts, a single in-line skate, a deflating basketball—before lifting a few objects to the sky, as if to inspect them in the dwindling daylight.

"Sorry? Who's this?"

"It's me, dummy."

Who? "Who?"

"Anita!"

"*Anita?*"

I felt one of my old selves tap me on the shoulder and take up residence in me once more. My ears rang and my eyes filled with something briny—not tears, no. Something else was happening because of the presence of an old creature, a creature to which I was a little allergic.

"Yeah, her, me."

"*Anita?* How'd you get my number?"

"Uh, I kept it. I got a new one in college. Okay. Maybe I should have started differently. How's this? Hi. Hello, again."

"I, er—I saw your mom the other day."

"I heard."

"And Prachi saw *you*—it's like—" I almost said *It's like I conjured you.* "Small world."

"It's always been a little claustrophobic to be an ABCD," Anita said. "No exit."

The tarp's resident—and I—watched a yellow windbreaker try to make its way downriver. It caught on a rock and flapped, an accidental flag.

"Prachi looked right through me," Anita continued. "She never did like me."

"That's not true." The man was removing his shoes and wading into the river to unhook the windbreaker. Freed, it was soon carried out of view. "I hear you're not getting married."

She laughed. "If there's an extreme opposite of *getting married*, I'm that."

My chest untightened, as it had when Anjali Auntie had denied it; there was something about hearing Anita's own coarse dismissal of the possibility. It confirmed that she had not chosen the life that could have by now subsumed her—Prachi's life, the life of a future-oriented South Asian professional.

"I think that's just called being single."

The man sent several more objects from his shopping cart downriver. I discerned a piece of wire, a saucepan, a red bandanna. I had a terrible thought that he was ridding himself of all this in preparation for some self-obliteration. I started to walk down the slope toward him.

"Somehow that doesn't seem strong enough," she said. "Hey. I googled you. You're a historian? Sorry, do I have to say *an* historian?"

"You don't have to say either. I'm just a grad student."

Close up, this man didn't look like a person about to absent himself. He just looked leathered by sun and time. He pointed over my shoulder. Behind me, to the west, the sun was setting over the bursting red of the Bok-Kai temple.

The man splashed the river onto his face, lifted his eyes to the sky, then walked back to his tarp. I pictured Snider making these gestures, kneeling at the bank, brushing the water.

Had I been silent too long? "Your mom," I said. "She looked different."

"Yes," Anita said. "Actually, that's why I'm calling. It's about my mom."

I followed the man's tread marks down to the water and dipped my fingers in as he had. The lick of the cold Yuba on my hand made me shudder, and a wave of visceral déjà vu passed over me. After a moment, the initial uncanny jitter ceased, but I still felt like the very surface of the Yuba was glistening with recognition.

Of course, though, it was just the girl on the line, Anita's old voice, skewing time.

"Listen," she went on. It was as though her words were reaching me not across miles but across decades. I had to ask her to speak up. "I'm out of town for a few weeks hustling up vendors for this ridiculous event I'm working on, a bridal expo," she said, louder. "I'll be back in two weeks. I know it's been ages. But can we meet up?"

7.

Those next two weeks were a kind of bardo; I hung between lifetimes. Flashes of who I had been ten years ago struck me in the mornings. One time I rolled over, my eyes foggy as strange dreams receded, to see that it was eight a.m.—*I have a chemistry test!* I thought, before realizing I was not sixteen. It was early August; San Francisco's most flamboyant denizens had caravanned off to Burning Man, and Berkeley's college students had been replaced by talented youths attending debate camps, science camps, philosophy camps, summer honors colloquia. I stepped into the sunlight only to buy the crap I ate but couldn't call food, spicy hot Cheetos and ramen, and one afternoon bumped into a short brown boy with a bowl cut, maybe twelve years old. His bright blue shirt read BERKELEY SUMMER HONORS ENRICHMENT PROGRAM. Go on, enrich yourself, I considered shouting. Look at how wealthy all that enrichment made *me*. The boy spied something unstable in my pupils and bolted.

Another time, on the way back from meeting Chidi's dealer, I passed the shop on University that sold Bollywood cassette tapes and georgette saris and Nepali prayer flags. Through the window I saw the owner in his full Indian dad attire—hoodless Hanes sweatshirt and white socks tugged halfway up his shins. He was still, taking in the passersby, his whole figure milky colored through the glass. His face did not warm when I stopped to reread, for the thousandth time, the yellow lettering. SHREE KRISHNA'S—BERKELEY. SINCE 1976. He simply held his arms behind his back and regarded me as though he had seen me a thousand times before, his expression as precise and calculating as my father's as he readjusted the pharmacist coat in the mirror. The drugs were hot against my thigh. *Are you making use of all you took?* I raced home to suck the fresh, pure powder up my nose until my sinuses froze over with this so requited cold, as I did it again, again.

Led by the bumps, I met with my one welcome ghost, Isaac Snider. I was writing things down about him, things I intuited but could not yet prove. It was the first time I'd written like this, with something that felt like truth flowing through me so quickly my hands struggled to keep up. Cold academic work yielded none of this transcendence; the many baffling components of my life had never converged so clearly as they did when I wrote toward Isaac Snider. I let myself forget the professionalization of the study of the past, because my private project felt like a purer communion. Maybe I looked at him because it was easier than looking at myself. He, my Bombayan gold digger, and the story I spun of him, was just about the only thing that took my mind off the impending meeting.

THE TALE OF ISAAC SNIDER

He was an immigrant, like all those forty-niners who crossed Death Valley or rode the Pacific or braved the

Great Basin, tempted by the Californian promise. In later years, as he assimilated, the Bombayan would claim he crossed the United States from St. Louis. By then his English was passably American and he had changed his name—Isaac Snider, a moniker to mask his origins.

Watch him, as I watched him, climbing aboard an East India ship bound for China. His lanky body wedged among the wares that came from ravagings. "Colonization of India was primarily economic," a professor lectured in college, which made the whole thing sound like the Brits had merely pickpocketed a few wallets. But in the gold digger, see the emasculation of colonization. The only way out is as an export. Through the porthole, his motherland shrinks.

In China, he trades labor for a ride to Hong Kong, and then for a foot of space aboard one of the vessels carrying migrants to California—Gold Mountain, the Chinese call it. Even the foul smells of pork and men relieving themselves and the queasiness of the voyage are preferable to shouldering tea onto a company ship.

In California, he barters his way to a pan of his own; the most basic technology suffices when gold runs free and clear in streams. Those early rush days are marked more by chaos than by calculation. There is no point in musing about geology, trying to figure out what caused the earth to bubble up such a product. The gold digger follows rumors, the gossip, if you will. He sleeps near other laborers, often Chinese, occasionally Mexican. Transient tent cities bordering the goldfields. Waking up with the dawn to the yellow landscape. More than once he thinks California is burning, burning, but that is just what light looks like when skies are clear.

When the easiest of plunders of a given deposit have been shaken clear of quartz sand and water and dried in the sun, then the metal is *yours*—not to be plucked from your arms by a leering Company man. He presses the nuggets and dust to his skin. It warms him as the sun falls.

He is surviving, a solo man among solo men, until that day, recorded in Ramesh Uncle's German travelogue, when the whites capture him. But he escapes.

I picture it like this: The gold digger, hunched on the ground, sustaining the beating, says a very rapid, old prayer. He places two golden nuggets in his mouth and swallows, thinking wildly that in these nuggets lie the very blessing and promise of America. He prays that this blessing be given him. He feels the nuggets melt in his mouth, like ghee on one's tongue. Warm and sweet and full of hope. Briefly, he wonders if he's gone mad: Did he just drink away wealth? But then something calms him, and says to wait, wait for the blessing.

A blessing—some blessing—comes: the whites cannot find any gold on him, only his empty poke and useless sheath knife. He runs; a few of them, drunk, follow, shooting as he races through woods as dark as a grave. He trips over the leg of a corpse that an animal has tugged from the dirt. And then he's struck.

A bullet tears through his flank. All goes black. When he looks up, he is not in the woods but on the banks of the Yuba River, where it meets the Feather.

He thinks of the holy Ganges, how auspicious it is to die near its banks. He edges to the river and begins to whisper prayers into it, all of his past selves floating downstream. He dips one hand in the water and a shudder runs through his body. A sacred river. The world-splitting pain halts, as quickly as it began. He lifts himself to his feet, presses his hand to the spot where the bullet ripped through him, and finds closed, healthy flesh.

He weeps, and as tears fall, the whole river turns the color of gold, like the water lifting Midas's curse. I see all this as clearly as the shape of my own hands above the keyboard as I type. The Bombayan, Isaac Snider, was saved, was preserved in history, was let into America by pure Californian gold.

He camps that night near Marysville and is kept awake by the drunken hoots of other gold diggers pushing through clacking saloon doors, wasting gains on games of monte and drink. In the morning, the call goes up: a gulch nearby, full of riches. Instead of following the line of sunburnt men scurrying out of town, the gold digger looks up at the sky. Rain is bulging in the air. It seems obvious. Instead of going to the north side of the gulch, he treks to a flat bank just south. When the rain strikes, the Bombayan is the only miner working that territory. There is the precious metal, washing toward him.

On he goes like this, beginning to make sharp calculations, returning to places where the top of the gold has been skimmed off, but digging deeper—sometimes banding with Mexican laborers. They dig until that sight: a veiny pattern of gold in the bedrock. The immigrant work ethic couples with luck. Now he does not chase blindly but instead plots the habits of the gold—how it appears, where it might show itself next.

He practices English, becomes literate. He writes and reads whatever he can—dispatches from the Midwest and East Coast, letters other miners send to loved ones. Even after a long day of labor, he studies. He loses the accent—might his skin even lighten a little? He insists upon a new name. Isaac Snider, Isaac Snider; he repeats it like a prayer.

No longer does he have to pay that foreigner's tax of three dollars a month to dig. He slips in step with the region's Jews, many of them only a few years removed from their own migrations—from Poland, from Prussia. Perhaps the blessing of the gold makes passing possible. Perhaps there is a quiet understanding, a solidarity, an invitation to hide among other outsiders.

With the help of his adoptive community, he goes on, hiring subcontractors to dig in places others believe tapped out. He offers a third of anything they strike. "Just one third?" they sometimes demand. But Snider taps his temple and points out, using reason to delight a Silicon Valley intellectual property lawyer, that the idea to dig in this unlikely place had been his.

Snider is hardly the only person discovering that the rush is not just a loner's game. Solo panners are taking up in groups to mine with Long Toms. Enterprise flourishes. American corporations germinate. Wells Fargo, Levi Strauss. Few call this new force *greed*. No, we say *ambition*.

In June 1859, Snider rests in the back of a general store with two Mormons who have taken a liking to his scrappy doggedness. They are reviewing an idea of his with skepticism. Consider them his investors, him their entrepreneur. The notion: to build a dam on the Yuba River—the same waters that once saved him. He swears there is gold beneath those rapids, worth extracting. Privately, he knows he won't just turn that gold into money; he'll consume some of it, and its blessing and power will let him into the main corridor of American history.

It takes five men over a month to pile up the rocks for the dam. It is physically risky, and each worker fears he is forfeiting easier gains. But when the month closes and the dam is finished, the cry goes up, one that rhymes with Sam Brannan's original call, the one that knocked down the first domino: "Gold! Gold! Gold in the Yuba River!"

Isaac Snider's ambition is not, however, to be some great figure in history. He only wishes to possess the singular identity of an uncolonized man. As the rush abates, like the last days of a war, he finds that he has built himself a network of allies. He marries the young niece of a local Bavarian immigrant. Adah. Adah

Eckman. He meets her in her uncle's dry-goods store. On the night of their wedding, she notices something—a central flaw in his claim to be Jewish. She says nothing at the sight of his foreskin. As though she knew all along? As though the gold's power occludes her vision.

Snider begins editing a newspaper—the ultimate hiding place, for who would suspect a professional writer of English to be an outsider? Make use of all you took. Write yourself into America.

It is after covering one particular event that Snider's identity is strained. The locals have never spared much love for the Chinese laborers living on the edge of town, praying in that Bok-Kai temple, wearing their hair in pigtails, working endless hours for astonishingly low pay. By the late 1860s, a new restlessness grows. California is settled. People live not in lean-tos but in houses; the currency is coin, not gold dust. Some bristle at the prospect that the Chinese might actually stick around. People say such things about Snider's community, too—there's talk of a Jewish tax, more than once.

One evening, a group of drunken white men comes upon one such Chinese fellow stepping out of the Bok-Kai temple. The whites believe they recognize the man: the proprietor of an opium den in San Francisco, since shut down by vice laws. A man who cheated countless smokers out of gold as they lay half-comatose in his sinners' palace. These white men are the same sort who, decades earlier, took it upon themselves to

form committees of vigilance, to prosecute Snider
when he was still brown. They are the same sort who
developed a protocol for lynching disruptive blacks
and Mexicans and Chileans and Native Americans.
They are the same sort who will, in another few
decades, form a mob in Oregon to murder more than
thirty Chinese miners; the same sort who will, soon
after that, chase throngs of Sikhs from Washington.
These white men beat the Chinese man and hang him
from a tree overlooking the Yuba. Later, it's revealed
that he was no opium supplier, but the owner of a
small laundry.

It is Snider's unhappy job to write up the incident
in the local paper: brutality, obviously brutality! But
his colleagues say it would be folly to pretend the
mob did not circle some fair point, that now that
American jobs are scarcer, it is time for these coolies
to go home, to take with them their pigtails and opium
and work ethic. And so Snider, sick with himself but
afraid of reminding people of the darkness of his
skin, condemns the Chinese as much as he does the
assailants. The best gesture he can offer, at the end of
his editorial, is a plea to end the rhetoric of ridding the
whole nation of the Chinese, for . . . *How costly would
this effort be? Let foreigners sink quietly into our new
society.*

Cresting into the 1870s, Snider has watched the
Indian struggles from afar. American papers report
on it occasionally, with indifference, but he risks it,
writing in the *Gold Star*: *As Americans have given up*

*the castes of nobility, Lord, Duke, and aristocracy, in
favor of Democratic ideals, so their Revolutionary
brethren wish to cast off unearned hierarchies, across the
seas. . . .* Ah, who would read such musings of an old
man, these vain gestures of the mind? But it means
something to a dislocated young man in Berkeley. I
experience a twitch of recognition, the shudder of time
folding in on itself, a shiver, an intuition. Time,
perhaps the truest magic, full of the unprovable.

The Bombayan is aging. Soon he will die, as will his
secret. When he boarded that East India Company
ship some thirty years earlier, he had hoped to cheat
history, to eschew his fate as a colonized man. Now, on
the other side of the planet, as he rubs his eyes in the
dim newspaper office and steps into the lowering
yellow light of a Marysville evening, he sees that he
did not manage to cheat history, which is inescapable.
No, he raced right into it with all the force of someone
swimming upstream. History let him live in its hot,
complex swirl for a few decades. And soon it will close
in on him, as it takes us all. He shuts the newspaper
door and walks to town, where, against all odds, and
at all costs, he has made himself a home.

ON THE DAY I roared down the 880 to meet Anita, Isaac Snider,
marvelous distraction though he'd been, was relegated to the back
of my mind. As I swung through the bosomy yellow hills on
the San Francisco Peninsula, I kept remembering the intensity of

adolescence, how everything Anita had said or left unsaid could send pin prickles along my flesh.

I parked my Honda in a venture capitalist office lot with a view: yellow headlands, highway curve. Buildings down here were invariably beige or brown or other neutral or neutered colors, earthlike tones that blended into the landscape, as though to normalize Silicon Valley wealth, as though to pretend there was something natural about such vertiginous valuations, such sums passing through term sheets every day.

Anita had asked me to meet her at a restaurant in a posh hotel called the Sonora. She stayed alone in an apartment in the terrible suburban purgatory that was the peninsula; she'd moved there when she was working at Galadriel, she said, which was headquartered on moneyed Sand Hill Road, and she hadn't yet bothered to relocate. "Sit at the far end of the bar," she'd said. "Beneath the TVs. It's quieter." The lobby was all smooth tile floors, high stone ceilings. An austere chandelier with iron limbs dripped from its apex. Above the bar hung bare bulbs, Californian minimalism. The walls looked to be made of redwood. The bartender wore a blue corduroy vest over a navy plaid button-down. Above him, in a half-hearted gesture at proper bar culture, two screens showed the Giants playing. I sat.

Around me: older women, several surgically enhanced, wearing cashmere sleeveless sweaters and tight suede skirts and leather pants that hugged their lifted asses; men in T-shirts beneath tossed-on sport coats, flat sneakers, dark jeans—conspicuously casual. A pruny-skinned man in a Cardinal red Stanford hat threw an arm around a younger woman in a corner booth. "You know a little guy," he said into the woman's cocked ear, loud enough that I could hear him, "named *Mark Zuckerberg*?" She sipped her wine, tolerated him. "I knew him *when*!"

"Neil!"

Anita stood in front of me for a dreadfully long moment. She wore a rose-red silky blouse with a ruffle interrupting her breasts, black pleated dress pants, and silver earrings.

"You look exactly the same," she said. There was her unblinking gaze. And there, too, was some reverberation of my old desire—to make those eyes look at nothing but me.

"You don't."

She didn't. And, actually, I resented the notion that I did. I was now six-one—some three inches taller than when she'd last seen me. I'd filled out. I maintained a good beard line. I'd figured out how to do this thing with my hair, thanks to some pomade Prachi had bought me. In the Bay Area, where a Los Angeles four is a seven or an eight, I'd come a long way.

She was leaner in the cheeks, muscled in the arms. Her hair was shorter, angled, streaked with chestnut brown, still thick. It was a good result, if you considered the countless ways time could affect people. I dredged her external appearance for signs of the gossip about her at Prachi's party. What I saw: a woman, comfortably adult. Straight-from-work attire. Quick, evaluating expression. Having located her there, I immediately granted her, once more, power over me. Highly functional, decisive, competent women have always compelled me. The world is enough for them, and they are enough for the world.

"I'm wrong," she said, sitting down. I realized we hadn't hugged, so I leaned over, but we were on barstools and mine was uneven, and I sort of toppled, and she stopped me with her knee. We tried again. A real hug. Warmth. Even a bit of an up-down stroke of her flat palm on my upper back. "You *do* look different. Older, but also . . ." She paused, reassessing.

I took it up for her. "Weathered. Wiser. More gallant?" I said. "Wiser? Philosophical."

A full laugh erupted, like a hiccup. "Looser. That's what I mean. Looser. I always think that when I see people from high school, you know? I saw your friend Wendi Zhao one time at this sushi place on Castro Street and she was slouching a little. She *never* slouched."

"Never."

"Oh, and Manu!"

"I see him sometimes."

"He's lovely. Super successful, and now he's getting very *political*, isn't he?"

"I think that's relative. The political part."

Anita was trying to catch the bartender's eye and missed my response. "I like their Napa chardonnay. A little oaky, but."

"You know wine? Classy."

"The basic adjectives. My college roommates only want to hang out by taking these wine tours of Sonoma, and if I want to have any social life at all, well."

I ordered an Anchor Steam. The bartender poured Anita's chardonnay and cranked the tap forward for my beer. Anita pressed her knuckles to the glass and frowned. "I'm sorry, but it's warm," she said. The bartender nodded rigidly, and went back for a more properly chilled bottle.

"Neil," she said, after taking a sip of the corrected drink, "I'm truly glad to see you."

"Me, too."

"I'm sorry it was so long."

"Me, too."

"I didn't mean for it to be so long, but you look up and all this time's gone by." She blinked. Her eyes, though wide, with a tendency to catch the light, revealed little about her emotions—as though something constricted them from behind the pupils. "How's your sister?"

"*Settled*, as my dad says. My mom's over the moon about the wedding."

"Is she chasing after you about your turn?"

I grimaced. "I'm far from that—what was it you said? The *way* opposite of engaged?"

Her lips quivered, as if to imply that she was unsurprised, or maybe that my singlehood was not quite like hers.

We drank, both of us. A swish, a thud of the glasses back on the bar, and I slid mine to admire the rings it made on the dark wood, also so I could have something in motion to look at.

"Tell me about your *history* work."

"Uh, well. I don't know. I'm supposed to be writing about the Gilded Age. But I've been messing with some stuff about an Indian dude in the gold rush." I shifted uncomfortably. I hadn't tried to explain Snider to anyone. It felt strange to try to account for what I'd been doing for the past weeks. "But really, mostly it's the Gilded Age."

It suddenly seemed that without directly discussing the span of time that had passed since we'd last seen each other, we would, in fact, have nothing to say.

"I watched your video," I said, before my bravery dissipated. "Your speech." She squinted, honestly; perhaps she'd given many speeches. "Miss Teen India?"

"*Oh*, yeah?" She shook her hair so it curtained her face, briefly, then re-parted it. "I got in trouble for that. They gave me three minutes to blabber about tech, and I went rogue."

I bristled to see that she'd considered invoking Shruti a radical act. "You're proud of it."

"I mean, yes. I was given a platform. I wanted to *say* something with it. I was *angry* with that organization—it made girls anorexic and anxious, and I didn't grasp how much damage all the high school messaging had done until I got to college. . . ." She slowed as her eyes flicked across my face. "Huh," she said, almost disinterestedly. "You're pissed."

"Yeah." I was speaking with an assurance that would have eluded a younger me. And yet I was afraid to push too hard, in case she retreated back to whatever world had possessed her for so long. "You traded on it."

"What do you think I traded it *for*?"

My hand shook and beer sloshed. "You don't think you got credit for being this . . . prophetess of mental health? You didn't feel hypocritical? You just tied everything up. Like it was all way back in the past."

"But it is, Neil," she said sadly. "It *is* way back in the past. That doesn't make it any less horrible. But it's there. It's too late."

The bartender was forming a kind of metronome, clinking liquor bottles against each other and stacking glasses. I turned to Anita and was surprised to find her unblinking eyes still on me. All her concentration seemed to be focused on convincing me—of something.

"You think about her a lot, don't you?" Anita said more softly.

"Most days." I drew on my beer glass with my pinky. "I've never told anyone."

"Why not? I don't mean about the lemonade. I mean about—her."

"How could I have?" I'd considered making Shruti my great confession in college. I wanted to erupt with the unsayable story of her during beer-foamy make-outs. When a girl began to tell me about her trauma, which she had learned to wrap in the language of a white therapist, I considered hissing her name, *Shruti*, daring the girl to ask further. "There's no language for what happened."

"No language? Or language you don't want to have to use?" The space behind my sternum burned. "Anyway," she added, "aren't you quite good with language?"

I had worried sometimes, with Wendi, with Arabella, that my capacity to feel immense emotions—not just grief or terror, but the kind of rich aches that remake you—had died with the end of the Lemonade Period. What they say about addicts: in the end, the brain is fried, and the daily dramas of life become doldrums. But sitting in the Sonora, with Anita's gaze haloing me for the first time in years, a glimmer of all that returned, and it felt like grace.

"I *am* sorry," she said. "For being cold to you for so long."

"Cold? You ignored me. I had nobody—"

"I couldn't have helped you. I needed space. And you'd made me feel so dirty, Neil. That night stuff happened with you and me? I could feel her in my bedroom with us as soon as I realized what you'd done. I swore I could just see her glaring at me. She liked you. That's all I could think about, how much she'd liked you, and I just couldn't look at you again."

"Yeah," I said. It was the first time I had ever been told by someone else what I had done. And I felt less shame than relief, for at least here was someone corroborating the lonely certitude I'd lived with for years; here was one of two other people alive who knew what I was. "I couldn't look at me, either."

Anita ran a hand through her bob as though to pull out tangles, but there were none. "I was also mad because I thought my mother pushed me too hard when I was already running myself ragged. And then I thought she forgave you too fast, and that she was doing this thing my grandma did with her kids, like, favoring boys."

The bartender shook out a new bowl of peanuts. I crammed some into my mouth. "You never told anyone?"

She chewed her bottom lip vigorously. I waited for a zipper of blood to appear on that plump mouth. "I don't really like having to sit with myself. But I had to go to therapy eventually, and I talked around it there, got some emotional vocabulary, which *isn't* a bad thing. And my ex knew the non-gold parts."

"When did, ah, when did you break up?"

"Which time?" she laughed. "He moved out earlier this year. For good, finally. But we'd been on and off since college."

"What's his deal?" My curiosity about how Anita had spent the past ten-odd years overwhelmed the sense of violation that came with hearing about a guy who'd been in and out of her bed for half that decade. And anyway, I had come to understand, through those many beer-foamy make-outs, that telling a story of who you were before a particular moment is a romantic activity, because the moment of the telling, the moment of you two sitting with each other, is the endpoint to the narrative, and that makes you, the hearer, indispensable to the story.

"He's older," she said. "From this oligarch-rich family. They split their time between Delhi and London. The wealthy Indian-Indians at Stanford had none of the baggage of us ABCDs. They're, frankly, bored of all our identity shit. You couldn't call him fresh off the boat—he was fresh off a private jet, you know? Jimmy—that's his name, Jimmy—just waltzed into Stanford and owned the place. Me along with it. He believed in me, you know? I was overwhelmed there—everyone was *so* smart—and he still looked at *me* and said I could be someone. He just *handled* life for me. He'd read my papers, fix my résumé, help me get job interviews—we actually worked at the same venture firm. And I knew I'd only been hired because of him. He gave me pictures of the world in a way my parents never could. . . ."

As she went on about what it was like to vacation with Jimmy's mother in the Maldives and catch his father on a layover in Dubai, and how they never worried about what tomorrow would bring, they simply incarnated the future they desired, sometimes buying it, other times negotiating for it, I understood something new about her. We were both conceptual orphans. Perhaps that is the condition of any second generation. In the space between us and the rest of adulthood lay a great expanse of the unknown. We had not grown up imbibing stories that implicitly conveyed answers to the basic questions of being: What did it feel like to fall in love in America, to take oneself for granted in America? Starved as we were for clues about how to live, we would grip like mad on to anything that lent a possible way of being.

"Did he have to do with what you talked about in that MTI video? Leaving Stanford?"

"He was part of it. He broke up with me after graduating to go to Oxford for a year, and that unleashed a lot of stuff I hadn't dealt with yet. I stopped eating and sleeping, and my grades slipped, and my mom and I were in a cold war because I'd said a bunch of awful things to her about how she'd fucked up my life. So, I withdrew. There was this farm-retreat place that a girl in my sorority had gone when *she* cracked up—it's not uncommon, at Stanford, to suddenly . . . *run out* of whatever got you there. Anyway, I stayed at that farm for about a year."

"I'm sorry. *You* lived on a farm?"

"I was shit at it."

"What's there to be shit at?"

"An ostrich attacked me once."

I chuckled. She was laughing, too. The air lightened. My belly and throat were bloated with beer, and I was aware of how the drive to Berkeley would feel—fizzy and swimming.

"Did you feel different? After the ostrich incident?"

"Yes, I did," she said. "After the farm—not just the ostrich—I was less . . . ruthless."

"*You?*"

Now Anita was looking at *me* funnily, surprised. "You're letting me go on and on."

"You never used to tell me so much. It's a nice change. Less ruthless, you were saying?"

"Well. After Shruti, I wished I'd wanted less. If I had just been okay being average—"

"You were never at risk of average."

"If I had been okay being any old *person*, not obsessed with being *the best*, there would've been no lemonade. And the same thing with Jimmy—if I hadn't needed someone to tell me I was *going places*, I could have picked a boyfriend I just liked spending time with. But I needed Jimmy because I needed what he promised me about my future."

I remembered one of Anita's old Halloween costumes when we were in elementary school. She'd gone as a businesswoman, in my mother's black suit jacket, nineties shoulder pads and all, wielding her father's briefcase and PalmPilot. "Your mom seemed unhappy that you'd quit your VC job."

"Frankly, she's never really *worked*," Anita snapped, "so she has no idea."

"Ani," I said. "She worked, just not—"

"She has no idea what it felt like to be there as Jimmy's nepotism hire. I had to get out, and I couldn't stomach walking into another office on Sand Hill Road and starting over on this path that belonged to *him*. Anyway, my old boss at Galadriel got pregnant and those assholes didn't give her flexible hours, so she quit and started this event firm. She's giving me some work. I'll have to figure out what to do, soon. But for once it doesn't feel like I need to obsess about tomorrow today. I think that . . . shrinking of things—I think it's saved me."

I nodded. She didn't seem shrunken. She seemed more real. I remembered how her ambition had sometimes made her almost illegible to the present. This Anita felt honest.

Around us, people had begun pairing off and making their way to their rooms. I'd heard about the Sonora from Chidi—it had a reputation for being not only the site of handshake agreements for exorbitant sums of money but also a meeting spot for high-end escorts and their clients. It was the kind of place that prides itself on discretion. I had not yet realized that this quality was exactly why Anita had chosen it that night. She looked to the farthest side of the bar, which was empty. She gestured in that direction, and we absconded into the shadows.

Anita pulled a pack of gum from her purse. "Nicorette," she said. "I smoked for a few years." Then: "Listen. Did you think my mom seemed—"

"Different?"

Anita nodded.

"I guess. It's been a while." I picked at the table in front of me, hesitating. "She was on campus for something—a memorial. For a man."

Anita sighed. "I knew someone important to her had died. And I suspected he was more than just a *dear friend*, or however she kept putting it." Anita clenched her fist a few times, like she was warming up for something. "Whatever's going on with her," she said, "that's what I need to talk to you about. I need your help. *She* needs our help."

ANJALI JOSHI MET HER husband-to-be on the green IIT Bombay campus in 1988. Her brother Vivek, in his second year at the elite institution, was earning C's and D's in everything save the joke class, Indian philosophy.

"Mama told me Vivek swore off the gold as soon as he got to IIT," Anita said, swirling her wine. "He never forgave himself for what he saw as stealing his neighbor Parag's spot, and he refused to acquire gold from his batchmates. He must have been very strong to white-knuckle his way through the withdrawal. I sometimes imagine that he wanted something else enough to make it bearable. He loved theater, and music, you know. Maybe he would have ended up an artist."

Happy, or average, or artistic, or whatever he was, Vivek was enjoying himself for the first time in years, playing guitar, sustaining flirtations with girls from nearby schools.

"I've pieced all this together over the last few months," Anita went on. "Talking to my mother, and my grandmother."

Anjali, who lived at home and commuted south to a women's college, used to visit Vivek sometimes. The Joshi parents abided this; they considered IITians harmless and presumed Vivek looked out for his baby sister. He did. He wouldn't let her near the minority cohort of boys who smoked ganja or got drunk, but he did let her pass rowdy evenings as a guest in the mess hall while he and his friends had endless conversations about American rock and roll. She was always packed off home before the real raucousness began in the hostels. Vivek was developing quite the foul lexicon, trading friendly insults in rough Marathi and Hindi late into the night. For now that he had reached this vaunted place, there was joy, and a chance to be young, at last.

Anjali—who'd grown into a striking woman—felt more comfortable among the IIT boys than with her female classmates. The others at her college, where she was a scholarship student (having been encouraged for the first time by a chemistry teacher in her final year), were products of upper-crust schools in Malabar Hill and Fort. They spoke in Oxford-tinged accents; some had boyfriends with whom they flitted into the Royal Willingdon Sports Club or the Bombay Gymkhana. The school's pink walls and the surrounding streets of foreign consul general offices, even the name of the neighborhood—Breach Candy—all rang of a place beyond sealess Dadar, its ruck, its clamor.

The first time Anjali visited IIT, she debarked from the paint-peeling city bus and spied a single female passing into a boxy beige building. "Are there *any* girls here?" she asked Vivek's Bengali roommate. They were filling up metal trays with mess hall vada pav. "Thirteen," the Bengali replied. "Of two hundred fifty." Perhaps those thirteen had been raised by mothers who brewed them the right drinks at the right hours.

The Bengali excused himself to join a scruffy curly-haired boy wearing glasses and a khadi kurta, messenger bag slung across his chest. They were off to protest one of the evening socials being held at a hostel; women from colleges like Anjali's were bussed up to keep young men company. "Socials are an American imperialist form of engaging!" the comrades chanted, pumping fists as they filed out. Hardly a catchy slogan. Which was when a plump young man with thick eyebrows adjusted his spectacles and cleared his throat.

"His hostel couldn't get anyone to come if they paid for it," he said. His voice sounded like an out-of-tune violin, but it was also hefty. He spoke as though he'd been practicing the line.

"They're communists," Anjali offered. "I don't think they want to pay."

The plump boy began to spout more insults about the Bengali, likely less because he disliked him than because the chap had served as a conversational entry point.

Anjali interrupted. "He's my brother's best friend."

"You're Vivek Joshi's sister?"

"Yes."

"Oh, god," Pranesh Dayal whimpered. "Oh, god, don't tell him I harassed you or something, na." He scuttled away.

When Anjali sat down across from her brother and inquired about the boy, Vivek and his friends laughed as they slopped up bhaji.

"Sad fellow, what to do," Vivek said. "Too studious, total pain. Gets ragged."

"Class topper, though," one of the friends said. "Got to respect it."

"You don't rag him, do you, bhau?"

Vivek mussed her hair with one large mitt of a hand. "Don't be bothered, Anju."

Anjali pictured a table of her classmates having this sort of exchange about her: *Anjali Joshi, sad girl, don't talk to her, her father is just an excise tax officer. . . .* And so when she came to visit Vivek every month or so, she kept an eye out for Pranesh. She'd notice him crossing the grass with a robotic gait, and she'd jog to catch him up.

"What do you want from me," he once demanded, in that voice of his that did not seem to contain in its repertoire question marks. She was taken aback. Gone was the boy who'd approached her to impress, replaced by a defensive creature. They stood in the shade of a flame-of-the-forest tree, but still they sweated. Fat brown pods dangled above them. Anjali tore one off.

"I hear you're the class topper," she said, fiddling with the pod. She took a finger to her loose hair and twirled it, as the Malabar Hill girls did. "I've never been much good at school."

She was not sure what had come over her. Maybe it was that Pranesh seemed harmless, someone to practice on. Likelier, she was genuinely curious about his intellectual prowess. She was standing in the vicinity of the thing she'd been trained to recognize as power: academic achievement. She thought of how Vivek had described *ambition* years earlier, as an energy that runs in some bodies and not in others. She had begun to wonder what would happen if someone drank one of *her* gold earrings. Nothing, she suspected. Her wants were too nebulous.

"I used to use those as swords, when I was small," Pranesh said, pointing at the pod. He took it and stabbed the air. He was so like a child. All that studying could not grow you up.

Slowly, they became friendly. Anjali shared a milky-sweet chai with him a few times. He reminded her of a teenage Dhruv, who had also been plump and bookish, to the extent that he barely existed outside his turning pages, his pencils on graphing paper. She felt for Pranesh when she learned he had been orphaned at fourteen; it explained—did it?—his coldness. Was there romance? There was a thrill in discovering that men harbored secrets, and that this thing called love might consist in part of teasing such privacies out, learning to hold them yourself. The fact that he told her so little gave her labor to perform, made her feel useful.

Vivek and his mates found the friendship odd. Particularly perturbed by Anjali's affection for dumpy Pranesh was Rakesh Malhotra, a good-looking Punjabi with a reputation for being the hostel's worst ragger. He dragged first-years from bed and made them march naked, gripping each other's penises. When Anjali failed to notice Rakesh, he began to talk about her as a calculating manipulator of male attention—a portrayal that would make its way to my mother's ears through his family, the Bhatts of Hammond Creek. *Gold digger.*

But things rolled on with Pranesh. When they strolled around the lake, she grilled him on his plans. He was going to get a PhD, in America.

"It's cutthroat," he told her expertly. "They do not let just anybody in."

She began to tell him about Dhruv in North Carolina, the Lynyrd Skynyrd tapes, the Jolen hair cream. Pranesh asked where Dhruv had been in school.

He shook his head. "I will go somewhere better. Do not worry. I'll do much more than all those people."

She felt, for the first time, included in the fringes of someone else's future.

. . .

IN THE SPRING OF his final year, Vivek went on holiday. He was riding with friends on the roof of a train from Bombay to Kanya-kumari. They had their guitars up there, and they were strumming Dire Straits the whole way south. There was a disconnect between landscape and soundscape—their twangs did not match the dry fields laden with yellow-green brush, baking beneath the cloudless sky. They felt thick with the possibility of what awaited them over the next several years, as some of them prepared to cross oceans, to make lives of their own.

The car passed under a low electrical wire. All ducked but Vivek. Beneath the relentless Andhra Pradesh sun, having brushed twenty-five thousand volts, he sustained third-degree burns. He died atop the train, miles from his parents, from his sister, from the elder brother who had set such a standard for him.

"My dad used to call Uncle Vivek's death very *Indian*," Anita said. "A third world way to go, that's what he'd say. He had a lot of anger against India for things like that. His parents died in a ter-rible bus crash in Himachal Pradesh." She shivered and continued.

The following months were brutal at the Joshis'. Dhruv did not come home. He was waiting for his American residency to go through and claimed leaving the United States would boot him to the back of the queue. Lakshmi Joshi never forgave her firstborn. She was territorial about her grief, snapping at anyone who tried to join her weeping. "My child, *my* child," she wailed. Anjali could not help thinking that her mother's overwhelming woe was an-other sign that she, the daughter, was inadequate.

As the year went on, Anjali completed her exams, earning poor marks. All auspicious events, engagements included, were postponed in the wake of death, so she had some time. But soon, she would be noticed for what she was—a daughter who needed to be married off. And who could say to what type of man? It seemed a horrible fate to have to live your life with someone whose mind was smaller than your own. She wanted someone who was more than she was.

So, she had an idea. To take what she needed. A few weeks after her exams, she rode the bus to Powai with some of her classmates to attend Mood Indigo, the big music festival hosted each year by IIT Bombay. Vivek had played with his band on those stages. It was stomach-clenching to be back in his territory, but she'd arrived on a mission. She skirted the edge of the party, passing greasy-haired communists. One of them handed her a bright flyer reading BAN ROCK SHOW: AMERICAN IMPERIALIST TRADITION before sighing, shoving the rest of his papers into a cloth messenger bag, and moseying back to his hostel, defeated that night by cultural globalization. A doomed student band from St. Xavier's began to play George Michael's "Careless Whisper," and as the frank roar of boos followed, Anjali knew it was only a matter of time before someone began throwing rotten bananas and tomatoes onto the stage.

Then, at the fateful swell of a Police song, she found herself blinking at Pranesh Dayal. They had not seen each other since Vivek's death. "I'm sorry," he shouted through the noise.

Their recommenced walks along the lakeside in Powai were longer now. Lakshmi believed her daughter to be studying in town with her posh friends. Pranesh told her stiffly, as though he'd copped the line from a film, that she was *the very picture of beauty*. For his part, he had begun jogging and doing push-ups; he was, briefly, almost handsome.

When he graduated and told her he was moving to a place called

Atlanta, where he had been accepted into Georgia Tech (he'd wanted Stanford), she told him to write. His letters rolled in. *There are no good rotis to be found. I hope you are learning your mother's/chachi's recipes etc because all of us students are homesick for proper food.* She held on to them as her parents began to trot grooms through the living room, each one promising her a smaller life than the last. Finally, she announced the fact of Pranesh and his correspondence. A *love match* to a foreign-dwelling boy was a surprise, but acceptable. There was little to arrange between families, given that Pranesh was an orphan. He came to marry and collect her. As they circled the wedding fire, she watched smoke obscure the back of his head and imagined there was more inside him she did not know.

It turned out that behind Pranesh Dayal's plump belly and thinning hair there was no secretly compassionate man. Anjali decided the remedy was a daughter. She learned to drive so she could take herself to the Hindu temple in Riverdale and make offerings of fruit and flowers. Kneeling before the stone Venkateshwara, she named Anita long before she was conceived. She would have had three, five more children if she could have—yes, she wanted a son, too, whom she imagined naming Vivek. But Pranesh got a vasectomy one summer when Anjali took Anita back to Bombay, telling her later that he did not plan on funneling his money to support a whole brood.

On the occasions Anjali considered her domestic situation, she developed a castor oil taste in her mouth. America: once metonymy for *more*. Here, was there more? She possessed a life of her own. Her husband left for California and she could breathe. It was something. She wanted *more*—infinitely more—for her daughter. She would do anything to give it to her.

. . .

ABOUT A YEAR before this reunion at the Sonora, Anjali's father died. She and her brother Dhruv had, over the years, remitted enough money that their parents could shift to be near some better-off relatives in Navi Mumbai. But after Mr. Joshi's death, the relatives whispered at how Lakshmi's wealthy children neglected the old woman, whispering of the disloyalty America bred. Anjali and Dhruv discussed things. Dhruv's wife did not want to take in Lakshmi. "You have much more than we do," the sister-in-law told Anjali—which was true, because Pranesh had recently sold his company for, as Chidi said, a fuckload. (Anjali did not contribute financially; she'd never restarted her catering business out west and struggled to hold jobs. She was an unreliable employee, forgetful and scattered.)

At any rate, the domino effect of family obligations and rivalries began, and Lakshmi came to live in Sunnyvale. How ironic to find that a doted-upon son would, in adulthood, kowtow to a cold wife. But the daughter didn't dwell on ugly history. Daughters had forgiveness in their bones. Up into the dry California sky went the resentments that might have been spoken about Dadar, about Parag the neighbor, about Vivek, about how Lakshmi had allocated love.

Lakshmi arrived in California just as Pranesh instigated divorce proceedings. Over the years, Anita's father had grown angry with Anjali for doing too little domestically, for why should a man like him be married to a woman like her, except for the sake of the household? But these days, she was not cooking, she did not work, they had nothing to say to each other. And sufficient money had led Pranesh to a conclusion that would have been unheard of some years earlier: he could afford now to exit the inconvenience of his marriage.

He nabbed the best lawyer in the region and met with many others, barring them from working with Anjali. Pranesh's attorney was arguing Anjali's irrelevance to her husband's company, litigating her out of a decent settlement. And the stress was taking its toll—"as you might have noticed," Anita said.

Anjali initially tried to pass off the fact that Pranesh was living in Portola Valley as temporary—she told Lakshmi that he wanted a retreat up in the hills, with fewer distractions, to begin ideating a new company. Lakshmi knew better. "I have seen things change in Bombay," she informed Anjali. The relatives in Navi Mumbai had a divorced son; the daughter was not even married to the man she lived with. Lakshmi was not unwise to the changing of the times. Perhaps she surprised herself with the expandable scope of her motherhood, how it swelled to make space for things previously unacceptable.

Lakshmi summoned her granddaughter to Sunnyvale, where Anjali had remained. (Anita's mother's sole victory in the divorce would be getting to keep the house she'd never wanted, in the suburb she'd always hated.) Anjali was asleep when Anita arrived. She poked her head in to see her mother breathing shallowly, her sharp wristbones and vertebrae visible through her oddly papery skin.

"There is something very wrong with your aiyee," Lakshmi said sternly, bustling over the stove. Anita tried to make the chai, but her grandmother scorned her attempts.

"She's depressed," Anita said, taking her tea.

Lakshmi clicked her tongue to dismiss the Western psychobabble. "What is wrong, see, is this. I made a very big mistake. I fixed up your uncles' lives. Got all their studies in order. Gave your uncle Vivek all kinds of special boosts. All this you know." Anita nodded. "But I did not arrange anything proper for your mother. She needed some kind of boost, too. Understand?"

"Ajji," Anita said. "Isn't that all in the past? You can't fix it now."

They were quiet for a while, drinking their chai, and then Anita began to wash their emptied mugs. From behind the sink, she could see the Sunnyvale cul-de-sac, cousin to the Hammond Creek cul-de-sac, only with squatter houses and more citrus trees. The sight gave her hot pangs between her ribs. Her mother had spent so many years here, in this place meant for certain types of families, certain types of lives. Was there no way out for Anjali Dayal— no, Anjali Joshi? No other way of being on offer?

"What *could* you do now, Ajji?" she said.

"I would not have given your mother the same-same kind of gold drink I gave your uncle," Lakshmi said. She came to stand by Anita. Together they surveyed the street. "What I should have given was a good gold tonic to ensure her marriage and home life were happy."

The blatant inequality of the statement made Anita roll her eyes. But she couldn't deny that those things—marriage and domestic life—were exactly what were going wrong for her mother now. It was far too late for Anjali to attend IIT. But maybe it was *not* too late for her to be, in some way, settled. Adjusted.

"What sort of gold does that come from?" Anita asked.

She thought she heard her mother shifting in the bedroom. Anjali would be furious to imagine beginning the cycle again.

"Good happy-home happy-life blessing? Where else? From wedding gold," Lakshmi said. "Actually, gold given just *before* a wedding. When everything is all, how to put it, *promise*. Absolutely fresh wedding gold, understand?" Anita's eyes widened. Lakshmi went on: "You have this bridal event you are planning, isn't it? That is what has given me this idea. There you will have good jewelers, with all kinds of handmade pieces and what all? Yes? Come. Let us talk about helping your mother."

"*THAT'S* WHY YOU CALLED ME? After all this time?" I lowered my voice. "You want me to do *it* again?" I inched my stool away. The intensity of her attention on me earlier in the night, the willingness to confess heartbreaks—all a calculation. To get me on her side. For a ridiculous cause! Anita seemed unperturbed. She signaled to the bartender for water.

"For a proper Indian wedding," she explained, willfully ignoring my agita, "you need certain things, as I've discovered over the past few years of every brown girl I know shaadi-ing up. You need someone to do mehendi—henna. You need a DJ, a caterer. Someone to tailor your lehenga. Get the point? Yes. And these vendors may not be available if you live in, say, some bumblefuck American suburb. So people come to these big convention centers to do all their wedding shopping."

"And some people get jewelry there." I felt spittle fly from my lips.

She swigged, then replied. "Yes. Some people have their inherited wedding trousseaus, though not everyone. These days women want modern, lighter gold or they rent. But desi brides *always* get high quality, high karat. And that gold—it contains—"

"Well-adjustment." I remembered Prachi's party, seeing happily engaged Maya's earrings and wondering at all they contained, at all I could have if I took them.

The faith to make it from day to day. Faith to lead Anjali Joshi out of bed, to new life.

The bartender was mopping up after a clumsy guy who had just spilled his cocktail. I had to imagine last call was soon; it was past midnight. The klutz had been eyeing Anita hungrily. Her bony knee knocked against mine, and she left it there.

"Don't you have enough money to buy wedding gold yourself?"

"You know how this works." Of course—if she bought it, it'd be her own luck, her own energy, her own ambition. Which was insufficient.

And then Anita's hand was briefly—so briefly—cupping my knee, calling on the old me. A shiver at the hand of that girl, the only girl, touching me, needing me. I felt that old Neil jonesing, his wants deep in my tissue. I pictured three generations, Lakshmi and Anjali and Anita, huddled around a huge pot on the stove on some sunny afternoon, a concoction bubbling. I, in the corner, inhaling the fumes. Intoxicated. Wedging between the women. Bringing the pot to my lips.

"Your mom doesn't know about this."

She shook her head.

"Because it's insane."

"She'd worry."

"Because it's insane."

"To a degree," Anita hedged. "But I'm in charge of this expo, Neil. I know how to manipulate things, and we'd take so little, out of so much stock—and not all from one store. It isn't like . . . with Shruti. We're not going to unhook some poor bride's necklace on her wedding day. We'll take it from vendors, a single earring, one bangle. They'll think they just lost it."

"Are you sure the gold would contain—everything we, I mean *you*, need?"

Her inky eyes flashed nervously at the bartender, who was still ignoring us. "When we drink the *stuff*, we're drinking the intention that the owner has imbued the gold with. Yes? Yes. But the gold's power begins earlier than that. Remember how my mom explained it years ago? A jeweler imbues his pieces with intentions when he's making it—when he sources the gold itself, when he starts to design, et cetera. Picture some desi jewelry maker in Bombay or Dubai or wherever. If he's bad at his job, he's working mindlessly, and we get shoddy craftsmanship. Drinking that crap is as useless as drinking seltzer.

"But if he's a *good* artisan—and my expo jewelers only stock the best artisans' work—he's making it with awareness that someone's going to get married in this. Indians have a lot of gold made *specifically for a wedding*. Mangalsutras, big maang tikkas, Mughalstyle matha pattis, South Indian–style temple gold, bajubands, kamarbandhs, naths—the big-ass nose rings . . . These are pieces you simply don't wear any other time. So someone making a highquality—"

"Bajuband?" I didn't know most of the words Anita had just recited.

"That's the fat gold armband. Or mangalsutra, the marriage necklace—your mom wears one. Someone making that bajuband or nath is infusing it *only* and *intensely* with the intention for domestic settlement."

"I get the point."

"No, the *point*, Neil," Anita said, positively clenching her fists in a way that suggested she did *not* believe I'd gotten it, "the point is that in India *and* America, something *powerful* happens at the start of marriage, something we can take for my mother. The start of the marriage, when two people are optimistic about each other— the American rom-com, love-shuv version.

"But we *also* want the old conservative Indian thing. And in some versions of India, the wedding is when the whole community is behind you, aunts and grandmothers and everyone who's been trying to get you married. For some families, and the Joshis were like this, marrying off a daughter makes her theoretically *safe*. Plus, historically some desi brides got that gold as a backup in case the marriage went wrong, for their own financial security—"

I couldn't help but think of even my thoroughly modern sister, how something in her had stabilized as soon as Avi slid the conflict-free diamond onto her ring finger. How in a rare moment of reflection, she'd told me once that the bulimia had finally ended with Avi, how the ground beneath your feet stopped shaking when you knew you had a partner in all things.

"Tell me your 'plan.'" I used air quotes.

Anita was panting from the exertion of explaining the Indian wedding industrial complex. But she nodded invitingly, in the same fashion Chidi did when he was asked a probing question about his start-up, as if to imply there was nothing he'd rather be doing than assuaging the asker's doubts.

"We've got to deal with security. Metal detectors, guards, cameras. Then, discretion. How to do it without alerting the jewelers. Plus, getaway."

"That wasn't a plan. That was a list of problems. And who's 'we'?"

"For now, just me."

"A crack team, huh."

"You're the only person I'd imagine trusting with this."

"You don't even know me anymore."

She was unscathed. "Maybe I don't."

My voice fell to a near whisper. "You really think it wouldn't hurt anyone?"

I looked around the room, on instinct. Shruti didn't step from the shadows to remind me about the unspeakable costs of fulfilling unnameable lusts. It was just me, Anita, and the bartender, who'd turned the TV to a black-and-white Japanese film.

"Yes, Neil," she said. "I really think it wouldn't hurt anyone."

"And would the gold contain . . . actual *happiness*, you think?"

"Something close to it," Anita said. And there her hand was, on my knee again. I was dizzy, as I hadn't been in years. "But, honestly, I'm not sure my mother's familiar enough with the real thing to discern."

I tried not to move, not to lose her touch. I nodded. A question formed in my throat, but I didn't say it aloud. *Could I have some, too?* "I'm not sure I'd know the difference, either," I said.

8.

It had come time for the suitable families to meet. Prachi and Avi were beginning to look for houses, and the Kapoor clan, self-identified Los Altos natives, had taken the opportunity to invite my parents out for a visit. Houses. Homes! These things were my mother's purpose. She was only too happy to lend her expertise to the hunt. We were to troop around, my whole family and Avi (his parents pled fatigue re: Bay Area real estate), working through as many open houses as could be crammed into one August Sunday.

I'd been conscripted into joining. "You'll have to do this one day, too," my father insisted, just as when we'd toured colleges for Prachi. There, the ever-dangling threat of the future.

I picked my parents up from my uncle Gopi and aunt Sandhya's house in Fremont, then gathered Prachi and Avi from the city.

"How *mad* that my brother lives so near your parents, Avi," my mother said merrily, as everyone squished into the backseat of my knee-knocking Honda. (Avi was lingering on the waitlist for a Tesla, and Prachi had never liked driving, not since her traumatic year of lessons from my father.) And yet it was not mad at all, because the Bay Area is the upper-middle-class Indian American promised land. These sunny small towns, with their citrus trees, their tidy main streets—all these qualities make the place peaceful in a way that promises an end to competition, suggesting (incorrectly, of course) that the game has been won.

"We should have rented a car," my father said when my Honda took too long to start.

Avi attempted to soothe nerves. "We can take my mom's other car tomorrow, Uncle."

My mother fluttered. "Oh, no. No. We would not put your parents out. We can rent."

I was exhausted from a week of pushing further into the Tale of Isaac Snider. He'd be back from Indonesia the following week, and we were scheduled for a check-in to ensure I was on track for the proposal defense in November. I was aware that I'd produced more on Snider than on the Gilded Age. I was aware, too, that the sentences pulsed in the former pages, and lay limp in the latter. I still had time, though, to try to breathe some life into my sample chapter on religious messaging surrounding money during the period.

I'd been further discombobulated thinking about Anita—the new Anita, who'd said she *needed* me, bringing forth a rocket of old wants. I hadn't yet given her an answer to her wild pitch. She'd been texting me occasionally to prod my decision along. Each buzz in my pocket drew me further away from this world, of my family, of houses, of the basic arrangements of life.

To see Prachi's and my mother's dreamy expressions upon entering each low-slung on-the-market California home was to feel that I had been locked out of one of the great secrets of the world. Each house shared a few things: a single story with sparse grass marking a front "lawn," a tinlike flat roof, pale paint—orange sherbet, cotton candy pink. Inside: sunbeams on hardwood, lanky windows. Citrus trees, tomatoes. Discussions of how to keep the squirrels from the plants. These were, by most standards of the country, modest buildings. But here, the land upon which they sat, which had once been dotted with flappy tents as gold hunters fled inland, was worth millions. A century and a half ago, to stand on this terrain would have made Prachi and Avi pioneers; even a well-to-do woman like my sister would have struggled to hire someone to build her a house, for all the able-bodied men would have been in the goldfields.

Now, though. Now Prachi and Avi would step into a home full of smart thermostats and smart fridges. They would drive Avi's Tesla, order groceries for delivery, stream any entertainment they liked, while Avi nursed his side-project start-ups, nail-bitingly hoping against hope that one of those could bloom into a lucky billion-dollar idea, the gold in the dirt.

We considered the city—Glen Park, Noe Valley—but mostly the suburbs on the peninsula: Burlingame, San Mateo, Menlo Park, Redwood City. The latter was the ideal location in Prachi and Avi's new collective couple consciousness—near their jobs and Avi's parents in Los Altos. (Who else would watch the future off-spring?) Redwood City's heart: a pedestrian mall, streets lined with Mongolian BBQ and AMC Super 3D Cineplex and the Cheesecake Factory.

"You will have everything you need right here," my father said.

"Convenience factor, very important," my mother agreed.

The third or fourth Redwood City house: lemon yellow, squat. A wooden slatted fence ringed a small yard, on which a tricycle currently lay, its front pink wheel spinning slowly. Sesame-colored walls, polished appliances. The floral smell of the potpourri in the pink-wallpapered powder room elicited coughs. Prachi and Avi said, "Is this it?" "This is it," quietly to each other, as we stepped into a final room, painted seafoam green.

I'd gone out with Chidi's crowd two nights earlier: MDMA at a warehouse party in Oakland. Forty-eight hours later, I was in the depths of cold, abject nihilism. Suicide Sunday. It hit me just then, as Prachi and Avi said *This is it*, and the comedown darkened until I was in the throes of one of my occasional panics.

"Is it a home office?" my father asked.

"No," Prachi said very quietly, and my mother took her hand.

"It's perfect for kids?" the strawberry-blond real estate agent uptalked.

"Yes," my mother said.

"Oh," my father said.

"Wow," Avi said.

"Uh," I said, "I have a headache." I dropped to my knees and pushed my face to the ground. Footsteps moved away—the real estate agent, excusing herself; I was making a *scene*. Everyone's ease was galactically distant. I wanted to disdain this prescribed life and yet I could not help it, I regretted that it seemed so out of reach; I wanted what it gave everyone else. I lifted my head from the floor. The carpet looked to be breathing as the indentation my forehead had made in it unflattened. My throat was growing smaller; now it was the size of a dime. Somewhere nearby the Caltrain rumbled, and I thought of the people who lay down in front of it every year, how their gray matter and organs and eyelashes and fingernails salted the tracks for miles.

I remembered the fizzing relief of a fresh glass of lemonade. I was parched with the memory.

My mother knelt next to me. Put a hand between my shoulder blades. Rubbed.

"Breathe, rajah," she said. "Breathe." She kept her hand there until the worst of it abated.

EVERYONE WAS STILL EYEING ME nervously at dinner, except that it was a festive occasion, the melding of two families, the mutually achieved immigrant dream hanging like a plump cloud over us.

We sat beneath the wooden trellis in the Kapoors' backyard. The domed sky was flecked with constellations. This was why people loved Northern California; its buildings did not pollute the sky. You could remember the stars, their dead light, their gold dust.

"You have to move fast in the Bay Area," said Mr. Kapoor, agreeing with someone that it was a good idea for Prachi and Avi to snap up the Redwood City house.

"Everything one big race here," Mrs. Kapoor supplied, with the even breathing of someone who has not been running it herself.

My father sniffed his red—it was the first time I'd seen my parents not scorn alcohol outright, because we were in the company of wealthy Punjabis who took drink seriously. Mr. Kapoor swirled his whiskey. The dinner conversation swarmed with swapped gossip. One can fill in the rest of the clanging of glasses and clacking of silverware and pass-the-paneer-phulka-tacos, how's-your-cholesterol exchanges that formed the backdrop to the evening's entertainment:

MY MOTHER: . . . So, see, first Indian I ever heard of coming to America, this family sent him off to college here when he was maybe sixteen.

SANDHYA: So young!

PRACHI: Too young.

MY MOTHER [*head shaking*]: Much, *much* too young, yes, anyway! So he's sixteen and in college, somewhere, say, Maine, maybe Nebraska, I don't know. And he has no friends. Until these Christian fellows come catch hold of him.

MRS. KAPOOR: They *do* that.

MY MOTHER: Yaa, yaa. So they say Jesus saves Jesus saves, whatever they say, and then he goes along and becomes one de*vout* Christian. His poor Brahmin mother, so confused when he came home shaking crucifixes and whatnot! Strict vegetarian, she was! And now he's eating chicken-schmicken. So they took him out of college. And now they decide ki he needs some job. Off he goes to work in the Gulf.

MY FATHER [*with affable recognition of the pattern of my mother's stories*]: Ayyo, Ramya.

MY MOTHER: But then guess what happens! These Muslims he's working with, *they* catch hold of him and give him beef and all and abhi? He's one de*vout* Muslim.

[*A chorus of laughter. Affectionate eye rolls. Prachi and Avi catching each other's gazes with stifled giggles. Sufficiently a part of this, sufficiently apart from it.*]

MR. KAPOOR: Now, think, such a fellow would not even get into these American colleges.

AVI: What do you mean, Dad?

MRS. KAPOOR: Avinash, he's just saying, these colleges have it out for our kind now. Very hard for Pratyusha's children; you can only get into Berkeley as some *other* minority.

AVI: What do you think, Neil? You TA for all these Berkeley kids, don't you? Prachi says you're always writing them letters of recommendation and stuff.

PRACHI [*glowing*]: My brother is a very popular teacher.

NEIL: I don't think there's a shortage of high-achieving Asians at Berkeley, Auntie. Honestly, I wonder if someone told them, "Stop racing, there are too many of you," if they'd wind up having to do something more *interesting* with themselves.

SANDHYA: Pinky, I teach, too, you know, eleventh grade, and Neil, they want it for themselves. You tell them they can't do it, their eyes pop out of their heads.

MRS. KAPOOR: You're in Fremont, isn't it? Say, what about these robberies and all?

MR. KAPOOR: Neil, this is a story for you. You must write this. Get him a notebook, Pinky.

PRACHI: He's not a journalist, Uncle.

MRS. KAPOOR: Why not try it? We could say we know this Pulitzer fellow Neil Narayan!

NEIL: I've considered it.

MY FATHER [*concerned*]: Journalism?

NEIL: A Pulitzer.

MR. KAPOOR: Point is, Neil, nobody's telling *our* stories. I have a colleague, he is a Jew—

AVI: Dad, say Jew*ish*, not *a* Jew.

MR. KAPOOR: Jewish-Jewish yes, anyway, he is a Jewish. They have their own proper magazines, we have just *India Abroad* bullshit—excuse me, Pinky, but that is what it is. Neil, why don't *you* start up some publication for desis! It's a good a time for starting up!

MY FATHER: Well, as Prachi is saying, Neil writes *history*—

MR. KAPOOR: What is history but an explanation for the present!

NEIL: I wouldn't put it like that.

MY MOTHER: Pinky, you're talking about gold robberies? This happened in Atlanta, too!

NEIL: In Atlanta? When?

MRS. KAPOOR: See, it's these Colombian gangster fellows. They come and hold Indians up inside their own homes at gunpoint and they make off with all the gold.

PRACHI: How do they know which houses belong to Indians?

GOPI: Stakeout, must be.

MY MOTHER: No, no, see, I have one other theory. From when it happened all over Atlanta.

MY FATHER: No proof for this theory!

MY MOTHER: You agreed just the other day, Raghu.

MY FATHER [*genially*]: Did I? [*to Mr. Kapoor*] Sometimes you have to!

MRS. KAPOOR: *What* was your theory, Ramya?

MY MOTHER: See, Pinky. See. It *has* to be Indians. Who else?

MRS. KAPOOR: What? Indians with guns?

MY MOTHER: No, no, in Atlanta there were no guns.

NEIL: *When* in Atlanta?

PRACHI: What do you mean, Amma? What Indians? Neil, don't sigh so loudly, it's rude.

MY MOTHER: It was all very well planned. The person would know exactly when a family was going to India. Savitri Reddy lost her mother out of nowhere, okay? She raced off to Hyderabad, then someone set in on her house the very next day. These people knew exactly where to go; they took all of it from her big suitcase in the guest bedroom, poor thing. They even found the pieces she kept hidden in Godiva chocolate containers in the pantry! Five, ten thousand dollars in all.

MRS. KAPOOR: No one should have so much in the house anymore!

PRACHI: Amma, when did all this happen, Neil was asking.

MY MOTHER: Few years back. Two thousand-leven. You were in college, Neeraj. I *told* you, you just never listen to me. See, and now only he listens—

NEIL: It never happened before that? When we were still at home?

GOPI [*heartily*]: Indians are not heisty-schmeisty material, Ramya.

MY MOTHER: See, *that's* why they were not caught! Who would suspect?

MRS. KAPOOR [*flushing*]: I picture them coming in all crowbars and guns sometimes and . . .

MR. KAPOOR: She gets scared.

MY MOTHER: I would be frightened, too, Pinky, except we have a *very* good neighborhood watch.

MY FATHER: Ramya, I'm sure they have a neighborhood watch here, too.

PRACHI: Auntie, if you're spooked, maybe you should get another security system.

AVI: Actually—that guy we were talking about the other day? [*turning to Prachi*] Pranesh Dayal? The company he sold does smart devices and stuff. Thermostats, fridges, internet-of-things-enabled security cameras. You can save all the images to the cloud, you know?

MY MOTHER: How do *you* know about Pranesh Dayal?

AVI: He's well known! Dad, he's that IIT Bombay dude—Harita Auntie's cousin?

NEIL: Actually, I ran into—

MY MOTHER: It *may* be that Pranesh Dayal is very smarty-smart, but that *wife* of his—actually, these days I'm hearing *ex*-wife—Avinash, just listen . . .

MY FAMILY DISTRIBUTED various tokens of advice before we parted ways again. As we hugged good-bye in Alamo Square, Prachi told me to call Keya, who was capable and cute and had (against all odds) *liked* me. As I dropped my parents at SFO the next day, my father reminded me about the existence of law school, and I shook it off before he could offer to pay for it with money he did not really have. My mother whispered into my hair that she was going to do some "health research," which meant she'd go digging through Ayurvedic remedies for malaise; she would fall asleep with her face on my horoscope and implore her cousins in Mysore to visit the family sage. (She had begun to swear on his precognition. "Rusyendra has foreseen this," she'd said of Prachi's match to Avi. "He said Prachi would choose outside of her community." "He's *Indian*, Mom," I said. "*Punjabi*, Neeraj," she'd replied. "Entirely different." "What about me?" "Rusyendra says you are very difficult to perceive, Neeraj.")

A few days later, on the eve of my appointment with Wang, I got a terse email from him reminding me that I still had not sent over any new work. *Making your adviser chase you down is less than ideal*, he wrote. I was forty milligrams of Adderall into my day. I opened my two projects, the sober and the intoxicated. On one hand: *Mythologies of Money in the Gilded Age.docx*—it was fragments and bullet points, full of my notes to myself, "ADD LATER" and "NEED MORE ON THIS." On the other: *Snider-draft-8.rtf*—full paragraphs. Images. A human, breathing on the page, speaking, wanting, accounting for time's passage. An argument about history. I remembered Wang, during our last meeting, telling me my sentences had an overboiled-spinach quality—tasteless, unappetizing. Remembered him accusing me of having a surface-level relationship to my material.

I chose the second document, then went out to buy more protein bars, and crashed late.

When I woke up before our meeting, my head thudded with regret and embarrassment.

In his office, Wang chewed the inside of his cheek and smoothed the T-shirt he wore beneath a light navy blazer. He pushed his glasses atop his head and frowned as he paged through a printout of my Isaac Snider chapters.

A few uncannily quiet minutes passed. The only sound was the scuffle of Wang's archless sneakers on the floor as his feet tapped.

"I wasn't aware," he said, "that you had an interest in writing fiction."

"I, well—"

"It isn't a terrible side hobby." He tented his fingertips, the veins in his sinewy forearms popping, and in a nauseating moment, I saw that he was offering me a way out. "I'd be happy to see more people in the academy thinking about art alongside their work."

"Yes," I said, in a very small, very breathy voice.

"But between you and me, Neil, I wouldn't make a habit of passing around your fiction until you've earned yourself a stable floor as a historian. Yes?"

I nodded. My mouth was thick with saliva; I couldn't have spoken if I'd tried.

"And you might explicitly indicate, when you're sending someone something, that you *intend* it to be fiction. Otherwise your diligent reader might start looking for citations, and proof, and clear argumentation. Of course, once one lets go of such expectations, this little *Tale of Isaac Snider* is quite a thrill."

"It is," I said. "It was. A thrill, I mean. To, erm, to write."

"You know, I almost did an MFA myself," Wang said. "Poetry. In Austin."

"*Really?*" Wang always struck me as a hardheaded, practical sort.

"But. You can't eat poetry. You can barely eat history. It's a few chunks of stale bread."

"Do you still write?"

"Of course I still write," he said, a bit haughtily. "*This* is a creative pursuit, getting in touch with the past. I used to write letters to the people I was studying, you know? In a journal. I'd say, TO: EUGENE DEBS, 1883. I'd tell young Eugene everything I thought he might be interested in about life today. Which as it happened, was a whole lot. And then I'd hear him talk back to me. And I'd come to understand where I should be looking in his life, in his story, et cetera. That's a kind of art, though my colleagues from *The Harvard Advocate* might not agree." He chuckled. "If you find that you have extra energy for external, ah, diversions, by all means— but if I were you, I'd be sure it wasn't coming at the expense of the thing you *can* eat. Understand? You don't need me to rehash the requirements for you to keep your funding."

I gulped. I did not.

"Want to catch me up on what you got through this summer, aside from this . . . story?"

I found my voice and spent the next half hour discussing my incomplete chapter, overstating its readiness and exaggerating my claims about late-nineteenth-century Protestantism; it was xeno-phobic, capitalistic, a precursor to think-your-way-to-wealth Sand-bergian hogwash.

"Sounds better," Wang said, a little bemused. He gazed out the window of his top-floor Dwinelle Hall office, at the sea of Medi-terranean red roofs that rolled across campus. The slender campa-nile pierced the sky north of us. Gaggles of undergraduates were pouring out of lecture halls, their first classes back. "I'd like to see that and the new chapter by October."

I left Dwinelle, reeling from what I'd promised, and walked through the redwood-shaded trails and along the edge of the north side of campus. I took out my phone to scroll through the texts that had been dribbling in from Anita over the two weeks since I'd met her at the Sonora. She'd gone down to Los Angeles to rustle up some vendors from Little India; this morning, she'd pressed yet again: *Do you have an idea? If you're in?*

My thumb hovered over the keyboard. I traipsed along in the wake of some chattering brown undergraduate girls, around Memorial Glade, toward the life sciences building, not far from where I'd bumped into Anjali Auntie earlier that summer. The campanile sounded again, heralding the fall. All around me, the chattering sounds of new-semester autumnal excitement.

And then these girls collided with another pack of sorority desis. There were screams that at first startled me; someone was hurt, I thought, from the timbre and pitch of the shriek. But, no—it was just old friends re-encountering one another after a summer apart. Names were shrieked. Ohmigodyouresotan. Priya! Ranjana! Shehzeen! I skirted them, then looked back once I'd passed to see that one throng of girls had blended into the other. They were so packed together, a single amoebic blob, that they blocked the whole walk.

As they began to move, one girl slipped off the trail and onto the high point of a ravine. In her instant of solitude, I saw Shruti—not the menacing ghost of Shruti stealing this girl's likeness, but the echo of Shruti, the kind of memory normal people see all the time. I thought of Anita saying, *It is way back in the past.* Perhaps holding the most abstract version of Shruti, as a blur of my own regrets and the generalized pain of the world, was all wrong. Perhaps I should have been trying to remember *her.* What she looked like. How she used to gather herself in a beat of silence against the lockers when a swarm of girls pushed past her. The fierce narrowing of her eyes when someone said something harsh to her. The way she searched herself for a retort, and fought her way back into a world that made her life so unpleasant, how she waged that fight over and over again, for years.

This girl, who was not Shruti, tugged on her fat braid and stepped back onto the cement, jogging a little to catch up.

I opened a new text to Anita: *you free tonight?*

ANITA LIVED IN ONE of those sandy-colored buildings off Embarcadero Road that put me in mind of a Florida beachside motel, and whose facade belied its exorbitant rent. I found my way to her one-bedroom on the third floor. She'd pulled out the deadbolt against the frame so the door remained ajar. I knocked, heard her call, "Come in," and pushed it open.

There were only two pieces of furniture in the living room, a black leather sofa with wooden legs and a gray crocheted ottoman that looked like it had been purchased from a dorm furniture bin at Target. No television. The kitchen—cellblock-gray granite countertops, dark wooden cabinets. A single wineglass on the counter, next to a hardback copy of *Sapiens*. A three-quarters-full bottle by the sink, uncorked. Not a stain anywhere. I recalled Anjali Auntie's kitchen—the imperfection of the white grouting always hued a little bit orange from turmeric; the general scent of pungent asafetida and browned onions lingering. This was a sterile, somehow anonymous life, as though Anita wanted to erase herself.

"I've been meaning to move," she said apologetically, emerging from what I presumed to be a bathroom, wearing a black sleeveless tank top and, noticeably, no bra. Her nipples lifted through the shirt, and the room seemed incandescent. Below, maroon athletic shorts displayed her quads, taut from years of running and tennis. It was so little clothing as to be nearing none at all. "I keep selling my stuff, and then getting stuck on the next step. Anyway, that's why it's so empty. I can't justify staying on here alone much longer." She bit her lip. "We lived together. Here. But until I figure out where my next job-job is, I don't know where to look, or what my budget should be, and it's all one big crazy-making loop, so I end up back in Palo Alto." She looked around the living room. "I know, it has no personality."

"If furniture reflects our personalities, I'm not sure what it says that all my roommate and I have in our common area is a futon and a bong. And these alpaca rugs he brought back from an aya-huasca retreat in Peru."

"That says *something*." She grinned. "Speaking of weed. Weed?"

"You're offering? Sure."

She nodded, gestured to the couch. I sat. The leather was cold on my back. Anita went to fiddle in the kitchen, returning with the bougiest piece I'd ever seen, foldable, with a balsa-wood-type finish. She offered me the first hit.

"So, what kind of job *do* you want?" I asked.

"You and my mother and everyone else wants to know."

"Sorry."

She shrugged. "It was *so* easy to slide into the tech world from Stanford. I did a training program at a good company right out of school, and then Galadriel happened, and you *don't* ask questions when Galadriel wants you. Which means you miss that they believe so intensely in this crazy science-fiction future—we're all going to live in space and live a thousand years and be married to software, or whatever—they believe in it *so* strongly that nothing that happens between now and then really matters. Screw privacy, harassment, whatever. You didn't happen to see our founder address the Republican National Convention, did you?"

I had. Galadriel also happened to be one of Chidi's investors, which had been a source of some debate in our home.

"So. Yeah," she said. "I've figured out I don't want to help robotic white men build robots, but that doesn't mean I know what comes next. You're lucky. I thought you were unfocused as a kid, but you actually just had likes and dislikes."

"You were too good at everything," I said. "I was lucky to only be good at a few things, and no one will pay me for them, which significantly lowers the chance I'm accidentally evil."

She handed me the piece again. "I told you all my shit last time. You go now. Who'd you lose your virginity to?"

"Erm." I took a pull. "Wendi Zhao."

Anita doubled over in hysterics, her legs curved into her stomach. She rolled her forehead on her knees. "Jeez," she said. "I called that, didn't I?"

"You get me." That seemed to tighten her. I worried that I'd transgressed, moving too quickly to close the nine years that still lay between us. "*Got* me," I amended.

Anita took a hit. "Don't give me too much credit," she said, with the smoke still caught in her throat. Exhale. "Any idiot could look at a tape of us back then and tell who liked who. It was all so obvious. You especially. You have no poker face."

"You always knew?" I said softly. "About me?"

"Of course I did. Why do you think I was so skittish with you? You had this way of looking at me that was *very* intense, Neil. Like you were stripping me naked, and not just sexually. Like, existentially. It was a lot for a fifteen-year-old."

"That's embarrassing," I said. I groped for the piece on the coffee table. Was the indignity of your teenage self always so close at hand, long after you thought you'd escaped?

She sucked in, held her puff, and then breathed out a slender rope of smoke. "Some girls, all they ever want is someone to look at them that way, you know? And I just ignored you."

"Because you weren't one of those girls." I waved my hand, refusing another puff. "I drove. I should stop. If I want to drive back."

"Those girls, though, they're happy now. Their lives don't look like *this*." Anita glanced around at the emptiness of the apartment, and I followed her gaze. There was just one shelf across from us, with a few books, Bluetooth speakers, and a framed photo of Anita in cap and gown, flanked on either side by her mother and what I presumed to be her ajji—a fair-skinned woman with light eyes and the same Mona Lisa smirk as Anita. Next to it was her diploma: BA, magna cum laude, double major in economics and sociology. "Want less, and you can have everything you want. *I* always thought of those girls as *unambitious*."

She was still waving the piece in my face, loopily.

"I can't be too baked," I said. "I have to drive home."

"You don't have to drive," she said. She scooted closer. Her knee knocked mine. She didn't move hers away. I didn't move mine away. "What about you? What do you want? Love? Fame? Fortune?" She folded a heel into her crotch and dropped her bare thigh on my quad. Before I could answer, she added, in a newscaster baritone: "The chance to pull off the biggest known bridal gold heist in American desi history?"

My hand landed centimeters from her lower thigh, testing. I knew things about lust now. Could she tell? Could she sense that I'd *become*, in some way?

"You don't want me to drive," I said.

"Not if you don't want to," she said.

"Hang on." I reached into my pocket and pulled out my wallet, a beat-up brown imitation-leather hand-me-down from my father, the same thing I'd been carrying since high school. I reached behind the driver's license and pulled out the two golden hoops I'd taken from Anita's nightstand ten years earlier. They had lived with me all this time, out of habit.

"Here." I unlocked her knuckles from their hard fist and pressed the cold circles into her palm. "These belong to you."

I felt the phantom of them on my skin then, all the times in Hammond Creek and Athens and Berkeley when I'd fingered them and placed them under my tongue, as though if I swallowed, I'd possess all Anita was—all we were—back then. And there, in the lingering cool circles of those hoops, those last physical mementos of the Lemonade Period, was one answer to what Anita had asked me. What did I want? It was impossible; all I wanted was what had already been lost. I wanted more than to change the past. I wanted to be consumed by it, to go back to a moment when all was still potential and I had ruined nothing, no one.

But absent that, there was this—Anita's eyes widening as she slid each hoop through her bare earlobes and fingered them as though surprised they still fit. Then she was leaning over, her palms taking my head with surprising force, pressing me to her chest, as she whispered *thank you*, more than once, so I was sure she was not only speaking about the earrings.

"I need you, Neil," she said. "Will you do it? Will you help?"

I brought my hands to her wrists and pressed them against the back of her couch. I nodded then, my cheek moving against her braless breasts, and I breathed, hot and hard, on the poke of her left nipple through the cotton, then the right. I looked up to see her eyes closed, her own mouth open. I didn't know what private dreamscapes passed behind her lids, and yet I had a sense of the pattern, a collage of what had been lost, and what she craved.

"Yeah," I said. I brushed my lips on her neck, still pressing her wrists into the sofa, as though we'd done this a thousand times before. "Yeah. I'll do it. I have some terms, though."

Her eyes opened. I loosened my grip on her wrists. "You want some," she said.

I thought about hiding my need, but I couldn't. "Yes," I said into her skin.

"I gathered," she said, husky but measured. "I need her covered first."

"You must want some, too, right?"

"Oh, Neil," she said. "I can't—"

But I hardly heard the rest, because my mouth had reached her earlobe. I felt against my lips the cool shape of the old gold hoops. "I like them on you," I said.

"They're familiar," she whispered back, and then I was upon her, and her lips were at first surprisingly clumsy, but endearingly, flatteringly so—was *she* nervous?

The last time I had been so close to her body, there had been someone else in the room. I waited for Shruti's voice (*Aren't you two, like . . . ?*), waited for her to wander in and blink at us intently, as though at her dissected frog on the biology lab table. But—nothing. We were alone. My hands were heavy when I pushed them into her hair, a little roughly. I felt, with enormous joy, the little puff of air her mouth expelled at that display of control. I tugged again, my hand on her neck, the years of want that I had worried were weakening me now becoming something like strength. There was a flesh and flop to her breasts as they bounced against her compact body—more than I expected. Jigsawed flashes of all the girls I'd ever fucked—not that many, never a brown girl—swished by me and then were lost. Her darkness was new. The black hair, the blanket of peach fuzz on her belly. I imagined Adah Eckman's eyes on Isaac Snider, the Snider I'd dreamt up, those eyes erasing the difference between him and the rest of his homeland. Him, disappearing into her. And me, in the present, not disappearing into Anita but becoming *more* of a person as the friction grew. Me, my uncut foreskin that had made me nervous around anybody new in bed, but Anita was not anybody, hers not any body. She shuddered at my teeth on her neck, her thigh. Her voice lifted, turning vaporous at my tongue, my fingers. "That, yeah, that, unh," I heard her say, like we were swapping promises, her *yeah* meeting my *yeah*.

9.

A miracle: here, within groping distance, was the body kept secret for so long. I discovered Anita's dramatic particularity. Things both attractive and mundane. That her mouth smelled like pungent yogurt in the mornings. That sharpness of her pelvis, that feel of her elfish little hands digging into my lats. What had once been a brick wall between her sexual self and her life-self now became a permeable membrane, and I could and did reach through whenever I liked, to nip the edge of her ear with my teeth as she wrote a grocery list, to cup her breasts in the kitchen as she poured wine, to press myself into her hips while she talked on the phone.

After just a few nights, she left me a key. "We have to do some planning as soon as I get home," she said sheepishly. "So you don't need to drive back to Berkeley, and waste all that time." She'd return to find that I'd been lying on her floor most of the day, reading, working. (Yes, working! For something about her presence had revived my commitment to the discipline of history. I saw how people did jobs. I could look upon my sample chapters with a kind of aloof pragmatism, because Anita would be home in a few hours, and we had something that needed us, which meant we needed each other.)

There we were: me, shaking myself off when she opened the door at six p.m., going on a run around the sterile Palo Alto streets. Me, permitted to be myself with dangerous ease in her company. Me, there must be something badly wrong with her if she could tolerate me, like this. Me, you *know* what's wrong with her, it's cousin to what's wrong with you. Her, in bed, where she was surprisingly muted and mousy, that girlish tongue stealing out adorably between her teeth, that tightening concentration of her features before she undid my pants.

The revelations came like this: a week or so in—we were in bed. She had her back to me. I pushed my fingers against the nape of her neck and considered my thumb impression. There I was, briefly settled into her skin, and then I was gone.

"That feels nice," she said, though I hadn't entirely meant it to. "My mother used to rub her nails up and down my back when I was a kid."

"This way?"

"Softer," she said.

I tried again. Through her west-facing windows, the sun was lowering, darkening her. I had the impression that the years had accumulated on her skin and I was pulling them off, slight scratch by gentle scratch.

Wendi was the only person I'd ever really dated, and with her there had been a similar sense of having been vetted on some prior occasion, so that when things accelerated, it seemed the jolt had come from somewhere, from before, and there were no mundane introductions. After Wendi, I always wished I could walk into something having been seen in all the necessary ways, so bodies could be bodies and history lighter.

"You've done this a lot," Anita said. It wasn't a question. "Slept with someone quickly."

"*Quickly?*"

"You know what I mean."

I returned my nails to her back. "I find—found—it easier to sleep with someone when I didn't know a whole story about them," I said. "I'd start to feel entangled. The more you know, the more, I don't know, narrative responsibility you have. You have to make sure you're not one of those other terrible guys they tell you about."

"Whereas if they hadn't told you anything?"

"I wouldn't have to think about what patterns they're repeating or trying to correct with me." I nuzzled her neck. "But that's not an issue . . . here." I waited to see if I would be bold enough to say more. "We've always known each other."

She was silent for a beat too long. I heard only my own thumping pulse. I regretted that I'd spoken—maybe she fancied her inner self a mystery to me still, or wanted to maintain some psychic distance.

But: "Yeah," she echoed eventually. "Yeah, I guess we have."

She didn't seem quite as relieved by that sentiment as I did.

EIGHT WEEKS TILL THE EXPO, then six, then four. When we *were* talking, it was mostly about our unlikely jewelry heist. Anita had snagged a whiteboard from the events office and propped it between her kitchen and her hollow living room. Many evenings that early fall were like this one: I sat in my boxers on her leather sofa, shoving lukewarm takeout noodles into my mouth while she contorted herself on a yoga mat in a sports bra and tiny shorts. She talked, smacking Nicorette between clauses.

She tugged her foot up behind her, arch in elbow crease, her purple toenails touching the bottom of her bra. Her glutes flexed mightily. "Are you *listening*?" she said, her chin jutting toward the whiteboard—on it, a scribbled map of the planned plays, like a football coach's blocking. "You don't seem to be getting it."

"I'm *getting* it." I plopped to my knees on her yoga mat and pressed one side of my face to the rise of her thigh. My forehead lined up with the crease where her leg met her ass. I looked out the window to see the weird darkness of Palo Alto at the witching hour—the crisscross of the streets around University Avenue all dead by eleven p.m. How odd yet apposite to be back with Anita, brewing strange schemes in a suburb! With little to do, in nowhere-nothing places, you turn to queer, harebrained plans. . . .

"I heard you," I said into her flesh. I was feeling slow; I'd popped Adderall all day as I plowed through work and had therefore forgotten to eat until just now. "The raffle. You've got it set up and the winner gets the designer whatsit, the gown, by Mani—erm. Manilala Megatron."

"Not a *gown*," she said. She did not tug her leg away from me, but pressed one too-cold palm against my exposed ear. "A lehenga. By Manish Motilal."

"That."

"And?"

"Annnnd . . ." She flicked the top of my ear, hard, the sound of her fingernail on my skin like a woodblock being banged. "*Ow.*"

"I'm going to put on real clothes. Sit up."

"Please, god, don't."

"Pay attention, then." She stood. Her body was ruddy from her stretches. She pointed to the whiteboard: beneath the column *Tasks*, squeezed into the right-hand side, her centipede-shaped girly handwriting read *Prachi*.

I had slacked. I had yet to invite my sister to the bridal expo, courtesy of Anita Dayal. (*What!* she would say. *Anita*-Anita? *You guys are in* touch?)

Prachi, our bride, was to win a rigged raffle. Was to step onto the runway where, moments before, girls would have just modeled the high, fine fashions of brown bridal couture. Prachi was to flutter her French-manicured hands in delight at winning. She was to receive as bounty a designer lehenga—*heavy*, it was to be *heavy*, can-can skirt, brocading on the silk. Prachi would watch the dress's mirrorwork reflecting the light staggering out from the gaudy oversize chandeliers in the convention center. She would feel tizzies being pulled backstage. A tailor would measure her for alterations. Prachi was to feel (Anita promised *all* girls feel this way) the creep of recognition as the tailor fitted the cloth to her, that sense that the world wished you to look this way.

Prachi was never to know that her brother had come along to this menagerie in order to stuff golden chains and bangles and tikkas into loose folds and trick pockets in the liner of the skirt, already so hefty one would not notice the extra weight. Anita would tell her, *Let Neil take it to the tailor.* I would gather it up. Carry it to Anita's green Subaru parked in the employee back lot, through the doors without metal detectors. I would drive with the windows down on the highway and listen to the airstream whooshes and make straight for Sunnyvale.

We would give most of the bounty to Anjali Auntie, of course, but surely both of us would take a few fated sips. We would be foolish not to accept the blessing it could confer on our little union. Because now we were *together.* Because gold was what we did. Because I still badly needed it. Which meant she must need it, too. No matter that she claimed otherwise.

The junkie's plan. The belief that another hit, the right hit, will settle everything.

"If anything goes wrong," Anita said as she paced, "you do what?"

"Leave you." I'd recited the words so often they'd become devoid of meaning. "Leave you, take the gold to your mother and grandmother."

"And I do the same."

Our eyes met. I rolled over on my stomach so that I did not have to return that stony stare for too long. I did a push-up, feeling strong.

"Your core is flopping." She tapped me in the protruding belly with her big toe. "So," she went on. "The lehenga's down in L.A. with that tailor, and he's not concerned why we might be tricking it out. People want weird shit on their wedding days. Little holders in dupattas and skirt hems to keep lucky charms, something borrowed and blue, blah, blah. But the point is, *none* of that matters unless you talk to your sister, you understand?"

She clasped her palms above her, and her stomach tautened. It was not as pillowy as it had been when we were younger. But what was I good for if not softening her?

"Mmhmm." I reached for her hips, pulling her pelvis to my forehead.

"I'm putting on clothes." She removed my hands from her flanks.

"No, keep talking," I said. "Tell me more problems, I'll fix them all."

"You used to do this when we studied together. You'd be paying zero attention, and as soon as I said we had to stop, you'd snap to." She was twirling an Expo marker as she examined the map of which shops and stalls would be located where, along with an estimate of the location of all the Santa Clara Convention Center's security cameras. I was struck by the sense that she was getting off on the planning, that it wasn't just her mother's well-being motivating her. She'd been itching for a challenge. God, she really did need a new job.

The convention center, like many of the industrial buildings in the Bay Area, employed Anita's father's technology, meaning it was studded with hundreds of small, beady lenses, each one like a nerve ending connecting to the brain of the whole beast—a cloud server. Every image collected beamed back to it. What the eyes saw, the brain would record indelibly. We had a notion, formed based on Anita's understanding, which I gathered *she'd* gathered from a flirtation with one of her father's old interns: a Wi-Fi interferer could knock out the images streaming to the server, sweeping clean the record of all we would do. As long as Anita could draw the security attendant's gaze away from the live feed for an hour or so, he'd never notice the signal had gone out. It was one of those oddities of life in the Valley—with so much technology at hand, people presumed its infallibility.

"You really don't want to taste even a bit of it?" I said. I felt terribly sad, looking around at her life, the granite and the wineglasses and the eerie nothingness of Palo Alto outside. "You don't miss it?" And didn't she miss her old self? The one who would have demanded more?

"Sometimes I manage to go months without thinking about it," Anita said softly. "But then I remember that what we were consuming each time we drank some lemonade was an ambition or energy or power that once *belonged to someone else.* Which means some people come by this stuff honestly. And I guess I'd like to be one of those people. At some point."

I swiveled her around to face me. I could do this now—move her, demand her gaze. But she shimmied away, and my palms went cold. For the first time since we'd begun whatever we were now doing, it occurred to me that perhaps we did not fully understand each other.

"I'm getting ready for bed. Just please contact Prachi, like, *now,*" she added, in a voice a less enlightened man than I would have called shrill.

She excused herself to the bathroom. (That sound of her in the shower in the next room now slightly less extraordinary than it had been when I was fifteen, yet still marvelous.) I began typing a note to my sister: *Anita Dayal hit me up the other day* . . . Deleted it. *So it was Anita you saw* . . . Deleted that, too. Clicked *forward* on the flyer Anita had emailed me a few days before: 15% OFF EVERYTHING FOR VIP SHAADI EXPO GUESTS.

Subject line: *Fw: Random but* . . . The body text: *Hey this is random but Anita Dayal hit me up the other day and we've hung out a few times. Turns out that* was *her you saw. Anyway, she's running this big Indian wedding thing, maybe you can make it? She says you get a discount with this coupon. Lmk if I can tell her you're coming. She'd like to say hi she says.*

I shut my laptop—that note had taken a half hour of dithering and blithering. In the bedroom, I found a damp-haired Anita asleep, a water stain blooming onto the cotton pillowcase. One hand rested on her stomach as it rose and fell. I turned out the light and tumbled into this, my new normal. Sometimes, it is *not* so hard to *ad-just*, not even to the most sublime unrealities. The new magic seeps into the old world, becomes as commonplace as the hoops strung through Anita's small ears.

Our plan, I calculated quickly on pen and paper as I sprawled on Anita's floor one weekday morning, would involve the abduction of several thousand dollars' worth of property. Grand theft. Up to ten years in prison.

I wish I could have said I felt the kind of thrill a man is supposed to feel when he is released from the confines of daily existence in late capitalism and offered a chance to *truly live*. To overthrow the system, in some small way! Unfortunately, I was a coward rather than a revolutionary. My stomach gave a growl that suggested I had eaten something rotten. When Anita got home after working a late charity gala, I was on the toilet, reading *Crime and Punishment*. I came out waving it, only a little embarrassed to have been caught with a book in the bathroom.

"We are not Raskolnikov." She rolled her eyes when I insisted on reading aloud the gory details of the old woman's death, how her sister appeared at the wrong instant and the criminal had to kill twice. Blood, unplanned-for blood. "This isn't a *murder*, Neil. We're being sensible. There's hardly even real security—there will be no weapons. I mean, I'm in *control*—"

I couldn't help it, though. I was seeing a carousel of possible obstacles. I heard the convention center door banging open behind me as I laid hands on the car. Saw a figure standing there, twice my size, a great bearded Sikh vendor leading with a paunch, lifting a single brawny hand that could pound my brain into the wall. Me, pissing myself with fear. Or what about this? A train of cars, women leaving early to *beat traffic*, that signature desi move (arrive late, leave at odd times), blocking our route. Me, dropping the lehenga on the asphalt, gold winking on blackness, conspicuously brightened by the California sunshine. Gold, covered in my prints . . . Anita, racing past me, grabbing the stolen goods, turning her head only briefly before gunning it to Sunnyvale, leaving me alone. . . .

Her, reminding me: *I'm just following the plan. Don't take it personally.*

"If you don't think *I'm* sick about it . . ." She coughed. "But I'm being rational. I'm accounting for everything. If you're nervous, put that energy toward working as hard as I am."

I went into Anita's room that night. She rolled over, and there she was, again, ready for me. She liked to feel small in bed, she'd whispered not long ago. I had the sense it was the first time she'd made that admission, clearly full of tempest and drama for her. She liked a little shove, a strength around her neck. She liked me to toss her here and there.

"Hey," she whispered after we'd finished. She'd asked me to try *calling her things.* I was too awkward to comply. The daylight Anita bossed me through heist planning with the same efficiency she'd once used to run our childhood games of house, but the bedroom Anita wanted this constructed cruelty. I couldn't always reconcile the two. "I feel weird about that stuff."

"You shouldn't," I said, as I knew I was supposed to. "If it's what you like."

She bit her lip, weighing something, before speaking the next part at a rapid pace. "I saw my dad hit my mom once. I was eleven." She drew me closer with her heels. "My mom never talked to me about it, but she saw me seeing it. I was kind of hiding in the hallway, and they were in the kitchen. She made eye contact with me, over his shoulder."

"Fuck," I said, and left it there, because it seemed like she wanted to add more.

"It never happened again in front of me," she said. "But sometimes that image pops into my mind at the wrong moment. Like, before sex. Or during sex."

"Did Jimmy—?"

"No. But control comes naturally to him. And I liked that. And *that* made me feel wrong. Like I was just like my mom. Like I needed someone else to tell me what I was."

She fell quiet. I meant to reply, but as I began to calculate the appropriate response, I was seized with exhaustion. The moment ballooned; my silence became outsize, and it was too late to say anything. But our limbs were entangled, and I felt her hot and close, and it seemed clear that whether or not I was prepared, I was inextricably, obviously *in*—for this, and for all else she entailed.

I'D BARELY RETURNED to Berkeley over the course of those first weeks with Anita, and when I had driven up 880, I'd just dipped into my apartment to grab more clothes. Chidi knew I'd started sleeping with a childhood friend in Palo Alto, though nothing more. And while I believed my near-constant presence at Anita's had been mostly productive and pleasurable for both of us, we had begun to prickle at each other here and there: She woke up very early; I sometimes didn't clean dishes properly. It was mostly stuff that could be fucked away, until one morning she came back sooner than I'd expected from a cloud-computing conference she'd been contracted to oversee. She found me pacing her apartment in my boxers, listening to a podcast on double speed and picking at my facial hair.

"I thought you were working," she said thinly. She glanced around the apartment, which had grown untidier since I'd arrived. Some of the mess was due to our shared task—the whiteboard and markers, legal pads, piles of brochures featuring the hundred-plus expo vendors and their respective wares. But some of it was only mine—my library books, my preferred snacks (Cheetos, protein bars), the hoodies I put on and pulled off during the day as my body temperature shifted.

I *had* been working. It had been an Adderall day—it's best for sustained mental labor; coke is all fragile flashes. As I came up, however, I made a crucial mistake, and instead of turning to my sample chapter Word doc, I'd gone down a rabbit hole of lefty talking heads discussing the election.

"Why aren't *you* working? It's only five."

"I was. And anyway, this is *my* home. I don't have to tell you when or why I'm back." She tapped her foot; she was still wearing her work shoes, and the knocking sound they made on her floor was menacing, like the sound of a teacher smacking your knuckles with a ruler. She kicked the pumps off and came nearer to me. She paused. "Are you *on* something?"

"Just Adderall." I waved my phone to indicate that I was occupied; my earbuds were in, and the podcasters were still yammering.

"Jeez, Neil. Aren't you a little old for this?"

"I have a prescription," I lied.

"It's an amphetamine. You're high on an amphetamine. Look at you, you're picking your face like a fucking meth-head." She walked away, just as my mother did when indicating that the final word had been uttered. She opened the fridge. "And you ate the takeout already."

"I didn't eat all day. *You* finished the takeout last night, remember? You got up after we had sex and you finished the yellow tofu because you couldn't sleep."

"I've done Adderall, Neil." She slammed the fridge door and a red Stanford magnet clunked to the ground. "I liked it, too. Too much. And I have to say that I don't think you should plan on drinking the expo lemonade if you haven't done some serious work on your addiction tendencies."

"I don't see how that's your choice."

"What the *fuck* does that mean?"

"It means," I said, yanking out my earbuds, "I've been giving as much to this as you. And I don't see how it's your call whether or not I get a share of the gold I'm putting *my* ass on the line for."

"I think you should go home for a while, Neil," Anita said. "Like, now-ish."

She stomped into her bathroom, and I waited for her to re-emerge for another round of argument, but instead there was just the tap water running. I could see her wiping her face clear of makeup, shedding her daytime sheen.

I sped the whole way back to the East Bay, too irate to absorb anything as my podcasters wrapped up their doomed polling predictions, all of them so certain about the future.

I decided to hang around Berkeley for at least a few days, to cool off and (I told myself) to immerse in work in a way that had been less possible with an often-pantsless girl wandering around the house. I wrote all morning, then found, in the afternoon, that I needed a book I'd left in the TA office a few weeks earlier. So, into Dwinelle I went, fat noise-canceling headphones on to ward off small talk. I nabbed the book from the bottom drawer of the desk I nominally shared with two other PhD candidates, and was on my way back out when I stopped, absently, to check my mailbox. Few people ever sent me mail, save some librarians who'd kick over reserved copies of requested books or specially called-up archives. But sitting in the wire tray labeled NEIL NARAYAN, GRAD '20, was a mustard-yellow unmarked legal-size envelope. There was no return address.

"Do you know who dropped this off?" I asked the admin, who was watching reality television clips on her laptop.

"Not a clue." She returned to *The Bachelorette*.

I peeked inside and extracted a photocopied newspaper page. *The San Francisco Call*, it read. The date of the paper was smudged, but I made out *185*—1850-something. Below was a headline, above a single cold paragraph.

AN HINDOSTAN FOUND DEAD IN MINING CAMP.

Coroner Michael Rogers was yesterday called to hold an inquest upon the body of an Hindostan who was found dead from debility and injuries in Yuba County, near the banks of the Yuba River in Marysville. Nearby miners identified the man as a migrant from the East Indian city of Bombay, though at least one individual identified him in contradiction as Mamhood, of Egypt. The man has also been named as a known thief of gold dust. Injuries may have been visited upon him as a result, and the Coroner's verdict was in agreement with the above statement.

There was nothing else.

I left Dwinelle Hall, stepping into the startlingly unrelenting

East Bay sunshine, envelope in hand. So, the Bombayan was real. He had made it to Marysville. But no one knew him. I supposed he had never been my Isaac Snider. Isaac Snider was an unproven theory of history, formulated solely to explain *me*. I would never have a corollary in the past, never have a legible American ancestor to provide guidance on how to make a life. I would just have to keep on trying, tomorrow and tomorrow.

I found my vape in my room and took it, along with the clipping, to sit in the park around the corner from my apartment. As I got stoned a few feet from some junkies busking, I read and reread the Bombayan gold digger's obituary—if those few lines could be called such a thing. What made some people's lives worth remembering, and what rendered others' forgettable? Did it have something to do with belonging? If the Bombayan had been at home in America—settled, adjusted, seen, witnessed, loved—would someone today know his name?

I lay back on the grass, trying not to smell the sweat and grime of the burnouts drumming next to me. I closed my eyes and imagined that the yellow envelope containing the only record I truly had of the gold digger had not been placed unceremoniously in my history mailbox by a research librarian. I imagined, instead, that I had done Wang's little thing: TO: THE BOMBAYAN GOLD DIGGER, 1851, written back to him—and that he had received my letter and been meaning to reply when he had the chance. And that he had whispered instructions to whatever being was nearest to him as he died; that said person had raced to the local paper to give news that a peculiar, unlikely American had died; and that the newspaper office had posted the clipping to me, with an apology for some details getting lost along the way.

. . .

I CALLED ANITA from a trail up to Wildcat Peak. I'd hiked it solo, legs jiggly and weak after my midday weed, but I sobered the higher I went. The silhouette of San Francisco was muted by fog, of course, but the evergreens and yellow-leafed oaks of the East Bay slanted down and lolled out to the water. There was enough space up there to see what Anita was right about. That there were parts of me, still, that were dangerous—parts that lacked a firm grasp on reality, parts that wanted something impossible. A certain story of history, a perfect fix, all of her.

"I'm sorry," I said.

"You're stressed," she said. It was not forgiveness, but it was maybe sympathy. "Your dissertation. We haven't talked that much about it. You're trying to do that, and do our thing, and I googled a bunch of blogs about what it's like to be a grad student, and then I felt bad. Are you starving, Neil? Are you burning out or being abused as a nonunionized worker? Are you concerned about job prospects?"

I started to laugh. It was growing dark, so I began downhill, my tractionless shoes slipping on the path. "Maybe I'm all of those things. But I'm union."

If I were to stick it out in the history academy, I would never find myself in the past. I would find images and characters who meant something to the present. I might even enjoy the rigor required to make an argument of those elements. But I couldn't call what I felt for the study of history *love*, for the study of history had come to feel separate from the spiritual reality that Ramesh Uncle had once promised me to be true, that every timeline was unfolding simultaneously, over and over.

"I just don't know what to do with all we took," I said. "I don't know how to make it all mean something."

"Me, either," she said.

I paused as I reached the flattening of the trail, to get one more look at California's many geographies—the hills and rivers and coastline that once stood for nothing except themselves. It took gold-lust to make it into the place it was today, a palimpsest of errors and triumphs.

"I should get back to my apartment," I said. "I'm supposed to meet my roommate, Chidi. We haven't seen each other in—" I'd reached the neighborhood at the base of the peak, with its wide, child-friendly sidewalks. "Wait. Chidi. *Chidi.* Chidi can do replacements!" I shouted. "Chidi can do them!"

With just under three weeks left till the expo, Anita and I had still been wondering if there was a way to buy ourselves more time— true forgeries seemed too onerous and traceable to invest in. But I'd just remembered Chidi's first start-up, the one that had earned the grant from the billionaire—the 3D printing company. He had *made* jewelry before. Cubic zirconia bearing a discomfiting resemblance to real diamonds. I'd once watched him trick female shoppers at a Berkeley tech fair. He'd even done gold-colored products; holding one, I'd been briefly reminded of the rush that came from grasping a piece of newly acquired gold; it was that convincing.

"WHERE THE FUCK have you been?" Chidi asked when I got back to the apartment.

He folded his arms; his muscles were veiny and casual. His cheeks were still sweetly chubby, boyish, augmenting his hacker- wunderkind identity. Together we got a little stoned and a little drunk—a rarity, as Chidi's longevity company, with its youngblood transfusions and telomere-lengthening studies, had caused him to drop alcohol in his effort to live a thousand years. Perhaps it was the months that had passed since he and I had truly talked, or perhaps it was the particular melding of the substances that night that created the right alchemy, but I wanted—was surprised to find myself longing for—a chance to speak some truths aloud at last. Or maybe it was just that I needed his help, and knew first I would have to spill.

He sat on a meditation bolster on the floor while I sprawled on the futon. And I began to try to fit the basic story of who Anita was to me into twenty or thirty minutes. There were some elisions and omissions, and I felt, as I spoke, like one of those accordion files we used to use in debate; stretched out they held hundreds of pages, but pressed into a purple Rubbermaid tub they became meek and discreet.

"Is it just sex now?" Chidi asked.

And that was when I knew I had to go back, to fill in what I had left out. The magic, and all we'd broken. Was it just sex? It had never been *just* anything.

"Well," I said, "there's a lot more."

"You know how little you tell me about yourself, Neil?"

I shook my head.

"I've been wondering when you'd actually decide I deserved to know things about you. I've never understood *privacy*." He kicked his legs up and began to do bicycle crunches, saying the next part through gritted teeth. "It's a social world for a reason."

"Chidi," I interrupted, in part to get him to stop before he began to tell me about Twitter's crucial import to humanity, but in part because he was right, because now that Anita was around again, I'd *seen* that he was right—the past was lighter when I wasn't the only one shouldering it. "If you're free now . . ."

It was to Chidi's great credit as a friend and a general believer in the improbable that as I talked on for nearly another hour, describing the Lemonade Period, he asked only a few clarifying questions. I explained things like the properties of the gold, and the matter of Shruti.

"I feel like I . . . did it," I admitted. It was the first time I had ever said it this way, with the neatness I'd begrudged Anita. I waited to see how it felt on my tongue. The short sentence, with no ambiguity, no spirit to it. "I did it."

"You probably did." He had switched from crunches to push-ups on the hardwood while I talked, but he halted when it became clear the story was darkening. He now lay on his belly. "Maybe it was like a firing squad, though, man. A bunch of people's guns pointed at her. Yours, too. You all pulled triggers. But you can't be certain which bullet was responsible."

And then, unbidden, came a memory. A field trip in middle school. We were on a school bus going somewhere—up into the North Georgia mountains. It might have been to Helen or Dahlonega, one of those boomtowns shaped by the twenty-niners' rush, the one that followed the Carolinas' and preceded California's. What I remembered was Shruti sitting alone at the far front of the bus. And I remembered Manu, my seatmate, looking at her the way he often did, with fellow-outsider sympathy, and saying, *I'm going over there*. I remembered shaking my head vigorously and saying, *She likes to sit alone*. But Manu stood and made his way up to her, and because we were jerking up a hill full of switchbacks, it meant the whole bus saw him wobbling to reach Shruti Patel. That was a naked risk, seeking her so publicly. The teacher didn't even yell at him to sit down when she saw that he was coming to Shruti. I remember them sharing silence as we wound higher. She *likes* to sit alone, I kept thinking, even as I bristled at Manu for having left me all by myself.

To: Shruti Patel, 2004. (I could write, in Wang's fashion.) *When, exactly, was the beginning of your end? Is suicide a complex concatenation of chemistry, culture, and cruelty? Or was yours never suicide, only a theft and murder? When someone says you took your own life, should I be stopping them to shout, no, I did? I study causality, Shruti. I try to understand how economies grow and collapse, and how one zeitgeist blows into another. When I'm doing my job well, I can see truths that politicians and financiers of their days missed. But I have never come close to grasping such patterns on the level of the personal.*

"No, no, no." And then I was saying it over and over—*I did it*—almost becoming addicted to the sound of the sentence, but then I stopped, lest it become itself a kind of absolution, like the rhythm of a bodily penance. "I did it, and I just live with that. Always."

Chidi bowed his head. He waited for me to catch my breath.

"If you insist on carrying that around," he said, "find a way to make it make you better."

We talked still later into the night, and eventually reached the matter of the bridal jewelry and Anita's mother, the suspected affair, and Lakshmi Joshi's inkling that wedding gold could contain the particular energy Anjali Auntie needed to get back on her feet.

"It sounds risky," he said. He was rubbing his palms together with glee. Chidi considered himself antiestablishment. He was all free information this and end copyrights that; during his youth he'd even once tried to release monkeys from a Berkeley primate lab. He was better suited for outlaw life than I. "Is it all planned out?"

"Actually, I could use your help. Could you still print good imitation gold?"

"Ohhh. To replace the shit? I'd need photographs."

"Anita could do that . . . take pictures of a few vendors' stock for, say, an ad brochure."

He nodded. "I could manage. Nothing fantastic, but convincing at a glance."

"Fuck," I said. "I mean. That'd be amazing—I could—would you *want* some? Lemonade, I mean? In exchange?"

He shook his head. "I've been meaning to tell you. Judith and I are moving in together."

I stared around our apartment, thinking how it would never be able to contain three bodies comfortably—and then I realized.

"You want to leave." I managed not to say the full sentence: you want to leave *me*.

"Yeah," he said. "So I don't really want the knockoff version of this happy-home-happy-life-happy-wife shit. But *you're* not seriously going to start all that all over again, are you?" He glanced around the room awkwardly. "I wasn't expecting to come back from summer to find so much of my coke gone. Were you partying that much?"

"I'll pay you back. And I've switched back to Adderall," I said. "Better for endurance."

"I just . . . I get your thing with substances a little better now."

"You *love* drugs, Chidi."

"I do them no more than once a week, as a strict rule."

"Do you have it on your calendar or something?"

"My point is, Neil, that you've got this relationship now. Something that means something. I mean, do you see it with her?"

"*It* being . . ."

"You know what I mean. I saw it with Judith, really fast."

"You wouldn't want security? To have something to fall back on if it didn't work out?"

"What does 'work out' mean? Living together for a hundred years? At least we could say we'd been something to each other for a while. Maybe Anita doesn't have to be, like, the start of your nuclear family. I mean, why do you devote your life to these institutions we invented for different times—universities, marriage?" He was back to the push-ups now, which made everything he said come out in a rapid, sweaty pant. "The fun of California, I mean, the whole point of this place, is that there are other ways to *be*. Be fucking polyamorous. Be an entrepreneur. Live *some other way* than what they sold you on."

Chidi had grown up with difference more readily at hand—his family did not ask him to be something specific; he was a programmer with sellable skills . . . there was no shortage of objections I could raise. But also, I didn't want to start a fight, not when I'd just revealed so much about myself for the first time.

I talked over him: "I can't let you do this without giving you something. It seems unfair."

He dropped from the plank he'd been holding and raised his index finger in a little Eureka flourish. "I want to meet Anita's mother or grandmother."

"What? Why?"

"You said they've been studying the properties of gold for years."

"Yes." I rubbed my forehead.

"You've lived with me *how* long, and you can't guess what I want from them?" Chidi went into the kitchen and poured from a cloudy brown growler of Judith's homemade kombucha.

"That stuff is alive," I said. "It grosses me out."

"You drink *gold*, man."

I laughed—actually laughed. A millimeter of this secret's power had loosened.

Chidi was rolling on. "Those women, Lakshmi and Anjali? They must know a thing or two about alchemy."

"*Alchemy?* You want to talk to them about pseudoscience?"

"Alchemy was about the pursuit of longer life. Lon-*gev*-i-ty! People across tons of cultures thought drinking or making gold might help prolong the human life span, you know?"

I remembered, then, Anjali Auntie talking about things like this here and there, on those afternoons while she cooked and made up lemonade batches, as I snacked greedily.

"Wait. Right," I said, recalling a spare detail from long ago. "It came from China?"

Chidi shrugged. "China, maybe—I think it started there and traveled to India, and the Europeans got ahold of it at some point. But see—thousands of years ago these alchemists were looking into the same thing I'm studying now. Everyone wants *more time*, Neil. For so many reasons. So they don't have regrets. So they can just go on a few more hikes, or meet a few more grandchildren or great-grandchildren, or see the world change. We all just want *time*. And soon, we'll actually be able to give it to them." I nodded and sighed audibly, so Chidi would remember how many times I'd heard this spiel.

"Come on," I said. "There's magic, and then there's *nonsense*."

10.

His name, I found out later, was Mukund Jhaveri, though he preferred Minkus. This was a sobriquet of his own choosing, because the other option, first floated in second grade by an unoriginal bully, was Monkey. Minkus had purchased his first gun ten years earlier and taken his first shots eight years before that.

Anita had invited the Decatur, Georgia–based Jhaveri Bazaar Jewelers to the Santa Clara expo along with many other renowned gold dealers nationwide. Jhaveri was one of those Atlanta shops whose wares Anjali Auntie had always praised—high quality, intentionally designed, "as good as what Kaveri Padmanaban brings back from Tanishq." Anita had not expected Mr. Jhaveri to accept a cross-country summons. It was merely good practice to get the expo's name out there for future events. But the elder Jhaveri had given her an eager call back, saying his son was opening a new branch in Fremont—"Same-caliber pieces, I assure"—and could use the exposure.

When Anita met Minkus at the new store, he looked everywhere but at her. His eyes remained on his phone, and she thought she heard pornographic grunts streaming from it when she returned from the bathroom. Distractible, perfect, she thought. He was large, though not intimidating. She shook his hand and told him his wares would be *most* welcome at the expo.

She did not know then that Minkus was the proud owner of a Smith & Wesson 9-millimeter, or that he possessed a concealed-carry permit in Georgia, though not yet in California. Minkus's love affair with guns had begun in part because Jhaveri Bazaar Jewelers had been the target of an armed robbery when Minkus was ten. He was doing his homework in the back room. The sun was setting, the whole strip mall closing up. Gopi D-Lites Idli Shop and Kulkarni Sweets and Merchant Grocers were lowering their metal grates for the night. The elder Jhaveri was puttering around, slow in closing, flimsy in a way his son, who was coming to believe in manhood as an essential concept, loathed. When the men in balaclavas, burly and big-voiced, kicked open the door and waved their pistols, the father put one hand on his son's head and said, "Down, beta."

Ineradicable was the feeling of his father's hand bowing him before the men, who took some forty thousand dollars' worth of gold and cash that night. He remembered it when his neighbors said he could come deer hunting with them anytime he liked. He remembered it when his father said he didn't think going and shooting-shmooting things was such a nice hobby. He remembered it when he returned home from hunting, suffused with the splendid smell and smoke of the reeling weapon.

Minkus Jhaveri, the unlikely violent offender arrested at the Santa Clara bridal expo on October 22, 2016, told the *India Abroad* reporter who came to visit him in jail that one of the things that most disgusted him about the modern Indian American identity was just how *weak* we as a people had turned out to be. "The guys

I grew up around," he said—and here the reporter rather dramatically described him as leaning forward with *panther-like eyes*— "they knew. They knew the only thing that stops a bad guy with a gun is a good guy with a gun. And I keep telling everyone who asks, I was right about that little fucker. He was a bad guy."

THE CONVENTION CENTER looked like a spaceship, its body outfitted with high white sails peacocking at you. Gaggles of desi women poured out of Hondas and Toyotas, eyes ablaze with the reflected red text of the conference center Jumbotron—DULHANIA BRIDAL EXPO 2016: TRY ON YOUR FUTURE.

I parked . . . aisle C, row 32, memorize it . . . All around me were brides and their mothers and their cousins and their friends. "Mehendi, you do, I'll talk to caterers . . ." "Why does he want a horse like some flashy-splashy Punjabi?" "Ankit did his baraat in one Rolls-Royce; these days everything is very *post*-horse."

I located Prachi in the doorway. Around her neck hung a hot pink lanyard and a laminated card announcing KISS ME, I'M A BRIDE! She twirled it so I could see the back. Fat green bubble letters stacked to form the shape of a wedding cake: PRIZES PRIZES PRIZES! WIN FREE TRIP TO INDIA. WIN COUPLES CRUISE TO BAHAMA'S.

"I can't believe Anita *works* here," my sister said.

"She doesn't work *here*. She's just doing some freelance stuff between jobs. But we should find her at some point."

We passed through the metal detectors. A single chubby guard was half-heartedly scanning women whose jewelry, belts, shoes, and multiple electronic devices kept setting off the alarms. "Keep it moving, keep it moving," he intoned, unconcerned.

I took out my phone, seeing that I had few bars and shoddy 4G once inside. I assumed Anita's Wi-Fi interferers were already at work. Chidi had helped us choose and test them at our house, and once briefly as we did a lap around the future crime scene. The melee would also serve as neat cover. This place was (ironically, despite the demography of the expo) not equipped for tech support. A failure would be difficult to amend.

"I'm surprised you wanted to come, little brother." Prachi pulled me in for a hug.

I flushed, afraid that when she released me she might see my shadow of shame. I looked away from her, over at a cluster of flat-chested prepubescent girls practicing a sangeet-ready Bollywood routine, bony hips popping. "Don't go shimmying the booty on 'Sheila ki Jawani,'" one scolded. "It's on 'I'm too sexy for you!'"

We wandered for the first thirty minutes, gazing upon the carnival, Prachi with wide eyes that were somehow *moved*. I recalled that she'd believed in the promise of the Miss Teen India crown, too, believed that a room full of desis fetishizing a culturally commodified India together could access some truth about *what it meant to be both Indian* and, *like, American*.

"Wouldn't you groomsmen look *wonderful* in that pistachio color? Oh, yuck, look, up close it's sort of more vomit-green . . . Neil, duck, that's Gayathri, Renuka Auntie's daughter, and we didn't send them a save-the-date. . . ." Someone in full whiteface sobbed at a makeover counter. "All the foundations, they're making me look like a freaking *ghost*."

A food court on the second floor gave brides the opportunity to sample the samosas and paneer that would inevitably end up on their wedding menus. (Prachi: "Hey, do you think someone would do *collard green* pakoras?") A runway show was scheduled on the third floor at noon. (Prachi: "You're kidding me—Bubu Mirani?

Manish Motilal? Monika Dongre?") A fashion show, followed by a raffle—*the* raffle—at four. (Prachi, unbidden, pulling a ticket from a dispenser: "Let's not miss that!")

In the mix was a DJ booth manned each hour by a new spinner; notepads were extracted from purses and people listened, seeking the right mix of Pitbull and Pritam. We stopped so Prachi could swoon at one bearded artiste—DJ Jai Zee—wearing dark gas-station-quality sunglasses and beating an enormous dhol.

I was finding it hard to breathe. The smell of baby powder and rose-water perfumes mingled with something deep-frying in the food court. Above us, the sun peeked through, throwing rhomboid patches of light on an Indian flag dangling from one of the beams.

I had the last of my summer's coke supply in my pocket. I hadn't touched the stuff since before things had begun with Anita, and I hadn't made up my mind about whether I wanted to make use of it today. But I was weighing what that bump or two could bring me. I shoved my hand in my pocket. Help was just a trip to the bathroom away.

PRACHI AND I DISEMBARKED from the escalator on the third floor to find Anita power-stomping through a swarm of photographers. Girls posed in front of white backdrops. ("Toss your dupatta, now, it's your wedding day, best damn day of your life, that's it.") Wearing a black pencil skirt and blazer and a black almost-pleather top, Anita looked like a candle wax, whip-wielding dominatrix. I was not opposed to the sartorial choices. She waved a walkie-talkie.

"Guess who demanded a location switch-up at the last second," she said through clenched teeth. "The photographers wanted to be near the retail people, so girls could have their 'pics snapped.'" (Air quotes, demarcating the fobby phrasing.) "Oh gosh, *hi*, Prachi."

The former pageant rivals hugged.

Prachi glanced curiously at a square-jawed photographer cleaning his lens in front of a banner reading RAJA RANI PHOTOS: BE ROYALTY ON YOUR SPECIAL DAY. Behind him, so many people's special days collaged on top of one another. Dark brown eyes and richly hennaed hands stroking bearded jawlines.

"Ooh, I'd love a photo." My sister pointed.

Something sputtered on Anita's walkie-talkie.

"Linda?" Anita pressed her lips to the speaker. "All good?"

"Ooh, honey!" came the voice. "Just playing around! These are so new . . ."

Anita lowered the device and rolled her eyes. "This event liaison I have to coordinate with from the convention center is a *moron*; anyway, I tried to leave her with the interns . . ."

"The raffle?" I reminded Prachi.

"Yes, have you got your ticket?" Anita said. "You don't want to miss that."

"I think so . . ." Prachi dug in her purse, then pulled out the ticket with her left hand, which allowed Anita to squeal: "Oh, my god—can I see the ring?" She gripped my sister's palm gleefully, staring at the ticket rather than the conflict-free diamond, memorizing the fated-to-win numbers. "It's *elegant*; he did well, your man. Hey. I'll catch you guys in a little, yeah?"

The play, beginning. I had hoped that at this moment my mind would go suddenly clear, my stomach would stop flipping, and I would automatically slide into the script, which we had so carefully written, edited, and rehearsed. But instead, I felt myself rap-

idly reduced to some liquid approximation of myself. I was going
to fuck it up if I didn't do something—

"Prachi," I said. "Can I leave you here for your photo?"

I veered away and met Anita in front of the black curtain cordon-
ing off a temporary office for her on the margins of the event. She
pulled me through the drapery and reached under the metal folding
table she'd set up as a desk, extracting a tote bag filled with several
jewelry-crammed Ziplocs. Chidi's forgeries, which he'd dropped at
her apartment en route to an investor meeting that morning.

"Divided by vendor, right?" I pulled one up. It was labeled in
Sharpie with a private code in Anita's bubble handwriting.

Several camera lenses fell on us: beady eyes where the walls met
the ceilings. Black ringed by flashing dark blue, a cop car's lights
at night.

"The Wi-Fi interferer's working already," Anita said softly. "I
had to bring it in before they turned on the metal detectors. And
the security booth guy is a nonissue. I brought him a tray full of
free chai and spilled it all over the controller." I realized her corsety
top was streaked with dark stains. She pressed the tote to my chest.
Her eyes were wide and her limbs trembling. I kissed her dryly on
her forehead and stuffed the tote into my messenger bag.

"Let's go," I said. "And congrats—this is a total shitshow. I
never imagined *you'd* be able to plan something so disorganized."

"Thanks," she said. She sniffed. "It ought to keep the interns
busy. But I'm not sure . . ." She seemed to be gripped by an atmospheric agitation. "I just need to know," she said in a brittle voice.
"Like, you're okay here, right? You're in control?"

"What does that mean?"

"Don't get pissed. I just need to know," she stammered, "that
you remember why we're doing this. That it's for my mother, first

and foremost. And we can talk about whether it's a good idea for
you to have some later, but my mom—"

The walkie-talkie on her desk crackled.

"After everything," I said, "you don't trust me."

"Anita?" came Linda-events-liaison's wheedling voice through
the walkie-talkie. "Are you free? I've got a confused lost old lady
and I can*not* understand her accent."

"I *said*, don't get pissed. I trust you. I just want you to remember
this is about my mother, who would do anything for you—"

"I won't fuck up," I said, as lightly as I could manage. Perhaps
she had never forgiven me for the Lemonade Period. Perhaps she
could never believe in a better Neil. And if Anita didn't know a
redeemed Neil, then maybe he didn't exist.

I lifted the curtain and the first thing I saw, like a beacon, was
a navy blue sign for the men's room. I would just be a minute. I
slipped in. When I stepped out, I was back, edges thrumming and
eyesight clear. It was good product. I'd probably feel it for as long
as an hour. An hour of this borrowed selfhood, an hour of trusting
myself. Someone had to. I reentered the swarm.

I found Prachi preening for Raja Rani Photos. "So special,"
the square-jawed man said. "You look so special, see, I see many
brides all the time, *you* look special, though."

"Prachi." I waved. "Anita wants you to meet a couple of the
jewelry people so she can hook you up with some discounts."

"It's everything all in one place, Neil!" She panted as she tried
to keep pace with me. "I've gotten, like, three things checked off
my list. But Anita . . . Are you two . . . ?"

"Something," I said, stopping so she could reach me. "I don't know what though."

Prachi dropped her purse on the floor and actually squealed. I reached down to pick it up, feeling my bag swing. I was aware of its new weight. "*Neil!* You haven't said a thing! When did it *start*? But not that long ago—when I saw her—you weren't even in *touch* then! How freaking random! Wait, so is she, like, a *career* event planner? And, oh, Amma, well—deal with her later. Neil, it's ex-*citing*! I want you to have this feeling, I just *knew*, I saw it so fast with Avi . . ."

I was sweating. "Prach, that's all a longer thing, and I'm not ready."

Anita appeared behind Prachi. "Ready for what? Ready to see the jewelers?"

Prachi began to walk quickly in front of us toward the banner reading JEWELRY BAZAAR. She peeked back several times, twinkling.

"Did you tell her something?" Anita elbowed me.

"She guessed." (Anita's breath sharpened.) "About us. She guessed about us. She could tell. She could tell we like each other. She could tell there is something *serious* going on here."

"Oh." Her chest rose and fell more slowly. "Well," she said. "Fuck."

I started. "Excuse me. Excuse me. You didn't want her—other people—to know?"

Anita shook her head. "We can have this conversation later, Neil."

"A conversation? It needs a conversation? What kind of conversation do you want to have? We can talk. We can talk later, or we can talk now—"

"Ohmigod!" Prachi was leaning over the counter at CREATIVE JEWELZ: GOLD AND DIAMONDS ALL KINDS. "That's a classic mangalsutra; you know, we hadn't decided . . ."

"Actually, Prachi, I have this VIP badge for you." Anita handed a laminated pink card to Prachi, glancing at me a moment, briefly, with a twinge of suspicion. "Let's go over there." She pointed. I shoved my hand in the tote, fingers widening the mouth of that first Ziploc, where I felt a cold 3D-printed fake, a smooth bangle. It seemed terribly flimsy, like if I squeezed it too hard, it might melt, staining my palm yellow.

Prachi was trying on a stack of bangles at MEHTA GOLD when someone else began our first job for us. A heavyset man knocked into her and mumbled a harried *sorry* before scurrying on. I only had to complete the action, grabbing her as if to pull her up but instead dropping both of us to the floor. My sister landed in an embarrassed squat, as the bangles and two fat armbands (Anita having chosen several too large for Prachi's wrist) slipped off.

I had replacements in my bag for several of the thinnest bangles. The mess of the real ones littered the floor. For a millisecond, before instinct kicked in, I blinked stupidly at the gold on the vacuumed gray carpet.

I knelt and began to gather the real gold, swapping in the fakes, which were lost among the authentic things quite quickly. Anita waved her clipboard in the owner's face, demanding his signature on photo releases.

Mr. Mehta pushed Anita aside to help Prachi stand. By then I had made the swap. My hands were clammy. But it was done—three pieces of bridal gold were stuffed in the inside pocket of my messenger bag. We had hurt no one. It hadn't been that hard.

"You know," I said conversationally, dusting my hands off, for part of my role was to be blithe and dumb, "I think someone was trampled to death in an Indian mall the other day."

Mr. Mehta glared at me. "Not nice to generalize like that."

We arrived at the second target: SCREWVALA PURVEYORS OF BOMBAY GOLD. Hovering over the glass jewelry case stood the spitting image of grown-up Shruti Patel as I had seen her more than once now.

"I'm Dia," said Shruti.

The moment of our most complex handoff was about to occur—we needed this stuff, and I saw, beneath Shruti's—Dia's—hands, through the glass, why. The pieces had a compact density to them. I thought again of Anita's description of the right kind of toiling artisan, the one who kept the purpose of this wedding gold in the foreground of his mind as he worked. The Screwvala gold had clearly, even to someone as clueless as me, been made by such a hand. A row of rings, both simple bands and dramatic statement pieces stacked on top of one another in merry columns along disembodied white mannequin fingers. A few thin anklets, and an armband and one thicker tikka to drip onto a traditional bride's forehead, plus a few sets of jhumka earrings that Chidi had mimicked in all their grooves. Pièces de résistance: two mangalsutras, the essential wedding necklace. In my bag, along with the forgeries: Anita's ajji's defunct mangalsutra, of no use to her now, as a widow.

I heard myself say to Dia, "You remind me of someone. You look just like her. I almost would actually say you were her. It's funny how that can happen, isn't it?"

"Yes, sir," Shruti, Dia, agreed. "It is. It is funny how that can happen."

And I was positive that she knew me just then. Knew not just who I was now but who I had been before. Knew, too, how the mad lust I felt now, for her gold, was one long continuation of the desire she had met with in Hammond Creek.

"*Neil.*" Anita's eyebrows soared first in annoyance, and then, as she turned to Dia, recognition. "Oh. Oh."

"Actually." I saw it then, the way out, and I improvised thusly: "Ani, you see it, too, don't you? Dia, you look just like our friend who introduced us to each other. You know, while we have a minute. While we're waiting for Prachi. Why don't you look at a few pieces, Ani? See, Dia, Ani's been so busy. So busy organizing *this*. That she hasn't been able to look for herself. And we're behind. On our *own* wedding planning." I cleared my throat. Tried it on: "Babe?"

Her eyes widened and the dark brown took on a sparkle of the fluorescent convention center lights. We had never been outside her apartment long enough to attempt pet names or public displays of affection. I placed my hand on her hip. Pulled her to me. Felt her stiffening through the black pleather. But going along with it.

"He's right," she said. Shruti's, Dia's, small eyes flitted between us, and then to Anita's bare left ring finger. "I never wear it, it's inconvenient when I'm working." Anita waved her hand as if to cool it from a burn. "But, Dia, could I?"

Shruti blinked rapidly. "Of course." She extracted a key and opened the case.

"Dia, what kind of set did you go with?" Anita asked. Dia maintained a blank expression. "I thought you mentioned, when we talked on the phone—weren't you getting married soon?"

"Ah." Dia gave a muted smile as she covered the case with gold, gold, gold. "That did not work out, madam. The boy's family had been dishonest about their financial situation, and even about his educational credentials. They were after our business success. But what to do? Everyone wants something from someone else."

"Oh, Dia, that's terrible," Anita said. "I'm sorry I asked."

"Yes, it was too bad," Dia, Shruti, said. "He was nice-looking. And it's a nice thing, a nice wedding. But you do not want to wind up with someone who just needs you for this, that, or the other. It should be a good match, all around." She slid some bangles onto Anita's forearm and considered them wistfully. "My grandmother had given me all of her old wedding gold. It is out of fashion, but we were planning to melt it down to make something new. Your wrists are very delicate. If you have any family heirlooms, we can of course do that for you, create something absolutely custom."

"Yes," Anita said, pointing at several pieces. "I probably wouldn't want my mother's wedding gold." I felt her eyes on me.

She turned back to Shruti, to Dia. *Everyone wants something from someone else, isn't that true, Neil* (came Shruti's voice, in its careening, angled pitch). "Go on, let's see that one," she said, "and, oh, Dia, that's *lovely*," and so on. I lifted the curtain, on alert, seeing nothing but hordes of brown limbs and dark hair, hordes who (I could not suddenly help but feel, acutely) were dumb to the great power of what they were shopping for today. They believed they were planning *weddings*. Did any of them smell the ugly, world-inverting lusts undergirding the romantic ones? *Everyone wants something from someone else.*

I felt fingers clasping my wrist and turned. It was Dia's hand on my arm, gesturing toward the woman she believed to be my bride.

"Look at her," she said, as though she had made Anita herself. "Doesn't she look lovely."

The diamond-shaped tikka connected to those jhumkas dripping against a fat choker. Her arm jangled with bangles. She'd clipped a huge ring to her nose. Perhaps it was regressive of me, but that picture of her—a demure, historical bride on top, the dominatrix-clad body beneath—was enormously appealing. I grabbed her face and kissed, wetly, but as the heat rose in my cheeks, my eyes flashed open a millisecond and through their slitted vision I saw Dia, saw Shruti, looking right at us, not glancing away, following the basic script of propriety, but *looking* with an intensity that implied she was seeing more than this moment. Her shaggy hair shook, and her marble eyes bore into the back of Anita's gold-draped head, and there was something grisly about the way she was taking us in, as though this kind of perpetual, even haunting would always be her very basic right, having been denied the chance to live this way herself.

And then I heard Shruti's voice. *Just like you kissed me.* There was a satisfied squeal at the fact that we had kissed. *You're kissing her just like you kissed me, look at you, Neil. Everyone wants something from someone else. You* like-like *Anita for the same exact reason you went out with me. Everyone wants something from someone else.*

I withdrew from Anita. I muffled a gag.

Prachi, wandering up, cheerily: "Did I miss something?"

"Dia," Anita mumbled, wiping her mouth with the back of her hand and beginning to remove all the pieces. "I wanted you to show Prachi the more South Indian designs—could you?"

Dia, cheeks tinting violet, dipped below the glass counter. Prachi stumbled over. The moment during which Prachi and Dia were fully occupied was so brief that Anita couldn't get everything we'd planned. She managed to knock the mangalsutra and a few rings off the counter, into my open palm, before I tossed her ajji's necklace and two forgeries onto the glass. Surely—I hoped—surely I'd chosen the right pieces, the ones for which we had Chidi's replacements.

Dia rose. "Do you have a date set?" she asked Anita.

Prachi's eyebrows furrowed, but Anita spoke forcefully before questions could be raised. "Dia, thank you *so* much, we'd better get going."

Before following Anita out, my eyes fell on Dia, who was rearranging a necklace on a velvet bust. She felt me looking too hard at her. Shruti raised a thick eyebrow.

"I'm sorry," I mumbled. To the wrong person. At the wrong time.

"Excuse me, sir?" Dia said.

"I'm so sorry," I said. "For what you went through. With that boy. That man. Your wedding. He sounded. He sounds . . . like a really bad guy."

ANITA HAD TO tap Minkus Jhaveri on his shoulder several times before he would look up from his phone. His single flimsy stall was only a few inches wider than his sizable waist on either side, and he yet he had crammed perhaps thirty or forty pieces into the glass case.

"Mukund," she said. "I'm sorry, *Minkus*."

Prachi leaned over his messy tangle of jewelry—gold, silver, precious and semiprecious stones. She rapped on the glass. "Do you think you could open this? I may like that bangle set, if I could see it—and those chokers."

Minkus drew a key from his pants pocket. He was wearing a faded jacket that looked as though it had once been emblazoned with camouflage print. The jacket shifted as his arm shifted, and that was when I saw the shape of something black and bulky wedged between his back fat and jeans. I had never seen a gun from so close before. I glimpsed it so briefly, and Minkus was so big, that I didn't immediately identify the object. It might have been a retro cell phone holster.

His large hands dug into the case, and he began to roughly pull the pieces loose.

"Oh, be *care*ful," Prachi said. Minkus's eyes flashed up at her. His pupils tightened and I did not see what Anita had seen—a lazy layabout—but a man defensive about his manhood.

As Minkus Jhaveri thrust a baroque choker at Prachi, and as Anita instead requested the one for which we had a Chidi-forged replacement, a woman I identified as Linda came bustling up the jewelry aisle, shouting, "I've been *looking* for you, where's your walkie-talkie?" Bright orange hair crested above her head; she wore a pink sweater bedazzled with butterflies.

Tottering behind Linda was a decrepit auntie in a sari. Her Coke bottle glasses were slipping down her nose.

"This little old lady has lost her family," Linda heaved when she approached Anita. "I did warn you this is what happens when you don't go with outside security firms, see, I did tell you that I'd have to be chasing *you* down, now, can you talk to her, sweet little thing I'm sure but I keep on trying to tell her please talk slower, all right, and your interns, I can't find them an-y-where." She began massaging the dimpled flesh above her knees.

"Neil," Anita said. The tense articulation of my name, and the surmised plea within it, was all she could get out, for Linda was steering Anita toward the auntie, who had removed her glasses to reveal eyes misting up with fear. I heard Anita snap, "She's speaking *English*, Linda . . ." and realized I was on my own. If we had not just failed to get the best of the Screwvala gold, I might have walked away from Minkus, and all might have gone differently. But we had only eight pieces in my bag. We'd wanted closer to thirty.

From the loudspeaker, "DJ Jai Zee in the house from Dil Se Entertainment letting you know we gonna have a *hella*-tight raffle following a fashion show in five-ten minutes."

Very briefly, my own eyes came into significant contact with Minkus's gloomy ones. We shared something, a stab of scorn for this, our milieu.

I cleared my throat, then brandished one collar-like necklace at Prachi. I'd forgotten the long list of proper Indian names that Anita had assigned each product. "This is cool."

She glanced sidelong at Minkus, and half shrugged. "Kind of a mess," she said to me, but her voice was not quiet enough; Minkus Jhaveri's hairy right ear cocked—a hunter's ear, alert.

"Anita says they source everything from, like, this one really good dude, somewhere in . . . uh, India . . . Anita says this is who *she'd* most want to go with—"

I was growing frantic, for Anita had been drawn to the Jhaveri Bazaar wares not just for Minkus's wandering eye but for his father's taste. He was a gentle man, she'd said, who relished stocking wedding wares in particular; her mother had known him to receive invitations from the brides he outfitted, so warm was their relationship after the selling. His gold was the stuff of solid relationships and sturdy happiness. She wanted *these* pieces, for her mother. I wanted them for me.

DJ Jai Zee, amplified: "If y'all are excited about your wedding days give it up give it up," and a smattering of applause. "Oh god I hope y'all's grooms didn't hear that. Hey look, I see one dude out there he's like I wanna be watching football, amirite?"

Anita, behind me: "Auntie, do you *remember* where you saw your granddaughter last?"

Minkus Jhaveri wasn't turning away. Prachi was trying to get cell service. Anita was preoccupied. I didn't know what else to do. I toppled forward and caught the Jhaveri Bazaar cart as I collapsed. The pieces on the case clattered to the ground. Minkus crouched over me. His gaze fell on my hands while I clenched my fists around whatever gold I could grab. No time to replace anything.

He snarled, savagely. "Don't fuck with me." His arm shifted. The jacket rode up his back. And I saw for sure this time that it was not a cell phone holster but a goddamn gun.

One hand formed into a fist and he raised it above me. The other jerked backward, heel nudging the handle of the weapon.

"Lord almighty!"

The squeal belonged to Linda, who grabbed Minkus by the collar with surprising strength. "Sir, we do not want to have to ask you to leave . . ."

A small circle of people had gathered around me. Prachi's hand rested on my head. I saw Anita's black heels. I held my fists steady, afraid to let slip what I had grabbed. A few earring backs poked my palms. The silkiness of at least one ring and possibly a pendant. I stood, shoved my hands, and the gold, in my back pocket. By the time Minkus Jhaveri had shunted Linda aside, I was already apologizing, straightening his cart.

At last I saw Anita. She was walking to the fashion show to join

DJ Jai Zee. She didn't nod, smile, or pretend at concern. That vision I'd had of her here and there, in the days leading up to the expo—gold slicking her lips before she brought them to mine—went out, like a light suddenly cut.

I reached a point of clarity as I heard her voice reciting the names of the fashion show sponsors over the loudspeaker before DJ Jai Zee ignited the soundtrack, thumping Goa trance.

It was all for her mother. She didn't think I could be *trusted*. She thought I was smaller than the sum of my lusts.

"We'd better get to that raffle, Prachi," I muttered. I didn't dare look at Minkus, who was still being scolded by Linda.

"Now, I told her she'd better hire a security firm, sir," she was saying, "but I am only too happy to escort you out, I will not have this behavior, I don't know how you people do things."

A swell of voices intervened, some woke ABCD suggesting Linda ought not use that phrase, *you people*; a fobby uncle addressing Minkus, "Mr. Jhaveri, do not make us look so bad, like this only people will think Indians are trampling on each other, sets very bad reputation."

Freed by the nosy, gossipy horde, Prachi and I arrived at the packed fashion show. The Jhaveri gold prodded me through my jeans but I didn't dare transfer it to my bag. Anita stood on the raised platform while DJ Jai Zee polished his sunglasses on a bright red mesh Adidas T-shirt. Beneath, he wore '90s Reebok track pants, white stripes on black. His hair was buzzed. His chin dimpled. He was grinning at Anita lasciviously.

"So hot," a girl behind me whispered.

The models swished up and down the runway. On one skeletal girl: a crimson hoop skirt large enough to hide a flock of small children. On another: a corset-like bodice, scaly as a mermaid tail, culminating in ruffled pants. Prachi pooh-poohed a few. ("Gaudy," she whispered.) She began taking notes as DJ Jai Zee name-dropped designers and Anita interspersed commentary. I turned my head, slowly as possible. I saw no sign of my armed rival. Still, I sweated.

When the white-clad women completed their walk, Anita declared that it was time for the raffle announcement. She held up a red box, shook it, then extracted a green ticket. She mouthed the numbers back to herself. I could see, from my seat, the fear passing over her, the momentary terror that she'd misremembered. But then she spoke them aloud. Some hundred brides fiddled with purses and wallets. Prachi was still writing on her legal pad when a lovely tall dark-skinned girl stood, only to have someone else say, "No, Sonia, that's not you."

"Prachi?" I whispered. "Check and see?"

Behind us: "Ey, wave yours, who says they'll look?"

Prachi laughed. "I never win anything," but then she dug in her purse as Anita read the numbers out once more. Prachi's head swiveled in my direction, her face tainted with suspicion.

"Here!" A helpful auntie raised my sister's hand high in the air. Prachi yelped, because said auntie's hand was done up with still-wet mehndi. The fecal henna oozed down Prachi's arm. "Go on, go on," the auntie said, and up Prachi went. There, Anita held Prachi's new deep red Manish Motilal lehenga. It was enormous, with enough fabric to be fitted to the body type of any possible winner. The blouse was silk starred with golden pricks; muslin overlaid the shoulders. It culminated in a huge fanned skirt.

Behind me, someone said, "Look at that girl. Too-too skinny."

"Stop telling *me* to lose weight then, hanh, Mummy?"

"There's curves, then there's fat, Rupali."

Prachi's limbs buckled when the dress made contact with her arms.

"Congrats, wow, that's some dress, huh—sorry, not dress, lehenga—are you going to wear it? Do you think Mom will like it?" I said to the bundle of fabric blocking Prachi's face.

We followed Anita to the tailor, a bespectacled uncle wearing pleated brown pants and a half-sleeve collared shirt, relic of a closet-sized Bangalore shop. "This is Mr. Harsh," Anita said. We absconded to a cluster of conference rooms at the west side. Feet away: two staircases. Exits sans metal detectors. The highway coiling toward the sea.

Prachi deposited the Manish Motilal on the table and Mr. Harsh, tape measure round his neck like a garland, beckoned Prachi to stand before a three-sided mirror. Anita dragged out a bamboo room divider to hide Prachi from my view, and more important, me from hers.

"I'll just be over here," I called unnecessarily. "I'll just be over here while you guys do your girl thing over there, don't worry."

I fingered the lehenga, laid out on the conference table. It was surprisingly rough.

"It's amazing, don't get me wrong, but I'm not sure it's totally my style, Anita," Prachi said. "And it's a summer wedding, in Georgia—it'll be so hot."

"Give yourself a chance to get it altered," Anita said. "You'll fall in love with it when Mr. Harsh sizes it perfectly. Trust me, I've seen Deepika Padukone in this, you two have the same figure, and it looks like a lot, yes, but when it hangs on you, ooh, it's stunning. If you *hate* it, give it to a cousin or something. Mr. Harsh will leave space for a few sizes, right?"

I began to pull the Jhaveri gold from my pockets and the Screwvala and Mehta pieces from the bag; felt inside the skirt for the trick pockets, each one sewn into the middle liner . . . there, there was the first one. I grabbed at the loose thread and felt something give way. I shoved the first bangles in, then retied the string.

It was so much less gold than we'd planned on. What if I didn't bother with smuggling it in the lehenga, just carried it out on me? But then came Anita's determined eyes, peering round the bamboo. She didn't know how little I'd gathered. And besides, what if someone—what if Minkus Jhaveri, or the single security guard—demanded I empty my bag? No one would guess about these trick pockets. I kept at it. I tried to work without the awareness of Anita's gaze on me. *Leave you,* she'd made me recite how many times. *If something goes wrong, I leave you, and I take everything to Anjali Auntie.*

You know I'd have to leave you, too, right, Neil? she'd said to me. *You understand that if something goes wrong, I will get to my mom first?*

"Turn. Arms up."

"I hate to ask, Anita, but . . ." Prachi was saying on the other side of the divider.

"Arms down."

"It was all . . . fair and square, wasn't it? I mean, I don't want you to do something, like, to get me to *like* you. Because you feel you need approval from our family?"

"Of course it isn't that."

I finished tying up the gold in the skirt. I smoothed the lehenga.

I stepped back and saw Mr. Harsh gripping my sister's hips like they were flanks of meat.

The tailor drew a datebook from his breast pocket. "Thursday after next," he said, head waggling, that indeterminate promise.

Anita removed the bamboo divider to see what was happening on the other side: I was lifting the lehenga, gathering it up to me. Her eyes landed on mine, and I saw some comprehension dawn on her.

"You all good with that, Neil?" she said.

"Neil, what are you doing, be careful!" Prachi cried.

"I thought," I said, stealing the line in the script that was supposed to belong to Anita, "I thought I might take it to Mr. Harsh's; didn't one of you say it's on my way back up to Berkeley? I'm actually pretty tired of all this, Prachi, it's very girly, and I'm exhausted, I have to get home and do a whole lot of work on my dissertation, and if I just drop this off, I'll just zip over to Berkeley, and—"

Anita reached for the lehenga. "Neil," she said. And I could tell that now she didn't want to abide by that original plan; she didn't want me to be alone with the goods. Her fingers closed around the silk, but they were so small, and I was stronger than she was. "Why don't you let *me* take the lehenga to Mr. Harsh's shop? And he and I should talk more about, as you say, *girly* design issues."

"I wish I had you guys fighting to run my errands all the time!" Prachi said, mildly bewildered.

"No," I said. "Really, it's no trouble. It's no trouble at all." I reached for Mr. Harsh's card, which he'd left on the table for Prachi, and in the same movement, I hugged Prachi with one arm. My sister was looking strangely at me and Anita, and I rolled my eyes, hoping to signify that it was just an innocent romantic spat. And then I turned, pulling the lehenga from Anita's grasp with ease. I pushed the conference room door open, and the last thing I saw behind me was Anita's mouth hanging half-open, as I proved right every doubt she'd ever had about me.

The door banged shut behind me. Little puffs of the sleeves poked me in my eyes. I thought of Chidi admonishing me when I worked out with him and pled exhaustion . . . *Neil, you can do anything for thirty seconds.* I moved through the next minutes in thirty-second blocks. Nudge open the conference room door, hustle down the hallway, thirty seconds. Clunk downstairs, each footstep echoing cavernously. At the bottom door, work knob; thirty seconds of fear at its stickiness, as the lehenga dropped to my ankles. Thirty seconds as I realized I'd been turning it the wrong way. Outside. Thirty seconds, into the parking lot. Thirty seconds of terror as I realized a horde of women were exiting the front entrance en masse, slowed, presumably, by the metal detectors restricting that door . . . I had parked, where, in aisle A, row 30? Aisle B, row 20? Fucking *where*?

I tried my key. Heard the *poink-poink* of my car. Saw women caroming away from the main entrance as, through them, came the thumping feet of Minkus Jhaveri.

"That's the fucking punk!" he shouted. He was perhaps eight feet to my right. My car had *poink-poinked* perhaps ten feet to my left. I felt the heat of a cocked weapon that has eyes only for you. My hands gave way. The lehenga landed at my feet. My arms rose, instinctively, white-flagging. I saw him in full profile: Minkus Jhaveri, buzzed hair and hefty belly, leading with the Smith & Wesson, hands clasped with purpose.

"I know your type," I heard him say. "Some people have the balls to at least come armed. But the sneaky ones. That's how fucking Indians do it. Little pussy pickpockets. Like beggars. Where'd you put it? Where'd you put it all?"

"I don't," I whispered, "know. I don't know what you're talking about."

The gun shook—not because of fear, no, it was thrill. Sweat beads formed on his brow. Behind Minkus Jhaveri, women crouched behind their cars. I felt sure I could hear everyone breathing, shallowly and gaspingly.

And then, over Minkus's shoulder, I saw orange-haired Linda approaching, her eyes narrowing. She knelt. She was lifting up her pant leg and loosening something around her ankle. I tried to mouth *Don't*, but Minkus saw my lips move, and he jerked his head around, taking with him the gun. I heard the shot, but I dove for the lehenga, and didn't see whose weapon fired. I collected the dress, bear-crawled to my Honda. I drove with my head low like I'd seen in movies, eyes beneath the steering wheel, not straightening till I had to look at the main road.

The convention center became a half-moon in my rearview. The sky blooming out in all directions was clear, but through it the smoke of an unlikely pistol still coiled. I was three miles, then five miles away, and my sister and Anita were back there, in the vicinity of the shots.

Q: If something happens?

A: Go straight to Sunnyvale. The faster the lemonade gets made, the sooner the evidence is gone.

My phone was vibrating atop the tulle, making a frizzy noise. I saw the waning power, 3 percent battery, as Prachi's name dissipated on the screen. It began again, Prachi once more. The ringing abated. Then started again.

It went like that for a few minutes. I never saw, not once, *Anita Dayal* flash up. Then the phone blackened. I had no charger. And I was still going, driving not southwest to Sunnyvale but instead wailing northeast on 680, approaching Berkeley, then passing it. Behind me the sky and the highway, that mingling of blue and gray that had always been the Georgia horizon, too, twined south, running the spine of the state all the way to Los Angeles. This endlessly striving state at the end of America, where everyone was always going somewhere, and fast.

11.

I took a seventy-dollar motel room outside Marysville. I'd zoomed there on instinct, as if toward some holy ground. I could not go *home*, where I might be found so easily. The motel seemed the thing to do. The owners, I was disappointed to discover, were Gujaratis, and gave me that knowing one-two sweep of brown on brown.

In my room, I stalked the grainy local news channels and found nothing about shots fired at a desi bridal expo. No talk of a *mass* shooting, certainly. But I refused myself optimism. The events at a parochial convention in Santa Clara might simply have been forgotten. Especially amid the nonstop election coverage: leaked emails, leaked tapes. I turned off the TV, took a walk to a corner store a half mile away, bought Jim Beam and a phone charger, began drinking from the bottle.

Somewhere nearby was a river that I'd once imagined saving my gold digger, turning him from an outlaw to a man at home in America. Somewhere nearby, a story of this country I'd wanted to believe in. But the magic I'd dreamt up had been carried downstream with the arrival of that news clipping in my wire mailbox.

I didn't plug in my phone. I sat on the floor of the motel room and ran my hands along the rough carpeting—ridiculously, I thought, *Good, my prints are being callused away.* I listened to the raspy air-conditioning unit and the pipes full of other people's fluids swishing through the thin walls. I stared at the drawn drapes, expecting them to become suddenly illumined with kaleidoscopically spinning red and blue lights as sirens sounded and law enforcement screeched in. In the back of their vehicle I would watch the red and blue fall in long columns along the rippled cornfields and the apricot orchards.

But no lights came, no yowl of sirens.

I drank, drank more.

Night fell and, in the darkness, I finally dared bring the Manish Motilal lehenga up from the trunk of the car—I'd moved it there at a piss stop on the way north, the same place I did the last of the coke and tossed the baggie. I'd been afraid to carry the dress to my room in the daylight; I didn't know what I might look like to the thin-lipped girl staffing the front desk. A runaway groom, having murdered his bride, on the lam, prepared to engage in some kind of necrophiliac ritual with her couture? I laid out the lehenga atop the faded floral duvet and observed it like it was in fact a body. What *was* my body count now? Just Shruti? Linda the liaison? One of the aunties cowering behind her car in the expo parking lot? Would they keep amassing over the years? I wondered not for the first time if one day Jay Bhatt or one of our other Hammond Creek victims would turn up dead and someone would mutter, in hushed gossip at the funeral, "It all started when he stopped excelling at math—what *happened*?" Or *Prachi*—

if one day Prachi would suddenly weaken, and as she declined, confess that in the summer of 2006, she had been sapped of something unnamable yet essential, and had never quite recovered.

There was nothing to do but throw the skirts up and begin gnawing on the tight strings with my teeth. I loosened each secret pocket like this. The sexual tantrum of it all was not lost on me. Next door: an unarousing moan. Downstairs: one of the owners' voices calling, *Shubhaaaa!*

I lined up the pieces on the peeling wooden desk and switched on the lamp. One mangalsutra. Three rings. Five bangles. A single jhumka earring. A tiny flower-shaped stud—for a nose? A rhomboid tikka. A few thousand dollars—grand theft—and yet only six or so months of lemonade. About the quantity I'd hoped to nab for myself, leaving the rest to Anjali Auntie.

I drank. The liquor stung. The warmth encircled my core.

The room, suddenly stifling. I jimmied the window, opened the drapes. That unpolluted night—not a lick of moon, no clouds within the gloaming, just an unmoving tarmac sky.

Everyone wants something from someone else. I paced and eyed the gold pieces and swigged again, stomach sloshing acidly. Did I owe Anjali Dayal anything? She, like her daughter, had left me alone with grief and guilt for ten years. I grunted massively and threw myself on the bed next to the rumpled Manish Motilal.

I remembered how to do it, didn't I? Fire. Flux. Lemons and sugar. I recalled with clarity the singsong of those foreign words; the incantation had meandered in and out of my dreams for years. But there were other substances that went into the vessels whose names I'd never learned. When I'd asked, Anjali Auntie had brushed me off—*It's untranslatable*, she'd say.

The truth: I didn't know how to make the damned thing on my

own. I was useless without the Dayals. They had made me. I couldn't remake myself. I was going to be sick. I slept.

THE POUNDING ON THE DOOR—it could only be the cops. I smelled something on the floral duvet, dribbles of my own vomit. I rubbed the duvet into itself to spread the vomit, as though that would limit the stench. My eyes filled. I tasted sweat and metal as tears and snot slicked down my cheeks. I wiped and wiped on my T-shirt, staining it like a little boy. I had only wanted to see that *it* everyone kept talking about. That thing they all *knew.* That conviction about love, about the absolution love brings. I saw myself in the mirror, the T-shirt discolored with bodily gunk, cheeks beginning to darken with stubble. Redness veined my eyes.

When the cops cuffed me, what motives could I offer? That I'd only wanted to give the girl I loved a bit of jewelry? I pictured it like that—me, declaring I loved her, articulating the thing I'd not spoken aloud, saying it for the first time in salacious newsprint.

The pounding again. "Sir, sir, sir." I wondered if an officer of the law would be so respectful. "*House*keeping, sir."

I gagged and this time made it to the bathroom.

"Not right now!" I shouted after I'd rinsed my mouth.

I plugged my phone in to tap around on the Wi-Fi. What would I search: *sanskrit gold smelting rituals? Shooting santa clara bridal expo?* As soon as the white light flickered back on, glowing lustrous, the thing freaked, buzzing and buzzing, text after text, voice mail after voice mail, from my parents and Prachi. My eyes stabilized on the last message shuddering on the screen as the phone finally lay limp on the nightstand.

From Anita: *Neil. I know you're okay. I *know* you're not doing something stupid. We just need to hear from you. I trust you. I love you.*

"Marysville?" she said when I called. "Where the fuck is that?"

"I just got on the highway and started heading toward Berkeley and then realized I couldn't stop there if anyone was, I don't know, *after* me? So I kept driving and when I saw Marysville, I thought, oh, yeah—"

"Your mind is a messy place, isn't it?"

I was crying again, hadn't in ages and now couldn't stop, tears of shock or relief or just the slackening of a body tightened by years of time and fear.

"You can't drive, can you?" She sounded soggy, too.

I sniffed. "I'm crashing. I was kind of high. And then drunk. I think I'm still drunk."

I could hear her head shake through the speaker. "*Marysville?*" I began to explain where it was, but someone said something I couldn't hear on the other side. "Huh," she said. "Apparently my mom knows where it is. We're coming to you. Stay put."

"Ani," I squeezed out pleadingly. "What happened? Back there?"

"Which part?"

MINKUS JHAVERI WAS TAKEN into custody on the count of un-lawful possession of a concealed firearm. But first, he went to the hospital for the bullet wound he had inflicted on his own left calf. The utter shock of seeing his new rival, Linda, heroically reaching for what he perceived to be a pistol but was, in fact, a mace gun bearing the empowering label SEE SOMETHING SPRAY SOMETHING

SANJENA SATHIAN

caused him to lower his hand a few inches in surprise. He jumped at the sound of Linda's mace popping, then pulled the trigger, visiting said injury upon himself.

That no one had died did not alleviate my dread or guilt. Regarding the first, there was still the matter of Minkus's opportunity to out me to the police. And indeed, in the weeks following the expo, a pair of portly disgruntled cops would arrive at my Ashby Avenue apartment to follow up on Mr. Moo-koond Juvvery's complaints about my odd behavior, his insistent claim that I was a *bad guy*. But by then, the evidence of our crime had long since been smelted away, and little came of the inquiry; perhaps the cops in the end found the whole thing to be a weird cultural entanglement beneath the dignity of the state.

"What he was doing was illegal either way," Anita said over the phone, as the three generations of women sped northeast from Sunnyvale. "The guy didn't have the right permits. He must have just skirted the metal detectors. But, Neil. Call your sister. Tell her you and I had a fight earlier, and that's why you were weird, and then when Minkus came at you, you just freaked, you're a panicky guy so you panicked, et cetera. Then we'll get there and do the thing. It'll all be over soon."

I left the television on mute while I called my parents, then Prachi. A crime procedural played. Two detectives surveyed the bloody floor of a New York apartment, traded morbid puns. I was telling my family, then Chidi, that I was *okay*, that the dude had seemed to have it out for me since I fell down on his cart, that some primal instinct had sent me fleeing.

My mother was weepy, which was infectious, and before I could stop myself, I was crying again. "It's okay, rajah," she said. "It's okay now." (For a long while after, she talked often, and scathingly, of Minkus, as though critiquing him could undo the horror he had nearly inflicted on her baby boy; she told people *this was what happened* when you let your brown children go off copying the ways of white people—hunting-schmunting, shooting-wooting.)

I apologized to Prachi—I didn't have the lehenga, I said. I wasn't sure where it was.

"Honestly," she said, after assuring me that what mattered most was my safety. "Don't worry about it. I'm going to wear white, and Amma can suck it up."

Chidi just whistled. "Fucking A," he said. "How are we supposed to live forever if you plonk yourself in the middle of shit like this, huh?"

When I was done reassuring everyone, I shoved all the gold under the mattress, left the lehenga on the duvet, and half jogged back to the corner store to buy a toothbrush, toothpaste, and deodorant. From the Goodwill next door I grabbed a cheap Hanes T-shirt. Arriving back at the motel, clutching my loot, I found three willowy Indian women, all with the same thick hair, the same sudden widening of the hips, the same swanlike neck, standing outside room 214. One of them was pounding, deliberate and furious.

"Ani," I said. Three faces turned toward me. Each one a startling inheritor of another. Lakshmi Joshi's face was lined, but she was curiously youthful in the eyes, which were lighter—wet sand, rather than muddy brown—and more judgmental than Anita's or Anjali Auntie's as they assessed me. Anjali Auntie looked the oldest—older even than her mother. Her hair was white and gray in the front, though black around the top and back—it had only been streaked with silver when I saw her in June. It was as though age were imperfectly, somehow unscientifically encroaching.

Each woman had a large bag slung over her shoulder—supplies,

I thought, relieved. We could, in moments, eliminate all evidence of the crime.

For a wild moment I had the urge to touch Anjali Auntie's feet the way my mother once forced me to touch my ajji's.

"Hi," I said, and let us all into the room.

Anjali Auntie smiled irresolutely. The frailness of her hand was matched in her face, too.

"This is my grandmother." Anita lifted her elbow unnecessarily in her ajji's direction.

Lakshmi Joshi sniffed pointedly.

"Yeah, um. I should shower." I lifted the mattress up, handed the gold to Anita. In the bathroom, I left the water scalding. Burn me away, I wished it. I emerged, smelling better, to find Anita and her mother watching as Lakshmi swirled some clear liquid in a dish soap bottle.

We gathered into an assembly line, intuitively. I stood at the far edge, pulling tools from bags. Me and the witches three.

The procedure this time was different—a distinct recipe. I laid out on the table several round steel boxes, three long spoons, two more of those dish soap bottles. Lakshmi muttered rapidly, monotonously, trailing through a longer invocation I didn't recognize. The old woman was efficient, hiking her lavender pallu up her shoulder a few times as it slipped, barely stopping to breathe as she placed each piece of gold in a stone basin. I handed Anita the bottles; she passed them to her ajji. The few times our eyes met I saw that she was as disoriented by the changed procedure as I was. Were we brewing another potion entirely?

Anjali Auntie seemed to need a wall or a chair to hold her up. Once or twice Anita's ajji looked at her and paused her recitation so the daughter could repeat after the mother in a faint voice. Various liquids were squeezed out, and Lakshmi began to massage the gold. It didn't liquefy as I remembered. It took on a batter-like quality, thick and jiggly on the surface.

"Light," Lakshmi Joshi said, breaking her rhythm. Anita extracted a butane canister. I took so many steps backward, I nearly buckled onto the bed.

Anita flicked on the blue flame, which angled steeply over the basin. Then she withdrew the butane. The flame shuddered.

I stepped close enough to feel that halo of heat that still ringed the basin and saw the lavalike bubbling of our now-molten gold. There was so little. But at least the stolen goods were one step more alien, one step removed from the crime.

"Where are the lemons?" I asked, pawing through the bags.

"Mama, we forgot them." Anita's voice caught.

Lakshmi Auntie's hand appeared on mine. She steered Anita and me away from the supplies. Her grip was gentler than I'd expected.

"What's wrong, Auntie?" I said.

"You listen Anita's mother, now," the old woman said.

"We won't need those lemons and all this time," Anjali Auntie said.

"You're not going to drink it?" Anita said.

"Come." Anjali Dayal ran a hand through her strange hair, that weird striping of black and gray. The already stuffy room was suffused with the dizzying smell of the molten metal.

"Sit," she said. "Let me tell you some things first."

ANJALI DAYAL TREASURED the Hammond Creek years when her life was solely hers. Well—hers and her daughter's. She wanted those precious years to go on forever. She believed they could.

Pranesh, on the West Coast, is at first content to split the family across the coasts. He builds his company in California, while Anjali manages hers (he never thinks of her work as a *company*, but she does) in Georgia. But after a few years, Pranesh grows tired of living alone, in a rented townhouse, like a bachelor, subsisting on Maggi noodles. His wife and daughter need to follow him west— it's past time. They rehearse this fight many times.

One night, during the fall of our freshman year of high school, the Dayals snipe at each other over the move for the hundredth time. Pranesh does not want to go on paying a mortgage *and* rent. Rent, at their age. He is trying to do what he came to America to do, to build something—can't Anjali see that? And Anjali: Can't Pranesh see that the thing you come to America to build isn't software, but a home for a new generation? She invokes Anita. *Anita* cannot move. Anita's just started high school. Anjali isn't sure where her needs end and her daughter's begin.

They strike a bargain on this fall evening: Anjali tells Pranesh that Anita will have a better shot at Harvard from a private school in Atlanta. "These public schools in the Bay Area, they're full of too many too-too brilliant Asian kids," she pitches. Pranesh, who never debates the importance of education, assents. If Anita can get into a private school with a track record of strong Ivy League admissions—a better track record than a South Bay public school— he'll pay for it, and the women can stay put a few more years.

So, Anjali needs a guarantee. For herself, and for Anita. She knows what a guarantee looks like. She's seen it bubbling on a stove. She's even tasted it, once.

Anjali and Lakshmi are not speaking regularly at this point in time. Anjali still nurses the snub of her childhood. That she was never given a dose of the gold her brother drank. That she had to take ambition on Pranesh's lips, secondhand. She has no desire to humble herself; doing so would mean returning to silenced parts of the past—to Vivek. The Joshis do not talk about Vivek.

But Anjali needs the gold.

So instead she hunts around online. Stumbles upon a few academic publications by a white man, a professor at Emory University, inside the perimeter. His name is Lyall Pratt. He's written on alchemical and Tantric texts. She decides to seek him out; perhaps whatever her mother did all those years ago belongs to some branch of philosophy or ritual practice that this South Asianist has studied.

In his office, she works up to it, asks him questions about gold, plays a curious, bored housewife. She's taken with him. He's a widower, twelve years older than she. Tall, salt-and-pepper-haired, with a background in philology and anthropology and a lithe, yogic body. His eyes are a surprisingly dark brown. By the end of that first meeting, she risks it. Tells him everything she saw her mother do years ago. He is suddenly animated. Keeps saying he heard of these kinds of things when living in the Indian hinterlands. Stories of kings drinking the plunder of their conquered subjects.

He had, he tells her, even trekked with some swamis in search of the mythical gold-laden Saraswati River. The swamis told him that if he brought his wife's ashes there, the holy water might revive something of what had been lost.

It drove Lyall nearly mad when they couldn't find the river.

I saw it then: Anjali Dayal and Lyall Pratt leaning into each other beneath the autumn Atlanta sun that year, daring to brush hands as they walk along the old Decatur homes, gold and myth on their tongues, gold and crimson leaves canopying above them.

Lyall helps Anjali confirm Anita's place at the new school, no

gold required. He is from an old Atlanta family; he knows everyone. He makes a call. Anjali listens in as he chats up the admissions committee. She's in his office, admiring the late-afternoon
sunbeams warming the sleek wood of his floors and bookshelves.
Dripping from his walls are Indian fabrics, mirrorwork and tinsel,
ikat and chungadi prints. India itself is decoration for him. Outside: Atlanta's Bradford pears are stripped of their foliage. Dead
branches rap against windowpanes. Undergraduates scurry to the
library. Lyall's is a security Anjali has never before seen, so free is
it of the elbowing and clawing of Hammond Creek. He belongs,
effortlessly.

But getting Anita into her new school is not enough. Lyall's
money and power are white. She needs more for her daughter.
That spring, the acquisitions begin. Anjali, creeping through suburban homes as onions brown and sabzis simmer in the kitchen.
The sizzle and crack of jeera in hot oil as she steals into bedrooms,
closets, jewelry cabinets. Choosing the small pieces no one will
miss. Reciting to herself: *You are the wife of a rich man*. You are not
the help. If she were caught—and she nearly is, a handful of times—
she could talk her way out of it. Snooping, someone would gossip.
Who would imagine Pranesh Dayal's wife to be a cat burglar?

In a chemistry lab at the university, she and Lyall iterate the
lemonade formula. At night, she fiddles in her kitchen. At last, she
gets it. It doesn't taste quite the way she remembers her mother's
concoction—she still recalls, vividly, that single stolen sip of Vivek's brew, decades ago. Lakshmi's potion was ugly, sour. Anjali
has made the lemonade sweet. She's made it a delight to drink.
She's made it *craveable*.

At this point in the telling, Anjali Auntie's eyelids looked heavy, like the weight of the story was exerting excess gravity on her. She turned her face to the window. The drapes were still drawn, but her eyes bore through the curtain, like they were witnessing a private play. Lakshmi Auntie was pacing around the motel room with the energy of a much younger woman.

Anjali has the recipe for Anita's and my lemonade in hand now. She doesn't need Lyall anymore, not officially; she could make do alone. But she keeps visiting Decatur. To see him. She stands in Lyall's backyard in his house off West Ponce de Leon Avenue, clinking white-wine glasses while sitar and tabla music plays. A portrait of Lyall's late wife, Miranda, eyes them from his bookshelves. They talk about gold, its strange properties, its beguiling histories.

"And I wasn't only interested in *him*," Anjali Auntie said now— and this was the first time she had stated it so boldly. "He and I shared a certain fascination. With alchemy."

"Alchemy promises *more time*," she went on. "See? And he and I both felt we had lost things to time. He had lost years watching his wife die, and grieving her, and all that aged him prematurely.

"Me, I suppose I felt something had been taken from me. I had never been given quite the same chances as my brother, or even Anita. I thought—more time . . . well, it seemed my due." Her voice turned a little bleating at that last part.

Lakshmi Auntie glanced at the basin. The gold congealed at its edges, a duller shade than I'd seen before. She lifted her sari to her mouth, as though to cover some impolitic expression. She closed her eyes. I was not sure how much she understood of the English, word by word—we were moving quickly. I wondered if Anita's ajji was attempting to hear as little as possible about the events leading to today, reserving her energy for the aftermath; she was not there to condone or analyze what had occurred, only to try to put it all to rest as best she could.

And so the affair begins, and with it, Anjali and Lyall's shared project.

Hours bent over old texts, hours of his hands unfurling in her hair, of forgetting responsibility and risk. They discover ancient recipes, and something begins to change. Anjali is lighter, happier. Her smooth, bronze-patina cheek presses against Lyall's lighter one, mildly shaded by his graying stubble, which browns with the potions. They must indeed be cheating time, because how else could she be here, how else could the two of them possess all this life and heat when she is supposed to be raising a daughter, being a wife? This is all she's wanted, for years, though she never had the language for it: a space apart from expectation, purloined pockets of time where she is permitted the sprawl of youth.

Lyall's emptied garage in the Ponce de Leon Avenue home: bodies knock into beakers. Strange smells, some pungent as fresh ginger, others hot like chili powder. Eerie columns of smoke rise from the vessels. Blue and orange flames irradiate the windowless bunker. Nothing here is as pretty as her lemonade. Often, it's gloopy, cinnabar red. Another, like souring milk—it comes up from her mouth in foamy vomit; she is rabid. He won't let her stop. He pushes the vial to her lips, holds her head back, tips it down her throat. "You have to, darling," he whispers. "You have to." For the first time, she wonders, as she swallows her bile, if they've gone a little mad.

But she's come to crave these drinks, just as we crave the lemonade. It's an addiction—to the brews, and to him. She aches for both equally. Once or twice, he wonders aloud if they should slow up. She never allows it.

Lyall and Anjali have had a year together.

But then Pranesh restarts the old fight. Anjali and Anita must move. To California. He plans to put the Hammond Creek house on the market. He needs liquidity for the company, and claims Anita stands a chance at Harvard from the South Bay public schools. He says it wouldn't matter, anyway, if she got into Harvard and he couldn't pay. Anjali fights back. Which causes Pranesh to suspect something. He threatens to cut her off. "I have been patient," he warns her. "Indulgent."

And then, Shruti.

When I tell Anjali the news, she thinks bitterly: *Perhaps* this *is why we age*, placing a hand on my neck. *So that someone makes the right decisions.* The world seems to be telling her that leaving Hammond Creek, and Lyall, is the adult thing to do. He tries to reason with her, even arrives at the mustard yellow house on the night the Dayals are hosting a party, the very last night I see Anjali Dayal for a decade. I catch a glimpse of him, pulling up by the Walthams' house. I walk home while they argue in plain sight. He begs her to consider being with him, not to be so trapped in her own *culture*. She dares him: Would *he* pay for Harvard? Parent Anita? His silence is all the answer she needs; her daughter is just a story to him.

NEXT TO ME, Anita sniffed. She had been as stony as a practiced meditator as we listened to her mother; her ajji, across the room, was similarly unmoving. I was afraid to look at Anita, for she had never liked anyone witnessing her vulnerability. I reached to hold her small hand in my larger one, gripped it so my muscles clenched and my ears popped.

Anjali Auntie, drawing me out of myself, just as she used to in the Hammond Creek basement: "Do you know why so many alchemists died, Neil?"

I shook my head—I didn't seem to know anything at all, in that moment—but then a phrase returned to me, from a college history-of-science class. *Mad as a hatter.*

"Mercury poisoning is often incurable and often deadly," she said in a terrible monotone. "And it's a key ingredient in most alchemical rituals. You end up ingesting fumes. We drank it, too. A lot of it. I thought I'd found some methods the rasasiddhis—the Hindu alchemists—never knew in order to make it safe." She scoffed. "Lyall believed me. That, or he was too hooked to object. The trouble is that it's hard to tell when mercury starts affecting you. The symptoms can seem like something else. Depression, Alzheimer's, Parkinson's." Her hand—her shaky hand—clutched her kneecap. "Your kidneys fail. A lot fails after that."

"Why couldn't you have drunk all the gold *we* were taking?" I burst.

"So much," Anita whispered. "There was so much, Mama."

Anjali Auntie shook her head, a professorial reprimand. We knew better. "Alchemy is bigger than that. We didn't want to steal someone else's ambitions. That's petty, small-time. We were trying to steal from the universe, you could say. Steal *time* itself."

Lakshmi Joshi stood, tracing the basin with her finger. Her eyes bore into that lumpy smelted metal. More than ever now, she seemed deaf to what we had just listened to; she was pacing some other plane, a plane where it was not too late.

"I didn't see symptoms for a while," Anjali Auntie said.

In Sunnyvale, she is miserable. She cannot find work. Her daughter hardly speaks to her, blaming her for Shruti's death. Pranesh says he's heard things. Says he knows what she is. He has learned the phrase *gold digger*—it's on every radio station, on all the airwaves that year; even Pranesh cannot avoid it. He pushes, he pounds things, he shouts.

Slowly, Anjali starts to notice she is growing older. Lines and spots and a need for reading glasses and a back that twinges, sometimes spasms. She thinks at first that it is just the natural process. But then it seems to speed up. Isn't she too young to have these tremors? To be forgetting things with enough frequency that she loses multiple jobs? She develops abstract suspicions: that time, in a way, is having its revenge on her. And then finally she admits it to herself. The mercury—and a few of the other untranslatable substances—are extracting their particular biochemical price. She researches chelation therapy, but what would she tell the internist when the lab work comes back?

She does not know how much damage she did to herself. Is she dying, too? Well, we're all dying; is she dying *faster*, sooner, *now*? Is it the *quality* of time she's ruined? Is it why she has a prescription for sleeping pills, why she sometimes shakes them out on her bathroom counter to imagine all of them clunking against one another in her stomach?

Anita inched away from me and placed her head in her mother's lap. Anjali Auntie ran one hand through her daughter's hair, her gaze fixed on the wall opposite, as though she was reading what came next on the sickly yellow motel wallpaper.

"Lyall got back in touch two years ago. He showed up at the house."

Pranesh: answering the door, belly protruding, eyebrows grown into one long caterpillar, facing this man in horn-rimmed glasses with now fully white hair. Lyall was always slender but is now emaciated. A neighbor in a sun hat fiddles in his garden, pausing his spade at the surface of the soil, craning his neck to gauge what juicy scene is playing out at the Dayals' front door.

Lyall tells Anjali he's at Berkeley now. He, too, is sick. He blacks out, hallucinates. He is aging unnaturally. Anjali speaks with him in the backyard, beneath the citrus trees. She stays feet away from him, her back against the sliding glass door, while Pranesh harrumphs in the kitchen, eyes on them both. Anjali suspects Lyall has gone on drinking the brews from the Hammond Creek days, that he never detoxed as she did. Which explains why he looks so much worse, as though he's survived a war.

After that, she goes to see Lyall at Berkeley a few times. They aren't *together*-together. He needs tending. At this point, it's a battle for months, maybe a year. "There must be something I can do," she insists, because this is something she knows how to do—to orient her life around another person's problems.

He says he has one hope—part of the reason he came to California. He still thinks about the promise the swamis made him. About the placer-lined Saraswati River, containing the holiest gold. Gold untouched by human madness and cravings. Gold that's pure enough to extend one's time. He knows there are only meager flecks left in Californian rivers. But he prays these waters can heal him. He and Anjali drive out to the American River, to the Sacramento, to the Trinity, to the Feather, to the Yuba.

She is always at the wheel, while he sits in the passenger's seat. His forehead bounces against the glass as he dozes. Rainless clouds obscure the Sacramento Valley sun. Cornfields reach for the dry gray sky. Each time they arrive at a riverbank, they remove their shoes and wade into the water, splashing each other, copying gestures described in texts. Once, a historical reenactor in suspenders and Levi's warns them not to keep their mouths open if they don't want the worst fucking runs for weeks.

And?

And, nothing. The rivers are just rivers.

There is a moment, though. Once, at the South Yuba River State Park. When they step toward each other in the water. They swivel their heads to the far bank to see a white woman and a brown man. Lyall sobs. Anjali breathes heavily. The woman looks so like Miranda. The man reminds Anjali of Vivek. They paddle across the water.

When they reach the other side, their bare feet slip on the slimy rocks, and the woman is laughing and the man is not Indian but Hispanic. "What are you guys doing in there?" the woman asks. Her accent is all middle America twang. Miranda was English. "You really meet some crazies in California."

Lyall dies. There wasn't enough pure gold left in the waters to undo the mercury poisoning. It's nearly all sapped up, by pans, by Long Toms, by barges, by dredges, by hydraulics, by the interminable yearning we share with so many other players in the long drama of history.

ANJALI AUNTIE LIFTED HER shirtsleeve to her eyes. "I'm sorry you put yourselves at such risk. If I'd known—if my mother had clued me in, or one of you . . . I would have told you, there's no point. It's too late for whatever blessing that wedding gold might've given me."

Anita began to dig in the bags. "Mama," she said metallically, "you need ibuprofen. A hot water bottle? Or, no. Is there an ice machine?" Her hair fell over her face, obscuring her features. Here she was, taking refuge in the hard edges of efficiency. Never one to dwell in grief or fear, or love. Then she looked at the basin next to her, at the gold that had settled into something pudding-like. "What do we *do* with this?" she muttered.

Which was when Lakshmi Joshi rose from her position perched on the desk chair. Her light eyes flicked themselves alive. Had we reached her plane now? A plane where something could be done?

Lakshmi Auntie said, matter-of-factly, her English clear but tentative, "We put it in river."

Like dumping a body.

"That's it?" I said.

Anita's grandmother rapped the vessel. "You take. Neeraj, you take."

"You didn't know about any of it?" I asked her, hoisting the basin to my hips obediently. "The alchemy, the—the affair?"

"Absolutely I did not know. If I knew, I would not have said go chase bridal gold. I would have done some other thinking." She took my elbow, unconcerned about overburdening me, and shuffled beside me. "So last night after Anita's mother tells me all this, I sit and think for a long time. New rite I am trying. Let us see."

"Where did you learn all this, Auntie?"

She pursed her lips and smacked them a few times. "You pick up things from mother, mother's mother, mother's sister. Like recipes. Cannot remember who starts it all."

Behind me, Anita carried out the Manish Motilal lehenga. We descended the stairs to the parking lot. I placed the basin in my passenger's seat, covered it with my dirty T-shirt.

Anita was in an authoritative mood now. "Drive. We'll follow you, Neil."

We squeezed through the narrow streets in that neatly gridded downtown and arrived at Sally's Saloon, with its swinging doors. We parked and passed the red Taoist Bok-Kai temple. I was holding the basin against my belly like a large pumpkin. Anjali Auntie stopped for a moment in front of the temple's high red gate. Anita was helping her grandmother up the steps that preceded the slippery gravel slope down to the riverbank.

Anjali Auntie turned from the red pillars of the temple.

"Do you know . . . ?" I began, and then stopped myself.

"How long I have?" Those white-gray streaks framing her face were handsome.

"Yeah."

"No." Her voice didn't break. "It's been bad since moving here. But the last few months, since Lyall died, have been even worse." Above us were the two dark shapes of Anita and her ajji, blending into each other. Anjali Auntie's eyes flitted a few centimeters to the right, locking on the taller, slimmer figure. "Ani must be furious at how little I told her." Her bark-colored eyes locked on mine. "But I haven't seen much of her in the last two months. She has secrets, too."

I looked away, flushing.

So up the steps we went, Anita's mother's elbow crooked through mine, until the four of us stood looking down at the sand-and-pebble bank. We were alone, us and the slow, gurgling rapids.

"Ajji won't be able to make it down," Anita said. Lakshmi Auntie spoke quickly in Marathi, gestured, and then tapped the basin.

Anita blinked very fast a few times as though to beat back emotion. I had almost forgotten my own heightened pulse from earlier in the day when I'd seen three words beaming up from my phone: *I love you.* It seemed wrong that the declaration had not been followed by a sudden stabilizing of the world.

"Anita," I said, still gripping the basin. The gold clotted at its edges like dairy left in the heat. It seemed eons away from what I'd been stuffing into my pockets and bag at the expo. "Can I have a word with you?"

She glanced over the water, at the lowering sun, and said, "Yes, but quickly, Neil." And I was consumed with a version of the feeling I'd had all the time as a child, that sense that privacy draped her, that she could not or would not lift it long enough to look directly at me. Except this time she turned, followed me a few paces away from her mother and grandmother, and let her lips briefly brush my clavicle. I felt the hot poignancy of her breath on my T-shirt, on my chest hairs. Her hands gripped the basin; her touch was so light that it was at first just there for balance, but then, before I knew it, she had taken the full weight of it out of my hands and into hers. The air felt icy on my palms.

"I just wanted some help," I said. "From this gold. I know it's too late now, I know it's probably not potable, or whatever." She was shaking her head rapidly. "I'm not asking for it. I'm not. But I want you to understand why I let it make me crazy. I just wanted something to make everything less scary. Sometimes I can't imagine ever feeling at home anywhere in the world, or with anyone at all."

"I know," she said. "Everyone's afraid, Neil." Then she whispered, "Would it be so wild to try to do this relationship on realist terms?"

The evening was going dark around us. "Look at them, my grandma and my mom," she said, glancing over her shoulder at her two progenitors. Her mother was looking decidedly away, while Lakshmi Auntie's gaze remained on us. "Look how far they've had to travel in their lifetimes. We don't have to do those distances, Neil. We just have to figure out how to be at home right here. That's so much easier. That's so lucky."

There were her lips on my clavicle again, and everything was both the same as always and also entirely, infinitely, promisingly new.

I WAITED AT THE TOP of the hill with Lakshmi Auntie while Anita and her mother picked down the slope together. Anita with the gold. Her mother, holding her wrist. The two of them faded into each other in a single shared form. I had that sense I'd had about them when I was a teenager—that some part of each one was indistinguishable from the other. I felt awkward and tongue-tied standing next to Anita's ajji.

"So. You are writer," she said.

"Oh! No. Just a grad student." I turned to see that her lined face was impassive.

"Anita says you are writer. You're writing book."

"No, no, no," I said. "Only a dissertation no one will ever read."

She folded her arms. Surveyed the beach. Anita and her mother were now lost to the darkness. "You *should* write book," she said.

"That is how you make career." I imagined Lakshmi Joshi looming over Vivek as he turned wraithlike from all the swotting. She was so small, and yet imposing, and had that older-Indian manner about her that refuses excuses.

"Okay," I said.

"Good," she said. "Write a big book. Adventure story. Mystery story. Sell many copies. I tell Anita these things, too. Your parents did not come so far for you to write nothing-things, for her to plan parties."

"Okay," I said.

"Good boy."

Then the sound I'd been waiting for rose up from the bank—a splash, like a bundle of heavy bricks puncturing the surface of still water. The gold, in the river. And I remembered then, that story Anjali Auntie had told me years earlier, about King Midas. How he shook his fingers into a river to wash away the curse he'd wished upon himself, which he'd first believed to be a blessing. How when the water took the golden touch from him, the earth earned back some of its precious stores. How other people panned for it, amassing little synecdoches of Midas's fortune for generations. How the burden was lifted and shared, and in that way turned back into a gift.

"Hai Raam," whispered Lakshmi Joshi, which meant she saw what I saw. "I hoped. Something to happen." Right at the spot where the two rivers forked into each other, the twin waters shuddered, briefly, like a fault line had been activated. And then came a flash, soundless, and the river turned a pale yellow, the hue of the dregs of lemon juice.

I raced downward. The sky above was still alight. The river, still that lemon shade. I approached the riverbank, where I dipped my fingers into the yellow water. I kicked my shoes off, rolled up my jeans, and stepped in. It was not as cold as it should have been.

I thought I saw, to my left, Anita and her mother standing ankle-deep in the river, but my eyes were not on them. I was looking instead across the water.

Crouched on the far side of the river was a dark man. His hair was rumpled and full of cowlicks. I recognized him. I might have called out, but I did not know his true name. His sleeves were rolled up past his elbows, and his arms were partially submerged in the water, as though he was collecting something.

A trickle of gold—brighter and bolder than the yellow of the rest of the water—was swimming neither downstream nor upstream but from our bank to his. Briefly, I tore my eyes away to see if Anita and her mother were looking, too. They were. I snapped my head back, half-afraid he'd be gone. He wasn't. He bent over, arms in the water. We all stood there like hunters watching a deer pad through brush. After a minute, or a few, the yellow began to fade, and the stream of gold grew distant until it all seemed to gather on the other side. My Bombayan gold digger was standing and shaking a pan.

And from the pan drifted the misty shape of a man; his white hair caught the moon's glow. His head was turned in the direction of Anjali Auntie, as though he could not see me at all. And another figure: a young man, early twenties at best, whose impish smile I could see even from here; he, too, looked at Anjali Auntie, his younger sister. And then a third: a girl with frizzy hair and a glower that I couldn't see from here but that was surely there, wrinkling her face. I waited to make out her expression—if I could just see how she looked upon me from death to life, then maybe I'd know if I had been or would be forgiven, one day. But it was just the shape of her, distinct yet cloudy, so all I knew was that she was regarding me. I didn't know if I'd ever know how to parse that regard. I took one step toward them on the rocky bank, but their figures seemed to quiver, as though at risk of dissipating if I got too close, so I stayed where I was.

The three of them, Shruti and Lyall and Vivek, and perhaps still others I couldn't even see at all, bent alongside the gold digger and plunged their hands into the river, collecting whatever we were giving back to them.

Our offering seemed meager, but they shone at the sight of it.

The Bombayan began to recede first, like fog lifting, and then the others followed him. In a moment, there was again a sudden shock of crooked yellow light. It came and was gone so quickly, and the night went dark as all the shapes from our past took rest.

I dipped my hand into the now alarmingly cold river, disturbing its stillness.

I didn't and don't have a name for what happened that night. In the months that followed, all I got from Lakshmi Joshi and her non-hermeneutical approach to history was that there are some mysteries a person needs to accept, some logics to which we are all subject, whether or not we believe we opted into them.

"We had to give it back," she said of the gold. "I was not sure. But thought maybe something would happen. To think about gold like some offering."

Or, like returning offspring to its ancestor.

Perhaps when Anita and Anjali Auntie delivered gold to the river that had run dry of it for so long, they unskewed some sins. Perhaps that night granted Anita's mother time. For there *was* time, time during which three generations of women were together, and closer, and known to one another. Time that, over the next few years, came to seem like incontrovertible magic, as Anjali Auntie had good days, days during which she told stories of Bombay in her living room and passed on recipes (to me, never Anita, who was clumsy in the kitchen). Time that, as Chidi would always say, was all everyone wanted—more time for the big and the small, a chance to undo resentments, a chance to witness your child's future slowly unfurling, a chance to go on another walk around the sun-warmed cul-de-sac.

Then again, perhaps the earth took the gold for itself, sparing us no boon. Perhaps the only magic that night was that a grandmother and a mother and a daughter saw each other more clearly, and that I glimpsed that truth about history, that it flows toward us as we flow toward it, that we each shine sense on the other.

12.

Prachi Narayan and Avinash Kapoor were married on Memorial Day weekend. I announced the matter of Anita to my parents a few months before the wedding. Relations with the Narayan headquarters back in Hammond Creek were chilly, as I'd consulted no one before taking a leave of absence from Berkeley. I needed a chance to write something grounded in the present for a while. I was using the next year to try my hand in the magazine world. History would wait for me.

"We've only been seeing each other for about four months," I reassured my parents. "It's new." We'd chosen to begin our count after the expo, rather than before. But I added that it was serious, and that Prachi had invited Anita, and I hoped they'd be welcoming, and that being welcoming entailed not mentioning the Dayal divorce.

My father attempted heartiness: "The whole gang back together again!"

"I'm only saying what everyone's saying," my mother said. "Which is that she took him for all he's worth, poor fellow. Anyway, it is not her fault, that girl growing up in a tarnished home and all.

What is Anita doing with herself now? Gotten a good job, I hope? One of you needs to be making *some* kind of money, what money is there in *writing*, at least people understand what a professor is.

"Oh! But, Neeraj, have I told you who's bought the old Dayal house? Third fresh-off-the-boat family moving into the subdivision in six months. I am starting to wonder where all the Americans have gone. Would you believe it, the other day a white family drove into the neighborhood looking for their friend's house, and they asked some auntie on her afternoon walk if she knew where the Georgemeisters or the Johnsmiths or whoever lived. And this auntie, you know what she said? She told them, 'There are no foreigners on this street, you are in the wrong place.' Pah! These new immigrants, very arrogant, they have much more money than Daddy and I did when we moved here, they waltz-faltz into Hammond Creek, and we had to scrimp and save, no idea how hard it was for *us* . . ."

On the Saturday of the wedding weekend, my father and I vaguely attempted to help with the setup for the mehendi in our backyard but were rendered useless by our masculinity. We stood on the fringes, eating catered samosas, taking in the pleasant chaos playing out in front of us. Cousins and neighbors and the new generation of Hammond Creek Indians gyrated to songs in languages only a fraction of them spoke. Keya and Hae-mi and Maya were all there, having their henna done. Across the grass, Anita was placing one hand on my mother's shoulder. My mother gestured inside, and Anita entered our basement—which had been finished during the past year, bearing lovely cream carpeting and an untouched exercise room. She came out wielding a flower arrangement in the shape of a heart that read PRACHI WEEDS AVI. She caught my eye through the mess and gave a small, sweet shrug.

"She is a good girl," my father said stiffly. "Attractive, too." I badly wished he hadn't added that. "Make sure she does not steam-roll you. Other than that, I think she may be a very good match." He belched, a big rippling sound. "Samosas are very oily today."

I'd been conscripted into folding name cards according to the seating chart, since Prachi had fired her wedding planner at the last minute in a rare fit of fury. This was how I came across a row of Bengali names—*cousins of Avi's sis-in-law*, Prachi had written above them on the legal pad. And one name stood out: Ramesh Chakraborty.

It might not be *him*. Ramesh—a common-enough name. And there were no shortage of Bengalis in Atlanta. But just in case. I moved myself to that table, leaving poor Anita seated with my family.

Sunday morning: a Marriott ballroom inside the perimeter. Prachi, who in the end wore the standard red-and-gold when my mother threatened hunger strike at the prospect of white, led Avi around the fire, which flickered a subdued orange. I found my-self scanning the room for the massive shape of Ramesh Uncle. He was such an immense man that I should have seen him if he was there.

On the marital platform there came a hubbub as the officiant—not a priest, but an amateur Sanskrit scholar, a family friend of a family friend—was revealed to have sent Prachi and Avi the wrong way around the fire. My mother's sister, Kalpana Auntie, hurdled onto the stage, braced Prachi by the shoulders to physically turn her around, and in the process trampled upon the edge of Avi's trailing sherwani, causing him to knock his forehead against Pra-chi's. They righted themselves and laughed, Prachi's mehendied hand pressing tenderly against Avi's receding hairline. The error undone, they decided, for good measure, to circle fourteen times rather than the prescribed seven, to plentiful chortles.

I used the commotion as an excuse to stand, making as though I was preparing to help with things up front. I once more swept the bobbling heads. (No tears were visible. This was an unsentimental affair, and besides, too many of us were lost among the Sanskrit. Who knew what promises were being uttered through the untranslated chants?) I thought I saw a knobbed nose, bushy salt-and-pepper eyebrows . . . but the profile was too low, belonging to a shorter man . . . oh, but a few rows back, there were Anita's perennially roving eyes, and she, like me, was glancing about, fidgeting with her old simple gold hoop earrings. Those eyes landed on mine and lit, and lingered, and I momentarily forgot the quest.

One of Prachi's white sorority sisters leaned over her husband. "Do you throw rice at Indian weddings or is that offensive?" she whispered.

"Why would that be offensive?"

"Because people are starving in India."

"Sit *down*," my cousin Padma hissed. I obeyed. It was the kind of weekend during which one must obey any and all Indian women's orders. When it was over, Padma and I processed together back down the aisle. Anita smirked gently, for reasons I couldn't entirely ascertain—maybe at the formalities, or just at how time had landed us in this room now. Padma and I trailed the newlyweds and cousins and Hae-mi and Avi's best friend from his Hindi a cappella group. The aisle: a facet of the wedding that, during the planning phases, my mother had deemed American *nonsense*, but that caused her to beam as she, in her emerald-green sari, clutched my father's arm. For a moment, all the eyes of Hammond Creek were upon her. Her long earlobes sagged from the burden of her jewels.

THE RECEPTION, in the early evening: a buffet line beneath a large white tent in Piedmont Park. Duke white girls stumbled over the hems of their newly purchased saris. Anita was being passed between Hammond Creek aunties who sought news of her mother and, secondarily, her own professional path. She reported to them that she had recently signed up for a computer programming boot camp to become more employable, which garnered her nearly enough favor among the older generation to overshadow the hullaballoo about the divorce. Occasionally, though, she waved me over to rescue her, once even kissing me dramatically on the mouth in front of Mrs. Bhatt. "That'll give her something else to talk about," she said, steering me toward the bar for another Mango Monsoon cocktail. "Anjali Joshi's slutty daughter."

An hour or so in, I was lurking alone by the buffet, still scanning for the old man. Manu Padmanaban startled me.

"I've got literally twenty minutes," he said, shoving a chunk of pakora in his mouth. He'd moved back to Georgia to attempt to flip the sixth congressional district, which included Hammond Creek. "I'm thinking I'll live like this for a while," he said, with a sincerity that felt increasingly rare. "I'll just go wherever there's a chance of purpling or bluing a place. It'll give me a chance to really see America. *America*-America."

"Brave of you," I said, which I meant, though it came out sardonically.

And then I saw him—being led from a maroon sedan parked

too close to the tent: an older man, leaning on someone. He had grown smaller. Those intervening years had rubbed away some of his stature, along with the sense I once had of him as standing cosmically outside of time. People parted, seeing only what was visible—an old man being helped to his table.

"Manu!" I shouted. "Best of luck with the blue wave, buddy, but I have to go—"

By the time I reached my table, the son had deposited his father and gone off to the snaking buffet line.

"Ramesh Uncle," I said, taking my seat next to him.

"Hallo, hallo," he said, fiddling with the collar of his black button-down. It was poorly tucked into his slacks. He was marvelously underdressed.

"Do you remember me?"

"Very good to see you," he said, sticking a hand out to shake mine. The knuckles were like ancient tree roots, bumped and ribbed and holding him to the earth.

"We used to talk at the public library, ten—*eleven*—years ago."

He blew his nose in a dark gray handkerchief.

"My name's Neil," I tried. "You used to tell me all these great historical stories."

"A very good subject, history," Ramesh Uncle said, his eyes locking on me. Did any part of his consciousness recognize me?

"I'm studying, well—I sort of study history," I said. "What I mean to say is that I got into the whole racket in part because of you."

The other Chakraborty returned. He was all elbows, slight and dark, with handsome white hair. He spoke in the easy Americanized accent my parents had also settled into over the past five or six years.

"Shondeep." We shook hands. "Cousin of the sister-in-law of the groom."

"I'm Neil. Brother of the bride. I've met your father before."

Ramesh Uncle's treelike hands got to work on a mound of white rice and dal makhani.

"We used to hang out, like, over ten years ago, actually," I said. "At the public library."

Shondeep's eyes effervesced. "That was *you*!"

"He talked about me?"

"Relentlessly! He went on and on about the young man keeping him company in his 'studies,' and he was so lonely that summer, my kids had no interest—Baba, do you remember Neil? You two were such good friends!"

Ramesh Uncle looked up from his food. "Quite a long time," he pronounced.

Indian weddings are memory dungeons. You wander through them and everyone is throwing some version of your past self at you: I saw you when you were sho-sho-shmall . . . sho-sho shweet . . . Remember when you and Prachi did your Radha-Krishna dances and you wanted to be Radha, wore Prachi's skirt and all? . . . And now, the one person whose memories I *hoped* would bubble up had, it seemed, no access to them.

"Where did you—where did he go, that summer?" I said. "He just disappeared in July."

Shondeep thought a moment. "Oh, yes, his brother, my kaka, passed away back in Calcutta, so we left suddenly. He wasn't so old. But that air, over there . . ."

The woman next to him tapped his shoulder. "Excuse me," he said to me. They began to chat.

Was this just what time did to a person? Would Anjali Auntie look at me soon with those same cloudy, roving eyes? These days, she was prone to long spells of what she called "dreary mind." She still seemed herself, at least for now—a blessing I privately attributed to that mysterious yellow light flashing above the Yuba River. I wondered, though, if she woke up every morning preparing to do battle with her own memory. If she had to fight daily to hold on to the past, both the precious and the painful parts.

"Ramesh Uncle," I said. "Do you remember the Bombayan gold digger?"

Ramesh Uncle lowered his dal-encrusted hand from his mouth. "My god, such a tale!"

"You remember?"

"You may find it absurd, young fellow"—*I won't*, I nearly said—"but some stories do not leave you alone."

"Yes," I whispered.

"Still, sometimes, it's quite difficult to reach the past. Almost as though we do not have the right address." I considered telling Ramesh Uncle that our Bombayan gold digger had likely died months or a year after the beating we'd read about. That no one had known his name at the time of his death. That we were perhaps the only two people who'd sought him. Or that maybe two people looking for you in the past was something, a humble, belated mourning.

A beat, two beats of silence, and I swore I saw something swelling in his expression, but then he trained his attention back on the rice. He glanced up a minute later.

"Good evening, young fellow," he said. "How is your medical school going?"

A pleasant, dreamy expression took his mouth and eyes. Perhaps it was not frightening to find one's mind unmoored from time and place; perhaps it was freeing to leave yourself behind.

I felt a hand on my neck, scratching affectionately. Anita. "Your mother wants you," she said, and I went on looking helplessly at Ramesh Uncle. "Actually, she's quite annoyed you're sitting all the way over here, and I am, too. . . . Your cousin Deepak is a nightmare; he's told me three times how much his Tribeca apartment costs."

And then I was carted away; hands were on me, and someone pinched my cheeks and told me how much I looked just-the-same, only sho-sho-handsome now, what was I doing these days, *writing?!* Really?! Well, what did I hope to *do* with that?! ("Write," I said, to no laughs.) There was saffron pound cake being shoved in my mouth by fingers adorned with gemstones, and photographers wanted the families here, then there, and then here again. There was my brief toast—I was still known, unfairly, as the public speaker of the family; I read a Neruda poem in lieu of offering original thoughts, in part to keep from choking on the something sentimental that was coursing through the air. Soon, Prachi, feeling empowered on wedding champagne, summoned the Narayan nuclear family onto the dance floor and made us sway in a tiny circle with her to some high-pitched Hindi croon.

The next time I looked, after the Narayan family dance and the Kapoor family dance and the Narayan-Kapoor family dances, he was gone.

Anita suffered through several songs, patiently screwing-in-the-lightbulb and patting-the-dog at my mother's elbow, before tugging me over to the dessert table, where we were hidden from view by the vat of gulab jamuns. Her skin glistened with sweat, nearly as bright as the silver-gray glimmer of her blouse. She mopped her brow with her pale pink dupatta.

She pulled her heels off and rested her wrist on my knee with just enough flounce to indicate tipsiness.

"I'm sorry about the table settings." I took a breath, preparing to explain all about Ramesh Uncle, and the matter of the Bombayan gold digger, and all that I felt had been lost. The fiction I'd wished was true. But I exhaled, and the words left me along with the breath. "And I'm especially sorry about Deepak."

"He kept hitting on me." My face must have puckered. "I told him you and I had been promised to one another years ago and that our families are expecting a suitable shaadi any day now."

She was rolling her eyes as I stared at her very seriously. "Oh, I was *joking*," she said. "Don't be *gooey*."

I brought my face close to hers. Our lives existed in this realer plane now, the one she'd exhorted me to accept. And while sometimes that meant I missed the mysterious patina that had once shrouded her, at other times, times like this, I saw that everything I'd ever wondered about was much closer at hand.

Just then, I looked at her and thought it seemed less that things had been lost than that they were being found, over and over again.

BEFORE THE FORTY-NINERS, in California, were the twenty-niners, in Georgia. They stole the land first from the Cherokee Nation, and then they stole and stole the gold until it was nearly all tapped. And then, after the Cherokee had been forced out, after home itself was purloined, many of those twenty-niners caught wind of Sam Brannan's call and went West. It was that loud: *Gold, gold, gold in the American River!* It was the same call my parents heard across oceans, over a century later; the same one Prachi followed to her Victorian on Alamo Square; the same one that had made me both at home in this country and responsible for a great evil.

The morning after the wedding, I had a few precious hours, and a small pilgrimage to make. I gunned my mother's car north toward Lumpkin County, and pulled over at a diner near the Dahlonega public square. I ordered sweet tea and a cinnamon roll, and I took out my notebook. I began writing a letter, the kind Wang had told me about. *To: Shruti Patel, 2007.* I remembered Ramesh Uncle's philosophy—eternalism. That the past lies just around every bend in the mountain highway. That you can spy it from the right summits. That if the fog lifts without warning, you might find yourself face-to-face with its most vivid outline in the sudden sunshine. That if you kneel by the right stretch of land under the right constellations, it might even rise from a river and acknowledge you.

To: Shruti Patel, 2007. I wrote to her, as I always do, about the day-to-day rhythms of my life at a given moment. I write until it leads back to her, as it always does. I told her I was sitting in North Georgia, near the place where she and I had been on a field trip during her first years in America. I told her about Prachi's wedding, about Manu leaving California to try to make Georgia a better home, about how little Anita and I still understood about how to make use of all we'd taken, but about how we were trying to figure that out these days. About how it seemed the most important question we could set our minds to.

I told her she would have been good at journalism, which was still new and intimidating to me, or at coding, which stumped Anita every day. I wrote to her about how the hardest thing about adulthood, for her, would not have been work, or money, or even making friends, or finding love—she would have met her tribe in college or graduate school, I was sure. *You would have had to forgive people, if you'd gone on,* I wrote. *You would have had to believe that idiots grow up and change. You would have had to be big enough to accept that, or the bitterness might have eroded you. But you would have. You would have found a way to be generous to everyone who was never generous to you. You would have figured out that thing historians and politicians and all the world today is struggling with— the moral weight of the past, how to hold it.*

I finished, signing as I always do: *I'm sorry, still sorry, will never not be sorry, your friend, Neil.*

I shut the notebook and got back in the car.

The historic downtown area was all kitsch and crowds. Pink-skinned people, turkey legs in hand; children on parents' shoulders, faces painted and stickered. All around, the jangling sounds of the Dahlonega Gold Festival, and the burst of the summer green foliage.

A man on a stage in high boots and Levi's was narrating a drama. "That gold fever, kids," he was telling his audience of open-mouthed children, "it just gets into ya and it won't leave ya. It's always there." A family band strummed banjos. People were clapping and dancing beneath the early June sunshine, elbows linking elbows. A few women in laced faux corsets and men in panners' trousers meandered, passing out brochures for gold hikes and ghost tours. The day, terribly easy. History on everyone like a shrugged-on costume.

Peals of children's laughter behind me, as an older sister chased her brother. He toppled, and a decked-out miner raced to help him up, offering the handle of his pick, and life persisted like this, blithe.

I drove northwest from the square, tailing a station wagon with two bicycles affixed to the top. At some point the wagon pulled off and I followed signs to a trailhead. I set out, hands in pockets. The path was deserted but for a few runners and one old woman walking her regal husky.

Above, a flutter of warbling birds flapped together, then suddenly split apart, disturbed by something I couldn't discern. The husky barked. And soon, I found myself on a ridge overlooking the splay of the North Georgia mountains, those rich evergreen summits that rolled out into distant blue shapes just shades away from the sky. Runners' voices echoed behind me, but I couldn't make out their words. Cotton ball clouds ringed the higher peaks.

Below plunged the valley, the state sinking low and deep. Through the trees came an interrupting vein of murky water. A river—perhaps one where, as in the American and the Yuba, someone waded two hundred years ago, caught a bounty in his hands, shouted, *Gold, gold, gold in the river*, shouted something about the American promise, and intoxicated the world.

I squatted low on the trail so that the river bled out of view, becoming just a ropy shape hanging between the trees. I knelt, teetering on the precipice, gravity threatening, and dropped my head as in accidental prayer. My vision was filled half by the dimming blue sky and half by the trees blooming verdant before autumn's hot flare-ups, before winter's dulling.

I still want, sometimes, to stand in front of time, to dam it up, halt or reroute its current. But as I pressed myself to that earth, I thought about Anjali Joshi shrinking under the weight of time and Anita beginning to grow larger in it and me, about to take some important strides toward a tomorrow that had long seemed elusive, and I thought that perhaps all this was good, or at least natural. Because I suspect that if I *were* to change the past, I would have to trace its river back to its primordial estuaries, to some place where all desire began, to the universe before neutron stars rained gold onto Earth. I don't think I would find, even in those elemental waters, the pure beginning of history, but instead the future already rising up, silt and gold and sweat, slicking across the surface of the water like oil and then drifting on.

Acknowledgments

I owe many thanks. Here are some. To Gita Krishnankutty, for the literary genes.

To Andrew Ridker, who believed in *Gold Diggers* first and fervently. Without his wisdom and friendship, it would not exist. To Ayana Mathis, for lending her considerable intelligence to an early draft. To *Gold Diggers'* other pivotal readers: Lee Cole, Pooja Bhatia, Sarah Thankam Mathews, and Wes Williams. To Janelle Effiwatt, who lived with and tended to this book, too. To Charlie D'Ambrosio, for pointing to where the story lay.

To Amy Parker, Ariel Katz, Diana Saverin, Patrick Doerksen, Ren Arcamone, Sib Mahapatra, and Ted McCombs, for years of literary friendship. To Ginny Fahs, for unswerving support.

To Varun Nagaraj for furnishing details on 1980s Bombay and IIT. To Shivani Radhakrishnan for shedding light on academic life. To Malathi Nagaraj and Tyler Richard for Sanskrit assistance, Arati Nagaraj for Marathi, and Ishita Chordia for Hinglish. To Rajesh Jegadeesh for lending Neil his old screen name.

To Sam Chang for making the Iowa Writers' Workshop what it is. To all those who make the Workshop run, and who funded me there and immediately after, including the Maytag Fellowship, James Patterson, and the Michener-Copernicus Foundation. To the Clarion Writers' Workshop. To Daisy Soros and the PD Soros fellowship team.

To Lasley Gober, who made me at home in American literature. To John Crowley, for reading mountains in 2013 and encouraging me after. To Anne Fadiman and Fred Strebeigh, whose teachings remain the cornerstone of my writing education. To several more teachers: Aaron Ritzenberg, Charlie Finlay, David Drake, David Heidt, Emily Barton, Gavin Drummond, Jenny Achten, Josue Sanchez, Justin Neuman, Rae Carson, Rick Byrd, and Tiffany Boozer.

Finally, to my brilliant agent, Susan Golomb, for her faith, advocacy, and warmth; to Mariah Stovall for the careful reads and for seeing something in the manuscript, and to Writers House Literary Agency. To Ginny Smith Younce, my astute editor and fellow Georgian, whose deep and generous understanding of this book was a boon, and to Caroline Sydney, who read shrewdly and kept everything running smoothly. And to everyone else at Penguin Press: Ann Godoff, Scott Moyers, Aly D'Amato, Matthew Boyd, Shina Patel, Katie Hurley, Kym Surridge, Juli Kiyan, Sarah Huston, and Mollie Reid. There was no better team to give *Gold Diggers* a home.

A Note on Research

I made use of many books while researching this novel. Epigraphs come from the following sources: *The Sacred Books of the East, vol. 30,* edited by Max Mueller (1892); *The Alchemical Body: Siddha Traditions in Medieval India* by David Gordon White (2012); *Manu Smriti* via the Sacred Texts archive, and *The Age of Gold: The California Gold Rush and the New American Dream* by H. W. Brands (2002).

The Tale of the Bombayan Gold Digger is based on "the Hindu," one of the chapters in a German travelogue by Friedrich Gerstäcker called *Scenes of Life in California,* which I accessed via the Library of Congress online. *The San Francisco Call* announced the death of a "Hindostan" in Happy Valley in 1850. I have borrowed some of its language directly here.

I further relied on the following texts about the gold rush and its ensuing eras in California, in addition to Gerstäcker and Brands: *Roaring Camp: The Social World of the California Gold Rush* by Susan Lee Johnson (2000); *Foreigners in the California Gold Rush* by Seville A. Sylva (1932); *Gold Rush: A Literary Exploration* edited by Michael Kowalewski (1997); *Gold Dust and Gunsmoke: Tales of Gold Rush Outlaws, Gunfighters, Law Men, and Vigilantes* by John Boessenecker

(1999); *The Rush: America's Fevered Quest for Fortune, 1848–1853* by Edward Dolnick (2014); *California as I Saw It* by William McCollum (1960); *Riches for All: The California Gold Rush and the World* edited by Kenneth N. Owens (2002); *Returning Thanks: Chinese Rites in an American Community* by Paul Anderson Chace (1992 via ProQuest dissertations), and the Virtual Museum of the City of San Francisco.

On alchemy, in addition to White, I referred to *The Alchemy Reader: From Hermes Trismegistus to Isaac Newton* edited by Stanton J. Linden (2003); *Indian Alchemy: Soma in the Veda* by S. Kalyanaraman (2004); "Alchemy: Indian Alchemy" by David Gordon White in *Encyclopedia of Religion* edited by Lindsay Jones (2005); and *Chinese Alchemy: the Taoist Quest for Immortality* by J. C. Cooper (1899).

I also read and learned from *The Power of Gold: The History of an Obsession* by Peter L. Bernstein (2000) and *The Early History of Gold in India* by Rajni Nanda (1992).

The history Ramesh Uncle refers to comes from many sources, but I want to thank Barnali Ghosh and Anirvan Chatterjee for running the Berkeley South Asian Radical History Walking Tour. Anirvan surfaced the *San Francisco Call* article. Thank you as well as to Samip Mallick and the South Asian American Digital Archive.

About the Author

A Paul and Daisy Soros fellow, Sanjena Sathian is a 2019 graduate of the Iowa Writers' Workshop. She has worked as a reporter in Mumbai and San Francisco, with non-fiction bylines for the *New Yorker*, the *New York Times*, *Food & Wine*, the *Boston Globe*, the *San Francisco Chronicle* and more. Her award-winning short fiction has been published in *Boulevard*, *Joyland*, *Salt Hill Journal* and *The Masters Review*.